The Editors

WILLIAM L. ANDREWS is E. Maynard Adams Professor of English at the University of North Carolina at Chapel Hill. He is general editor of *Wisconsin Studies in Autobiography* and *The Literature of the American South: A Norton Anthology*, and co-editor of *The Oxford Companion to African American Literature* and *The Norton Anthology of African American Literature.* Other works include the Norton Critical Edition of *Up From Slavery; The Literary Career of Charles W. Chesnutt; To Tell a Free Story: The First Century of Afro-American Autobiography, 1760–1865; Sisters of the Spirit; The Curse of Caste* by Julia C. Collins; *Life of William Grimes, the Runaway Slave*; and *Slave Narratives after Slavery.*

WILLIAM S. MCFEELY is Abraham Baldwin Professor of the Humanities, Emeritus, at the University of Georgia. He is the author of *Yankee Stepfather: General O. O. Howard and the Freedmen; Grant: A Biography,* for which he was awarded the Pulitzer Prize and the Parkman Prize; *Frederick Douglass,* which received the Lincoln Prize; *Sapelo's People: A Long Walk into Freedom;* and *Proximity to Death.*

NORTON CRITICAL EDITIONS
AMERICAN REALISM & REFORM

ALCOTT, Little Women
ALGER, Ragged Dick
ANDERSON, Winesburg, Ohio
CHESNUTT, The Conjure Stories
CHESNUTT, The Marrow of Tradition
CHOPIN, The Awakening
CRANE, Maggie: A Girl of the Streets
CRANE, The Red Badge of Courage
DOUGLASS, Narrative of the Life of Frederick Douglass
DREISER, Sister Carrie
DU BOIS, The Souls of Black Folk
EMERSON, Emerson's Prose and Poetry
FULLER, Woman in the Nineteenth Century
HAWTHORNE, The Blithedale Romance
HAWTHORNE, The House of the Seven Gables
HAWTHORNE, Nathaniel Hawthorne's Tales
HAWTHORNE, The Scarlet Letter and Other Writings
HOWELLS, The Rise of Silas Lapham
JACOBS, Incidents in the Life of a Slave Girl
JAMES, The Ambassadors
JAMES, The American
JAMES, The Portrait of a Lady
JAMES, Tales of Henry James
JAMES, The Turn of the Screw
JAMES, The Wings of the Dove
LINCOLN, Lincoln's Selected Writings
MELVILLE, The Confidence-Man
MELVILLE, Melville's Short Novels
MELVILLE, Moby-Dick
MELVILLE, Pierre
MONTGOMERY, Anne of Green Gables
MOODIE, Roughing It in the Bush
NORRIS, McTeague
NORTHUP, Twelve Years a Slave
POE, The Selected Writings of Edgar Allan Poe
RIIS, How the Other Half Lives
SINCLAIR, The Jungle
STOWE, Uncle Tom's Cabin
THOREAU, Walden, Civil Disobedience, and Other Writings
TWAIN, Adventures of Huckleberry Finn
TWAIN, The Adventures of Tom Sawyer
TWAIN, A Connecticut Yankee in King Arthur's Court
TWAIN, Pudd'nhead Wilson and Those Extraordinary Twins
WASHINGTON, Up From Slavery
WHARTON, The Age of Innocence
WHARTON, Ethan Frome
WHARTON, The House of Mirth
WHITMAN, Leaves of Grass and Other Writings

For a complete list of Norton Critical Editions, visit
wwnorton.com/nortoncriticals

A NORTON CRITICAL EDITION

Frederick Douglass

NARRATIVE OF THE LIFE OF FREDERICK DOUGLASS, AN AMERICAN SLAVE, WRITTEN BY HIMSELF

AUTHORITATIVE TEXT

CONTEXTS

CRITICISM

SECOND EDITION

Edited by

WILLIAM L. ANDREWS
UNIVERSITY OF NORTH CAROLINA AT CHAPEL HILL

and

WILLIAM S. McFEELY
UNIVERSITY OF GEORGIA

W • W • NORTON & COMPANY • *New York • London*

W. W. Norton & Company has been independent since its founding in 1923, when William Warder Norton and Mary D. Herter Norton first published lectures delivered at the People's Institute, the adult education division of New York City's Cooper Union. The firm soon expanded its program beyond the Institute, publishing books by celebrated academics from America and abroad. By midcentury, the two major pillars of Norton's publishing program—trade books and college texts—were firmly established. In the 1950s, the Norton family transferred control of the company to its employees, and today—with a staff of four hundred and a comparable number of trade, college, and professional titles published each year—W. W. Norton & Company stands as the largest and oldest publishing house owned wholly by its employees.

Printed in the United States of America

Library of Congress Cataloging-in-Publication Data

Names: Douglass, Frederick, 1818–1895, author. | Andrews, William L., 1946– editor. | McFeely, William S., editor.
Title: Narrative of the life of Frederick Douglass, an American slave, written by himself : authoritative text, contexts, criticsm / edited by William L. Andrews (University of North Carolina at Chapel Hill) and William S. McFeely (University of Georgia).
Description: Second edition. | New York : W.W. Norton & Company, 2017. | Series: A Norton critical edition | Includes bibliographical references.
Identifiers: LCCN 2016015313 | **ISBN 9780393265446 (pbk.)**
Subjects: LCSH: Douglass, Frederick, 1818–1895. | African American abolitionists—Biography. | Abolitionists—United States—Biography. | Douglass, Frederick, 1818–1895. Narrative of the life of Frederick Douglass, an American slave.
Classification: LCC E449.D75 D686 2017 | DDC 973.8092 [B]—dc23
LC record available at https://lccn.loc.gov/2016015313

W. W. Norton & Company, Inc., 500 Fifth Avenue, New York, NY 10110-0017
wwnorton.com

W. W. Norton & Company Ltd., Castle House, 15 Carlisle Street, London W1D 3BS

1 2 3 4 5 6 7 8 9 0

Contents

Preface

Frederick Douglass has grown. When, two decades ago, we first edited the *Narrative of the Life of Frederick Douglass* for critical attention, we were fully confident of the importance of the book in American literature. We are no less so today; on the contrary, it has been quite remarkable to note the increased gain in importance of both the man and his book in any appraisal of American culture. Even in 1997 there lingered a sense that Douglass mattered primarily in matters of race. No such categorical designation will any longer suffice. There were towering figures in nineteenth-century American history whose ideas are as potent in the twenty-first, and few would deny now that Douglass indisputably stands among them.

The *Narrative* remains one of the great first-person accounts of a life in literature, but increasingly it is also a reminder that slavery, far from being a thing of the past, has gained in significance in American history. Though over, its effect is not. Douglass gave the subject one of its most telling voices. *Narrative of the Life of Frederick Douglass, an American Slave, Written by Himself*, published in 1845, echoes in powerful prose the antislavery speeches given by an escaped slave across the Northern states of the United States. That power remains. When he sat down to write the book, Douglass gave us not only a story of his life but a remarkable indictment of American slavery. Abolition of slavery was the greatest moral cause in the years before the Civil War, and Douglass was proud to have his book be one of its most powerful tracts. In our time, the *Narrative* forces us to confront the inequality that still pervades American society.

From his forthrightly personal first words, "I was born," until his final public words, Douglass makes clear that his commitment is to the antislavery cause. His hope is "that this little book may do something toward throwing light on the American slave system." Finally he made the public words firmly personal: "solemnly pledging my self anew to the sacred cause,—I subscribe myself FREDERICK DOUGLASS." By the fall of 1845, forty-five hundred copies of the *Narrative* were in circulation. With the exception of Harriet Beecher

Stowe's 1852 *Uncle Tom's Cabin; or, Life among the Lowly*, no other literary work contributed more to the beginning of the Civil War and the ending of slavery than did Douglass's book.

Slavery existed before anyone got around to recording its beginning. It came into particularly extensive use in the sixteenth century, with European exploitation of the rich natural resources of North and South America. In the United States it reached its peak in the nineteenth century when vast profits were gained from the sale of cotton raised by slave labor. In Great Britain, where cotton was made into cloth, Quakers and other nonconformists led by William Wilberforce organized to achieve slavery's elimination. They succeeded; slavery was abolished in Britain's Caribbean colonies in 1833. In the United States, late in the eighteenth century, Quakers were again pioneers in converting other reform-minded men and women to the cause. A major step in the growth of the abolitionist movement was taken by a Boston editor, William Lloyd Garrison, who, in 1831, in the first edition of his paper, *The Liberator*, proclaimed: "I will be heard." Antislavery societies formed and began drawing ardent adherents, but these abolitionists were never in the majority and faced ridicule and often violence for their beliefs. African American slaves and their free-born brethren had long dreamed of slavery's end. Frederick Douglass, living in New Bedford, was one these.

Douglass, born a slave in rural Maryland, had been sent as a boy to Baltimore where he taught himself to read and recite prose calling for liberty. A trained ship caulker by his late teens, he escaped to the Quaker port of New Bedford and worked on the docks. Hearing a rousing speech by Garrison and reading the *Liberator*, Douglass was inspired to make his first antislavery speech. When word of the power of his local oratory reached the Massachusetts Anti-Slavery Society, he was invited to address its annual 1841 meeting on Nantucket. The antislavery group was so impressed by his recounting of his own experiences as a slave that it hired him to give abolitionist speeches across the North. These became the raw material of his *Narrative*. Garrison was instrumental in its publication and wrote the famous preface to the book, which is included here.

Douglass's *Narrative* joined the remarkable books known as fugitive slave narratives in the middle of the nineteenth century. Many readers in the United States, Great Britain, and western Europe welcomed the publication of short, often sensational, autobiographies in which former slaves gave testimony of their experiences of slavery's terrors. *The Interesting Narrative of the Life of Olaudah Equiano* (1789), published in England, was the first former slave's autobiography to become an international best seller.

Douglass's narrative was followed by a number of widely read personal accounts by famous fugitives, such as *Narrative of William W. Brown, A Fugitive Slave* (1847), *Narrative of the Life and Adventures of Henry Bibb* (1849), and *Narrative of Henry Box Brown* (1849). Solomon Northup's *Twelve Years a Slave* (1853), the story of a free black man kidnapped and enslaved in Louisiana, gave graphic evidence of the terrors of slavery and of the extent of the lucrative interstate commerce in slaves. Harriet Jacobs's *Incidents in the Life of a Slave Girl Written by Herself* (1861) showed how its author fought back against sexual exploitation and ultimately gained her own freedom and that of her two children. The more than one hundred slave narratives separately published before Emancipation in 1865 contributed to the vast literature of slavery, which keeps growing as forgotten texts are recovered today. Most recently, economic historians have expanded the study of slavery to include its importance in the growth of capitalism's power. Douglass's varied experience of slavery in a major city and on a rural farm, as a house slave, field worker, and skilled tradesman, made him especially effective as an analyst of Southern slavery from multiple standpoints.

As famous as the *Narrative* was as an abolitionist tract, it was also a remarkable autobiography, one often compared to autobiographical books by Benjamin Franklin, Henry David Thoreau, and Jane Addams. Rich as is the narrative of his life, there is much Douglass does not tell us. We learn little about his remarkable grandmother who raised him as a child and even less about his numerous siblings and cousins. Poignantly, he tells us almost nothing of his mother, who was a slave on another plantation. Of his unknown father, he can only conjecture, which led him on a lifelong quest for more knowledge of his roots, including his birthday. In his *Narrative* he did not have room to go into great detail about his impressive African American family history or his wife's exciting separate escape from Maryland to Massachusetts. To do so would have disclosed to those eager to reenslave runaways how the Underground Railroad worked. Despite these omissions the *Narrative* became the way that many readers, then and now, first learned of slavery's true nature. But despite its picture of slavery, the *Narrative* is a remarkable story of a boy coming into manhood, of a person coming into his full strength.

Douglass published two autobiographies other than the *Narrative: My Bondage and My Freedom* (1855) and *Life and Times of Frederick Douglass* (1881, 1892), which with subtle differences retell his story and bring it up to date. By the time his third book was published, the white nation had lost interest in the lives of Americans who had been its slaves. America had put aside the problems of the freed people who had briefly had a chance at equality during

Reconstruction. Their basic needs and those of their descendants were ignored. They endured lynching, Jim Crow practices, the poverty of sharecropping, and disenfranchisement. The *Narrative* went into eclipse, to be returned to its relevance as African Americans began their long struggle for freedom that culminated in the civil rights movement of the 1950s and 1960s. Since then it has been on countless reading lists in high school and college courses not only as a document of African American history but as a work of literature. We urged scholarly attention to the book in the original Norton Critical Edition of the *Narrative* published in 1997. Now, in the twenty-first century, we reaffirm the book's historical importance and contemporary resonance and offer more critical perspectives on Douglass's art. His *Narrative* in hand, Frederick Douglass, standing taller than ever, summons us.

The heightened civil rights militancy of the 1960s, along with the rise of Black Studies in the academy, helped resurrect the *Narrative* and elevate Douglass to prominence as the key figure in the evolution of African American prose in the antebellum period. From the 1970s a wealth of useful studies of the *Narrative*'s artistry have demonstrated Douglass's centrality not only in early African American literature but in the mid-nineteenth-century American literary renaissance. In the 1980s and early 1990s discussion of the *Narrative* evolved from a predominately formalistic appreciation of Douglass's rhetorical art to increasingly widely ranging assessments of the relationship of the *Narrative* to historical trends and sociocultural norms and expressive traditions in the middle of the nineteenth century.

In this Norton Critical Edition, seven literary and cultural analyses of the *Narrative* published since 1979 have been selected to indicate some of the areas of investigation and evaluation that have engaged Douglass scholars over the past three decades. Drawing on his indispensable 1991 biography of Douglass, William S. McFeely initiates this review of criticism by situating the composition of *Narrative* in its own time and cultural circumstances. The selection from William L. Andrews's *To Tell a Free Story* explains the *Narrative*'s relationship to the American jeremiad, a popular literary and oratorical tradition that Douglass tried to adapt in order to appeal to his middle-class northern audience. The excerpt from Robert D. Richardson's biography of Henry David Thoreau attests to Douglass's influence on the antislavery message of Thoreau's classic *Walden* (1854). The selection from Houston A. Baker's *Blues, Ideology, and Afro-American Literature* shows how an economic reading of the text can yield significant insights into Douglass's development from slave to freeman to abolitionist lecturer. Surveying Douglass criticism since the 1960s, Deborah E. McDowell reads the *Narrative* through a feminist lens in "In the First Place: Making Frederick Douglass and the Afro-American Narrative Tradition." Selected from her book *Slavery on Trial,* Jeannine DeLombard's discussion of the *Narrative* reveals how adept Douglass was in fashioning his first-person witness into a quasi-legal indictment of slavery as a national crime. Finally, Henry Louis Gates, Jr.'s epilogue to *Picturing Frederick Douglass* on Douglass and photography dubs Douglass "the most photographed American of the nineteenth century" and goes on to help us understand why, starting with the frontispiece of his *Narrative,* Douglass self-consciously projected himself through the camera for the sake of sociopolitical reform and racial progress in America. The distinctive yet mutually reinforcing perspectives on Douglass and his *Narrative* in these seven essays testify to the richness of this text and its powerful ongoing engagement with twentieth- and twenty-first-century scholars and readers.

WILLIAM L. ANDREWS
WILLIAM S. MCFEELY

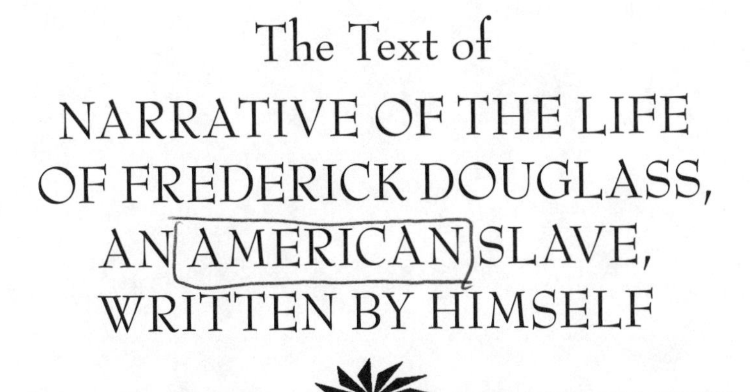

The Text of

NARRATIVE OF THE LIFE OF FREDERICK DOUGLASS, AN AMERICAN SLAVE, WRITTEN BY HIMSELF

Preface by William Lloyd Garrison[†]

In the month of August, 1841, I attended an anti-slavery convention in Nantucket, at which it was my happiness to become acquainted with FREDERICK DOUGLASS, the writer of the following Narrative. He was a stranger to nearly every member of that body; but, having recently made his escape from the southern prison-house of bondage, and feeling his curiosity excited to ascertain the principles and measures of the abolitionists,—of whom he had heard a somewhat vague description while he was a slave,—he was induced to give his attendance, on the occasion alluded to, though at that time a resident in New Bedford.[1]

Fortunate, most fortunate occurrence!—fortunate for the millions of his manacled brethren, yet panting for deliverance from their awful thraldom!—fortunate for the cause of negro emancipation, and of universal liberty!—fortunate for the land of his birth, which he has already done so much to save and bless!—fortunate for a large circle of friends and acquaintances, whose sympathy and affection he has strongly secured by the many sufferings he has endured, by his virtuous traits of character, by his ever-abiding remembrance of those who are in bonds, as being bound with them!—fortunate for the multitudes, in various parts of our republic, whose minds he has enlightened on the subject of slavery, and who have been melted to tears by his pathos, or roused to virtuous indignation by his stirring

† First printed in May 1845 by the Anti-Slavery Office in Boston, the source of the present text. Punctuation and hyphenation have been slightly regularized and a few typographical emendations have also been made. The spelling of names has not been altered.

When the *Narrative* was first published, the opening pages of the book were a "Preface" by William Lloyd Garrison and a "Letter from Wendell Phillips, Esq.," followed by Douglass's text as it appears in this volume.

William Lloyd Garrison (1805–1879) was the leading abolitionist at the time the *Narrative* was written. He was head of the New England Anti-Slavery Society and had founded the American Anti-Slavery Society, and he was the editor of the *Liberator.* He demanded "immediate and complete emancipation." Wendell Phillips (1811–1884), a lawyer, was scarcely less well known than Garrison as an antislavery advocate. Both were brilliant speakers who spoke often on behalf of the cause.

Garrison and Phillips were the most distinguished of the many important antislavery leaders who were present at the August 1841 antislavery meeting on Nantucket Island where Douglass gave his first great public antislavery speech. When Douglass had finished, Garrison rose to praise him warmly; immediately after the meeting, Douglass was hired as an agent of the New England Anti-Slavery Society and began his career as an orator, speaking across the North and in Great Britain in opposition to slavery.

The endorsements of Garrison and Phillips, published in the *Narrative*, served to assure white antislavery readers that the former slave's writing was to be trusted and to allay their own worries that Douglass, still technically a slave whom his master could attempt to recapture, was risking more than he should by publishing the book. Garrison and Phillips, like Douglass, were saying that having his story in print was too valuable to the cause not to have it published.

1. Douglass escaped from Hugh Auld's home in Baltimore in September 1838 and settled in New Bedford, Massachusetts, where he became active among the New Bedford abolitionists.

eloquence against the enslavers of men!—fortunate for himself, as it at once brought him into the field of public usefulness, "gave the world assurance of a MAN,"[2] quickened the slumbering energies of his soul, and consecrated him to the great work of breaking the rod of the oppressor, and letting the oppressed go free!

I shall never forget his first speech at the convention—the extraordinary emotion it excited in my own mind—the powerful impression it created upon a crowded auditory, completely taken by surprise—the applause which followed from the beginning to the end of his felicitous remarks. I think I never hated slavery so intensely as at that moment; certainly, my perception of the enormous outrage which is inflicted by it, on the godlike nature of its victims, was rendered far more clear than ever. There stood one, in physical proportion and stature commanding and exact—in intellect richly endowed—in natural eloquence a prodigy—in soul manifestly "created but a little lower than the angels"[3]—yet a slave, ay, a fugitive slave,—trembling for his safety, hardly daring to believe that on the American soil, a single white person could be found who would befriend him at all hazards, for the love of God and humanity! Capable of high attainments as an intellectual and moral being—needing nothing but a comparatively small amount of cultivation to make him an ornament to society and a blessing to his race—by the law of the land, by the voice of the people, by the terms of the slave code, he was only a piece of property, a beast of burden, a chattel personal, nevertheless!

A beloved friend[4] from New Bedford prevailed on Mr. DOUGLASS to address the convention. He came forward to the platform with a hesitancy and embarrassment, necessarily the attendants of a sensitive mind in such a novel position. After apologizing for his ignorance, and reminding the audience that slavery was a poor school for the human intellect and heart, he proceeded to narrate some of the facts in his own history as a slave, and in the course of his speech gave utterance to many noble thoughts and thrilling reflections. As soon as he had taken his seat, filled with hope and admiration, I rose, and declared that PATRICK HENRY,[5] of revolutionary fame, never made a speech more eloquent in the cause of liberty, than the one we had just listened to from the lips of that hunted fugitive. So I believed at that time—such is my belief now.

2. Shakespeare, *Hamlet* 3.4.62.
3. God created people "a little lower than the angels" (Psalms 8.5) to have authority over all other living creatures. Paul calls the Hebrews to look at Christ, who was made "a little lower than the angels" (Hebrews 2.7, 9).
4. William C. Coffin, New Bedford's leading abolitionist at the time.
5. U.S. patriot (1736–1799), famous for the words "I know not what course others may take, but as for me, give me liberty or give me death."

I reminded the audience of the peril which surrounded this self-emancipated young man at the North,—even in Massachusetts, on the soil of the Pilgrim Fathers, among the descendants of revolutionary sires; and I appealed to them, whether they would ever allow him to be carried back into slavery,—law or no law, constitution or no constitution. The response was unanimous and in thunder-tones—"NO!" "Will you succor and protect him as a brother-man—a resident of the old Bay State."[6] "YES!" shouted the whole mass, with an energy so startling, that the ruthless tyrants south of Mason and Dixon's line[7] might almost have heard the mighty burst of feeling, and recognized it as the pledge of an invincible determination, on the part of those who gave it, never to betray him that wanders, but to hide the outcast, and firmly to abide the consequences.

It was at once deeply impressed upon my mind, that, if Mr. DOUGLASS could be persuaded to consecrate his time and talents to the promotion of the anti-slavery enterprise, a powerful impetus would be given to it, and a stunning blow at the same time inflicted on northern prejudice against a colored complexion. I therefore endeavored to instil hope and courage into his mind, in order that he might dare to engage in a vocation so anomalous and responsible for a person in his situation; and I was seconded in this effort by warm-hearted friends, especially by the late General Agent of the Massachusetts Anti-Slavery Society, Mr. JOHN A. COLLINS, whose judgment in this instance entirely coincided with my own. At first, he could give no encouragement; with unfeigned diffidence, he expressed his conviction that he was not adequate to the performance of so great a task; the path marked out was wholly an untrodden one; he was sincerely apprehensive that he should do more harm than good. After much deliberation, however, he consented to make a trial; and ever since that period, he has acted as a lecturing agent, under the auspices either of the American or the Massachusetts Anti-Slavery Society. In labors he has been most abundant; and his success in combating prejudice, in gaining proselytes, in agitating the public mind, has far surpassed the most sanguine expectations that were raised at the commencement of his brilliant career. He has borne himself with gentleness and meekness, yet with true manliness of character. As a public speaker, he excels in pathos, wit, comparison, imitation, strength of reasoning, and fluency of language. There is in him that union of head and heart, which is indispensable to an enlightenment of the heads and a winning of

6. I.e., Massachusetts.
7. The boundary between Maryland and Pennsylvania, surveyed by Charles Mason and Jeremiah Dixon between 1763 and 1767.

the hearts of others. May his strength continue to be equal to his day! May he continue to "grow in grace, and in the knowledge of God,"[8] that he may be increasingly serviceable in the cause of bleeding humanity, whether at home or abroad!

It is certainly a very remarkable fact, that one of the most efficient advocates of the slave population, now before the public, is a fugitive slave, in the person of FREDERICK DOUGLASS; and that the free colored population of the United States are as ably represented by one of their own number, in the person of CHARLES LENOX REMOND,[9] whose eloquent appeals have extorted the highest applause of multitudes on both sides of the Atlantic. Let the calumniators of the colored race despise themselves for their baseness and illiberality of spirit, and henceforth cease to talk of the natural inferiority of those who require nothing but time and opportunity to attain to the highest point of human excellence.

It may, perhaps, be fairly questioned, whether any other portion of the population of the earth could have endured the privations, sufferings and horrors of slavery, without having become more degraded in the scale of humanity than the slaves of African descent. Nothing has been left undone to cripple their intellects, darken their minds, debase their moral nature, obliterate all traces of their relationship to mankind; and yet how wonderfully they have sustained the mighty load of a most frightful bondage, under which they have been groaning for centuries! To illustrate the effect of slavery on the white man,—to show that he has no powers of endurance, in such a condition, superior to those of his black brother,—DANIEL O'CONNELL,[1] the distinguished advocate of universal emancipation, and the mightiest champion of prostrate but not conquered Ireland, relates the following anecdote in a speech delivered by him in the Conciliation Hall, Dublin, before the Loyal National Repeal Association, March 31, 1845. "No matter," said Mr. O'CONNELL, "under what specious term it may disguise itself, slavery is still hideous. *It has a natural, an inevitable tendency to brutalize every noble faculty of man.* An American sailor, who was cast away on the shore of Africa, where he was kept in slavery for three years, was, at the expiration of that period, found to be imbruted and stultified—he had lost all reasoning power; and having forgotten his native language, could only utter some savage gibberish between Arabic and English, which nobody could understand, and which even he himself found difficulty in pronouncing. So much for the

8. 2 Peter 3.18.
9. Black leader of the antislavery movement (1810–1873), born free in Salem, Massachusetts; he traveled widely, often with Douglass, speaking for the abolitionist cause.
1. Irish statesman (1775–1847), fighter for Catholic emancipation and Irish independence, called the "Liberator."

humanizing influence of THE DOMESTIC INSTITUTION!" Admitting this to have been an extraordinary case of mental deterioration, it proves at least that the white slave can sink as low in the scale of humanity as the black one.

Mr. DOUGLASS has very properly chosen to write his own Narrative, in his own style, and according to the best of his ability, rather than to employ some one else. It is, therefore, entirely his own production; and, considering how long and dark was the career he had to run as a slave,—how few have been his opportunities to improve his mind since he broke his iron fetters,—it is, in my judgment, highly creditable to his head and heart. He who can peruse it without a tearful eye, a heaving breast, an afflicted spirit,—without being filled with an unutterable abhorrence of slavery and all its abettors, and animated with a determination to seek the immediate overthrow of that execrable system,—without trembling for the fate of this country in the hands of a righteous God, who is ever on the side of the oppressed, and whose arm is not shortened that it cannot save,—must have a flinty heart, and be qualified to act the part of a trafficker "in slaves and the souls of men."[2] I am confident that it is essentially true in all its statements; that nothing has been set down in malice, nothing exaggerated, nothing drawn from the imagination; that it comes short of the reality, rather than overstates a single fact in regard to SLAVERY AS IT IS. The experience of FREDERICK DOUGLASS, as a slave, was not a peculiar one; his lot was not especially a hard one; his case may be regarded as a very fair specimen of the treatment of slaves in Maryland, in which State it is conceded that they are better fed and less cruelly treated than in Georgia, Alabama, or Louisiana. Many have suffered incomparably more, while very few on the plantations have suffered less, than himself. Yet how deplorable was his situation! what terrible chastisements were inflicted upon his person! what still more shocking outrages were perpetrated upon his mind! with all his noble powers and sublime aspirations, how like a brute was he treated, even by those professing to have the same mind in them that was in Christ Jesus! to what dreadful liabilities was he continually subjected! how destitute of friendly counsel and aid, even in his greatest extremities! how heavy was the midnight of woe which shrouded in blackness the last ray of hope, and filled the future with terror and gloom! what longings after freedom took possession of his breast, and how his misery augmented, in proportion as he grew reflective and intelligent,—thus demonstrating that a happy slave is an extinct man! how he thought, reasoned, felt, under the lash of the driver, with the chains upon his limbs! what perils he encountered in his

2. Revelations 18.13.

endeavors to escape from his horrible doom! and how signal have been his deliverance and preservation in the midst of a nation of pitiless enemies!

This Narrative contains many affecting incidents, many passages of great eloquence and power; but I think the most thrilling one of them all is the description DOUGLASS gives of his feelings, as he stood soliloquizing respecting his fate, and the chances of his one day being a freeman, on the banks of the Chesapeake Bay—viewing the receding vessels as they flew with their white wings before the breeze, and apostrophizing them as animated by the living spirit of freedom. Who can read that passage, and be insensible to its pathos and sublimity? Compressed into it is a whole Alexandrian library[3] of thought, feeling, and sentiment—all that can, all that need be urged, in the form of expostulation, entreaty, rebuke, against that crime of crimes,—making man the property of his fellow-man! O, how accursed is that system, which entombs the godlike mind of man, defaces the divine image, reduces those who by creation were crowned with glory and honor to a level with four-footed beasts, and exalts the dealer in human flesh above all that is called God! Why should its existence be prolonged one hour? Is it not evil, only evil, and that continually? What does its presence imply but the absence of all fear of God, all regard for man, on the part of the people of the United States? Heaven speed its eternal overthrow!

So profoundly ignorant of the nature of slavery are many persons, that they are stubbornly incredulous whenever they read or listen to any recital of the cruelties which are daily inflicted on its victims. They do not deny that the slaves are held as property; but that terrible fact seems to convey to their minds no idea of injustice, exposure to outrage, or savage barbarity. Tell them of cruel scourgings, of mutilations and brandings, of scenes of pollution and blood, of the banishment of all light and knowledge, and they affect to be greatly indignant at such enormous exaggerations, such wholesale misstatements, such abominable libels on the character of the southern planters! As if all these direful outrages were not the natural results of slavery! As if it were less cruel to reduce a human being to the condition of a thing, than to give him a severe flagellation, or to deprive him of necessary food and clothing! As if whips, chains, thumb-screws, paddles, bloodhounds, overseers, drivers, patrols, were not all indispensable to keep the slaves down, and to give protection to their ruthless oppressors! As if, when the marriage institution is abolished, concubinage, adultery, and incest, must not necessarily abound; when all the rights of humanity are

3. Alexandria, in Egypt, housed the great library center of the Greco-Roman world.

annihilated, any barrier remains to protect the victim from the fury of the spoiler; when absolute power is assumed over life and liberty, it will not be wielded with destructive sway! Skeptics of this character abound in society. In some few instances, their incredulity arises from a want of reflection; but, generally, it indicates a hatred of the light, a desire to shield slavery from the assaults of its foes, a contempt of the colored race, whether bond or free. Such will try to discredit the shocking tales of slaveholding cruelty which are recorded in this truthful Narrative; but they will labor in vain. Mr. DOUGLASS has frankly disclosed the place of his birth, the names of those who claimed ownership in his body and soul, and the names also of those who committed the crimes which he has alleged against them. His statements, therefore, may easily be disproved, if they are untrue.

In the course of his Narrative, he relates two instances of murderous cruelty,—in one of which a planter deliberately shot a slave belonging to a neighboring plantation, who had unintentionally gotten within his lordly domain in quest of fish; and in the other, an overseer blew out the brains of a slave who had fled to a stream of water to escape a bloody scourging. Mr. DOUGLASS states that in neither of these instances was any thing done by way of legal arrest or judicial investigation. The Baltimore American, of March 17, 1845, relates a similar case of atrocity, perpetrated with similar impunity—as follows:—"*Shooting a Slave.*—We learn, upon the authority of a letter from Charles county, Maryland, received by a gentleman of this city, that a young man, named Matthews, a nephew of General Matthews, and whose father, it is believed, holds an office at Washington, killed one of the slaves upon his father's farm by shooting him. The letter states that young Matthews had been left in charge of the farm; that he gave an order to the servant, which was disobeyed, when he proceeded to the house, *obtained a gun, and, returning, shot the servant.* He immediately, the letter continues, fled to his father's residence, where he still remains unmolested."—Let it never be forgotten, that no slaveholder or overseer can be convicted of any outrage perpetrated on the person of a slave, however diabolical it may be, on the testimony of colored witnesses, whether bond or free. By the slave code, they are adjudged to be as incompetent to testify against a white man, as though they were indeed a part of the brute creation. Hence, there is no legal protection in fact, whatever there may be in form, for the slave population; and any amount of cruelty may be inflicted on them with impunity. Is it possible for the human mind to conceive of a more horrible state of society?

The effect of a religious profession on the conduct of southern masters is vividly described in the following Narrative, and shown to be any thing but salutary. In the nature of the case, it must be in the highest degree pernicious. The testimony of Mr. DOUGLASS, on this point, is sustained by a cloud of witnesses, whose veracity is unimpeachable. "A slaveholder's profession of Christianity is a palpable imposture. He is a felon of the highest grade. He is a man-stealer. It is of no importance what you put in the other scale."

Reader! are you with the man-stealers in sympathy and purpose, or on the side of their down-trodden victims? If with the former, then are you the foe of God and man. If with the latter, what are you prepared to do and dare in their behalf? Be faithful, be vigilant, be untiring in your efforts to break every yoke, and let the oppressed go free.[4] Come what may—cost what it may—inscribe on the banner which you unfurl to the breeze, as your religious and political motto—"NO COMPROMISE WITH SLAVERY! NO UNION WITH SLAVEHOLDERS!"

WM. LLOYD GARRISON.

BOSTON, *May* 1, 1845.

Letter from Wendell Phillips, Esq.

BOSTON, *April* 22, 1845.

My Dear Friend:

You remember the old fable of "The Man and the Lion," where the lion complained that he should not be so misrepresented "when the lions wrote history."

I am glad the time has come when the "lions write history." We have been left long enough to gather the character of slavery from the involuntary evidence of the masters. One might, indeed, rest sufficiently satisfied with what, it is evident, must be, in general, the results of such a relation, without seeking farther to find whether they have followed in every instance. Indeed, those who stare at the half-peck of corn a week, and love to count the lashes on the slave's back, are seldom the "stuff" out of which reformers and abolitionists are to be made. I remember that, in 1838, many were waiting for the results of the West India experiment,[1] before they could come into our ranks. Those "results" have come long ago; but, alas! few of that number have come with them, as converts. A man must be disposed to judge of emancipation by other tests than whether it

4. Isaiah 58.6.

1. The British Parliament abolished slavery throughout the empire in 1833, and so in the late 1830s Britain's West Indian sugar islands were undergoing a major transition from slavery to freedom. White planters were allotted a total of £20 million in compensation for their loss of "property," and a brief apprenticeship period was designed to prevent an immediate withdrawal of labor. However, many blacks left the plantations, established free villages, and became small landholders themselves. The consequent labor shortage caused bankruptcies and financial loss for many white planters in the 1840s as both sugar production and sugar prices fell, leading many white people to believe that the "experiment" had been a failure.

has increased the produce of sugar,—and to hate slavery for other reasons than because it starves men and whips women,—before he is ready to lay the first stone of his anti-slavery life.

I was glad to learn, in your story, how early the most neglected of God's children waken to a sense of their rights, and of the injustice done them. Experience is a keen teacher; and long before you had mastered your A B C, or knew where the "white sails" of the Chesapeake were bound, you began, I see, to gauge the wretchedness of the slave, not by his hunger and want, not by his lashes and toil, but by the cruel and blighting death which gathers over his soul.

In connection with this, there is one circumstance which makes your recollections peculiarly valuable, and renders your early insight the more remarkable. You come from that part of the country where we are told slavery appears with its fairest features. Let us hear, then, what it is at its best estate—gaze on its bright side, if it has one; and then imagination may task her powers to add dark lines to the picture, as she travels southward to that (for the colored man) Valley of the Shadow of Death,[2] where the Mississippi sweeps along.

Again, we have known you long, and can put the most entire confidence in your truth, candor, and sincerity. Every one who has heard you speak has felt, and, I am confident, every one who reads your book will feel, persuaded that you give them a fair specimen of the whole truth. No one-sided portrait,—no wholesale complaints,—but strict justice done, whenever individual kindliness has neutralized, for a moment, the deadly system with which it was strangely allied. You have been with us, too, some years, and can fairly compare the twilight of rights, which your race enjoy at the North, with that "noon of night"[3] under which they labor south of Mason and Dixon's line. Tell us whether, after all, the half-free colored man of Massachusetts is worse off than the pampered slave of the rice swamps!

In reading your life, no one can say that we have unfairly picked out some rare specimens of cruelty. We know that the bitter drops, which even you have drained from the cup, are no incidental aggravations, no individual ills, but such as must mingle always and necessarily in the lot of every slave. They are the essential ingredients, not the occasional results, of the system.

After all, I shall read your book with trembling for you. Some years ago, when you were beginning to tell me your real name and birthplace, you may remember I stopped you, and preferred to

2. Psalms 23.4, commonly recognized by nineteenth-century readers.
3. Typical abolitionist rhetoric, meaning that even the noonday sun was darkened by the moral blight of slavery.

remain ignorant of all. With the exception of a vague description, so I continued, till the other day, when you read me your memoirs. I hardly knew, at the time, whether to thank you or not for the sight of them, when I reflected that it was still dangerous, in Massachusetts, for honest men to tell their names! They say the fathers, in 1776, signed the Declaration of Independence with the halter about their necks. You, too, publish your declaration of freedom with danger compassing you around. In all the broad lands which the Constitution of the United States overshadows, there is no single spot,—however narrow or desolate,—where a fugitive slave can plant himself and say, "I am safe." The whole armory of Northern Law has no shield for you. I am free to say that, in your place, I should throw the MS. into the fire.

You, perhaps, may tell your story in safety, endeared as you are to so many warm hearts by rare gifts, and a still rarer devotion of them to the service of others. But it will be owing only to your labors, and the fearless efforts of those who, trampling the laws and Constitution of the country under their feet, are determined that they will "hide the outcast,"[4] and that their hearths shall be, spite of the law, an asylum for the oppressed, if, some time or other, the humblest may stand in our streets, and bear witness in safety against the cruelties of which he has been the victim.

Yet is is sad to think, that these very throbbing hearts which welcome your story, and form your best safeguard in telling it, are all beating contrary to the "statute in such case made and provided." Go on, my dear friend, till you, and those who, like you, have been saved, so as by fire, from the dark prison-house, shall stereotype these free, illegal pulses into statutes; and New England, cutting loose from a blood-stained Union, shall glory in being the house of refuge for the oppressed;—till we no longer merely "*hide* the outcast," or make a merit of standing idly by while he is hunted in our midst; but, consecrating anew the soil of the Pilgrims as an asylum for the oppressed, proclaim our *welcome* to the slave so loudly, that the tones shall reach every hut in the Carolinas, and make the broken-hearted bondman leap up at the thought of old Massachusetts.

God speed the day!
Till then, and ever,
Yours truly,
WENDELL PHILLIPS.

4. Isaiah 16.3.

Chapter I

I was born in Tuckahoe, near Hillsborough, and about twelve miles from Easton, in Talbot county, Maryland. I have no accurate knowledge of my age, never having seen any authentic record containing it. By far the larger part of the slaves know as little of their ages as horses know of theirs, and it is the wish of most masters within my knowledge to keep their slaves thus ignorant. I do not remember to have ever met a slave who could tell of his birthday. They seldom come nearer to it than planting-time, harvest-time, cherry-time, spring-time, or fall-time. A want of information concerning my own was a source of unhappiness to me even during childhood. The white children could tell their ages. I could not tell why I ought to be deprived of the same privilege. I was not allowed to make any inquiries of my master concerning it. He deemed all such inquiries on the part of a slave improper and impertinent, and evidence of a restless spirit. The nearest estimate I can give makes me now between twenty-seven and twenty-eight years of age. I come to this, from hearing my master say, some time during 1835, I was about seventeen years old.

My mother was named Harriet Bailey. She was the daughter of Isaac and Betsey Bailey, both colored, and quite dark. My mother was of a darker complexion than either my grandmother or grandfather.

My father was a white man. He was admitted to be such by all I ever heard speak of my parentage. The opinion was also whispered that my master was my father; but of the correctness of this opinion, I know nothing; the means of knowing was withheld from me. My mother and I were separated when I was but an infant—before I knew her as my mother. It is a common custom, in the part of Maryland from which I ran away, to part children from their mothers at a very early age. Frequently, before the child has reached its twelfth month, its mother is taken from it, and hired out on some farm a considerable distance off, and the child is placed under the care of an old woman, too old for field labor. For what this separation is done, I do not know, unless it be to hinder the development of the child's affection toward its mother, and to blunt and destroy the natural affection of the mother for the child. This is the inevitable result.

I never saw my mother, to know her as such, more than four or five times in my life; and each of these times was very short in duration, and at night. She was hired by a Mr. Stewart, who lived about twelve miles from my home. She made her journeys to see me in the night, travelling the whole distance on foot, after the performance of her day's work. She was a field hand, and a whipping is the penalty of not being in the field at sunrise, unless a slave has special permission from his or her master to the contrary—a permission which they seldom get, and one that gives to him that gives it the proud name of being a kind master. I do not recollect of ever seeing my mother by the light of day. She was with me in the night. She would lie down with me, and get me to sleep, but long before I waked she was gone. Very little communication ever took place between us. Death soon ended what little we could have while she lived, and with it her hardships and suffering. She died when I was about seven years old, on one of my master's farms, near Lee's Mill. I was not allowed to be present during her illness, at her death, or burial. She was gone long before I knew any thing about it. Never having enjoyed, to any considerable extent, her soothing presence, her tender and watchful care, I received the tidings of her death with much the same emotions I should have probably felt at the death of a stranger.

Called thus suddenly away, she left me without the slightest intimation of who my father was. The whisper that my master was my father, may or may not be true; and, true or false, it is of but little consequence to my purpose whilst the fact remains, in all its glaring odiousness, that slaveholders have ordained, and by law established, that the children of slave women shall in all cases follow the condition of their mothers; and this is done too obviously to administer to their own lusts, and make a gratification of their wicked desires profitable as well as pleasurable; for by this cunning arrangement, the slaveholder, in cases not a few, sustains to his slaves the double relation of master and father.

I know of such cases; and it is worthy of remark that such slaves invariably suffer greater hardships, and have more to contend with, than others. They are, in the first place, a constant offence to their mistress. She is ever disposed to find fault with them; they can seldom do any thing to please her; she is never better pleased than when she sees them under the lash, especially when she suspects her husband of showing to his mulatto children favors which he withholds from his black slaves. The master is frequently compelled to sell this class of his slaves, out of deference to the feelings of his white wife; and, cruel as the deed may strike any one to be, for a man to sell his own children to human flesh-mongers, it is often the dictate of humanity for him to do so; for, unless he does this, he must not only whip them himself, but must stand by and see one white son tie up his brother, of but few shades darker complexion than himself, and ply the gory lash to his naked back; and if he lisp one word of disapproval, it is set down to his parental partiality, and only makes a bad matter worse, both for himself and the slave whom he would protect and defend.

Every year brings with it multitudes of this class of slaves. It was doubtless in consequence of a knowledge of this fact, that one great statesman of the south predicted the downfall of slavery by the inevitable laws of population. Whether this prophecy is ever fulfilled or not, it is nevertheless plain that a very different-looking class of people are springing up at the south, and are now held in slavery, from those originally brought to this country from Africa; and if their increase will do no other good, it will do away the force of the argument, that God cursed Ham,[1] and therefore American slavery is right. If the lineal descendants of Ham are alone to be scripturally enslaved, it is certain that slavery at the south must soon become unscriptural; for thousands are ushered into the world, annually, who, like myself, owe their existence to white fathers, and those fathers most frequently their own masters.

I have had two masters. My first master's name was Anthony. I do not remember his first name. He was generally called Captain Anthony—a title which, I presume, he acquired by sailing a craft on the Chesapeake Bay. He was not considered a rich slaveholder. He owned two or three farms, and about thirty slaves. His farms and slaves were under the care of an overseer. The overseer's name was Plummer. Mr. Plummer was a miserable drunkard, a profane swearer, and a savage monster. He always went armed with a cowskin[2] and a heavy cudgel. I have known him to cut and slash the women's heads so horribly, that even master would be enraged at his cruelty, and would threaten to whip him if he did not mind himself. Master, however, was not a humane slaveholder. It required extraordinary barbarity on the part of an overseer to affect him. He was a cruel man, hardened by a long life of slaveholding. He would at times seem to take great pleasure in whipping a slave. I have often been awakened at the dawn of day by the most heart-rending shrieks of an own aunt of mine, whom he used to tie up to a joist, and whip upon her naked back till she was literally covered with blood. No words, no tears, no prayers, from his gory victim, seemed to move his iron heart from its bloody purpose. The louder she screamed, the harder he whipped; and where the blood ran fastest, there he whipped longest. He would whip her to make her scream, and whip her to make her hush; and not until overcome by fatigue, would he cease to swing the blood-clotted cowskin. I remember the first time I ever witnessed this horrible exhibition. I was quite a child, but I well remember it. I never shall forget it whilst I remember any thing. It was the first of a long series of such outrages, of which I was doomed to be a witness and a participant. It struck me with

1. The specious argument referred to is based on an interpretation of Genesis 9.20–27, in which Noah curses his son Ham and condemns him to bondage to his brothers.
2. A whip made of raw cowhide.

awful force. It was the blood-stained gate, the entrance to the hell of slavery, through which I was about to pass. It was a most terrible spectacle. I wish I could commit to paper the feelings with which I beheld it.

This occurrence took place very soon after I went to live with my old master, and under the following circumstances. Aunt Hester went out one night,—where or for what I do not know,—and happened to be absent when my master desired her presence. He had ordered her not to go out evenings, and warned her that she must never let him catch her in company with a young man, who was paying attention to her, belonging to Colonel Lloyd. The young man's name was Ned Roberts, generally called Lloyd's Ned. Why master was so careful of her, may be safely left to conjecture. She was a woman of noble form, and of graceful proportions, having very few equals, and fewer superiors, in personal appearance, among the colored or white women of our neighborhood.

Aunt Hester had not only disobeyed his orders in going out, but had been found in company with Lloyd's Ned; which circumstance, I found, from what he said while whipping her, was the chief offence. Had he been a man of pure morals himself, he might have been thought interested in protecting the innocence of my aunt; but those who knew him will not suspect him of any such virtue. Before he commenced whipping Aunt Hester, he took her into the kitchen, and stripped her from neck to waist, leaving her neck, shoulders, and back, entirely naked. He then told her to cross her hands, calling her at the same time a d——d b——h. After crossing her hands, he tied them with a strong rope, and led her to a stool under a large hook in the joist, put in for the purpose. He made her get upon the stool, and tied her hands to the hook. She now stood fair for his infernal purpose. Her arms were stretched up at their full length, so that she stood upon the ends of her toes. He then said to her, "Now, you d——d b——h, I'll learn you how to disobey my orders!" and after rolling up his sleeves, he commenced to lay on the heavy cowskin, and soon the warm, red blood (amid heartrending shrieks from her, and horrid oaths from him) came dripping to the floor. I was so terrified and horror-stricken at the sight, that I hid myself in a closet, and dared not venture out till long after the bloody transaction was over. I expected it would be my turn next. It was all new to me. I had never seen any thing like it before. I had always lived with my grandmother on the outskirts of the plantation, where she was put to raise the children of the younger women. I had therefore been, until now, out of the way of the bloody scenes that often occurred on the plantation.

Chapter II

My master's family consisted of two sons, Andrew and Richard; one daughter, Lucretia, and her husband, Captain Thomas Auld. They lived in one house, upon the home plantation of Colonel Edward Lloyd. My master was Colonel Lloyd's clerk and superintendent. He was what might be called the overseer of the overseers. I spent two years of childhood on this plantation in my old master's family. It was here that I witnessed the bloody transaction recorded in the first chapter; and as I received my first impressions of slavery on this plantation, I will give some description of it, and of slavery as it there existed. The plantation is about twelve miles north of Easton, in Talbot county, and is situated on the border of Miles River. The principal products raised upon it were tobacco, corn, and wheat. These were raised in great abundance; so that, with the products of this and the other farms belonging to him, he was able to keep in almost constant employment a large sloop, in carrying them to market at Baltimore. This sloop was named Sally Lloyd, in honor of one of the colonel's daughters. My master's son-in-law, Captain Auld, was master of the vessel; she was otherwise manned by the colonel's own slaves. Their names were Peter, Isaac, Rich, and Jake. These were esteemed very highly by the other slaves, and looked upon as the privileged ones of the plantation; for it was no small affair, in the eyes of the slaves, to be allowed to see Baltimore.

Colonel Lloyd kept from three to four hundred slaves on his home plantation, and owned a large number more on the neighboring farms belonging to him. The names of the farms nearest to the home plantation were Wye Town and New Design. "Wye Town" was under the overseership of a man named Noah Willis. New Design was under the overseership of a Mr. Townsend. The overseers of these, and all the rest of the farms, numbering over twenty, received advice and direction from the managers of the home plantation. This was the great business place. It was the seat of government for the whole twenty farms. All disputes among the overseers were settled here. If a slave was convicted of any high misdemeanor, became unmanageable, or evinced a determination to run away, he was brought immediately here, severely whipped, put on board the sloop, carried to Baltimore, and sold to Austin Woolfolk, or some other slave-trader, as a warning to the slaves remaining.

Here, too, the slaves of all the other farms received their monthly allowance of food, and their yearly clothing. The men and women slaves received, as their monthly allowance of food, eight pounds of pork, or its equivalent in fish, and one bushel of corn meal. Their yearly clothing consisted of two coarse linen shirts, one pair of linen trousers, like the shirts, one jacket, one pair of trousers for winter, made of coarse negro cloth, one pair of stockings, and one pair of shoes; the whole of which could not have cost more than seven dollars. The allowance of the slave children was given to their mothers, or the old women having the care of them. The children unable to work in the field had neither shoes, stockings, jackets, nor trousers, given to them; their clothing consisted of two coarse linen shirts per year. When these failed them, they went naked until the next allowance-day. Children from seven to ten years old, of both sexes, almost naked, might be seen at all seasons of the year.

There were no beds given the slaves, unless one coarse blanket be considered such, and none but the men and women had these. This, however, is not considered a very great privation. They find less difficulty from the want of beds, than from the want of time to sleep; for when their day's work in the field is done, the most of them having their washing, mending, and cooking to do, and having few or none of the ordinary facilities for doing either of these, very many of their sleeping hours are consumed in preparing for the field the coming day; and when this is done, old and young, male and female, married and single, drop down side by side, on one common bed,—the cold, damp floor,—each covering himself or herself with their miserable blankets; and here they sleep till they are summoned to the field by the driver's horn. At the sound of this, all must rise, and be off to the field. There must be no halting; every one must be at his or her post; and woe betides them who hear not this morning summons to the field; for if they are not awakened by the sense of hearing, they are by the sense of feeling: no age nor sex finds any favor. Mr. Severe, the overseer, used to stand by the door of the quarter, armed with a large hickory stick and heavy cowskin, ready to whip any one who was so unfortunate as not to hear, or, from any other cause, was prevented from being ready to start for the field at the sound of the horn.

Mr. Severe was rightly named: he was a cruel man. I have seen him whip a woman, causing the blood to run half an hour at the time; and this, too, in the midst of her crying children, pleading for their mother's release. He seemed to take pleasure in manifesting his fiendish barbarity. Added to his cruelty, he was a profane swearer. It was enough to chill the blood and stiffen the hair of an ordinary man to hear him talk. Scarce a sentence escaped him but that was commenced or concluded by some horrid oath. The field was the place to witness his cruelty and profanity. His presence made it both the field of blood and of blasphemy. From the rising till the going down of the sun, he was cursing, raving, cutting, and slashing among the slaves of the field, in the most frightful manner. His career was short. He died very soon after I went to Colonel Lloyd's; and he died as he lived, uttering, with his dying groans, bitter curses and horrid oaths. His death was regarded by the slaves as the result of a merciful providence.

Mr. Severe's place was filled by a Mr. Hopkins. He was a very different man. He was less cruel, less profane, and made less noise, than Mr. Severe. His course was characterized by no extraordinary demonstrations of cruelty. He whipped, but seemed to take no pleasure in it. He was called by the slaves a good overseer.

The home plantation of Colonel Lloyd wore the appearance of a country village. All the mechanical operations for all the farms were performed here. The shoemaking and mending, the blacksmithing, cartwrighting, coopering, weaving, and grain-grinding, were all performed by the slaves on the home plantation. The whole place wore a business-like aspect very unlike the neighboring farms. The number of houses, too, conspired to give it advantage over the neighboring farms. It was called by the slaves the *Great House Farm.* Few privileges were esteemed higher, by the slaves of the out-farms, than that of being selected to do errands at the Great House Farm. It was associated in their minds with greatness. A representative could not be prouder of his election to a seat in the American Congress, than a slave on one of the out-farms would be of his election to do errands at the Great House Farm. They regarded it as evidence of great confidence reposed in them by their overseers; and it was on this account, as well as a constant desire to be out of the field from under the driver's lash, that they esteemed it a high privilege, one worth careful living for. He was called the smartest and most trusty fellow, who had this honor conferred upon him the most frequently. The competitors for this office sought as diligently to please their overseers, as the office-seekers in the political parties seek to please and deceive the people. The same traits of character might be seen in Colonel Lloyd's slaves, as are seen in the slaves of the political parties.

The slaves selected to go to the Great House Farm, for the monthly allowance for themselves and their fellow-slaves, were peculiarly enthusiastic. While on their way, they would make the dense old woods, for miles around, reverberate with their wild songs, revealing at once the highest joy and the deepest sadness. They would compose and sing as they went along, consulting neither time nor tune. The thought that came up, came out—if not in the word, in the sound;—and as frequently in the one as in the other. They would sometimes sing the most pathetic sentiment in the most rapturous tone, and the most rapturous sentiment in the most pathetic tone. Into all of their songs they would manage to weave something of the Great House Farm. Especially would they do this, when leaving home. They would then sing most exultingly the following words:—

"I am going away to the Great House Farm!
O, yea! O, yea! O!"

This they would sing, as a chorus, to words which to many would seem unmeaning jargon, but which, nevertheless, were full of meaning to themselves. I have sometimes thought that the mere hearing of those songs would do more to impress some minds with the horrible character of slavery, than the reading of whole volumes of philosophy on the subject could do.

I did not, when a slave, understand the deep meaning of those rude and apparently incoherent songs. I was myself within the circle; so that I neither saw nor heard as those without might see and hear. They told a tale of woe which was then altogether beyond my feeble comprehension; they were tones loud, long, and deep; they breathed the prayer and complaint of souls boiling over with the bitterest anguish. Every tone was a testimony against slavery, and a prayer to God for deliverance from chains. The hearing of those wild notes always depressed my spirit, and filled me with ineffable sadness. I have frequently found myself in tears while hearing them. The mere recurrence to those songs, even now, afflicts me; and while I am writing these lines, an expression of feeling has already found its way down my cheek. To those songs I trace my first glimmering conception of the dehumanizing character of slavery. I can never get rid of that conception. Those songs still follow me, to deepen my hatred of slavery, and quicken my sympathies for my brethren in bonds. If any one wishes to be impressed with the soul-killing effects of slavery, let him go to Colonel Lloyd's plantation, and, on allowance-day, place himself in the deep pine woods, and there let him, in silence, analyze the sounds that shall pass through the chambers of his soul,—and if he is not thus impressed, it will only be because "there is no flesh in his obdurate heart."[1]

I have often been utterly astonished, since I came to the north, to find persons who could speak of the singing, among slaves, as evidence of their contentment and happiness. It is impossible to conceive of a greater mistake. Slaves sing most when they are most unhappy. The songs of the slave represent the sorrows of his heart; and he is relieved by them, only as an aching heart is relieved by its tears. At least, such is my experience. I have often sung to drown my sorrow, but seldom to express my happiness. Crying for joy, and singing for joy, were alike uncommon to me while in the jaws of

1. Cf. "The Time-Piece," book 2, line 8, in William Cowper's popular poem *The Task* (1785).

slavery. The singing of a man cast away upon a desolate island might be as appropriately considered as evidence of contentment and happiness, as the singing of a slave; the songs of the one and of the other are prompted by the same emotion.

Chapter III

Colonel Lloyd kept a large and finely cultivated garden, which afforded almost constant employment for four men, besides the chief gardener, (Mr. M'Durmond.) This garden was probably the greatest attraction of the place. During the summer months, people came from far and near—from Baltimore, Easton, and Annapolis—to see it. It abounded in fruits of almost every description, from the hardy apple of the north to the delicate orange of the south. This garden was not the least source of trouble on the plantation. Its excellent fruit was quite a temptation to the hungry swarms of boys, as well as the older slaves, belonging to the colonel, few of whom had the virtue or the vice to resist it. Scarcely a day passed, during the summer, but that some slave had to take the lash for stealing fruit. The colonel had to resort to all kinds of stratagems to keep his slaves out of the garden. The last and most successful one was that of tarring his fence all around, after which, if a slave was caught with any tar upon his person, it was deemed sufficient proof that he had either been into the garden, or had tried to get in. In either case, he was severely whipped by the chief gardener. This plan worked well; the slaves became as fearful of tar as of the lash. They seemed to realize the impossibility of touching *tar* without being defiled.

The colonel also kept a splendid riding equipage. His stable and carriage-house presented the appearance of some of our large city livery establishments. His horses were of the finest form and noblest blood. His carriage-house contained three splendid coaches, three or four gigs, besides dearborns and barouches[1] of the most fashionable style.

This establishment was under the care of two slaves—old Barney and young Barney—father and son. To attend to this establishment was their sole work. But it was by no means an easy employment; for in nothing was Colonel Lloyd more particular than in the management of his horses. The slightest inattention to these was unpardonable, and was visited upon those, under whose care they were placed, with the severest punishment; no excuse could shield them, if the colonel only suspected any want of attention to his horses—a supposition which he frequently indulged, and one which, of course, made the office of old and young Barney a very trying one.

1. Different kinds of carriages.

They never knew when they were safe from punishment. They were frequently whipped when least deserving, and escaped whipping when most deserving it. Every thing depended upon the looks of the horses, and the state of Colonel Lloyd's own mind when his horses were brought to him for use. If a horse did not move fast enough, or hold his head high enough, it was owing to some fault of his keepers. It was painful to stand near the stable-door, and hear the various complaints against the keepers when a horse was taken out for use. "This horse has not had proper attention. He has not been sufficiently rubbed and curried, or he has not been properly fed; his food was too wet or too dry; he got it too soon or too late; he was too hot or too cold; he had too much hay, and not enough of grain; or he had too much grain, and not enough of hay; instead of old Barney's attending to the horse, he had very improperly left it to his son." To all these complaints, no matter how unjust, the slave must answer never a word. Colonel Lloyd could not brook any contradiction from a slave. When he spoke, a slave must stand, listen, and tremble; and such was literally the case. I have seen Colonel Lloyd make old Barney, a man between fifty and sixty years of age, uncover his bald head, kneel down upon the cold, damp ground, and receive upon his naked and toil-worn shoulders more than thirty lashes at the time. Colonel Lloyd had three sons—Edward, Murray, and Daniel,—and three sons-in-law, Mr. Winder, Mr. Nicholson, and Mr. Lowndes. All of these lived at the Great House Farm, and enjoyed the luxury of whipping the servants when they pleased, from old Barney down to William Wilkes, the coach-driver. I have seen Winder make one of the house-servants stand off from him a suitable distance to be touched with the end of his whip, and at every stroke raise great ridges upon his back.

To describe the wealth of Colonel Lloyd would be almost equal to describing the riches of Job. He kept from ten to fifteen house-servants. He was said to own a thousand slaves, and I think this estimate quite within the truth. Colonel Lloyd owned so many that he did not know them when he saw them; nor did all the slaves of the out-farms know him. It is reported of him, that, while riding along the road one day, he met a colored man, and addressed him in the usual manner of speaking to colored people on the public highways of the south: "Well, boy, whom do you belong to?" "To Colonel Lloyd," replied the slave. "Well, does the colonel treat you well?" "No, sir," was the ready reply. "What, does he work you too hard?" "Yes, sir." "Well, don't he give you enough to eat?" "Yes, sir, he gives me enough, such as it is."

The colonel, after ascertaining where the slave belonged, rode on; the man also went on about his business, not dreaming that he had been conversing with his master. He thought, said, and heard nothing more of the matter, until two or three weeks afterwards. The poor man was then informed by his overseer that, for having found fault with his master, he was now to be sold to a Georgia trader. He was immediately chained and handcuffed; and thus, without a moment's warning, he was snatched away, and forever sundered, from his family and friends, by a hand more unrelenting than death. This is the penalty of telling the truth, of telling the simple truth, in answer to a series of plain questions.

It is partly in consequence of such facts, that slaves, when inquired of as to their condition and the character of their masters, almost universally say they are contented, and that their masters are kind. The slave-holders have been known to send in spies among their slaves, to ascertain their views and feelings in regard to their condition. The frequency of this has had the effect to establish among the slaves the maxim, that a still tongue makes a wise head. They suppress the truth rather than take the consequences of telling it, and in so doing prove themselves a part of the human family. If they have any thing to say of their masters, it is generally in their masters' favor, especially when speaking to an untried man. I have been frequently asked, when a slave, if I had a kind master, and do not remember ever to have given a negative answer; nor did I, in pursuing this course, consider myself as uttering what was absolutely false; for I always measured the kindness of my master by the standard of kindness set up among slaveholders around us. Moreover, slaves are like other people, and imbibe prejudices quite common to others. They think their own better than that of others. Many, under the influence of this prejudice, think their own masters are better than the masters of other slaves; and this, too, in some cases, when the very reverse is true. Indeed, it is not uncommon for slaves even to fall out and quarrel among themselves about the relative goodness of their masters, each contending for the superior goodness of his own over that of the others. At the very same time, they mutually execrate their masters when viewed separately. It was so on our plantation. When Colonel Lloyd's slaves met the slaves of Jacob Jepson, they seldom parted without a quarrel about their masters; Colonel Lloyd's slaves contending that he was the richest, and Mr. Jepson's slaves that he was the smartest, and most of a man. Colonel Lloyd's slaves would boast his ability to buy and sell Jacob Jepson. Mr. Jepson's slaves would boast his ability to whip Colonel Lloyd. These quarrels would almost always end in a fight between the parties, and those that whipped were supposed to have gained the point at issue. They seemed to think that the greatness of their masters was transferable to themselves. It was considered as being bad enough to be a slave; but to be a poor man's slave was deemed a disgrace indeed!

Chapter IV

Mr. Hopkins remained but a short time in the office of overseer. Why his career was so short, I do not know, but suppose he lacked the necessary severity to suit Colonel Lloyd. Mr. Hopkins was succeeded by Mr. Austin Gore, a man possessing, in an eminent degree, all those traits of character indispensable to what is called a first-rate overseer. Mr. Gore had served Colonel Lloyd, in the capacity of overseer, upon one of the out-farms, and had shown himself worthy of the high station of overseer upon the home or Great House Farm.

Mr. Gore was proud, ambitious, and persevering. He was artful, cruel, and obdurate. He was just the man for such a place, and it was just the place for such a man. It afforded scope for the full exercise of all his powers, and he seemed to be perfectly at home in it. He was one of those who could torture the slightest look, word, or gesture, on the part of the slave, into impudence, and would treat it accordingly. There must be no answering back to him; no explanation was allowed a slave, showing himself to have been wrongfully accused. Mr. Gore acted fully up to the maxim laid down by slaveholders,—"It is better that a dozen slaves suffer under the lash, than that the overseer should be convicted, in the presence of the slaves, of having been at fault." No matter how innocent a slave might be—it availed him nothing, when accused by Mr. Gore of any misdemeanor. To be accused was to be convicted, and to be convicted was to be punished; the one always following the other with immutable certainty. To escape punishment was to escape accusation; and few slaves had the fortune to do either, under the overseership of Mr. Gore. He was just proud enough to demand the most debasing homage of the slave, and quite servile enough to crouch, himself, at the feet of the master. He was ambitious enough to be contented with nothing short of the highest rank of overseers, and persevering enough to reach the height of his ambition. He was cruel enough to inflict the severest punishment, artful enough to descend to the lowest trickery, and obdurate enough to be insensible to the voice of a reproving conscience. He was, of all the overseers, the most dreaded by the slaves. His presence was painful; his eye flashed confusion; and seldom was his sharp, shrill voice heard, without producing horror and trembling in their ranks.

Mr. Gore was a grave man, and, though a young man, he indulged in no jokes, said no funny words, seldom smiled. His words were in perfect keeping with his looks, and his looks were in perfect keeping with his words. Overseers will sometimes indulge in a witty word, even with the slaves; not so with Mr. Gore. He spoke but to command, and commanded but to be obeyed; he dealt sparingly with his words, and bountifully with his whip, never using the former where the latter would answer as well. When he whipped, he seemed to do so from a sense of duty, and feared no consequences. He did nothing reluctantly, no matter how disagreeable; always at his post, never inconsistent. He never promised but to fulfil. He was, in a word, a man of the most inflexible firmness and stone-like coolness.

His savage barbarity was equalled only by the consummate coolness with which he committed the grossest and most savage deeds upon the slaves under his charge. Mr. Gore once undertook to whip one of Colonel Lloyd's slaves, by the name of Demby. He had given Demby but few stripes, when, to get rid of the scourging, he ran and plunged himself into a creek, and stood there at the depth of his shoulders, refusing to come out. Mr. Gore told him that he would give him three calls, and that, if he did not come out at the third call, he would shoot him. The first call was given. Demby made no response, but stood his ground. The second and third calls were given with the same result. Mr. Gore then, without consultation or deliberation with any one, not even giving Demby an additional call, raised his musket to his face, taking deadly aim at his standing victim, and in an instant poor Demby was no more. His mangled body sank out of sight, and blood and brains marked the water where he had stood.

A thrill of horror flashed through every soul upon the plantation, excepting Mr. Gore. He alone seemed cool and collected. He was asked by Colonel Lloyd and my old master, why he resorted to this extraordinary expedient. His reply was, (as well as I can remember,) that Demby had become unmanageable. He was setting a dangerous example to the other slaves,—one which, if suffered to pass without some such demonstration on his part, would finally lead to the total subversion of all rule and order upon the plantation. He argued that if one slave refused to be corrected, and escaped with his life, the other slaves would soon copy the example; the result of which would be, the freedom of the slaves, and the enslavement of the whites. Mr. Gore's defence was satisfactory. He was continued in his station as overseer upon the home plantation. His fame as an overseer went abroad. His horrid crime was not even submitted to judicial investigation. It was committed in the presence of slaves, and they of course could neither institute a suit, nor testify against him; and thus the guilty perpetrator of one of the bloodiest and most foul murders goes unwhipped of justice, and uncensured by the community in which he lives. Mr. Gore lived in St. Michael's, Talbot county, Maryland, when I left there; and if he is still alive, he very probably lives there now; and if so, he is now, as he was then, as highly esteemed and as much respected as though his guilty soul had not been stained with his brother's blood.

I speak advisedly when I say this,—that killing a slave, or any colored person, in Talbot county, Maryland, is not treated as a crime, either by the courts or the community. Mr. Thomas Lanman, of St. Michael's, killed two slaves, one of whom he killed with a hatchet, by knocking his brains out. He used to boast of the commission of the awful and bloody deed. I have heard him do so laughingly, saying, among other things, that he was the only benefactor of his country in the company, and that when others would do as much as he had done, we should be relieved of "the d——d niggers."

The wife of Mr. Giles Hick, living but a short distance from where I used to live, murdered my wife's cousin, a young girl between fifteen and sixteen years of age, mangling her person in the most horrible manner, breaking her nose and breastbone with a stick, so that the poor girl expired in a few hours afterward. She was immediately buried, but had not been in her untimely grave but a few hours before she was taken up and examined by the coroner, who decided that she had come to her death by severe beating. The offence for which this girl was thus murdered was this:—She had been set that night to mind Mrs. Hick's baby, and during the night she fell asleep, and the baby cried. She, having lost her rest for several nights previous, did not hear the crying. They were both in the room with Mrs. Hicks. Mrs. Hicks, finding the girl slow to move, jumped from her bed, seized an oak stick of wood by the fireplace, and with it broke the girl's nose and breastbone, and thus ended her life. I will not say that this most horrid murder produced no sensation in the community. It did produce sensation, but not enough to bring the murderess to punishment. There was a warrant issued for her arrest, but it was never served. Thus she escaped not only punishment, but even the pain of being arraigned before a court for her horrid crime.

Whilst I am detailing bloody deeds which took place during my stay on Colonel Lloyd's plantation, I will briefly narrate another, which occurred about the same time as the murder of Demby by Mr. Gore.

Colonel Lloyd's slaves were in the habit of spending a part of their nights and Sundays in fishing for oysters, and in this way made up the deficiency of their scanty allowance. An old man belonging to Colonel Lloyd, while thus engaged, happened to get beyond the limits of Colonel Lloyd's, and on the premises of Mr. Beal Bondly. At this trespass, Mr. Bondly took offence, and with his musket came down to the shore, and blew its deadly contents into the poor old man.

Mr. Bondly came over to see Colonel Lloyd the next day, whether to pay him for his property, or to justify himself in what he had done, I know not. At any rate, this whole fiendish transaction was soon hushed up. There was very little said about it at all, and nothing done. It was a common saying, even among little white boys, that it was worth a half-cent to kill a "nigger," and a half-cent to bury one.

Chapter V

As to my own treatment while I lived on Colonel Lloyd's plantation, it was very similar to that of the other slave children. I was not old enough to work in the field, and there being little else than field work to do, I had a great deal of leisure time. The most I had to do was to drive up the cows at evening, keep the fowls out of the garden, keep the front yard clean, and run of errands for my old master's daughter, Mrs. Lucretia Auld. The most of my leisure time I spent in helping Master Daniel Lloyd in finding his birds, after he had shot them. My connection with Master Daniel was of some advantage to me. He became quite attached to me, and was a sort of protector of me. He would not allow the older boys to impose upon me, and would divide his cakes with me.

I was seldom whipped by my old master, and suffered little from anything else than hunger and cold. I suffered much from hunger, but much more from cold. In hottest summer and coldest winter, I was kept almost naked—no shoes, no stockings, no jacket, no trousers, nothing on but a coarse tow linen shirt, reaching only to my knees. I had no bed. I must have perished with cold, but that, the coldest nights, I used to steal a bag which was used for carrying corn to the mill. I would crawl into this bag, and there sleep on the cold, damp, clay floor, with my head in and feet out. My feet have been so cracked with the frost, that the pen with which I am writing might be laid in the gashes.

We were not regularly allowanced. Our food was coarse corn meal boiled. This was called *mush.* It was put into a large wooden tray or trough, and set down upon the ground. The children were then called, like so many pigs, and like so many pigs they would come and devour the mush; some with oyster-shells, others with pieces of shingle, some with naked hands, and none with spoons. He that ate fastest got most; he that was strongest secured the best place; and few left the trough satisfied.

I was probably between seven and eight years old when I left Colonel Lloyd's plantation. I left it with joy. I shall never forget the ecstasy with which I received the intelligence that my old master (Anthony) had determined to let me go to Baltimore, to live with Mr. Hugh Auld, brother to my old master's son-in-law, Captain Thomas Auld. I received this information about three days before my departure. They were three of the happiest days I ever enjoyed. I spent the most part of all these three days in the creek, washing off the plantation scurf, and preparing myself for my departure.

The pride of appearance which this would indicate was not my own. I spent the time in washing, not so much because I wished to, but because Mrs. Lucretia had told me I must get all the dead skin off my feet and knees before I could go to Baltimore; for the people of Baltimore were very cleanly, and would laugh at me if I looked dirty. Besides, she was going to give me a pair of trousers, which I should not put on unless I got all the dirt off me. The thought of owning a pair of trousers was great indeed! It was almost a sufficient motive, not only to make me take off what would be called by pig-drovers the mange, but the skin itself. I went at it in good earnest, working for the first time with the hope of reward.

The ties that ordinarily bind children to their homes were all suspended in my case. I found no severe trial in my departure. My home was charmless; it was not home to me; on parting from it, I could not feel that I was leaving any thing which I could have enjoyed by staying. My mother was dead, my grandmother lived far off, so that I seldom saw her. I had two sisters and one brother, that lived in the same house with me; but the early separation of us from our mother had well nigh blotted the fact of our relationship from our memories. I looked for home elsewhere, and was confident of finding none which I should relish less than the one which I was leaving. If, however, I found in my new home hardship, hunger, whipping, and nakedness, I had the consolation that I should not have escaped any one of them by staying. Having already had more than a taste of them in the house of my old master, and having endured them there, I very naturally inferred my ability to endure them elsewhere, and especially at Baltimore; for I had something of the feeling about Baltimore that is expressed in the proverb, that "being hanged in England is preferable to dying a natural death in Ireland." I had the strongest desire to see Baltimore. Cousin Tom, though not fluent in speech, had inspired me with that desire by his eloquent description of the place. I could never point out any thing at the Great House, no matter how beautiful or powerful, but that he had seen something at Baltimore far exceeding, both in beauty and strength, the object which I pointed out to him. Even the Great House itself, with all its pictures, was far inferior to many buildings in Baltimore. So strong was my desire, that I thought a gratification of it would fully compensate for whatever loss of comforts I should sustain by the exchange. I left without a regret, and with the highest hopes of future happiness.

We sailed out of Miles River for Baltimore on a Saturday morning. I remember only the day of the week, for at that time I had no knowledge of the days of the month, nor the months of the year. On setting sail, I walked aft, and gave to Colonel Lloyd's plantation what I hoped would be the last look. I then placed myself in the bows of the sloop, and there spent the remainder of the day in looking ahead, interesting myself in what was in the distance rather than in things near by or behind.

In the afternoon of that day, we reached Annapolis, the capital of the State. We stopped but a few moments, so that I had no time to go on shore. It was the first large town that I had ever seen, and though it would look small compared with some of our New England factory villages, I thought it a wonderful place for its size—more imposing even than the Great House Farm!

We arrived at Baltimore early on Sunday morning, landing at Smith's Wharf, not far from Bowley's Wharf. We had on board the sloop a large flock of sheep; and after aiding in driving them to the slaughterhouse of Mr. Curtis on Louden Slater's Hill, I was conducted by Rich, one of the hands belonging on board of the sloop, to my new home in Alliciana Street, near Mr. Gardner's ship-yard, on Fells Point.

Mr. and Mrs. Auld were both at home, and met me at the door with their little son Thomas, to take care of whom I had been given. And here I saw what I had never seen before; it was a white face beaming with the most kindly emotions; it was the face of my new mistress, Sophia Auld. I wish I could describe the rapture that flashed through my soul as I beheld it. It was a new and strange sight to me, brightening up my pathway with the light of happiness. Little Thomas was told, there was his Freddy,—and I was told to take care of little Thomas; and thus I entered upon the duties of my new home with the most cheering prospect ahead.

I look upon my departure from Colonel Lloyd's plantation as one of the most interesting events of my life. It is possible, and even quite probable, that but for the mere circumstance of being removed from that plantation to Baltimore, I should have to-day, instead of being here seated by my own table, in the enjoyment of freedom and the happiness of home, writing this Narrative, been confined in the galling chains of slavery. Going to live at Baltimore laid the foundation, and opened the gateway, to all my subsequent prosperity. I have ever regarded it as the first plain manifestation of that kind providence which has ever since attended me, and marked my life with so many favors. I regarded the selection of myself as being somewhat remarkable. There were a number of slave children that might have been sent from the plantation to Baltimore. There were those younger, those older, and those of the same age. I was chosen from among them all, and was the first, last, and only choice.

I may be deemed superstitious, and even egotistical, in regarding this event as a special interposition of divine Providence in my favor. But I should be false to the earliest sentiments of my soul, if I suppressed the opinion. I prefer to be true to myself, even at the hazard of incurring the ridicule of others, rather than to be false, and incur my own abhorrence. From my earliest recollection, I date the entertainment of a deep conviction that slavery would not always be able to hold me within its foul embrace; and in the darkest hours of my career in slavery, this living word of faith and spirit of hope departed not from me, but remained like ministering angels to cheer me through the gloom. This good spirit was from God, and to him I offer thanksgiving and praise.

Chapter VI

My new mistress proved to be all she appeared when I first met her at the door,—a woman of the kindest heart and finest feelings. She had never had a slave under her control previously to myself, and prior to her marriage she had been dependent upon her own industry for a living. She was by trade a weaver; and by constant application to her business, she had been in a good degree preserved from the blighting and dehumanizing effects of slavery. I was utterly astonished at her goodness. I scarcely knew how to behave towards her. She was entirely unlike any other white woman I had ever seen. I could not approach her as I was accustomed to approach other white ladies. My early instruction was all out of place. The crouching servility, usually so acceptable a quality in a slave, did not answer when manifested toward her. Her favor was not gained by it; she seemed to be disturbed by it. She did not deem it impudent or unmannerly for a slave to look her in the face. The meanest slave was put fully at ease in her presence, and none left without feeling better for having seen her. Her face was made of heavenly smiles, and her voice of tranquil music.

But, alas! this kind heart had but a short time to remain such. The fatal poison of irresponsible power was already in her hands, and soon commenced its infernal work. That cheerful eye, under the influence of slavery, soon became red with rage; that voice, made all of sweet accord, changed to one of harsh and horrid discord; and that angelic face gave place to that of a demon.

Very soon after I went to live with Mr. and Mrs. Auld, she very kindly commenced to teach me the A, B, C. After I had learned this, she assisted me in learning to spell words of three or four letters. Just at this point of my progress, Mr. Auld found out what was going on, and at once forbade Mrs. Auld to instruct me further, telling her, among other things, that it was unlawful, as well as unsafe, to teach a slave to read. To use his own words, further, he said, "If you give a nigger an inch, he will take an ell.[1] A nigger should know

1. A measure of length; 27 inches in England.

nothing but to obey his master—to do as he is told to do. Learning would *spoil* the best nigger in the world. Now," said he, "if you teach that nigger (speaking of myself) how to read, there would be no keeping him. It would forever unfit him to be a slave. He would at once become unmanageable, and of no value to his master. As to himself, it could do him no good, but a great deal of harm. It would make him discontented and unhappy." These words sank deep into my heart, stirred up sentiments within that lay slumbering, and called into existence an entirely new train of thought. It was a new and special revelation, explaining dark and mysterious things, with which my youthful understanding had struggled, but struggled in vain. I now understood what had been to me a most perplexing difficulty—to wit, the white man's power to enslave the black man. It was a grand achievement, and I prized it highly. From that moment, I understood the pathway from slavery to freedom. It was just what I wanted, and I got it at a time when I the least expected it. Whilst I was saddened by the thought of losing the aid of my kind mistress, I was gladdened by the invaluable instruction which, by the merest accident, I had gained from my master. Though conscious of the difficulty of learning without a teacher, I set out with high hope, and a fixed purpose, at whatever cost of trouble, to learn how to read. The very decided manner with which he spoke, and strove to impress his wife with the evil consequences of giving me instruction, served to convince me that he was deeply sensible of the truths he was uttering. It gave me the best assurance that I might rely with the utmost confidence on the results which, he said, would flow from teaching me to read. What he most dreaded, that I most desired. What he most loved, that I most hated. That which to him was a great evil, to be carefully shunned, was to me a great good, to be diligently sought; and the argument which he so warmly urged, against my learning to read, only served to inspire me with a desire and determination to learn. In learning to read, I owe almost as much to the bitter opposition of my master, as to the kindly aid of my mistress. I acknowledge the benefit of both.

I had resided but a short time in Baltimore before I observed a marked difference, in the treatment of slaves, from that which I had witnessed in the country. A city slave is almost a freeman, compared with a slave on the plantation. He is much better fed and clothed, and enjoys privileges altogether unknown to the slave on the plantation. There is a vestige of decency, a sense of shame, that does much to curb and check those outbreaks of atrocious cruelty so commonly enacted upon the plantation. He is a desperate slaveholder, who will shock the humanity of his non-slaveholding neighbors with the cries of his lacerated slave. Few are willing to incur the odium attaching to the reputation of being a cruel master;

and above all things, they would not be known as not giving a slave enough to eat. Every city slaveholder is anxious to have it known of him, that he feeds his slaves well; and it is due to them to say, that most of them do give their slaves enough to eat. There are, however, some painful exceptions to this rule. Directly opposite to us, on Philpot Street, lived Mr. Thomas Hamilton. He owned two slaves. Their names were Henrietta and Mary. Henrietta was about twenty-two years of age, Mary was about fourteen; and of all the mangled and emaciated creatures I ever looked upon, these two were the most so. His heart must be harder than stone, that could look upon these unmoved. The head, neck, and shoulders of Mary were literally cut to pieces. I have frequently felt her head, and found it nearly covered with festering sores, caused by the lash of her cruel mistress. I do not know that her master ever whipped her, but I have been an eyewitness to the cruelty of Mrs. Hamilton. I used to be in Mr. Hamilton's house nearly every day. Mrs. Hamilton used to sit in a large chair in the middle of the room, with a heavy cowskin always by her side, and scarce an hour passed during the day but was marked by the blood of one of these slaves. The girls seldom passed her without her saying, "Move faster, you *black gip!*" at the same time giving them a blow with the cowskin over the head or shoulders, often drawing the blood. She would then say, "Take that, you *black gip!*"—continuing, "If you don't move faster, I'll move you!" Added to the cruel lashings to which these slaves were subjected, they were kept nearly half-starved. They seldom knew what it was to eat a full meal. I have seen Mary contending with the pigs for the offal thrown into the street. So much was Mary kicked and cut to pieces, that she was oftener called *"pecked"* than by her name.

Chapter VII

I lived in Master Hugh's family about seven years. During this time, I succeeded in learning to read and write. In accomplishing this, I was compelled to resort to various stratagems. I had no regular teacher. My mistress, who had kindly commenced to instruct me, had, in compliance with the advice and direction of her husband, not only ceased to instruct, but had set her face against my being instructed by any one else. It is due, however, to my mistress to say of her, that she did not adopt this course of treatment immediately. She at first lacked the depravity indispensable to shutting me up in mental darkness. It was at least necessary for her to have some training in the exercise of irresponsible power, to make her equal to the task of treating me as though I were a brute.

My mistress was, as I have said, a kind and tender-hearted woman; and in the simplicity of her soul she commenced, when I first went to live with her, to treat me as she supposed one human being ought to treat another. In entering upon the duties of a slaveholder, she did not seem to perceive that I sustained to her the relation of a mere chattel, and that for her to treat me as a human being was not only wrong, but dangerously so. Slavery proved as injurious to her as it did to me. When I went there, she was a pious, warm, and tender-hearted woman. There was no sorrow or suffering for which she had not a tear. She had bread for the hungry, clothes for the naked, and comfort for every mourner that came within her reach. Slavery soon proved its ability to divest her of these heavenly qualities. Under its influence, the tender heart became stone, and the lamb-like disposition gave way to one of tiger-like fierceness. The first step in her downward course was in her ceasing to instruct me. She now commenced to practise her husband's precepts. She finally became even more violent in her opposition than her husband himself. She was not satisfied with simply doing as well as he had commanded; she seemed anxious to do better. Nothing seemed to make her more angry than to see me with a newspaper. She seemed to think that here lay the danger. I have had her rush at me with a face made all up of fury, and snatch from me a newspaper, in a manner that fully revealed her apprehension. She was an apt woman; and a little experience soon demonstrated, to her satisfaction, that education and slavery were incompatible with each other.

From this time I was most narrowly watched. If I was in a separate room any considerable length of time, I was sure to be suspected of having a book, and was at once called to give an account of myself. All this, however, was too late. The first step had been taken. Mistress, in teaching me the alphabet, had given me the *inch*, and no precaution could prevent me from taking the *ell*.

The plan which I adopted, and the one by which I was most successful, was that of making friends of all the little white boys whom I met in the street. As many of these as I could, I converted into teachers. With their kindly aid, obtained at different times and in different places, I finally succeeded in learning to read. When I was sent of errands, I always took my book with me, and by going one part of my errand quickly, I found time to get a lesson before my return. I used also to carry bread with me, enough of which was always in the house, and to which I was always welcome; for I was much better off in this regard than many of the poor white children in our neighborhood. This bread I used to bestow upon the hungry little urchins, who, in return, would give me that more valuable bread of knowledge. I am strongly tempted to give the names of two or three of those little boys, as a testimonial of the gratitude and affection I bear them; but prudence forbids;—not that it would injure me, but it might embarrass them; for it is almost an unpardonable offence to teach slaves to read in this Christian country. It is enough to say of the dear little fellows, that they lived on Philpot Street, very near Durgin and Bailey's ship-yard. I used to talk this matter of slavery over with them. I would sometimes say to them, I wished I could be as free as they would be when they got to be men. "You will be free as soon as you are twenty-one, *but I am a slave for life!* Have not I as good a right to be free as you have?" These words used to trouble them; they would express for me the liveliest sympathy, and console me with the hope that something would occur by which I might be free.

I was now about twelve years old, and the thought of being *a slave for life* began to bear heavily upon my heart. Just about this time, I got hold of a book entitled "The Columbian Orator."[1] Every opportunity I got, I used to read this book. Among much of other interesting matter, I found in it a dialogue between a master and his slave. The slave was represented as having run away from his master three times. The dialogue represented the conversation which took place between them, when the slave was retaken the third time. In this dialogue, the whole argument in behalf of slavery was brought forward by the master, all of which was disposed of by the slave. The slave was made to say some very smart as well as impressive things in reply to his master—things which had the desired though unexpected effect; for the conversation resulted in the voluntary emancipation of the slave on the part of the master.

In the same book, I met with one of Sheridan's[2] mighty speeches on and in behalf of Catholic emancipation. These were choice documents to me. I read them over and over again with unabated interest. They gave tongue to interesting thoughts of my own soul, which had frequently flashed through my mind, and died away for want of utterance. The moral which I gained from the dialogue was the power of truth over the conscience of even a slaveholder. What I got from Sheridan was a bold denunciation of slavery, and a powerful vindication of human rights. The reading of these documents enabled me to utter my thoughts, and to meet the arguments brought forward to sustain slavery; but while they relieved me of one difficulty, they brought on another even more painful than the one of which I was relieved. The more I read, the more I was led to abhor and detest my enslavers. I could regard them in no other light than a band of successful robbers, who had left their homes, and gone to Africa, and stolen us from our homes, and in a strange land reduced us to slavery. I loathed them as being the meanest as well as the most wicked of men. As I read and contemplated the subject, behold!

1. A popular eloquence manual compiled in 1797 by Caleb Bingham.
2. Richard Brinsley Sheridan (1751–1816), Irish dramatist and political leader. The speech in the *Columbian Orator* to which Douglass refers was actually made by the Irish patriot Arthur O'Connor.

that very discontentment which Master Hugh had predicted would follow my learning to read had already come, to torment and sting my soul to unutterable anguish. As I writhed under it, I would at times feel that learning to read had been a curse rather than a blessing. It had given me a view of my wretched condition, without the remedy. It opened my eyes to the horrible pit, but to no ladder upon which to get out. In moments of agony, I envied my fellow-slaves for their stupidity. I have often wished myself a beast. I preferred the condition of the meanest reptile to my own. Any thing, no matter what, to get rid of thinking! It was this everlasting thinking of my condition that tormented me. There was no getting rid of it. It was pressed upon me by every object within sight or hearing, animate or inanimate. The silver trump of freedom had roused my soul to eternal wakefulness. Freedom now appeared, to disappear no more forever. It was heard in every sound, and seen in every thing. It was ever present to torment me with a sense of my wretched condition. I saw nothing without seeing it, I heard nothing without hearing it, and felt nothing without feeling. It looked from every star, it smiled in every calm, breathed in every wind, and moved in every storm.

I often found myself regretting my own existence, and wishing myself dead; and but for the hope of being free, I have no doubt but that I should have killed myself, or done something for which I should have been killed. While in this state of mind, I was eager to hear any one speak of slavery. I was a ready listener. Every little while, I could hear something about the abolitionists. It was some time before I found what the word meant. It was always used in such connections as to make it an interesting word to me. If a slave ran away and succeeded in getting clear, or if a slave killed his master, set fire to a barn, or did any thing very wrong in the mind of a slaveholder, it was spoken of as the fruit of *abolition*. Hearing the word in this connection very often, I set about learning what it meant. The dictionary afforded me little or no help. I found it was "the act of abolishing;" but then I did not know what was to be abolished. Here I was perplexed. I did not dare to ask any one about its meaning, for I was satisfied that it was something they wanted me to know very little about. After a patient waiting, I got one of our city papers, containing an account of the number of petitions from the north, praying for the abolition of slavery in the District of Columbia, and of the slave trade between the States. From this time I understood the words *abolition* and *abolitionist,* and always drew near when that word was spoken, expecting to hear something of importance to myself and fellow-slaves. The light broke in upon me by degrees. I went one day down on the wharf of Mr. Waters; and seeing two Irishmen unloading a scow of stone, I went, unasked, and helped them. When we had finished, one of them came to me and asked me if I were a slave. I told him I was. He asked, "Are ye a slave for life?" I told him that I was. The good Irishman seemed to be deeply affected by the statement. He said to the other that it was a pity so fine a little fellow as myself should be a slave for life. He said it was a shame to hold me. They both advised me to run away to the north; that I should find friends there, and that I should be free. I pretended not to be interested in what they said, and treated them as if I did not understand them; for I feared they might be treacherous. White men have been known to encourage slaves to escape, and then, to get the reward, catch them and return them to their masters. I was afraid that these seemingly good men might use me so; but I nevertheless remembered their advice, and from that time I resolved to run away. I looked forward to a time at which it would be safe for me to escape. I was too young to think of doing so immediately; besides, I wished to learn how to write, as I might have occasion to write my own pass. I consoled myself with the hope that I should one day find a good chance. Meanwhile, I would learn to write.

The idea as to how I might learn to write was suggested to me by being in Durgin and Bailey's ship-yard, and frequently seeing the ship carpenters, after hewing, and getting a piece of timber ready for use, write on the timber the name of that part of the ship for which it was intended. When a piece of timber was intended for the larboard side, it would be marked thus—"L." When a piece was for the starboard side, it would be marked thus—"S." A piece for the larboard side forward, would be marked thus—"L. F." When a piece was for starboard side forward, it would be marked thus—"S. F." For larboard aft, it would be marked thus—"L. A." For starboard aft, it would be marked thus—"S. A." I soon learned the names of these letters, and for what they were intended when placed upon a piece of timber in the ship-yard. I immediately commenced copying them, and in a short time was able to make the four letters named. After that, when I met with any boy who I knew could write, I would tell him I could write as well as he. The next word would be, "I don't believe you. Let me see you try it." I would then make the letters which I had been so fortunate as to learn, and ask him to beat that. In this way I got a good many lessons in writing, which it is quite possible I should never have gotten in any other way. During this time, my copy-book was the board fence, brick wall, and pavement; my pen and ink was a lump of chalk. With these, I learned mainly how to write. I then commenced and continued copying the Italics in Webster's Spelling Book,[3] until I could make them all

3. *The American Spelling Book* (1783) by Noah Webster, the leading American lexicographer of the time.

without looking on the book. By this time, my little Master Thomas had gone to school, and learned how to write, and had written over a number of copy-books. These had been brought home, and shown to some of our near neighbors, and then laid aside. My mistress used to go to class meeting at the Wilk Street meeting-house every Monday afternoon, and leave me to take care of the house. When left thus, I used to spend the time in writing in the spaces left in Master Thomas's copy-book, copying what he had written. I continued to do this until I could write a hand very similar to that of Master Thomas. Thus, after a long, tedious effort for years, I finally succeeded in learning how to write.

Chapter VIII

In a very short time after I went to live at Baltimore, my old master's youngest son Richard died; and in about three years and six months after his death, my old master, Captain Anthony, died, leaving only his son, Andrew, and daughter, Lucretia, to share his estate. He died while on a visit to see his daughter at Hillsborough. Cut off thus unexpectedly, he left no will as to the disposal of his property. It was therefore necessary to have a valuation of the property, that it might be equally divided between Mrs. Lucretia and Master Andrew. I was immediately sent for, to be valued with the other property. Here again my feelings rose up in detestation of slavery. I had now a new conception of my degraded condition. Prior to this, I had become, if not insensible to my lot, at least partly so. I left Baltimore with a young heart overborne with sadness, and a soul full of apprehension. I took passage with Captain Rowe, in the schooner Wild Cat, and, after a sail of about twenty-four hours, I found myself near the place of my birth. I had now been absent from it almost, if not quite, five years. I, however, remembered the place very well. I was only about five years old when I left it, to go and live with my old master on Colonel Lloyd's plantation; so that I was now between ten and eleven years old.

We were all ranked together at the valuation. Men and women, old and young, married and single, were ranked with horses, sheep, and swine. There were horses and men, cattle and women, pigs and children, all holding the same rank in the scale of being, and were all subjected to the same narrow examination. Silvery-headed age and sprightly youth, maids and matrons, had to undergo the same indelicate inspection. At this moment, I saw more clearly than ever the brutalizing effects of slavery upon both slave and slaveholder.

After the valuation, then came the division. I have no language to express the high excitement and deep anxiety which were felt among us poor slaves during this time. Our fate for life was now to be decided. We had no more voice in that decision than the brutes among whom we were ranked. A single word from the white men was enough—against all our wishes, prayers, and entreaties—to sunder forever the dearest friends, dearest kindred, and strongest ties known to human beings. In addition to the pain of separation, there was the horrid dread of falling into the hands of Master Andrew. He was known to us all as being a most cruel wretch,—a common drunkard, who had, by his reckless mismanagement and profligate dissipation, already wasted a large portion of his father's property. We all felt that we might as well be sold at once to the Georgia traders, as to pass into his hands; for we knew that that would be our inevitable condition,—a condition held by us all in the utmost horror and dread.

I suffered more anxiety than most of my fellow-slaves. I had known what it was to be kindly treated; they had known nothing of the kind. They had seen little or nothing of the world. They were in very deed men and women of sorrow, and acquainted with grief.[1] Their backs had been made familiar with the bloody lash, so that they had become callous; mine was yet tender; for while at Baltimore I got few whippings, and few slaves could boast of a kinder master and mistress than myself; and the thought of passing out of their hands into those of Master Andrew—a man who, but a few days before, to give me a sample of his bloody disposition, took my little brother by the throat, threw him on the ground, and with the heel of his boot stamped upon his head till the blood gushed from his nose and ears—was well calculated to make me anxious as to my fate. After he had committed this savage outrage upon my brother, he turned to me, and said that was the way he meant to serve me one of these days,—meaning, I suppose, when I came into his possession.

Thanks to a kind Providence, I fell to the portion of Mrs. Lucretia, and was sent immediately back to Baltimore, to live again in the family of Master Hugh. Their joy at my return equalled their sorrow at my departure. It was a glad day to me. I had escaped a [fate] worse than lion's jaws. I was absent from Baltimore, for the purpose of valuation and division, just about one month, and it seemed to have been six.

Very soon after my return to Baltimore, my mistress, Lucretia, died, leaving her husband and one child, Amanda; and in a very short time after her death, Master Andrew died. Now all the property of my old master, slaves included, was in the hands of strangers,—strangers who had had nothing to do with accumulating it. Not a slave was left free. All remained slaves, from the youngest to the

1. Cf. Isaiah 53.3.

oldest. If any one thing in my experience, more than another, served to deepen my conviction of the infernal character of slavery, and to fill me with unutterable loathing of slaveholders, it was their base ingratitude to my poor old grandmother. She had served my old master faithfully from youth to old age. She had been the source of all his wealth; she had peopled his plantation with slaves; she had become a great grandmother in his service. She had rocked him in infancy, attended him in childhood, served him through life, and at his death wiped from his icy brow the cold death-sweat, and closed his eyes forever. She was nevertheless left a slave—a slave for life—a slave in the hands of strangers; and in their hands she saw her children, her grandchildren, and her great-grandchildren, divided, like so many sheep, without being gratified with the small privilege of a single word, as to their or her own destiny. And, to cap the climax of their base ingratitude and fiendish barbarity, my grandmother, who was now very old, having outlived my old master and all his children, having seen the beginning and end of all of them, and her present owners finding she was of but little value, her frame already racked with the pains of old age, and complete helplessness fast stealing over her once active limbs, they took her to the woods, built her a little hut, put up a little mud-chimney, and then made her welcome to the privilege of supporting herself there in perfect loneliness; thus virtually turning her out to die! If my poor old grandmother now lives, she lives to suffer in utter loneliness; she lives to remember and mourn over the loss of children, the loss of grandchildren, and the loss of great-grandchildren. They are, in the language of the slave's poet, Whittier,[2]—

> "Gone, gone, sold and gone
> To the rice swamp dank and lone,
> Where the slave-whip ceaseless swings,
> Where the noisome insect stings,
> Where the fever-demon strews
> Poison with the falling dews,
> Where the sickly sunbeams glare
> Through the hot and misty air:—
> Gone, gone, sold and gone
> To the rice swamp dank and lone,
> From Virginia hills and waters—
> Woe is me, my stolen daughters!"

The hearth is desolate. The children, the unconscious children, who once sang and danced in her presence, are gone. She gropes her

2. John Greenleaf Whittier (1807–1892), American poet and abolitionist. The lines Douglass quotes are from Whittier's antislavery poem *The Farewell of a Virginia Slave Mother to Her Daughters, Sold into Southern Bondage* (1838).

way, in the darkness of age, for a drink of water. Instead of the voices of her children, she hears by day the moans of the dove, and by night the screams of the hideous owl. All is gloom. The grave is at the door. And now, when weighed down by the pains and aches of old age, when the head inclines to the feet, when the beginning and ending of human existence meet, and helpless infancy and painful old age combine together—at this time, this most needful time, the time for the exercise of that tenderness and affection which children only can exercise toward a declining parent—my poor old grandmother, the devoted mother of twelve children, is left all alone, in yonder little hut, before a few dim embers. She stands—she sits—she staggers—she falls—she groans—she dies—and there are none of her children or grandchildren present, to wipe from her wrinkled brow the cold sweat of death, or to place beneath the sod her fallen remains. Will not a righteous God visit for these things?

In about two years after the death of Mrs. Lucretia, Master Thomas married his second wife. Her name was Rowena Hamilton. She was the eldest daughter of Mr. William Hamilton. Master now lived in St. Michael's. Not long after his marriage, a misunderstanding took place between himself and Master Hugh; and as a means of punishing his brother, he took me from him to live with himself at St. Michael's. Here I underwent another most painful separation. It, however, was not so severe as the one I dreaded at the division of property; for, during this interval, a great change had taken place in Master Hugh and his once kind and affectionate wife. The influence of brandy upon him, and of slavery upon her, had effected a disastrous change in the characters of both; so that, as far as they were concerned, I thought I had little to lose by the change. But it was not to them that I was attached. It was to those little Baltimore boys that I felt the strongest attachment. I had received many good lessons from them, and was still receiving them, and the thought of leaving them was painful indeed. I was leaving, too, without the hope of ever being allowed to return. Master Thomas had said he would never let me return again. The barrier betwixt himself and brother he considered impassable.

I then had to regret that I did not at least make the attempt to carry out my resolution to run away; for the chances of success are tenfold greater from the city than from the country.

I sailed from Baltimore for St. Michael's in the sloop Amanda, Captain Edward Dodson. On my passage, I paid particular attention to the direction which the steamboats took to go to Philadelphia. I found, instead of going down, on reaching North Point they went up the bay, in a north-easterly direction. I deemed this knowledge of the utmost importance. My determination to run away was again revived. I resolved to wait only so long as the offering of a favorable opportunity. When that came, I was determined to be off.

Chapter IX

I have now reached a period of my life when I can give dates. I left Baltimore, and went to live with Master Thomas Auld, at St. Michael's, in March, 1832. It was now more than seven years since I lived with him in the family of my old master, on Colonel Lloyd's plantation. We of course were now almost entire strangers to each other. He was to me a new master, and I to him a new slave. I was ignorant of his temper and disposition; he was equally so of mine. A very short time, however brought us into full acquaintance with each other. I was made acquainted with his wife not less than with himself. They were well matched, being equally mean and cruel. I was now, for the first time during a space of more than seven years, made to feel the painful gnawing of hunger—a something which I had not experienced before since I left Colonel Lloyd's plantation. It went hard enough with me then, when I could look back to no period at which I had enjoyed a sufficiency. It was tenfold harder after living in Master Hugh's family, where I had always had enough to eat, and of that which was good. I have said Master Thomas was a mean man. He was so. Not to give a slave enough to eat, is regarded as the most aggravated development of meanness even among slaveholders. The rule is, no matter how coarse the food, only let there be enough of it. This is the theory; and in the part of Maryland from which I came, it is the general practice,—though there are many exceptions. Master Thomas gave us enough of neither coarse nor fine food. There were four slaves of us in the kitchen—my sister Eliza, my aunt Priscilla, Henny, and myself; and we were allowed less than half of a bushel of corn-meal per week, and very little else, either in the shape of meat or vegetables. It was not enough for us to subsist upon. We were therefore reduced to the wretched necessity of living at the expense of our neighbors. This we did by begging and stealing, whichever came handy in the time of need, the one being considered as legitimate as the other. A great many times have we poor creatures been nearly perishing with hunger, when food in abundance lay mouldering in the safe[1] and smoke-house, and our pious mistress was aware of the fact; and yet that mistress and her husband would kneel every morning, and pray that God would bless them in basket and store!

Bad as all slaveholders are, we seldom meet one destitute of every element of character commanding respect. My master was one of

1. A meat safe and smokehouse are structures for preserving food.

this rare sort. I do not know of one single noble act ever performed by him. The leading trait in his character was meanness; and if there were any other element in his nature, it was made subject to this. He was mean; and, like most other mean men, he lacked the ability to conceal his meanness. Captain Auld was not born a slaveholder. He had been a poor man, master only of a Bay craft. He came into possession of all his slaves by marriage; and of all men, adopted slaveholders are the worst. He was cruel, but cowardly. He commanded without firmness. In the enforcement of his rules he was at times rigid, and at times lax. At times, he spoke to his slaves with the firmness of Napoleon and the fury of a demon; at other times, he might well be mistaken for an inquirer who had lost his way. He did nothing of himself. He might have passed for a lion, but for his ears. In all things noble which he attempted, his own meanness shone most conspicuous. His airs, words, and actions, were the airs, words, and actions of born slaveholders, and, being assumed, were awkward enough. He was not even a good imitator. He possessed all the disposition to deceive, but wanted the power. Having no resources within himself, he was compelled to be the copyist of many, and being such, he was forever the victim of inconsistency; and of consequence he was an object of contempt, and was held as such even by his slaves. The luxury of having slaves of his own to wait upon him was something new and unprepared for. He was a slaveholder without the ability to hold slaves. He found himself incapable of managing his slaves either by force, fear, or fraud. We seldom called him "master;" we generally called him "Captain Auld," and were hardly disposed to title him at all. I doubt not that our conduct had much to do with making him appear awkward, and of consequence fretful. Our want of reverence for him must have perplexed him greatly. He wished to have us call him master, but lacked the firmness necessary to command us to do so. His wife used to insist upon our calling him so, but to no purpose. In August, 1832, my master attended a Methodist camp-meeting[2] held in the Bay-side, Talbot county, and there experienced religion. I indulged a faint hope that his conversion would lead him to emancipate his slaves, and that, if he did not do this, it would, at any rate, make him more kind and humane. I was disappointed in both these respects. It neither made him to be humane to his slaves, nor to emancipate them. If it had any effect on his character, it made him more cruel and hateful in all his ways; for I believe him to have been a much worse man after his conversion than before. Prior to his conversion, he relied upon his own depravity to shield and sustain him in his savage barbarity; but after his conversion, he found religious sanction and support for his

2. A popular form of 19th-century evangelical religious gathering.

slaveholding cruelty. He made the greatest pretensions to piety. His house was the house of prayer. He prayed morning, noon, and night. He very soon distinguished himself among his brethren, and was soon made a class-leader and exhorter. His activity in revivals was great, and he proved himself an instrument in the hands of the church in converting many souls. His house was the preachers' home. They used to take great pleasure in coming there to put up; for while he starved us, he stuffed them. We have had three or four preachers there at a time. The names of those who used to come most frequently while I lived there, were Mr. Storks, Mr. Ewery, Mr. Humphry, and Mr. Hickey. I have also seen Mr. George Cookman[3] at our house. We slaves loved Mr. Cookman. We believed him to be a good man. We thought him instrumental in getting Mr. Samuel Harrison, a very rich slaveholder, to emancipate his slaves; and by some means got the impression that he was laboring to effect the emancipation of all the slaves. When he was at our house, we were sure to be called in to prayers. When the others were there, we were sometimes called in and sometimes not. Mr. Cookman took more notice of us than either of the other ministers. He could not come among us without betraying his sympathy for us, and, stupid as we were, we had the sagacity to see it.

While I lived with my master in St. Michael's, there was a white young man, a Mr. Wilson, who proposed to keep a Sabbath school for the instruction of such slaves as might be disposed to learn to read the New Testament. We met but three times, when Mr. West and Mr. Fairbanks, both class-leaders, with many others, came upon with us with sticks and other missiles, drove us off, and forbade us to meet again. Thus ended our little Sabbath school in the pious town of St. Michael's.

I have said my master found religious sanction for his cruelty. As an example, I will state one of many facts going to prove the charge. I have seen him tie up a lame young woman, and whip her with a heavy cowskin upon her naked shoulders, causing the warm red blood to drip; and, in justification of the bloody deed, he would quote this passage of Scripture—"He that knoweth his master's will, and doeth it not, shall be beaten with many stripes."[4]

Master would keep this lacerated young woman tied up in this horrid situation four or five hours at a time. I have known him to tie her up early in the morning, and whip her before breakfast; leave her, go to his store, return at dinner, and whip her again, cutting her in the places already made raw with his cruel lash. The secret of master's cruelty toward "Henny" is found in the fact of her

3. A prominent English Methodist minister (1800–1841).
4. Luke 12.47.

being almost helpless. When quite a child, she fell into the fire, and burned herself horribly. Her hands were so burnt that she never got the use of them. She could do very little but bear heavy burdens. She was to master a bill of expense; and as he was a mean man, she was a constant offence to him. He seemed desirous of getting the poor girl out of existence. He gave her away once to his sister; but, being a poor gift, she was not disposed to keep her. Finally, my benevolent master, to use his own words, "set her adrift to take care of herself." Here was a recently-converted man, holding on upon the mother, and at the same time turning out her helpless child, to starve and die! Master Thomas was one of the many pious slave-holders who hold slaves for the very charitable purpose of taking care of them.

My master and myself had quite a number of differences. He found me unsuitable to his purpose. My city life, he said, had had a very pernicious effect upon me. It had almost ruined me for every good purpose, and fitted me for every thing which was bad. One of my greatest faults was that of letting his horse run away, and go down to his father-in-law's farm, which was about five miles from St. Michael's. I would then have to go after it. My reason for this kind of carelessness, or carefulness, was, that I could always get something to eat when I went there. Master William Hamilton, my master's father-in-law, always gave his slaves enough to eat. I never left there hungry, no matter how great the need of my speedy return. Master Thomas at length said he would stand it no longer. I had lived with him nine months, during which time he had given me a number of severe whippings, all to no good purpose. He resolved to put me out, as he said, to be broken; and, for this purpose, he let me for one year to a man named Edward Covey. Mr. Covey was a poor man, a farm-renter. He rented the place upon which he lived, as also the hands with which he tilled it. Mr. Covey had acquired a very high reputation for breaking young slaves, and this reputation was of immense value to him. It enabled him to get his farm tilled with much less expense to himself than he could have had it done without such a reputation. Some slaveholders thought it not much loss to allow Mr. Covey to have their slaves one year, for the sake of training to which they were subjected, without any other compensation. He could hire young help with great ease, in consequence of this reputation. Added to the natural good qualities of Mr. Covey, he was a professor of religion—a pious soul—a member and a class-leader in the Methodist church. All of this added weight to his reputation as a "nigger-breaker." I was aware of all the facts, having been made acquainted with them by a young man who had lived there. I nevertheless made the change gladly; for I was sure of getting enough to eat, which is not the smallest consideration to a hungry man.

Chapter X

I left Master Thomas's house, and went to live with Mr. Covey, on the 1st of January, 1833. I was now, for the first time in my life, a field hand. In my new employment, I found myself even more awkward than a country boy appeared to be in a large city. I had been at my new home but one week before Mr. Covey gave me a very severe whipping, cutting my back, causing the blood to run, and raising ridges on my flesh as large as my little finger. The details of this affair are as follows: Mr. Covey sent me, very early in the morning of one of our coldest days in the month of January, to the woods, to get a load of wood. He gave me a team of unbroken oxen. He told me which was the in-hand ox, and which the off-hand one.[1] He then tied the end of a large rope around the horns of the in-hand-ox, and gave me the other end of it, and told me, if the oxen started to run, that I must hold on upon the rope. I had never driven oxen before, and of course I was very awkward. I, however, succeeded in getting to the edge of the woods with little difficulty; but I had got a very few rods into the woods, when the oxen took fright, and started full tilt, carrying the cart against trees, and over stumps, in the most frightful manner. I expected every moment that my brains would be dashed out against the trees. After running thus for a considerable distance, they finally upset the cart, dashing it with great force against a tree, and threw themselves into a dense thicket. How I escaped death, I do not know. There I was, entirely alone, in a thick wood, in a place new to me. My cart was upset and shattered, my oxen were entangled among the young trees, and there was none to help me. After a long spell of effort, I succeeded in getting my cart righted, my oxen disentangled, and again yoked to the cart. I now proceeded with my team to the place where I had, the day before, been chopping wood, and loaded my cart pretty heavily, thinking in this way to tame my oxen. I then proceeded on my way home. I had now consumed one half of the day. I got out of the woods safely, and now felt out of danger. I stopped my oxen to open the woods gate; and just as I did so, before I could get hold of my ox-rope, the oxen again started, rushed through the gate, catching it between the wheel and the body of the cart, tearing it to pieces, and coming within a few inches of crushing me against the gate-post. Thus twice, in one short day, I escaped death by the merest chance. On my return, I told Mr. Covey what had happened, and how it happened. He ordered me to return to the woods again immediately. I did so, and he followed on after me. Just as I got into the woods, he came up and told me to stop my cart, and that he would teach me how

1. The one on the right of a pair hitched to a wagon. "In-hand ox": the one to the left.

to trifle away my time, and break gates. He then went to a large gum-tree, and with his axe cut three large switches, and, after trimming them up neatly with his pocket-knife, he ordered me to take off my clothes. I made him no answer, but stood with my clothes on. He repeated his order. I still made him no answer, nor did I move to strip myself. Upon this he rushed at me with the fierceness of a tiger, tore off my clothes, and lashed me till he had worn out his switches, cutting me so savagely as to leave the marks visible for a long time after. This whipping was the first of a number just like it, and for similar offences.

I lived with Mr. Covey one year. During the first six months, of that year, scarce a week passed without his whipping me. I was seldom free from a sore back. My awkwardness was almost always his excuse for whipping me. We were worked fully up to the point of endurance. Long before day we were up, our horses fed, and by the first approach of day we were off to the field with our hoes and ploughing teams. Mr. Covey gave us enough to eat, but scarce time to eat it. We were often less than five minutes taking our meals. We were often in the field from the first approach of day till its last lingering ray had left us; and at saving-fodder time, midnight often caught us in the field binding blades.[2]

Covey would be out with us. The way he used to stand it, was this. He would spend the most of his afternoons in bed. He would then come out fresh in the evening, ready to urge us on with his words, example, and frequently with the whip. Mr. Covey was one of the few slaveholders who could and did work with his hands. He was a hard-working man. He knew by himself just what a man or a boy could do. There was no deceiving him. His work went on in his absence almost as well as in his presence; and he had the faculty of making us feel that he was ever present with us. This he did by surprising us. He seldom approached the spot where we were at work openly, if he could do it secretly. He always aimed at taking us by surprise. Such was his cunning, that we used to call him, among ourselves, "the snake." When we were at work in the cornfield, he would sometimes crawl on his hands and knees to avoid detection, and all at once he would rise nearly in our midst, and scream out, "Ha, ha! Come, come! Dash on, dash on!" This being his mode of attack, it was never safe to stop a single minute. His comings were like a thief in the night. He appeared to us as being ever at hand. He was under every tree, behind every stump, in every bush, and at every window, on the plantation. He would sometimes mount his horse, as if bound to St. Michael's, a distance of seven miles, and in half an hour afterwards you would see him coiled up in the corner of the wood-fence,

2. I.e., of wheat or other plants. "Saving-fodder time": harvest time.

watching every motion of the slaves. He would, for this purpose, leave his horse tied up in the woods. Again, he would sometimes walk up to us, and give us orders as though he was upon the point of starting on a long journey, turn his back upon us, and make as though he was going to the house to get ready; and, before he would get half way thither, he would turn short and crawl into a fence-corner, or behind some tree, and there watch us till the going down of the sun.

Mr. Covey's *forte* consisted in his power to deceive. His life was devoted to planning and perpetrating the grossest deceptions. Every thing he possessed in the shape of learning or religion, he made conform to his disposition to deceive. He seemed to think himself equal to deceiving the Almighty. He would make a short prayer in the morning, and a long prayer at night; and, strange as it may seem, few men would at times appear more devotional than he. The exercises of his family devotions were always commenced with singing; and, as he was a very poor singer himself, the duty of raising the hymn generally came upon me. He would read his hymn, and nod at me to commence. I would at times do so; at others, I would not. My non-compliance would almost always produce much confusion. To show himself independent of me, he would start and stagger through with his hymn in the most discordant manner. In this state of mind, he prayed with more than ordinary spirit. Poor man! such was his disposition, and success at deceiving, I do verily believe that he sometimes deceived himself into the solemn belief, that he was a sincere worshiper of the most high God; and this, too, at a time when he may be said to have been guilty of compelling his woman slave to commit the sin of adultery. The facts in the case are these: Mr. Covey was a poor man; he was just commencing in life; he was only able to buy one slave; and, shocking as is the fact, he bought her, as he said, for *a breeder*. This woman was named Caroline. Mr. Covey bought her from Mr. Thomas Lowe, about six miles from St. Michael's. She was a large, able-bodied woman, about twenty years old. She had already given birth to one child, which proved her to be just what he wanted. After buying her, he hired a married man of Mr. Samuel Harrison, to live with him one year; and him he used to fasten up with her every night! The result was, that, at the end of the year, the miserable woman gave birth to twins. At this result Mr. Covey seemed to be highly pleased, both with the man and the wretched woman. Such was his joy, and that of his wife, that nothing they could do for Caroline during her confinement was too good, or too hard, to be done. The children were regarded as being quite an addition to his wealth.

If at any one time of my life more than another, I was made to drink the bitterest dregs of slavery, that time was during the first six months of my stay with Mr. Covey. We were worked in all weathers. It was never too hot or too cold; it could never rain, blow, hail, or snow, too hard for us to work in the field. Work, work, work, was scarcely more the order of the day than of the night. The longest days were too short for him, and the shortest nights too long for him. I was somewhat unmanageable when I first went there, but a few months of this discipline tamed me. Mr. Covey succeeded in breaking me. I was broken in body, soul, and spirit. My natural elasticity was crushed, my intellect languished, the disposition to read departed, the cheerful spark that lingered about my eye died; the dark night of slavery closed in upon me; and behold a man transformed into a brute!

Sunday was my only leisure time. I spent this in a sort of beast-like stupor, between sleep and wake, under some large tree. At times I would rise up, a flash of energetic freedom would dart through my soul, accompanied with a faint beam of hope, that flickered for a moment, and then vanished. I sank down again, mourning over my wretched condition. I was sometimes prompted to take my life, and that of Covey, but was prevented by a combination of hope and fear. My sufferings on this plantation seem now like a dream rather than a stern reality.

Our house stood within a few rods of the Chesapeake Bay, whose broad bosom was ever white with sails from every quarter of the habitable globe. Those beautiful vessels, robed in purest white, so delightful to the eye of freemen, were to me so many shrouded ghosts, to terrify and torment me with thoughts of my wretched condition. I have often, in the deep stillness of a summer's Sabbath, stood all alone upon the lofty banks of that noble bay, and traced, with saddened heart and tearful eye, the countless number of sails moving off to the mighty ocean. The sight of these always affected me powerfully. My thoughts would compel utterance; and there, with no audience but the Almighty, I would pour out my soul's complaint, in my rude way, with an apostrophe to the moving multitude of ships:—

"You are loosed from your moorings, and are free; I am fast in my chains, and am a slave! You move merrily before the gentle gale, and I sadly before the bloody whip! You are freedom's swift-winged angels, that fly round the world; I am confined in bands of iron! O that I were free! Oh, that I were on one of your gallant decks, and under your protecting wing! Alas! betwixt me and you, the turbid waters roll. Go on, go on. O that I could also go! Could I but swim! If I could fly! O, why was I born a man, of whom to make a brute! The glad ship is gone; she hides in the dim distance. I am left in the hottest hell of unending slavery. O God, save me! God, deliver me! Let me be free! Is there any God? Why am I a slave? I will run away. I will not stand it. Get caught, or get clear, I'll try it. I had as well die with ague as the fever. I have only one life to lose. I had as well be killed running as die standing. Only think of it; one hundred miles straight north, and I am free! Try it? Yes! God helping me, I will. It cannot be that I shall live and die a slave. I will take to the water. This very bay shall yet bear me into freedom. The steamboats steered in a north-east course from North Point. I will do the same; and when I get to the head of the bay, I will turn my canoe adrift, and walk straight through Delaware into Pennsylvania. When I get there, I shall not be required to have a pass; I can travel without being disturbed. Let but the first opportunity offer, and, come what will, I am off. Meanwhile, I will try to bear up under the yoke. I am not the only slave in the world. Why should I fret? I can bear as much as any of them. Besides, I am but a boy, and all boys are bound to some one. It may be that my misery in slavery will only increase my happiness when I get free. There is a better day coming."

Thus I used to think, and thus I used to speak to myself; goaded almost to madness at one moment, and at the next reconciling myself to my wretched lot.

I have already intimated that my condition was much worse, during the first six months of my stay at Mr. Covey's, than in the last six. The circumstances leading to the change in Mr. Covey's course toward me form an epoch in my humble history. You have seen how a man was made a slave; you shall see how a slave was made a man. On one of the hottest days of the month of August, 1833, Bill Smith, William Hughes, a slave named Eli, and myself, were engaged in fanning wheat.[3] Hughes was clearing the fanned wheat from before the fan, Eli was turning, Smith was feeding, and I was carrying wheat to the fan. The work was simple, requiring strength rather than intellect; yet, to one entirely unused to such work, it came very hard. About three o'clock of that day, I broke down; my strength failed me; I was seized with a violent aching of the head, attended with extreme dizziness; I trembled in every limb. Finding what was coming, I nerved myself up, feeling it would never do to stop work! I stood as long as I could stagger to the hopper with grain. When I could stand no longer, I fell, and felt as if held down by an immense weight. The fan of course stopped; every one had his own work to do; and no one could do the work of the other, and have his own go on at the same time.

Mr. Covey was at the house, about one hundred yards from the treading-yard where we were fanning. On hearing the fan stop, he left immediately, and came to the spot where we were. He hastily inquired what the matter was. Bill answered that I was sick, and

3. I.e., separating the wheat from the chaff.

there was no one to bring wheat to the fan. I had by this time crawled away under the side of the post and rail-fence by which the yard was enclosed, hoping to find relief by getting out of the sun. He then asked where I was. He was told by one of the hands. He came to the spot, and, after looking at me awhile, asked me what was the matter. I told him as well as I could, for I scarce had strength to speak. He then gave me a savage kick in the side, and told me to get up. I tried to do so, but fell back in the attempt. He gave me another kick, and again told me to rise. I again tried, and succeeded in gaining my feet; but, stooping to get the tub with which I was feeding the fan, I again staggered and fell. While down in this situation, Mr. Covey took up the hickory slat with which Hughes had been striking off the half-bushel measure, and with it gave me a heavy blow upon the head, making a large wound, and the blood ran freely; and with this again told me to get up. I made no effort to comply, having now made up my mind to let him do his worst. In a short time after receiving this blow, my head grew better. Mr. Covey had now left me to my fate. At this moment I resolved, for the first time, to go to my master, enter a complaint, and ask his protection. In order to do this, I must that afternoon walk seven miles; and this, under the circumstances, was truly a severe undertaking. I was exceedingly feeble; made so as much by the kicks and blows which I received, as by the severe fit of sickness to which I had been subjected. I, however, watched my chance, while Covey was looking in an opposite direction, and started for St. Michael's. I succeeded in getting a considerable distance on my way to the woods, when Covey discovered me, and called after me to come back, threatening what he would do if I did not come. I disregarded both his calls and his threats, and made my way to the woods as fast as my feeble state would allow; and thinking I might be overhauled by him if I kept the road, I walked through the woods, keeping far enough from the road to avoid detection, and near enough to prevent losing my way. I had not gone far before my little strength again failed me. I could go no farther. I fell down, and lay for a considerable time. The blood was yet oozing from the wound on my head. For a time I thought I should bleed to death; and think now that I should have done so, but that the blood so matted my hair as to stop the wound. After lying there about three quarters of an hour, I nerved myself up again, and started on my way, through bogs and briers, barefooted and bareheaded, tearing my feet sometimes at nearly every step; and after a journey of about seven miles, occupying some five hours to perform it, I arrived at master's store. I then presented an appearance enough to affect any but a heart of iron. From the crown of my head to my feet, I was covered with blood. My hair was all clotted with dust and blood; my shirt was stiff with blood. My legs and feet were torn in sundry places with briers and thorns, and were also covered with blood. I suppose I looked like a man who had escaped a den of wild beasts, and barely escaped them. In this state I appeared before my master, humbly entreating him to interpose his authority for my protection. I told him all the circumstances as well as I could, and it seemed, as I spoke, at times to affect him. He would then walk the floor, and seek to justify Covey by saying he expected I deserved it. He asked me what I wanted. I told him, to let me get a new home; that as sure as I lived with Mr. Covey again, I should live with but to die with him; that Covey would surely kill me; he was in a fair way for it. Master Thomas ridiculed the idea that there was any danger of Mr. Covey's killing me, and said that he knew Mr. Covey; that he was a good man, and that he could not think of taking me from him; that, should he do so, he would lose the whole year's wages; that I belonged to Mr. Covey for one year, and that I must go back to him, come what might; and that I must not trouble him with any more stories, or that he would himself *get hold of me*. After threatening me thus, he gave me a very large dose of salts, telling me that I might remain in St. Michael's that night, (it being quite late,) but that I must be off back to Mr. Covey's early in the morning; and that if I did not, he would *get hold of me*, which meant that he would whip me. I remained all night, and, according to his orders, I started off to Covey's in the morning, (Saturday morning), wearied in body and broken in spirit. I got no supper that night, or breakfast that morning. I reached Covey's about nine o'clock; and just as I was getting over the fence that divided Mrs. Kemp's fields from ours, out ran Covey with his cowskin, to give me another whipping. Before he could reach me, I succeeded in getting to the cornfield; and as the corn was very high, it afforded me the means of hiding. He seemed very angry, and searched for me a long time. My behavior was altogether unaccountable. He finally gave up the chase, thinking, I suppose, that I must come home for something to eat; he would give himself no further trouble in looking for me. I spent that day mostly in the woods, having the alternative before me,—to go home and be whipped to death, or stay in the woods and be starved to death. That night, I fell in with Sandy Jenkins, a slave with whom I was somewhat acquainted. Sandy had a free wife[4] who lived about four miles from Mr. Covey's; and it being Saturday, he was on his way to see her. I told him my circumstances, and he very kindly invited me to go home with him. I went home with him, and talked this whole matter over, and got his advice as to what course it was best for me to pursue. I found Sandy an old adviser. He told me, with great solemnity, I must go back to

4. I.e., his wife had been either born free or set free and was not legally a slave.

Covey; but that before I went, I must go with him into another part of the woods, where there was a certain *root*, which, if I would take some of it with me, carrying it *always on my right side*, would render it impossible for Mr. Covey, or any other white man, to whip me. He said he had carried it for years; and since he had done so, he had never received a blow, and never expected to while he carried it. I at first rejected the idea, that the simple carrying of a root in my pocket would have any such effect as he had said, and was not disposed to take it; but Sandy impressed the necessity with much earnestness, telling me it could do no harm, if it did no good. To please him, I at length took the root, and, according to his direction, carried it upon my right side. This was Sunday morning. I immediately started for home; and upon entering the yard gate, out came Mr. Covey on his way to meeting. He spoke to me very kindly, bade me drive the pigs from a lot near by, and passed on towards the church. Now, this singular conduct of Mr. Covey really made me begin to think that there was something in the *root* which Sandy had given me; and had it been on any other day than Sunday, I could have attributed the conduct to no other cause then the influence of that root; and as it was, I was half inclined to think the *root* to be something more than I at first had taken it to be. All went well till Monday morning. On this morning, the virtue of the *root* was fully tested. Long before daylight, I was called to go and rub, curry, and feed, the horses. I obeyed, and was glad to obey. But whilst thus engaged, whilst in the act of throwing down some blades from the loft, Mr. Covey entered the stable with a long rope; and just as I was half out of the loft, he caught hold of my legs, and was about tying me. As soon as I found what he was up to, I gave a sudden spring, and as I did so, he holding to my legs, I was brought sprawling on the stable floor. Mr. Covey seemed now to think he had me, and could do what he pleased; but at this moment—from whence came the spirit I don't know—I resolved to fight; and, suiting my action to the resolution, I seized Covey hard by the throat; and as I did so, I rose. He held on to me, and I to him. My resistance was so entirely unexpected, that Covey seemed taken all aback. He trembled like a leaf. This gave me assurance, and I held him uneasy, causing the blood to run where I touched him with the ends of my fingers. Mr. Covey soon called out to Hughes for help. Hughes came, and, while Covey held me, attempted to tie my right hand. While he was in the act of doing so, I watched my chance, and gave him a heavy kick close under the ribs. This kick fairly sickened Hughes, so that he left me in the hands of Mr. Covey. This kick had the effect of not only weakening Hughes, but Covey also. When he saw Hughes bending over with pain, his courage quailed. He asked me if I meant to persist in my resistance. I told him I did, come what might; that he had used me like a brute for six months, and that I was determined to be used so no longer. With that, he strove to drag me to a stick that was lying just out of the stable door. He meant to knock me down. But just as he was leaning over to get the stick, I seized him with both hands by his collar, and brought him by a sudden snatch to the ground. By this time, Bill came. Covey called upon him for assistance. Bill wanted to know what he could do. Covey said, "Take hold of him, take hold of him!" Bill said his master hired him out to work, and not to help to whip me; so he left Covey and myself to fight our own battle out. We were at it for nearly two hours. Covey at length let me go, puffing and blowing at a great rate, saying that if I had not resisted, he would not have whipped me half so much. The truth was, that he had not whipped me at all. I considered him as getting entirely the worst end of the bargain; for he had drawn no blood from me, but I had from him. The whole six months afterwards, that I spent with Mr. Covey, he never laid the weight of his finger upon me in anger. He would occasionally say, he didn't want to get hold of me again. "No," thought I, "you need not; for you will come off worse than you did before."

This battle with Mr. Covey was the turning-point in my career as a slave. It rekindled the few expiring embers of freedom, and revived within me a sense of my own manhood. It recalled the departed self-confidence, and inspired me again with a determination to be free. The gratification afforded by the triumph was a full compensation for whatever else might follow, even death itself. He only can understand the deep satisfaction which I experienced, who has himself repelled by force the bloody arm of slavery. I felt as I never felt before. It was a glorious resurrection, from the tomb of slavery, to the heaven of freedom. My long-crushed spirit rose, cowardice departed, bold defiance took its place; and I now resolved that, however long I might remain a slave in form, the day had passed forever when I could be a slave in fact. I did not hesitate to let it be known of me, that the white man who expected to succeed in whipping, must also succeed in killing me.

From this time I was never again what might be called fairly whipped, though I remained a slave four years afterwards. I had several fights, but was never whipped.

It was for a long time a matter of surprise to me why Mr. Covey did not immediately have me taken by the constable to the whipping-post, and there regularly whipped for the crime of raising my hand against a white man in defence of myself. And the only explanation I can now think of does not entirely satisfy me; but such as it is, I will give it. Mr. Covey enjoyed the most unbounded reputation for being a first-rate overseer and negro-breaker. It was of considerable importance to him. That reputation was at stake;

and had he sent me—a boy about sixteen years old—to the public whipping-post, his reputation would have been lost; so, to save his reputation, he suffered me to go unpunished.

My term of actual service to Mr. Edward Covey ended on Christmas day, 1833. The days between Christmas and New Year's day are allowed as holidays; and, accordingly, we were not required to perform any labor, more than to feed and take care of the stock. This time we regarded as our own, by the grace of our masters; and we therefore used or abused it nearly as we pleased. Those of us who had families at a distance, were generally allowed to spend the whole six days in their society. This time, however, was spent in various ways. The staid, sober, thinking and industrious ones of our number would employ themselves in making corn-brooms, mats, horse-collars, and baskets; and another class of us would spend the time hunting opossums, hares, and coons. But by far the larger part engaged in such sports and merriments as playing ball, wrestling, running foot-races, fiddling, dancing, and drinking whisky; and this latter mode of spending the time was by far the most agreeable to the feelings of our master. A slave who would work during the holidays was considered by our masters as scarcely deserving them. He was regarded as one who rejected the favor of his master. It was deemed a disgrace not to get drunk at Christmas; and he was regarded as lazy indeed, who had not provided himself with the necessary means, during the year, to get whisky enough to last him through Christmas.

From what I know of the effect of these holidays upon the slave, I believe them to be among the most effective means in the hands of the slaveholder in keeping down the spirit of insurrection. Were the slaveholders at once to abandon this practice, I have not the slightest doubt it would lead to an immediate insurrection among the slaves. These holidays serve as conductors, or safety-valves, to carry off the rebellious spirit of enslaved humanity. But for these, the slave would be forced up to the wildest desperation; and woe betide the slaveholder, the day he ventures to remove or hinder the operation of those conductors! I warn him that, in such an event, a spirit will go forth in their midst, more to be dreaded than the most appalling earthquake.

The holidays are part and parcel of the gross fraud, wrong, and inhumanity of slavery. They are professedly a custom established by the benevolence of the slaveholders; but I undertake to say, it is the result of selfishness, and one of the grossest frauds committed upon the downtrodden slave. They do not give the slaves this time because they would not like to have their work during its continuance, but because they know it would be unsafe to deprive them of it. This will be seen by the fact, that the slaveholders like to have their slaves spend those days just in such a manner as to make them as glad of their ending as of their beginning. Their object seems to be, to disgust their slaves with freedom, by plunging them into the lowest depths of dissipation. For instance, the slaveholders not only like to see the slave drink of his own accord, but will adopt various plans to make him drunk. One plan is, to make bets on their slaves, as to who can drink the most whisky without getting drunk; and in this way they succeed in getting whole multitudes to drink to excess. Thus, when the slave asks for virtuous freedom, the cunning slaveholder, knowing his ignorance, cheats him with a dose of vicious dissipation, artfully labelled with the name of liberty. The most of us used to drink it down, and the result was just what might be supposed: many of us were led to think that there was little to choose between liberty and slavery. We felt, and very properly too, that we had almost as well be slaves to man as to rum. So, when the holidays ended, we staggered up from the filth of our wallowing, took a long breath, and marched to the field,—feeling, upon the whole, rather glad to go, from what our master had deceived us into a belief was freedom, back to the arms of slavery.

I have said that this mode of treatment is a part of the whole system of fraud and inhumanity of slavery. It is so. The mode here adopted to disgust the slave with freedom, by allowing him to see only the abuse of it, is carried out in other things. For instance, a slave loves molasses; he steals some. His master, in many cases, goes off to town, and buys a large quantity; he returns, takes his whip, and commands the slave to eat the molasses, until the poor fellow is made sick at the very mention of it. The same mode is sometimes adopted to make the slaves refrain from asking for more food than their regular allowance. A slave runs through his allowance, and applies for more. His master is enraged at him; but, not willing to send him off without food, gives him more than is necessary, and compels him to eat it within a given time. Then, if he complains that he cannot eat it, he is said to be satisfied neither full nor fasting, and is whipped for being hard to please! I have an abundance of such illustrations of the same principle, drawn from my own observation, but think the cases I have cited sufficient. The practice is a very common one.

On the first of January, 1834, I left Mr. Covey, and went to live with Mr. William Freeland, who lived about three miles from St. Michael's. I soon found Mr. Freeland a very different man from Mr. Covey. Though not rich, he was what would be called an educated southern gentleman. Mr. Covey, as I have shown, was a well-trained negro-breaker and slave-driver. The former (slaveholder though he was) seemed to possess some regard for honor, some reverence for justice, and some respect for humanity. The latter seemed totally insensible to all such sentiments. Mr. Freeland had many of the faults peculiar to slaveholders, such as being very passionate and fretful; but I must do him the justice to say, that he was exceedingly free from those degrading vices to which Mr. Covey was constantly addicted. The one was open and frank, and we always knew where to find him. The other was a most artful deceiver, and could be understood only by such as were skilful enough to detect his cunningly-devised frauds. Another advantage I gained in my new master was, he made no pretensions to, or profession of, religion; and this, in my opinion, was truly a great advantage. I assert most unhesitatingly, that the religion of the south is a mere covering for the most horrid crimes,—a justifier of the most appalling barbarity,—a sanctifier of the most hateful frauds,—and a dark shelter under which the darkest, foulest, grossest, and most infernal deeds of slaveholders find the strongest protection. Were I to be again reduced to the chains of slavery, next to that enslavement, I should regard being the slave of a religious master the greatest calamity that could befall me. For of all slaveholders with whom I have ever met, religious slaveholders are the worst. I have ever found them the meanest and basest, the most cruel and cowardly, of all others. It was my unhappy lot not only to belong to a religious slaveholder, but to live in a community of such religionists. Very near Mr. Freeland lived the Rev. Daniel Weeden, and in the same neighborhood lived the Rev. Rigby Hopkins. These were members and ministers in the Reformed Methodist Church. Mr. Weeden owned, among others, a woman slave, whose name I have forgotten. This woman's back, for weeks, was kept literally raw, made so by the lash of this merciless, *religious* wretch. He used to hire hands. His maxim was, Behave well or behave ill, it is the duty of a master occasionally to whip a slave, to remind him of his master's authority. Such was his theory, and such his practice.

Mr. Hopkins was even worse than Mr. Weeden. His chief boast was his ability to manage slaves. The peculiar feature of his government was that of whipping slaves in advance of deserving it. He always managed to have one or more of his slaves to whip every Monday morning. He did this to alarm their fears, and strike terror into those who escaped. His plan was to whip for the smallest offences, to prevent the commission of large ones. Mr. Hopkins could always find some excuse for whipping a slave. It would astonish one, unaccustomed to a slaveholding life, to see with what wonderful ease a slaveholder can find things, of which to make occasion to whip a slave. A mere look, word, or motion,—a mistake, accident, or want of power,—are all matters for which a slave may be whipped at any time. Does a slave look dissatisfied? It is said, he has the devil in him, and it must be whipped out. Does he speak loudly when spoken to by his master? Then he is getting high-minded, and should be taken down a button-hole lower. Does he forget to pull off his hat at the approach of a white person? Then he is wanting in reverence, and should be whipped for it. Does he ever venture to vindicate his conduct, when censured for it? Then he is guilty of impudence,—one of the greatest crimes of which a slave can be guilty. Does he ever venture to suggest a different mode of doing things from that pointed out by his master? He is indeed presumptuous, and getting above himself; and nothing less than a flogging will do for him. Does he, while ploughing, break a plough,—or, while hoeing, break a hoe? It is owing to his carelessness, and for it a slave must always be whipped. Mr. Hopkins could always find something of this sort to justify the use of the lash, and he seldom failed to embrace such opportunities. There was not a man in the whole county, with whom the slaves who had the getting their own home, would not prefer to live, rather than with this Rev. Mr. Hopkins. And yet there was not a man any where round, who made higher professions of religion, or was more active in revivals—more attentive to the class, love-feast, prayer and preaching meetings, or more devotional in his family,—that prayed earlier, later, louder, and longer,—than this same reverend slave-driver, Rigby Hopkins.

But to return to Mr. Freeland, and to my experience while in his employment. He, like Mr. Covey, gave us enough to eat; but unlike Mr. Covey, he also gave us sufficient time to take our meals. He worked us hard, but always between sunrise and sunset. He required a good deal of work to be done, but gave us good tools with which to work. His farm was large, but he employed hands enough to work it, and with ease, compared with many of his neighbors. My treatment, while in his employment, was heavenly, compared with what I experienced at the hands of Mr. Edward Covey.

Mr. Freeland was himself the owner of but two slaves. Their names were Henry Harris and John Harris. The rest of his hands he hired. These consisted of myself, Sandy Jenkins[5] and Handy Caldwell. Henry and John were quite intelligent, and in a very little while after I went there, I succeeded in creating in them a strong desire to learn how to read. This desire soon sprang up in the others also. They very soon mustered up some old spelling-books, and nothing would do but that I must keep a Sabbath school. I agreed to do so, and accordingly devoted my Sundays to teaching these my loved fellow-slaves how to read. Neither of them knew his letters

5. "This is the same man who gave me the roots to prevent my being whipped by Mr. Covey. He was a 'clever soul.' We used frequently to talk about the fight with Covey, and as often as we did so, he would claim my success as the result of the roots he gave me. This superstition is very common among the more ignorant slaves. A slave seldom dies but that his death is attributed to trickery" [Douglass's note].

when I went there. Some of the slaves of the neighboring farms found what was going on, and also availed themselves of this little opportunity to learn to read. It was understood, among all who came, that there must be as little display about it as possible. It was necessary to keep our religious masters at St. Michael's unacquainted with the fact, that, instead of spending the Sabbath in wrestling, boxing, and drinking whisky, we were trying to learn how to read the will of God; for they had much rather see us engaged in those degrading sports, than to see us behaving like intellectual, moral, and accountable beings. My blood boils as I think of the bloody manner in which Messrs. Wright Fairbanks and Garrison West, both class-leaders, in connection with many others, rushed in upon us with sticks and stones, and broke up our virtuous little Sabbath school, at St. Michael's—all calling themselves Christians! humble followers of the Lord Jesus Christ! But I am again digressing.

I held my Sabbath school at the house of a free colored man, whose name I deem it imprudent to mention; for should it be known, it might embarrass him greatly, though the crime of holding the school was committed ten years ago. I had at one time over forty scholars, and those of the right sort, ardently desiring to learn. They were of all ages, though mostly men and women. I look back to those Sundays with an amount of pleasure not to be expressed. They were great days to my soul. The work of instructing my dear fellow-slaves was the sweetest engagement with which I was ever blessed. We loved each other, and to leave them at the close of the Sabbath was a severe cross indeed. When I think that those precious souls are to-day shut up in the prison-house of slavery, my feelings overcome me, and I am almost ready to ask, "Does a righteous God govern the universe? and for what does he hold the thunders in his right hand, if not to smite the oppressor, and deliver the spoiled out of the hand of the spoiler?" These dear souls came not to Sabbath school because it was popular to do so, nor did I teach them because it was reputable to be thus engaged. Every moment they spent in that school, they were liable to be taken up, and given thirty-nine lashes. They came because they wished to learn. Their minds had been starved by their cruel masters. They had been shut up in mental darkness. I taught them, because it was the delight of my soul to be doing something that looked like bettering the condition of my race. I kept up my school nearly the whole year I lived with Mr. Freeland; and, beside my Sabbath school, I devoted three evenings in the week, during the winter, to teaching the slaves at home. And I have the happiness to know, that several of those who came to Sabbath school learned how to read; and that one, at least, is now free through my agency.

The year passed off smoothly. It seemed only about half as long as the year which preceded it. I went through it without receiving a single blow. I will give Mr. Freeland the credit of being the best master I ever had, *till I became my own master.* For the ease with which I passed the year, I was, however, somewhat indebted to the society of my fellow-slaves. They were noble souls; they not only possessed loving hearts, but brave ones. We were linked and interlinked with each other. I loved them with a love stronger than any thing I have experienced since. It is sometimes said that we slaves do not love and confide in each other. In answer to this assertion, I can say, I never loved any or confided in any people more than my fellow-slaves, and especially those with whom I lived at Mr. Freeland's. I believe we would have died for each other. We never undertook to do any thing, of any importance, without a mutual consultation. We never moved separately. We were one; and as much so by our tempers and dispositions, as by the mutual hardships to which we were necessarily subjected by our condition as slaves.

At the close of the year 1834, Mr. Freeland again hired me of my master, for the year 1835. But, by this time, I began to want to live *upon free land* as well as *with Freeland;* and I was no longer content, therefore, to live with him or any other slaveholder. I began, with the commencement of the year, to prepare myself for a final struggle, which should decide my fate one way or the other. My tendency was upward. I was fast approaching manhood, and year after year had passed, and I was still a slave. These thoughts roused me—I must do something. I therefore resolved that 1835 should not pass without witnessing an attempt, on my part, to secure my liberty. But I was not willing to cherish this determination alone. My fellow-slaves were dear to me. I was anxious to have them participate with me in this, my life-giving determination. I therefore, though with great prudence, commenced early to ascertain their views and feelings in regard to their condition, and to imbue their minds with thoughts of freedom. I bent myself to devising ways and means for our escape, and meanwhile strove, on all fitting occasions, to impress them with the gross fraud and inhumanity of slavery. I went first to Henry, next to John, then to the others. I found, in them all, warm hearts and noble spirits. They were ready to hear, and ready to act when a feasible plan should be proposed. This was what I wanted. I talked to them of our want of manhood, if we submitted to our enslavement without at least one noble effort to be free. We met often, and consulted frequently, and told our hopes and fears, recounted the difficulties, real and imagined, which we should be called on to meet. At times we were almost disposed to give up, and try to content ourselves with our wretched lot; at others, we were firm and unbending in our determination to go. Whenever we suggested any plan, there was shrinking—the odds were fearful. Our path was beset with the greatest obstacles; and if we succeeded in gaining the end of it, our right to be free was yet questionable—we were yet liable to be returned to bondage. We could see no spot, this side of the ocean, where we could be free. We knew nothing about Canada. Our knowledge of the north did not extend farther than New York; and to go there, and be forever harassed with the frightful liability of being returned to slavery—with the certainty of being treated tenfold worse than before—the thought was truly a horrible one, and one which it was not easy to overcome. The case sometimes stood thus: At every gate through which we were to pass, we saw a watchman—at every ferry a guard—on every bridge a sentinel—and in every wood a patrol. We were hemmed in upon every side. Here were the difficulties, real or imagined—the good to be sought, and the evil to be shunned. On the one hand, there stood slavery, a stern reality, glaring frightfully upon us,—its robes already crimsoned with the blood of millions, and even now feasting itself greedily upon our own flesh. On the other hand, away back in the dim distance, under the flickering light of the north star, behind some craggy hill or snow-covered mountain, stood a doubtful freedom—half frozen—beckoning us to come and share its hospitality. This in itself was sometimes enough to stagger us; but when we permitted ourselves to survey the road, we were frequently appalled. Upon either side we saw grim death, assuming the most horrid shapes. Now it was starvation, causing us to eat our own flesh;—now we were contending with the waves, and were drowned;—now we were overtaken, and torn to pieces by the fangs of the terrible bloodhound. We were stung by scorpions, chased by wild beasts, bitten by snakes, and finally, after having nearly reached the desired spot,—after swimming rivers, encountering wild beasts, sleeping in the woods, suffering hunger and nakedness,—we were overtaken by our pursuers, and in our resistance, we were shot dead upon the spot! I say, this picture sometimes appalled us, and made us

> "rather bear those ills we had,
> Than fly to others, that we knew not of."[6]

In coming to a fixed determination to run away, we did more than Patrick Henry, when he resolved upon liberty or death. With us it was a doubtful liberty at most, and almost certain death if we failed. For my part, I should prefer death to hopeless bondage.

6. Shakespeare, *Hamlet* 3.1.81–82.

Sandy, one of our number, gave up the notion, but still encouraged us. Our company then consisted of Henry Harris, John Harris, Henry Bailey, Charles Roberts, and myself. Henry Bailey was my uncle, and belonged to my master. Charles married my aunt: he belonged to my master's father-in-law, Mr. William Hamilton.

The plan we finally concluded upon was, to get a large canoe belonging to Mr. Hamilton, and upon the Saturday night previous to Easter holidays, paddle directly up the Chesapeake Bay. On our arrival at the head of the bay, a distance of seventy or eighty miles from where we lived, it was our purpose to turn our canoe adrift, and follow the guidance of the north star till we got beyond the limits of Maryland. Our reason for taking the water route was, that we were less liable to be suspected as runaways; we hoped to be regarded as fishermen; whereas, if we should take the land route, we should be subjected to interruptions of almost every kind. Any one having a white face, and being so disposed, could stop us, and subject us to examination.

The week before our intended start, I wrote several protections, one for each of us. As well as I can remember, they were in the following words, to wit:—

> "This is to certify that I, the undersigned, have given the bearer, my servant, full liberty to go to Baltimore, and spend the Easter holidays. Written with mine own hand, &c., 1835.
>
> "William Hamilton,
>
> "Near St. Michael's, in Talbot county, Maryland."

We were not going to Baltimore; but, in going up the bay, we went toward Baltimore, and these protections were only intended to protect us while on the bay.

As the time drew near for our departure, our anxiety became more and more intense. It was truly a matter of life and death with us. The strength of our determination was about to be fully tested. At this time, I was very active in explaining every difficulty, removing every doubt, dispelling every fear, and inspiring all with the firmness indispensable to success in our undertaking; assuring them that half was gained the instant we made the move; we had talked long enough; we were now ready to move; if not now, we never should be; and if we did not intend to move now, we had as well fold our arms, sit down, and acknowledge ourselves fit only to be slaves. This, none of us were prepared to acknowledge. Every man stood firm; and at our last meeting, we pledged ourselves afresh, in the most solemn manner, that, at the time appointed, we would certainly start in pursuit of freedom. This was in the middle of the week, at the end of which we were to be off. We went, as usual, to our several fields of labor, but with bosoms highly agitated with thoughts of our truly hazardous undertaking. We tried to conceal our feelings as much as possible; and I think we succeeded very well.

After a painful waiting, the Saturday morning, whose night was to witness our departure, came. I hailed it with joy, bring what of sadness it might. Friday night was a sleepless one for me. I probably felt more anxious than the rest, because I was, by common consent, at the head of the whole affair. The responsibility of success or failure lay heavily upon me. The glory of the one, and the confusion of the other, were alike mine. The first two hours of that morning were such as I never experienced before, and hope never to again. Early in the morning, we went, as usual, to the field. We were spreading manure; and all at once, while thus engaged, I was overwhelmed with an indescribable feeling, in the fulness of which I turned to Sandy, who was near by, and said, "We are betrayed!" "Well," said he, "that thought has this moment struck me." We said no more. I was never more certain of any thing.

The horn was blown as usual, and we went up from the field to the house for breakfast. I went for the form, more than for want of any thing to eat that morning. Just as I got to the house, in looking out at the lane gate, I saw four white men, with two colored men. The white men were on horseback, and the colored ones were walking behind, as if tied. I watched them a few moments till they got up to our lane gate. Here they halted, and tied the colored men to the gate-post. I was not yet certain as to what the matter was. In a few moments, in rode Mr. Hamilton, with a speed betokening great excitement. He came to the door, and inquired if Master William was in. He was told he was at the barn. Mr. Hamilton, without dismounting, rode up to the barn with extraordinary speed. In a few moments, he and Mr. Freeland returned to the house. By this time, the three constables rode up, and in great haste dismounted, tied their horses, and met Master William and Mr. Hamilton returning from the barn; and after talking awhile, they all walked up to the kitchen door. There was no one in the kitchen but myself and John. Henry and Sandy were up at the barn. Mr. Freeland put his head in at the door, and called me by name, saying, there were some gentlemen at the door who wished to see me. I stepped to the door, and inquired what they wanted. They at once seized me, and, without giving me any satisfaction, tied me—lashing my hands closely together. I insisted upon knowing what the matter was. They at length said, that they had learned I had been in a "scrape," and that I was to be examined before my master; and if their information proved false, I should not be hurt.

In a few moments, they succeeded in tying John. They then turned to Henry, who had by this time returned, and commanded him to cross his hands. "I won't!" said Henry, in a firm tone, indicating his readiness to meet the consequences of his refusal. "Won't you?" said Tom Graham, the constable. "No, I won't!" said Henry, in a still stronger tone. With this, two of the constables pulled out their shining pistols, and swore, by their Creator, that they would make him cross his hands or kill him. Each cocked his pistol, and, with fingers on the trigger, walked up to Henry, saying, at the same time, if he did not cross his hands, they would blow his damned heart out. "Shoot me, shoot me!" said Henry; "you can't kill me but once. Shoot, shoot,—and be damned! *I won't be tied!*" This he said in a tone of loud defiance; and at the same time, with a motion as quick as lightning, he with one single stroke dashed the pistols from the hand of each constable. As he did this, all hands fell upon him, and, after beating him some time, they finally overpowered him, and got him tied.

During the scuffle, I managed, I know not how, to get my pass out, and, without being discovered, put it into the fire. We were all now tied; and just as we were to leave for Easton jail, Betsy Freeland, mother of William Freeland, came to the door with her hands full of biscuits, and divided them between Henry and John. She then delivered herself of a speech, to the following effect:—addressing herself to me, she said, "*You devil! You yellow devil!* it was you that put it into the heads of Henry and John to run away. But for you, you long-legged mulatto devil! Henry nor John would never have thought of such a thing." I made no reply, and was immediately hurried off towards St. Michael's. Just a moment previous to the scuffle with Henry, Mr. Hamilton suggested the propriety of making a search for the protections which he had understood Frederick had written for himself and the rest. But, just at the moment he was about carrying his proposal into effect, his aid was needed in helping to tie Henry; and the excitement attending the scuffle caused them either to forget, or to deem it unsafe, under the circumstances, to search. So we were not yet convicted of the intention to run away.

When we got about half way to St. Michael's, while the constables having us in charge were looking ahead, Henry inquired of me what he should do with his pass. I told him to eat it with his biscuit, and own nothing; and we passed the word around, "*Own nothing*;" and "*Own nothing!*" said we all. Our confidence in each other was unshaken. We were resolved to succeed or fail together, after the calamity had befallen us as much as before. We were now prepared for any thing. We were to be dragged that morning fifteen miles behind horses, and then to be placed in the Easton jail. When we reached St. Michael's, we underwent a sort of examination. We all denied that we ever intended to run away. We did this more to bring out the evidence against us, than from any hope of getting clear of being sold; for, as I have said, we were ready for that. The fact was, we cared but little where we went, so we went together. Our greatest concern was about separation. We dreaded that more than any thing this side of death. We found the evidence against us to be the testimony of one person; our master would not tell who it was; but we came to a unanimous decision among ourselves as to who their informant was. We were sent off to the jail at Easton. When we got there, we were delivered up to the sheriff, Mr. Joseph Graham, and by him placed in jail. Henry, John, and myself, were placed in one room together—Charles, and Henry Bailey, in another. Their object in separating us was to hinder concert.

We had been in jail scarcely twenty minutes, when a swarm of slave traders, and agents for slave traders, flocked into jail to look at us, and to ascertain if we were for sale. Such a set of beings I never saw before! I felt myself surrounded by so many fiends from perdition. A band of pirates never looked more like their father, the devil. They laughed and grinned over us, saying, "Ah, my boys! we have got you, haven't we?" And after taunting us in various ways, they one by one went into an examination of us, with intent to ascertain our value. They would impudently ask us if we would not like to have them for our masters. We would make them no answer, and leave them to find out as best they could. Then they would curse and swear at us, telling us that they could take the devil out of us in a very little while, if we were only in their hands.

While in jail, we found ourselves in much more comfortable quarters than we expected when we went there. We did not get much to eat, nor that which was very good; but we had a good clean room, from the windows of which we could see what was going on in the street, which was very much better than though we had been placed in one of the dark, damp cells. Upon the whole, we got along very well, so far as the jail and its keeper were concerned. Immediately after the holidays were over, contrary to all our expectations, Mr. Hamilton and Mr. Freeland came up to Easton, and took Charles, the two Henrys, and John, out of jail, and carried them home, leaving me alone. I regarded this separation as a final one. It caused me more pain than any thing else in the whole transaction. I was ready for any thing rather than separation. I supposed that they had consulted together, and had decided that, as I was the whole cause of the intention of the others to run away, it was hard to make the innocent suffer with the guilty; and that they had, therefore, concluded to take the others home, and sell me, as a warning to the others that remained. It is due to the noble Henry to say, he seemed almost as reluctant at leaving the prison as at leaving home to come to the prison. But we knew we should, in all probability, be separated, if we were sold; and since he was in their hands, he concluded to go peaceably home.

I was now left to my fate. I was all alone, and within the walls of a stone prison. But a few days before, and I was full of hope. I expected to have been safe in a land of freedom; but now I was covered with gloom, sunk down to the utmost despair. I thought the possibility of freedom was gone. I was kept in this way about one week, at the end of which, Captain Auld, my master, to my surprise and utter astonishment, came up, and took me out, with the intention of sending me, with a gentleman of his acquaintance, into Alabama. But, from some cause or other, he did not send me to Alabama, but concluded to send me back to Baltimore, to live again with his brother Hugh, and to learn a trade.

Thus, after an absence of three years and one month, I was once more permitted to return to my old home at Baltimore. My master sent me away, because there existed against me a very great prejudice in the community, and he feared I might be killed.

In a few weeks after I went to Baltimore, Master Hugh hired me to Mr. William Gardner, an extensive ship-builder, on Fell's Point. I was put there to learn how to calk. It, however, proved a very unfavorable place for the accomplishment of this object. Mr. Gardner was engaged that spring in building two large man-of-war brigs, professedly for the Mexican government. The vessels were to be launched in the July of that year, and in failure thereof, Mr. Gardner was to lose a considerable sum; so that when I entered, all was hurry. There was no time to learn any thing. Every man had to do that which he knew how to do. In entering the ship-yard, my orders from Mr. Gardner were, to do whatever the carpenters commanded me to do. This was placing me at the beck and call of about seventy-five men. I was to regard all these as masters. Their word was to be my law. My situation was a most trying one. At times I needed a dozen pair of hands. I was called a dozen ways in the space of a single minute. Three or four voices would strike my ear at the same moment. It was—"Fred., come help me to cant this timber here."—"Fred., come carry this timber yonder."—Fred., bring that roller here."—"Fred., go get a fresh can of water."—"Fred., come help saw off the end of this timber."—"Fred., go quick, and get the crowbar."—"Fred., hold on the end of this fall."[7]—"Fred., go to the blacksmith's shop, and get a new punch."—"Hurra, Fred.! run and bring me a cold chisel."—"I say, Fred., bear a hand, and get up a fire as quick as lightning under that steam-box."—"Halloo, nigger! come, turn this grindstone."—"Come, come! move, move! and *bowse*[8] this timber forward."—"I say, darky, blast your eyes, why don't you heat up some pitch?"—"Halloo! halloo! halloo!" (Three voices at the

7. Nautical term for the free end of a rope of a tackle or hoisting device.
8. To haul the timber by pulling on the rope.

same time.) "Come here!—Go there!—Hold on where you are! Damn you, if you move, I'll knock your brains out!"

This was my school for eight months; and I might have remained there longer, but for a most horrid fight I had with four of the white apprentices, in which my left eye was nearly knocked out, and I was horribly mangled in other respects. The facts in the case were these: Until a very little while after I went there, white and black ship-carpenters worked side by side, and no one seemed to see any impropriety in it. All hands seemed to be very well satisfied. Many of the black carpenters were freemen. Things seemed to be going on very well. All at once, the white carpenters knocked off, and said they would not work with free colored workmen. Their reason for this, as alleged, was, that if free colored carpenters were encouraged, they would soon take the trade into their own hands, and poor white men would be thrown out of employment. They therefore felt called upon at once to put a stop to it. And, taking advantage of Mr. Gardner's necessities, they broke off, swearing they would work no longer, unless he would discharge his black carpenters. Now, though this did not extend to me in form, it did reach me in fact. My fellow-apprentices very soon began to feel it degrading to them to work with me. They began to put on airs, and talk about the "niggers" taking the country, saying we all ought to be killed; and, being encouraged by the journeymen, they commenced making my condition as hard as they could, by hectoring me around, and sometimes striking me. I, of course, kept the vow I made after the fight with Mr. Covey, and struck back again, regardless of consequences; and while I kept them from combining, I succeeded very well; for I could whip the whole of them, taking them separately. They, however, at length combined, and came upon me, armed with sticks, stones, and heavy handspikes. One came in front with a half brick. There was one at each side of me, and one behind me. While I was attending to those in front, and on either side, the one behind ran up with the handspike, and struck me a heavy blow upon the head. It stunned me. I fell, and with this they all ran upon me, and fell to beating me with their fists. I let them lay on for a while, gathering strength. In an instant, I gave a sudden surge, and rose to my hands and knees. Just as I did that, one of their number gave me, with his heavy boot, a powerful kick in the left eye. My eyeball seemed to have burst. When they saw my eye closed, and badly swollen, they left me. With this I seized the handspike, and for a time pursued them. But here the carpenters interfered, and I thought I might as well give it up. It was impossible to stand my hand against so many. All this took place in sight of not less than fifty white ship-carpenters, and not one interposed a friendly word; but some cried, "Kill the damned nigger! Kill him! kill him! He struck a white person."

I found my only chance for life was in flight. I succeeded in getting away without an additional blow, and barely so; for to strike a white man is death by Lynch law,[9]—and that was the law in Mr. Gardner's shipyard; nor is there much of any other out of Mr. Gardner's ship-yard.

I went directly home, and told the story of my wrongs to Master Hugh; and I am happy to say of him, irreligious as he was, his conduct was heavenly, compared with that of his brother Thomas under similar circumstances. He listened attentively to my narration of the circumstances leading to the savage outrage, and gave many proofs of his strong indignation at it. The heart of my once overkind mistress was again melted into pity. My puffed-out eye and blood-covered face moved her to tears. She took a chair by me, washed the blood from my face, and, with a mother's tenderness, bound up my head, covering the wounded eye with a lean piece of fresh beef. It was almost compensation for my suffering to witness, once more, a manifestation of kindness from this, my once affectionate old mistress. Master Hugh was very much enraged. He gave expression to his feelings by pouring out curses upon the heads of those who did the deed. As soon as I got a little the better of my bruises, he took me with him to Esquire Watson's, on Bond Street, to see what could be done about the matter. Mr. Watson inquired who saw the assault committed. Master Hugh told him it was done in Mr. Gardner's ship-yard, at midday, where there were a large company of men at work. "As to that," he said, "the deed was done, and there was no question as to who did it." His answer was, he could do nothing in the case, unless some white man would come forward and testify. He could issue no warrant on my word. If I had been killed in the presence of a thousand colored people, their testimony combined would have been insufficient to have arrested one of the murderers. Master Hugh, for once, was compelled to say this state of things was too bad. Of course, it was impossible to get any white man to volunteer his testimony in my behalf, and against the white young men. Even those who may have sympathized with me were not prepared to do this. It required a degree of courage unknown to them to do so; for just at that time, the slightest manifestation of humanity toward a colored person was denounced as abolitionism, and that name subjected its bearer to frightful liabilities. The watchwords of the bloody-minded in that region, and in those days, were, "Damn the abolitionists!" and "Damn the niggers!" There was nothing done, and probably nothing would have been done if I had been killed. Such was, and such remains, the state of things in the Christian city of Baltimore.

9. I.e., to be subject to lynching, without benefit of legal procedures.

Master Hugh, finding he could get no redress, refused to let me go back again to Mr. Gardner. He kept me himself, and his wife dressed my wound till I was again restored to health. He then took me into the ship-yard of which he was foreman, in the employment of Mr. Walter Price. There I was immediately set to calking, and very soon learned the art of using my mallet and irons. In the course of one year from the time I left Mr. Gardner's, I was able to command the highest wages given to the most experienced calkers. I was now of some importance to my master. I was bringing him from six to seven dollars per week. I sometimes brought him nine dollars per week: my wages were a dollar and a half a day. After learning how to calk, I sought my own employment, made my own contracts, and collected the money which I earned. My pathway became much more smooth than before; my condition was now much more comfortable. When I could get no calking to do, I did nothing. During these leisure times, those old notions about freedom would steal over me again. When in Mr. Gardner's employment, I was kept in such a perpetual whirl of excitement, I could think of nothing, scarcely, but my life; and, in thinking of my life, I almost forgot my liberty. I have observed this in my experience of slavery,—that whenever my condition was improved, instead of its increasing my contentment, it only increased my desire to be free, and set me to thinking of plans to gain my freedom. I have found that, to make a contented slave, it is necessary to make a thoughtless one. It is necessary to darken his moral and mental vision, and, as far as possible, to annihilate the power of reason. He must be able to detect no inconsistencies in slavery; he must be made to feel that slavery is right; and he can be brought to that only when he ceases to be a man.

I was now getting, as I have said, one dollar and fifty cents per day. I contracted for it; I earned it; it was paid to me; it was rightfully my own; yet, upon each returning Saturday night, I was compelled to deliver every cent of that money to Master Hugh. And why? Not because he earned it,—not because he had any hand in earning it,—not because I owed it to him,—nor because he possessed the slightest shadow of a right to it; but solely because he had the power to compel me to give it up. The right of the grim-visaged pirate upon the high seas is exactly the same.

Chapter XI

I now come to that part of my life during which I planned, and finally succeeded in making, my escape from slavery. But before narrating any of the peculiar circumstances, I deem it proper to make known my intention not to state all the facts connected with the transaction. My reasons for pursuing this course may be understood from the following: First, were I to give a minute statement of all the facts, it is not only possible, but quite probable, that others would thereby be involved in the most embarrassing difficulties. Secondly, such a statement would most undoubtedly induce greater vigilance on the part of slaveholders than has existed heretofore among them; which would, of course, be the means of guarding a door whereby some dear brother bondman might escape his galling chains. I deeply regret the necessity that impels me to suppress any thing of importance connected with my experience in slavery. It would afford me great pleasure indeed, as well as materially add to the interest of my narrative, were I at liberty to gratify a curiosity, which I know exists in the minds of many, by an accurate statement of all the facts pertaining to my most fortunate escape. But I must deprive myself of this pleasure, and the curious of the gratification which such a statement would afford. I would allow myself to suffer under the greatest imputations which evil-minded men might suggest, rather than exculpate myself, and thereby run the hazard of closing the slightest avenue by which a brother slave might clear himself of the chains and fetters of slavery.

I have never approved of the very public manner in which some of our western friends have conducted what they call the *underground railroad,* but which, I think, by their own declarations, has been made most emphatically the *upperground railroad.* I honor those good men and women for their noble daring, and applaud them for willingly subjecting themselves to bloody persecution, by openly avowing their participation in the escape of slaves. I, however, can see very little good resulting from such a course, either to themselves or the slaves escaping; while, upon the other hand, I see and feel assured that those open declarations are a positive evil to the slaves remaining, who are seeking to escape. They do nothing towards enlightening the slave, whilst they do much towards enlightening the master. They stimulate him to greater watchfulness, and enhance his power to capture his slave. We owe something to the slaves south of the line as well as to those north of it; and in aiding the latter on their way to freedom, we should be careful to do nothing which would be likely to hinder the former from escaping from slavery. I would keep the merciless slaveholder profoundly ignorant of the means of flight adopted by the slave. I would leave him to imagine himself surrounded by myriads of invisible tormentors, ever ready to snatch from his infernal grasp his trembling prey. Let him be left to feel his way in the dark; let darkness commensurate with his crime hover over him; and let him feel that at every step he takes, in pursuit of the flying bondman, he is running the frightful risk of having his hot brains dashed out by an invisible agency. Let us render the tyrant no aid; let us not hold the light by which he can trace the footprints of our flying brother. But enough of this. I will now proceed to the statement of those facts, connected with my escape, for which I am alone responsible, and for which no one can be made to suffer but myself.

In the early part of the year 1838, I became quite restless. I could see no reason why I should, at the end of each week, pour the reward of my toil into the purse of my master. When I carried to him my weekly wages, he would, after counting the money, look me in the face with a robber-like fierceness, and say, "Is this all?" He was satisfied with nothing less than the last cent. He would, however, when I made him six dollars, sometimes give me six cents, to encourage me. It had the opposite effect. I regarded it as a sort of admission of my right to the whole. The fact that he gave me any part of my wages was proof, to my mind, that he believed me entitled to the whole of them. I always felt worse for having received any thing; for I feared that the giving me a few cents would ease his conscience, and make him feel himself to be a pretty honorable sort of robber. My discontent grew upon me. I was ever on the look-out for means of escape; and, finding no direct means, I determined to try to hire my time, with a view of getting money with which to make my escape. In the spring of 1838, when Master Thomas came to Baltimore to purchase his spring goods, I got an opportunity, and applied to him to allow me to hire my time. He unhesitatingly refused my request, and told me this was another stratagem by which to escape. He told me I could go nowhere but that he could get me; and that, in the event of my running away, he should spare no pains in his efforts to catch me. He exhorted me to content myself, and be obedient. He told me, if I would be happy, I must lay out no plans for the future. He said, if I behaved myself properly, he would take care of me. Indeed, he advised me to complete thoughtlessness of the future, and taught me to depend solely upon him for happiness. He seemed to see fully the pressing necessity of setting aside my intellectual nature, in order to [insure] contentment in slavery. But in spite of him, and even in spite of myself, I continued to think, and to think about the injustice of my enslavement, and the means of escape.

About two months after this, I applied to Master Hugh for the privilege of hiring my time. He was not acquainted with the fact that I had applied to Master Thomas, and had been refused. He too, at first, seemed disposed to refuse; but, after some reflection, he granted me the privilege, and proposed the following terms: I was to be allowed all my time, make all contracts with those for whom I worked, and find my own employment; and, in return for this liberty, I was to pay him three dollars at the end of each week; find myself in calking tools, and in board and clothing. My board was two dollars and a half per week. This, with the wear and tear of clothing and calking tools, made my regular expenses about six dollars per week. This amount I was compelled to make up, or relinquish the privilege of hiring my time. Rain or shine, work or no work, at the end of each week the money must be forthcoming, or I must give up my privilege. This arrangement, it will be perceived, was decidedly in my master's favor. It relieved him of all need of looking after me. His money was sure. He received all the benefits of slaveholding without its evils; while I endured all the evils of a slave, and suffered all the care and anxiety of a freeman. I found it a hard bargain. But, hard as it was, I thought it better than the old mode of getting along. It was a step towards freedom to be allowed to bear the responsibilities of a freeman, and I was determined to hold on upon it. I bent myself to the work of making money. I was ready to work at night as well as day, and by the most untiring perseverance and industry, I made enough to meet my expenses, and lay up a little money every week. I went on thus from May till August. Master Hugh then refused to allow me to hire my time longer. The ground for his refusal was a failure on my part, one Saturday night, to pay him for my week's time. This failure was occasioned by my attending a camp meeting about ten miles from Baltimore. During the week, I had entered into an engagement with a number of young friends to start from Baltimore to the camp ground early Saturday evening; and being detained by my employer, I was unable to get down to Master Hugh's without disappointing the company. I knew that Master Hugh was in no special need of the money that night. I therefore decided to go to camp meeting, and upon my return pay him the three dollars. I staid at the camp meeting one day longer than I intended when I left. But as soon as I returned, I called upon him to pay him what he considered his due. I found him very angry; he could scarce restrain his wrath. He said he had a great mind to give me a severe whipping. He wished to know how I dared go out of the city without asking his permission. I told him I hired my time, and while I paid him the price which he asked for it, I did not know that I was bound to ask him when and where I should go. This reply troubled him; and, after reflecting a few moments, he turned to me, and said I should hire my time no longer; that the next thing he should know of, I would be running away. Upon the same plea, he told me to bring my tools and clothing home forthwith. I did so; but instead of seeking work, as I had been accustomed to do previously to hiring my time, I spent the whole week without the performance of a single stroke of work. I did this in retaliation. Saturday night, he called upon me as usual for my week's wages. I told him I had no wages; I had done no work that week. Here we were upon the point of coming to blows. He raved, and swore his determination to get hold of me. I did not allow myself a single word; but was resolved, if he laid the weight of his hand upon me, it should be blow for blow. He did not strike me, but told me that he would find me in constant employment in future. I thought the matter over during the next day, Sunday, and finally resolved upon the third day of September, as the day upon which I would make a second attempt to secure my freedom. I now had three weeks during which to prepare for my journey. Early on Monday morning, before Master Hugh had time to make any engagement for me, I went out and got employment of Mr. Butler, at his ship-yard near the drawbridge, upon what is called the City Block, thus making it unnecessary for him to seek employment for me. At the end of the week, I brought him between eight and nine dollars. He seemed very well pleased, and asked me why I did not do the same the week before. He little knew what my plans were. My object in working steadily was to remove any suspicion he might entertain of my intent to run away; and in this I succeeded admirably. I suppose he thought I was never better satisfied with my condition than at the very time during which I was planning my escape. The second week passed, and again I carried him my full wages; and so well pleased was he, that he gave me twenty-five cents, (quite a large sum for a slaveholder to give a slave), and bade me to make a good use of it. I told him I would.

Things went on without very smoothly indeed, but within there was trouble. It is impossible for me to describe my feelings as the time of my contemplated start drew near. I had a number of warm-hearted friends in Baltimore,—friends that I loved almost as I did my life,—and the thought of being separated from them forever was painful beyond expression. It is my opinion that thousands would escape from slavery, who now remain, but for the strong cords of affection that bind them to their friends. The thought of leaving my friends was decidedly the most painful thought with which I had to contend. The love of them was my tender point, and shook my decision more than all things else. Besides the pain of separation, the dread and apprehension of a failure exceeded what I had experienced at my first attempt. The appalling defeat I then sustained returned to torment me. I felt assured that, if I failed in this attempt, my case would be a hopeless one—it would seal my fate as a slave forever. I could not hope to get off with any thing less than the severest punishment, and being placed beyond the means of escape. It required no very vivid imagination to depict the most frightful scenes through which I should have to pass, in case I failed. The wretchedness of slavery, and the blessedness of freedom, were perpetually before me. It was life and death with me. But I remained firm, and, according to my resolution, on the third day of September, 1838, I left my chains, and succeeded in reaching New York without the slightest interruption of any kind.[1] How I did so,—what means I adopted,—what direction I travelled, and by what mode of conveyance,—I must leave unexplained, for the reasons before mentioned.

I have been frequently asked how I felt when I found myself in a free State. I have never been able to answer the question with any satisfaction to myself. It was a moment of the highest excitement I ever experienced. I suppose I felt as one may imagine the unarmed mariner to feel when he is rescued by a friendly man-of-war from the pursuit of a pirate. In writing to a dear friend, immediately after my arrival at New York, I said I felt like one who had escaped a den of hungry lions. This state of mind, however, very soon subsided; and I was again seized with a feeling of great insecurity and loneliness. I was yet liable to be taken back, and subjected to all the tortures of slavery. This in itself was enough to damp the ardor of my enthusiasm. But the loneliness overcame me. There I was in the midst of thousands, and yet a perfect stranger; without home and without friends, in the midst of thousands of my own brethren—children of a common Father, and yet I dared not to unfold to any one of them my sad condition. I was afraid to speak to any one for fear of speaking to the wrong one, and thereby falling into the hands of money-loving kidnappers, whose business it was to lie in wait for the panting fugitive, as the ferocious beasts of the forest lie in wait for their prey. The motto which I adopted when I started from slavery was this—"Trust no man!" I saw in every white man an enemy, and in almost every colored man cause for distrust. It was a most painful situation; and, to understand it, one must needs experience it, or imagine himself in similar circumstances. Let him be a fugitive slave in a strange land—a land given up to be the hunting-ground for slaveholders—whose inhabitants are legalized kidnappers—where he is every moment subjected to the terrible liability of being seized upon by his fellow-men, as the hideous crocodile seizes upon his prey!—I say, let him place himself in my situation—without home or friends—without money or credit—wanting shelter, and no one to give it—wanting bread, and no money to buy it,—and at the same time let him feel that he is pursued by merciless men-hunters, and in total darkness as to what to do, where to go, or where to stay,—perfectly helpless both as to the means of defence and means of escape,—in the midst of plenty, yet suffering the terrible gnawings of hunger,—in the midst of houses,

1. See "Douglass on His Escape from Slavery," p. 100 herein.

yet having no home,—among fellow-men, yet feeling as if in the midst of wild beasts, whose greediness to swallow up the trembling and half-famished fugitive is only equalled by that with which the monsters of the deep swallow up the helpless fish upon which they subsist,—I say, let him be placed in this most trying situation,—the situation in which I was placed,—then, and not till then, will he fully appreciate the hardships of, and know how to sympathize with, the toil-worn and whip-scarred fugitive slave.

Thank Heaven, I remained but a short time in this distressed situation. I was relieved from it by the humane hand of MR. DAVID RUGGLES,[2] whose vigilance, kindness, and perseverance, I shall never forget. I am glad of an opportunity to express, as far as words can, the love and gratitude I bear him. Mr. Ruggles is now afflicted with blindness, and is himself in need of the same kind offices which he was once so forward in the performance of toward others. I had been in New York but a few days, when Mr. Ruggles sought me out, and very kindly took me to his boarding-house at the corner of Church and Lespenard Streets. Mr. Ruggles was then very deeply engaged in the memorable *Darg* case,[3] as well as attending to a number of other fugitive slaves; devising ways and means for their successful escape; and, though watched and hemmed in on almost every side, he seemed to be more than a match for his enemies.

Very soon after I went to Mr. Ruggles, he wished to know of me where I wanted to go; as he deemed it unsafe for me to remain in New York. I told him I was a calker, and should like to go where I could get work. I thought of going to Canada; but he decided against it, and in favor of my going to New Bedford, thinking I should be able to get work there at my trade. At this time, Anna,[4] my intended wife, came on; for I wrote to her immediately after my arrival at New York, (notwithstanding my homeless, houseless, and helpless condition,) informing her of my successful flight, and wishing her to come on forthwith. In a few days after her arrival, Mr. Ruggles called in the Rev. J. W. C. Pennington,[5] who, in the presence of Mr. Ruggles, Mrs. Ruggles, Mrs. Michaels, and two or three others, performed the marriage ceremony, and gave us a certificate, of which the following is an exact copy:—

2. A black journalist and abolitionist famous for his aid to fugitive slaves (1810–1849). Douglass stayed in Ruggles's house on his way to New Bedford in 1838.
3. Ruggles had been arrested in 1839 and charged with harboring a fugitive slave who had escaped from John P. Darg of Arkansas.
4. "She was free" [Douglass's note]. Anna Murray (d. 1882) had been a self-supporting domestic worker and a member of the East Baltimore Mental Improvement Society before moving to New York to marry.
5. Fugitive slave (also born on Maryland's Eastern Shore), abolitionist orator, and Congregationalist pastor (1807–1870).

"This may certify, that I joined together in holy matrimony Frederick Johnson[6] and Anna Murray, as man and wife, in the presence of Mr. David Ruggles and Mrs. Michaels.

"JAMES W. C. PENNINGTON

"New York, Sept. 15, 1838."

Upon receiving this certificate, and a five-dollar bill from Mr. Ruggles, I shouldered one part of our baggage, and Anna took up the other, and we set out forthwith to take passage on board of the steamboat John W. Richmond for Newport, on our way to New Bedford. Mr. Ruggles gave me a letter to a Mr. Shaw in Newport, and told me, in case my money did not serve me to New Bedford, to stop in Newport and obtain further assistance; but upon our arrival at Newport, we were so anxious to get to a place of safety, that, notwithstanding we lacked the necessary money to pay our fare, we decided to take seats in the stage, and promise to pay when we got to New Bedford. We were encouraged to do this by two excellent gentlemen, residents of New Bedford, whose names I afterward ascertained to be Joseph Ricketson and William C. Taber. They seemed at once to understand our circumstances, and gave us such assurance of their friendliness as put us fully at ease in their presence. It was good indeed to meet with such friends, at such a time. Upon reaching New Bedford, we were directed to the house of Mr. Nathan Johnson, by whom we were kindly received, and hospitably provided for. Both Mr. and Mrs. Johnson took a deep and lively interest in our welfare. They proved themselves quite worthy of the name of abolitionists. When the stage-driver found us unable to pay our fare, he held on upon our baggage as security for the debt. I had but to mention the fact to Mr. Johnson, and he forthwith advanced the money.

We now began to feel a degree of safety, and to prepare ourselves for the duties and responsibilities of a life of freedom. On the morning after our arrival at New Bedford, while at the breakfast-table, the question arose as to what name I should be called by. The name given me by my mother was, "Frederick Augustus Washington Bailey." I, however, had dispensed with the two middle names long before I left Maryland so that I was generally known by the name of "Frederick Bailey." I started from Baltimore bearing the name of "Stanley." When I got to New York, I again changed my name to "Frederick Johnson," and thought that would be the last change. But when I got to New Bedford, I found it necessary again to change my name. The reason of this necessity was, that there were so many Johnsons in New Bedford, it was already quite difficult to distinguish

6. "I had changed my name from Frederick *Bailey* to that of *Johnson*" [Douglass's note].

between them. I gave Mr. Johnson the privilege of choosing me a name, but told him he must not take from me the name of "Frederick." I must hold on to that, to preserve a sense of my identity. Mr. Johnson had just been reading the "Lady of the Lake,"[7] and at once suggested that my name be "Douglass." From that time until now I have been called "Frederick Douglass;" and as I am more widely known by that name than by either of the others, I shall continue to use it as my own.

I was quite disappointed at the general appearance of things in New Bedford. The impression which I had received respecting the character and condition of the people of the north, I found to be singularly erroneous. I had very strangely supposed, while in slavery, that few of the comforts, and scarcely any of the luxuries, of life were enjoyed at the north, compared with what were enjoyed by the slaveholders of the south. I probably came to this conclusion from the fact that northern people owned no slaves. I supposed that they were about upon a level with the non-slaveholding population of the south. I knew *they* were exceedingly poor, and I had been accustomed to regard their poverty as the necessary consequence of their being non-slaveholders. I had somehow imbibed the opinion that, in the absence of slaves, there could be no wealth, and very little refinement. And upon coming to the north, I expected to meet with a rough, hard-handed, and uncultivated population, living in the most Spartan-like simplicity, knowing nothing of the ease, luxury, pomp, and grandeur of southern slaveholders. Such being my conjectures, any one acquainted with the appearance of New Bedford may very readily infer how palpably I must have seen my mistake.

In the afternoon of the day when I reached New Bedford, I visited the wharves, to take a view of the shipping. Here I found myself surrounded with the strongest proofs of wealth. Lying at the wharves, and riding in the stream, I saw many ships of the finest model, in the best order, and of the largest size. Upon the right and left, I was walled in by granite warehouses of the widest dimensions, stowed to their utmost capacity with the necessaries and comforts of life. Added to this, almost every body seemed to be at work, but noiselessly so, compared with what I had been accustomed to in Baltimore. There were no loud songs heard from those engaged in loading and unloading ships. I heard no deep oaths or horrid curses on the laborer. I saw no whipping of men; but all

7. Sir Walter Scott's (1771–1832) poem *Lady of the Lake* (1810), a historical romance set in the Scottish highlands in the 16th century. Douglass's namesake is the wrongfully exiled Lord James of Douglas, a Scottish chieftain revered for his bravery and virtue. There is also the famous "black Douglas" in Scott's *Fair Maid of Perth*. The novelist was one of Douglass's favorites.

seemed to go smoothly on. Every man appeared to understand his work, and went at it with a sober, yet cheerful earnestness, which betokened the deep interest which he felt in what he was doing, as well as a sense of his own dignity as a man. To me this looked exceedingly strange. From the wharves I strolled around and over the town, gazing with wonder and admiration at the splendid churches, beautiful dwellings, and finely-cultivated gardens; evincing an amount of wealth, comfort, taste, and refinement, such as I had never seen in any part of slaveholding Maryland.

Every thing looked clean, new, and beautiful. I saw few or no dilapidated houses, with poverty-stricken inmates; no half-naked children and barefooted women, such as I had been accustomed to see in Hillsborough, Easton, St. Michael's, and Baltimore. The people looked more able, stronger, healthier, and happier, than those of Maryland. I was for once made glad by a view of extreme wealth, without being saddened by seeing extreme poverty. But the most astonishing as well as the most interesting thing to me was the condition of the colored people, a great many of whom, like myself, had escaped thither as a refuge from the hunters of men. I found many, who had not been seven years out of their chains, living in finer houses, and evidently enjoying more of the comforts of life, than the average of slaveholders in Maryland. I will venture to assert that my friend Mr. Nathan Johnson (of whom I can say with a grateful heart, "I was hungry, and he gave me meat; I was thirsty, and he gave me drink; I was a stranger, and he took me in"[8]) lived in a neater house; dined at a better table; took, paid for, and read, more newspapers; better understood the moral, religious, and political character of the nation,—than nine tenths of the slaveholders in Talbot county Maryland. Yet Mr. Johnson was a working man. His hands were hardened by toil, and not his alone, but those also of Mrs. Johnson. I found the colored people much more spirited than I had supposed they would be. I found among them a determination to protect each other from the blood-thirsty kidnapper, at all hazards. Soon after my arrival, I was told of a circumstance which illustrated their spirit. A colored man and a fugitive slave were on unfriendly terms. The former was heard to threaten the latter with informing his master of his whereabouts. Straightway a meeting was called among the colored people, under the stereotyped notice, "Business of importance!" The betrayer was invited to attend. The people came at the appointed hour, and organized the meeting by appointing a very religious old gentleman as president, who, I believe, made a prayer, after which he addressed the meeting as follows: *"Friends, we have got him here, and I would*

8. Cf. Matthew 25.35.

recommend that you young men just take him outside the door, and kill him!" With this, a number of them bolted at him; but they were intercepted by some more timid than themselves, and the betrayer escaped their vengeance, and has not been seen in New Bedford since. I believe there have been no more such threats, and should there be hereafter, I doubt not that death would be the consequence.

I found employment, the third day after my arrival, in stowing a sloop with a load of oil. It was new, dirty, and hard work for me; but I went at it with a glad heart and a willing hand. I was now my own master. It was a happy moment, the rapture of which can be understood only by those who have been slaves. It was the first work, the reward of which was to be entirely my own. There was no Master Hugh standing ready, the moment I earned the money, to rob me of it. I worked that day with a pleasure I had never before experienced. I was at work for myself and newly-married wife. It was to me the starting-point of a new existence. When I got through with that job, I went in pursuit of a job of calking; but such was the strength of prejudice against color, among the white calkers, that they refused to work with me, and of course I could get no employment.[9] Finding my trade of no immediate benefit, I threw off my calking habiliments, and prepared myself to do any kind of work I could get to do. Mr. Johnson kindly let me have his wood-horse and saw, and I very soon found myself a plenty of work. There was no work too hard—none too dirty. I was ready to saw wood, shovel coal, carry the hod, sweep the chimney, or roll oil casks,—all of which I did for nearly three years in New Bedford, before I became known to the anti-slavery world.

In about four months after I went to New Bedford, there came a young man to me, and inquired if I did not wish to take the "Liberator."[1] I told him I did; but, just having made my escape from slavery, I remarked that I was unable to pay for it then. I, however, finally became a subscriber to it. The paper came, and I read it from week to week with such feelings as it would be quite idle for me to attempt to describe. The paper became my meat and my drink. My soul was set all on fire. Its sympathy for my brethren in bonds—its scathing denunciations of slaveholders—its faithful exposures of slavery—and its powerful attacks upon the upholders of the institution—sent a thrill of joy through my soul, such as I had never felt before!

I had not long been a reader of the "Liberator," before I got a pretty correct idea of the principles, measures and spirit of the anti-slavery

9. "I am told that colored persons can now get employment at calking in New Bedford—a result of anti-slavery effort" [Douglass's note].

1. The first issue of Garrison's *Liberator* appeared in January 1831. Initially dependent on its black readership for support, it became the most eloquent and widely read of the abolitionist organs during more than thirty years of publication.

reform. I took right hold of the cause. I could do but little; but what I could, I did with a joyful heart, and never felt happier than when in an anti-slavery meeting. I seldom had much to say at the meetings, because what I wanted to say was said so much better by others. But, while attending an anti-slavery convention at Nantucket, on the 11th of August, 1841, I felt strongly moved to speak, and was at the same time much urged to do so by Mr. William C. Coffin, a gentleman who had heard me speak in the colored people's meeting at New Bedford.[2] It was a severe cross, and I took it up reluctantly. The truth was, I felt myself a slave, and the idea of speaking to white people weighed me down. I spoke but a few moments, when I felt a degree of freedom, and said what I desired with considerable ease. From that time until now, I have been engaged in pleading the cause of my brethren—with what success, and with what devotion, I leave those acquainted with my labors to decide.

Appendix

I find, since reading over the foregoing Narrative, that I have, in several instances, spoken in such a tone and manner, respecting religion, as may possibly lead those unacquainted with my religious views to suppose me an opponent of all religion. To remove the liability of such misapprehension, I deem it proper to append the following brief explanation. What I have said respecting and against religion, I mean strictly to apply to the *slaveholding religion* of this land, and with no possible reference to Christianity proper; for, between the Christianity of this land, and the Christianity of Christ, I recognize the widest possible difference—so wide, that to receive the one as good, pure, and holy, is of necessity to reject the other as bad, corrupt, and wicked. To be the friend of the one, is of necessity to be the enemy of the other. I love the pure, peaceable, and impartial Christianity of Christ: I therefore hate the corrupt, slaveholding, women-whipping, cradle-plundering, partial and hypocritical Christianity of this land. Indeed, I can see no reason, but the most deceitful one, for calling the religion of this land Christianity. I look upon it as the climax of all misnomers, the boldest of all frauds, and the grossest of all libels. Never was there a clearer case of "stealing the livery of the court of heaven to serve the devil in."[1] I am filled with unutterable loathing when I contemplate the religious pomp and show, together with the horrible inconsistencies, which every where surround me. We have men-stealers for ministers,

2. Douglass was licensed to preach in the African Methodist Episcopal Zion church in 1839.
1. From the Reverend Robert Pollok, *The Course of Time* (1827), book 8, 616–18.

women-whippers for missionaries, and cradle-plunderers for church members. The man who wields the blood-clotted cowskin during the week fills the pulpit on Sunday, and claims to be a minister of the meek and lowly Jesus. The man who robs me of my earnings at the end of each week meets me as a class-leader on Sunday morning, to show me the way of life, and the path of salvation. He who sells my sister, for purposes of prostitution, stands forth as the pious advocate of purity. He who proclaims it a religious duty to read the Bible denies me the right of learning to read the name of the God who made me. He who is the religious advocate of marriage robs whole millions of its sacred influence, and leaves them to the ravages of wholesale pollution. The warm defender of the sacredness of the family relation is the same that scatters whole families,—sundering husbands and wives, parents and children, sisters and brothers,—leaving the hut vacant, and the hearth desolate. We see the thief preaching against theft, and the adulterer against adultery. We have men sold to build churches, women sold to support the gospel, and babes sold to purchase Bibles for the *poor heathen! all for the glory of God and the good of souls!* The slave auctioneer's bell and the church-going bell chime in with each other, and the bitter cries of the heart-broken slave are drowned in the religious shouts of his pious master. Revivals of religion and revivals in the slave-trade go hand in hand together. The slave prison and the church stand near each other. The clanking of fetters and the rattling of chains in the prison, and the pious psalm and solemn prayer in the church, may be heard at the same time. The dealers in the bodies and souls of men erect their stand in the presence of the pulpit, and they mutually help each other. The dealer gives his bloodstained gold to support the pulpit, and the pulpit, in return, covers his infernal business with the garb of Christianity. Here we have religion and robbery the allies of each other—devils dressed in angels' robes, and hell presenting the semblance of paradise.

> "Just God! and these are they,
> Who minister at thine altar, God of right!
> Men who their hands, with prayer and blessing, lay
> On Israel's ark of light.[2]
>
> "What! preach, and kidnap men?
> Give thanks, and rob thy own afflicted poor?
> Talk of thy glorious liberty, and then
> Bolt hard the captive's door?

2. I.e., the Holy Ark containing the Torah; by extension, the entire body of law as contained in the Old Testament and Talmud.

"What! servants of thy own
 Merciful Son, who came to seek and save
The homeless and the outcast, fettering down
 The tasked and plundered slave!

"Pilate and Herod[3] friends!
 Chief priests and rulers, as of old, combine!
Just God and holy! is that church which lends
 Strength to the spoiler thine?"[4]

The Christianity of America is a Christianity, of whose votaries it may be as truly said, as it was of the ancient scribes and Pharisees,[5] "They bind heavy burdens, and grievous to be borne, and lay them on men's shoulders, but they themselves will not move them with one of their fingers. All their works they do for to be seen of men.—They love the uppermost rooms at feasts, and the chief seats in the synagogues, ... and to be called of men, Rabbi, Rabbi.—But woe unto you, scribes and Pharisees, hypocrites! for ye shut up the kingdom of heaven against men; for ye neither go in yourselves, neither suffer ye them that are entering to go in. Ye devour widows' houses, and for a pretence make long prayers; therefore ye shall receive the greater damnation. Ye compass sea and land to make one proselyte, and when he is made, ye make him twofold more the child of hell than yourselves.—Woe unto you, scribes and Pharisees, hypocrites! for ye pay tithe of mint, and anise, and cumin, and have omitted the weightier matters of the law, judgment, mercy, and faith; these ought ye to have done, and not to leave the other undone. Ye blind guides! which strain at a gnat, and swallow a camel. Woe unto you, scribes and Pharisees, hypocrites! for ye make clean the outside of the cup and of the platter; but within, they are full of extortion and excess.—Woe unto you, scribes and Pharisees, hypocrites! for ye are like unto whited sepulchres, which indeed appear beautiful outward, but are within full of dead men's bones, and of all uncleanness. Even so ye also outwardly appear righteous unto men, but within ye are full of hypocrisy and iniquity."[6]

Dark and terrible as is this picture, I hold it to be strictly true of the overwhelming mass of professed Christians in America. They strain at a gnat, and swallow a camel.[7] Could any thing be more true

3. Herod Antipas, ruler of Galilee, ordered the execution of John the Baptist and participated in the trial of Christ. Pontius Pilate was the Roman authority who condemned Christ to death.
4. These stanzas are from Whittier's antislavery poem *Clerical Oppressors* (1836).
5. Members of a powerful Jewish sect that insisted on strict observance of written and oral religious laws. The scribes were the Jewish scholars who taught Jewish law and edited and interpreted the Bible.
6. Cf. Matthew 23.4–28.
7. Matthew 23.24.

of our churches? They would be shocked at the proposition of fellowshipping a *sheep*-stealer; and at the same time they hug to their communion a *man*-stealer, and brand me with being an infidel, if I find fault with them for it. They attend with Pharisaical strictness to the outward forms of religion, and at the same time neglect the weightier matters of the law, judgment, mercy, and faith. They are always ready to sacrifice, but seldom to show mercy. They are they who are represented as professing to love God whom they have not seen, whilst they hate their brother whom they have seen. They love the heathen on the other side of the globe. They can pray for him, pay money to have the Bible put into his hand, and missionaries to instruct him; while they despise and totally neglect the heathen at their own doors.

Such is, very briefly, my view of the religion of this land; and to avoid any misunderstanding, growing out of the use of general terms, I mean, by the religion of this land, that which is revealed in the words, deeds, and actions, of those bodies, north and south, calling themselves Christian churches, and yet in union with slaveholders. It is against religion, as presented by these bodies, that I have felt it my duty to testify.

I conclude these remarks by copying the following portrait of the religion of the south, (which is, by communion and fellowship, the religion of the north,) which I soberly affirm is "true to the life," and without caricature or the slightest exaggeration. It is said to have been drawn, several years before the present anti-slavery agitation began, by a northern Methodist preacher, who, while residing at the south, had an opportunity to see slaveholding morals, manners, and piety, with his own eyes. "Shall I not visit for these things? saith the Lord. Shall not my soul be avenged on such a nation as this?"[8]

A PARODY[9]

"Come, saints and sinners, hear me tell
How pious priests whip Jack and Nell,
And women buy and children sell,
And preach all sinners down to hell,
  And sing of heavenly union.

"They'll bleat and baa, dona like goats,[1]
Gorge down black sheep, and strain at motes,
Array their backs in fine black coats,

8. Jeremiah speaks God's charges against the sins of the House of Israel (Jeremiah 5–9).
9. Douglass is parodying "Heavenly Union," a hymn sung in many Southern churches at the time. Douglass was famous for his sharp sense of humor and ability to mimic the Southern clergy.
1. Probably a printer's error for "moan like goats."

Then seize their negroes by their throats,
And choke, for heavenly union.

"They'll church you if you sip a dram,
And damn you if you steal a lamb;
Yet rob old Tony, Doll, and Sam,
Of human rights, and bread and ham;
Kidnapper's heavenly union.

"They'll loudly talk of Christ's reward,
And bind his image with a cord,
And scold, and swing the lash abhorred,
And sell their brother in the Lord
To handcuffed heavenly union.

"They'll read and sing a sacred song,
And make a prayer both loud and long,
And teach the right and do the wrong,
Hailing the brother, sister throng,
With words of heavenly union.

"We wonder how such saints can sing,
Or praise the Lord upon the wing,
Who roar, and scold, and whip, and sting,
And to their slaves and mammon[2] cling,
In guilty conscience union.

"They'll raise tobacco, corn, and rye,
And drive, and thieve, and cheat, and lie,
And lay up treasures in the sky,
By making switch and cowskin fly,
In hope of heavenly union.

"They'll crack old Tony on the skull,
And preach and roar like Bashan[3] bull,
Or braying ass, of mischief full,
Then seize old Jacob by the wool,
And pull for heavenly union.

"A roaring, ranting, sleek man-thief,
Who lived on mutton, veal, and beef,
Yet never would afford relief
To needy, sable sons of grief,
Was big with heavenly union.

"'Love not the world,' the preacher said,
And winked his eye, and shook his head;

2. Strong bulls mentioned in the Old Testament.
3. Wealth worshiped as a false god.

He seized on Tom, and Dick, and Ned,
Cut short their meat, and clothes, and bread,
  Yet still loved heavenly union.

"Another preacher whining spoke
Of One whose heart for sinners broke:
He tied old Nanny to an oak,
And drew the blood at every stroke,
  And prayed for heavenly union.

"Two others oped their iron jaws,
And waved their children-stealing paws;
There sat their children in gewgaws;
By stinting negroes' backs and maws,
  They kept up heavenly union.

"All good from Jack another takes,
And entertains their flirts and rakes,
Who dress as sleek as glossy snakes,
And cram their mouths with sweetened cakes;
  And this goes down for union."

Sincerely and earnestly hoping that this little book may do something toward throwing light on the American slave system, and hastening the glad day of deliverance to the millions of my brethren in bonds—faithfully relying upon the power of truth, love, and justice, for success in my humble efforts—and solemnly pledging my self anew to the sacred cause,—I subscribe myself,

FREDERICK DOUGLASS.

LYNN, *Mass., April* 28, 1845.

1845

CONTEXTS

MARGARET FULLER

Review of the *Narrative*†

[Margaret Fuller (1810–1850), one of the leading intellectuals of her day, had been editor of the literary journal *The Dial* before joining Horace Greeley's *New York Tribune*. It was a mark of the importance attached to Douglass's *Narrative* that Fuller, perhaps the most prominent book review critic of the era, reviewed the book for her influential newspaper.]

Frederick Douglass has been for some time a prominent member of the Abolition party. He is said to be an excellent speaker—can speak from a thorough personal experience—and has upon the audience, beside, the influence of a strong character and uncommon talents. In the book before us he has put into the story of his life the thoughts, the feelings, and the adventures that have been so affecting through the living voice; nor are they less so from the printed page. He has had the courage to name the persons, times and places, thus exposing himself to obvious danger, and setting the seal on his deep convictions as to the religious need of speaking the whole truth. Considered merely as a narrative, we have never read one more simple, true, coherent, and warm with genuine feeling. It is an excellent piece of writing, and on that score to be prized as a specimen of the powers of the Black Race, which Prejudice persists in disputing. We prize highly all evidence of this kind, and it is becoming more abundant. The Cross of the Legion of Honor has just been conferred in France on Dumas and Soulie, both celebrated in the paths of light and literature. Dumas, whose father was a General in the French Army, is a Mulatto; Soulie, a Quadroon. He went from New Orleans, where, though to the eye a white man, yet as known to have African blood in his veins, he could never have enjoyed the privileges due to a human being. Leaving the Land of Freedom, he found himself free to develop the powers that God had given.

Two wise and candid thinkers,—the Scotchman, Kinment, prematurely lost to this country, of which he was so faithful and generous a student, and the late Dr. Channing,—both thought that the African Race had in them a peculiar element, which, if it could be assimilated with those imported among us from Europe would give to genius a development, and to the energies of character a balance and harmony beyond what has been seen heretofore in the history of the world. Such an element is indicated in their lowest estate by

† The review appeared in the *New York Tribune* on June 10, 1845.

a talent for melody, a ready skill at imitation and adaptation, an almost indestructible elasticity of nature. It is to be remarked in the writings both of Soulie and Dumas, full of faults but glowing with plastic life and fertile in invention. The same torrid energy and saccharine fulness may be felt in the writings of this Douglass, though his life being one of action or resistance, was less favorable to SUCH powers than one of a more joyous flow might have been.

The book is prefaced by two communications—one from Garrison and one from Wendell Phillips. That from the former is in his usual over-emphatic style. His motives and his course have been noble and generous. We look upon him with high respect, but he has indulged in violent invective and denunciation till he has spoiled the temper of his mind. Like a man who has been in the habit of screaming himself hoarse to make the deaf better, he can no longer pitch his voice on a key agreeable to common ears. Mr. Phillips's remarks are equally decided, without this exaggeration in the tone. Douglass himself seems very just and temperate. We feel that his view, even of those who have injured him most, may be relied upon. He knows how to allow for motives and influences. Upon the subject of Religion, he speaks with great force, and not more than our own sympathies can respond to. The inconsistencies of Slaveholding professors of religion cry to Heaven. We are not disposed to detest, or refuse communion with them. Their blindness is but one form of that prevalent fallacy which substitutes a creed for a faith, a ritual for life. We have seen too much of this system of atonement not to know that those who adopt it often began with good intentions, and are, at any rate, in their mistakes worthy of the deepest pity. But that is no reason why the truth should not be uttered, trumpet-tongued, about the thing. "Bring no more vain oblations": sermons must daily be preached anew on that text. Kings, five hundred years ago, built churches with the spoils of war; Clergymen to-day command Slaves to obey a Gospel which they will not allow them to read, and call themselves Christians amid the curses of their fellow men. The world ought to get on a little faster than that, if there be really any principle of movement in it. The Kingdom of Heaven may not at the beginning have dropped seed larger than a mustard seed, but even from that we had a right to expect a fuller growth than can be believed to exist, when we read such a book as this of Douglass. Unspeakably affecting is the fact that he never saw his mother at all by day light. "I do not recollect of ever seeing my mother by the light of day. She was with me in the night. She would lie down with me, and get me to sleep, but long before I waked she was gone."

The following extract presents a suitable answer to the background argument drawn by the defender of Slavery from the songs of the Slave, and it is also a good specimen of the powers of observation and manly heart of the writer. We wish that every one may read his book and see what a mind might have been stifled in bondage—what a man may be subjected to the insults of spendthrift dandies, or the blows of mercenary brutes, in whom there is no whiteness except of the skin, no humanity except in the outward form, and of whom the Avenger will not fail yet to demand—"where is thy brother?"[1]

ANONYMOUS

Review of the *Narrative*[†]

Frederick Douglass appears as a Maryland slave, who escaped from his master in 1838, and, after working as a free labourer in the Northeastern States till 1841, was engaged by an American Anti-Slavery Society as itinerant lecturer. Having a natural force and fluency of language, and dealing with things within his own experience, he appears to have spoken with so much acceptance as to have been stimulated to commit to paper the autobiographical portion of his addresses, which is before us in a Dublin reprint.

In his life there is not much of hairbreadth escape. He is a Mulatto, and supposes that his first owner was his father. Time, to a slave, is not known in its particulars, such as birthdays and exact dates; so that he does not know his own age, but supposes it now to be about seven-and-twenty. According to this reckoning, he was sent in his sixth year from the estate where he was born to wait upon a little boy in Baltimore. Here he was treated kindly; and his mistress began to teach him to read, till his master forbade it: but Frederick, having, as he says, had his mind a little opened, persevered in teaching himself, and succeeded by dint of casual assistance from poor White boys in the street: and to reading, at a subsequent period, he added writing. When about fifteen, his owner in the country took him from his master in town, in consequence of a family quarrel; and Frederick was transformed from a sort of page or footman to a field-labourer. His first two country masters were religious men, but very cruel and exacting; so that he had no time to think of anything but work. His third master was more liberal; and, having time to

1. See Genesis 4.9. This review concludes by quoting the last four paragraphs of chapter 2 of the *Narrative*.

† The *Spectator*, an English journal first published in 1828, while not radical, generally supported reform movements. This review appeared on November 29, 1845. It was the custom for such reviews not to be signed. The European edition of the *Narrative* had been published in Dublin in 1845 and was widely read. Bracketed page numbers refer to this Norton Critical Edition.

meditate, he planned an escape, with some fellow-slaves: but it was detected; and Frederick, after being imprisoned and threatened with sale, was sent back to his old quarters in Baltimore, whence he finally managed to escape in reality. Up to this point his narrative is pretty full; but he designedly suppresses the particulars of his escape, lest he should expose others to danger, and prevent some unfortunates from attaining their freedom. In plain English, he was assisted by those secret agents who are scattered through some of the Southern States for the especial purpose of aiding the escape of runaway slaves.

We assume that Frederick Douglass is really what he professes, and not a Coloured free man in masquerade, upon the Jesuit's principle that the end justifies the means. On the one hand, we note the very extraordinary manner in which he taught himself to read; some contentions with different masters, in one case proceeding to a fight,—which seems an improbable insubordination in a slave country, though it may have been heightened to add dignity to Douglass; and a precocious air in the more youthful part of his career, but which also may have been unconsciously coloured by his feelings at the period of composition. On the other hand, the facts and incidents have a strong character of truth. Frederick deals a little in atrocities, though he admits them to be exceptions; but they do not make the greatest impression on the reader as to the horrors of slavery. This appears rather in the brutish degradation to which the mind of the slave is reduced, the destruction of all family ties which is systematically aimed at, and the reaction of the "institution" upon the whites themselves, lowering their character, and often, according to Douglass, wringing their affections in the case of their Coloured children.

> "It is worthy of remark, that such slaves [children of the planter] invariably suffer greater hardships, and have more to contend with than others. They are, in the first place, a constant offence to their mistress. She is ever disposed to find fault with them; they can seldom do anything to please her; she is never better pleased than when she sees them under the lash, especially when she suspects her husband of showing to his Mulatto children favours which he withholds from his Black slaves. The master is frequently compelled to sell this class of his slaves, out of deference to the feelings of his White wife; and, cruel as the deed may strike any one to be for a man to sell his own children to human fleshmongers, it is often the dictate of humanity for him to do so; for unless he does this, he must not only whip them himself, but must stand by and see one White son tie up his brother of but few shades darker complexion than himself, and ply the gory lash to his naked back; and if he

lisp one word of disapproval, it is set down to his parental partiality, and only makes a bad matter worse both for himself and the slave whom he would protect and defend." [14]

There is something natural and touching in this instance of maternal feeling.

"My mother and I were separated when I was but an infant—before I knew her as my mother. It is a common custom, in the part of Maryland from which I ran away, to part children from their mothers at a very early age. Frequently, before the child has reached its twelfth month, its mother is taken from it, and hired out on some farm a considerable distance off; and the child is placed under the care of an old woman, too old for field-labour. For what this separation is done I do not know, unless it be to hinder the development of the child's affection toward its mother, and to blunt and destroy the natural affection of the mother for the child. This is the inevitable result.

"I never saw my mother, to know her as such, more than four or five times in my life; and each of these times was very short in duration, and at night. She was hired by a Mr. Stewart, who lived about twelve miles from my home. She made her journey to see me in the night, travelling the whole distance on foot, after the performance of her day's work. She was a field hand, and a whipping is the penalty of not being in the field at sunrise, unless a slave has special permission from his or her master to the contrary; a permission which they seldom get, and one that gives to him that gives it the proud name of being a kind master. I do not recollect of ever seeing my mother by the light of day. She was with me in the night. She would lie down with me, and get me to sleep; but long before I waked she was gone." [13–14]

According to Frederick, slaveholders professing religion are a great deal worse than others; more gravely cruel, more exacting, and very mean—not even giving their people enough to eat, which in Maryland is very contrary to public opinion. "Not to give a slave enough to eat, is regarded as the most aggravated development of meanness even among slaveholders. The rule is, no matter how coarse the food, only let there be enough of it." This meanness the professors seem to carry into punishment; assigning Scriptural reasons for it. Here is a text for stripes.

"I have said my master found religious sanction for his cruelty. As an example, I will state one of many facts going to prove the charge. I have seen him tie up a lame young woman, and whip her with a heavy cowskin upon her naked shoulders, causing the warm red blood to drip; and, in justification of the

> bloody deed, he would quote this passage of Scripture—'He that knoweth his master's will, and doeth it not, shall be beaten with many stripes.'" [43]

If this narrative is really true in its basis, and untouched by any one save Douglass himself, it is a singular book, and he is a more singular man. Even if it is of the nature of the true stories of De Foe,[1] it is curious as a picture of slavery, and worth reading.

FREDERICK DOUGLASS

Preface to the Second Dublin Edition of the *Narrative of the Life of Frederick Douglass*†

In May last,[1] the present Narrative was published in Boston, Massachusetts, and when I sailed for England in September, about 4,500 copies had been sold. I have lately heard that a fifth edition has been called for. This rapid sale may be accounted for by the fact of my being a fugitive slave, and from the circumstance that for the last four years I have been engaged in travelling as a lecturing agent of the American Anti-slavery Society, by which means I became extensively known in the United States.

My visit to Great Britain had a threefold object. I wished to be out of the way during the excitement consequent on the publication of my book; lest the information I had there given as to my identity and place of abode, should induce my *owner* to take measures for my restoration to his 'patriarchal care.' For it may not be generally known in Europe, that a slave who escapes from his master is liable, by the Constitution of the United States, to be dragged back into bondage, no matter in what part of the vast extent of the States and their territories he may have taken refuge.

My next inducement was a desire to increase my stock of information, and my opportunities of self-improvement, by a visit to the land of my *paternal* ancestors.

My third and chief object was, by the public exposition of the contaminating and degrading influences of Slavery upon the

1. Daniel Defoe (1661?–1731), British journalist and novelist, most famous for his fictitious work *The Life and Adventures of Robinson Crusoe*. In his writing, Defoe would oftentimes "stretch the truth" or exaggerate to get his point across. By making a somewhat sarcastic reference to Defoe, the review implies that Douglass's story is embellished or even ghostwritten.

† Following the excellent reception of the *Narrative of the Life of Frederick Douglass*, published in 1845 in America and shortly thereafter in Ireland, Douglass arranged with his Irish publisher to issue a second Dublin edition. The following is a new preface that he wrote to accompany the text.

1. I.e., 1846.

slaveholder and his abettors, as well as the slave, to excite such an intelligent interest on the subject of American Slavery, as may react upon my own country, and may tend to shame her out of her adhesion to a system so abhorrent to Christianity and to her republican institutions.

My last object is, I am happy to say, in a fair way of being accomplished. I have held public meetings in Dublin, Wexford, Waterford, Cork, Youghal, Limerick, Belfast, Glasgow, Aberdeen, Perth, and Dundee, within the five months which have elapsed since I landed in England. An edition of 2000 copies of my Narrative has been exhausted, and I am in great hopes that before my visit to Great Britain shall be completed, thousands and tens of thousands of the intelligent and philanthropic will be induced to co-operate with the noble band of American abolitionists, for the overthrow of the meanest, hugest, and most dastardly system of iniquity that ever disgraced any country laying claim to the benefits of religion and civilization.

I beg to refer my reader to the Preface to the First edition, and the Letter which follows it; to some notices of my Narrative from various sources, which will be found at the end of the book;[2] and to the following notice of a public meeting held the evening previous to my departure from home, in the town of Lynn, Massachusetts, where I have resided for the last two years:—

"Last Friday evening a meeting was held in Lyceum Hall, for the purpose of exchanging farewells with Frederick Douglass and James N. Buffum,[3] prior to their departure, on the ensuing day, for the Old World. The spacious hall was crowded to its utmost capacity—hundreds of men and women being obliged to stand all the evening. This was a most gratifying fact, and spoke volumes for the onward progress of the anti-slavery movement—since but six or seven years back, the people, instead of meeting with two such anti-slavery men for the interchange of kindly feelings, would have been more likely to meet them for the purpose of inflicting some summary punishment. Hundreds of persons enjoyed on this occasion the first good opportunity they have had to judge of Frederick Douglass's ability as a speaker and a reasoner; and unless I am much mistaken, their judgment was such as not only to increase their respect for him, but for his race, and the great movement now on foot to release it from thraldom. He spoke twice, and both times with great power. His second effort sparkled with wit from beginning to end.

2. Douglass refers to excerpts from reviews of the *Narrative* published in U.S. and British newspapers [*editors*].
3. James Needham Buffum (1807–1887), businessman, Massachusetts politician, and civil rights activist [*editors*].

"The following resolutions were adopted, *nem. con.*[4]

> "RESOLVED—As the sense of this great gathering of the inhabitants of Lynn and vicinity, that we extend to our esteemed fellow citizens Frederick Douglass and James N. Buffum, whose proposed departure for England has brought this multitude together, our heartiest good wishes for a successful issue of their journey.
>
> "RESOLVED—That we are especially desirous that Frederick Douglass, who came to this town a fugitive from slavery, should bear with him to the shores of the Old World, our unanimous testimony to the fidelity with which he has sustained the various relations of life, and to the deep respect with which he is now regarded by every friend of liberty throughout our borders."

It gives me great pleasure to be able to add, in an Appendix to the present edition, an attempted Refutation of my Narrative, lately published in the "Delaware Republican" by Mr. A. C. C. Thompson. My reply will be found along with Mr. Thompson's letter. I have thanked him there; but I cannot refrain from repeating my acknowledgments for the testimony he bears to the substantial truth of my story. We differ in our details, to be sure. But this was to be expected. He is the friend of slave-holders; he resides in a slave state, and is probably a slave-holder himself. He dares not speak the whole truth, if he would. I am an American slave, who have given my tyrant the slip. I am in a land of liberty, with no man to make me afraid. He agrees with me at least in the important fact, that I am what I proclaim myself to be, an ungrateful fugitive from the 'patriarchal institutions' of the Slave States; and he certifies that many of the heroes of my Narrative are still living and doing well, as "honored and worthy members of the Methodist Episcopal Church."

FREDERICK DOUGLASS.

Glasgow, Feb. 6th, 1846.

Douglass on His Mother and His Father

[No aspect of the *Narrative* has proved more troubling to readers than Douglass's compelling references to his mother and father. It is clear, in fact, that his relationships to the two were deeply troubling to Douglass as well. He describes them differently in his three autobiographies, *Narrative of the Life of Frederick Douglass* (1845), *My Bondage and My Freedom* (1855), and *Life and Times of Frederick Douglass* (1892).]

4. Unanimously.

From *Narrative of the Life of Frederick Douglass* (1845)

* * *

My mother was named Harriet Bailey. She was the daughter of Isaac and Betsey Bailey, both colored, and quite dark. My mother was of a darker complexion than either my grandmother or grandfather.

* * * My mother and I were separated when I was but an infant—before I knew her as my mother. It is a common custom, in the part of Maryland from which I ran away, to part children from their mothers at a very early age. Frequently, before the child has reached its twelfth month, its mother is taken from it, and hired out on some farm a considerable distance off, and the child is placed under the care of an old woman, too old for field labor. For what this separation is done, I do not know, unless it be to hinder the development of the child's affection toward its mother, and to blunt and destroy the natural affection of the mother for the child. This is the inevitable result.

I never saw my mother, to know her as such, more than four or five times in my life; and each of those times was very short in duration, and at night. She was hired by a Mr. Stewart, who lived about twelve miles from my home. She made her journeys to see me in the night, travelling the whole distance on foot, after the performance of her day's work. She was a field hand, and a whipping is the penalty of not being in the field at sunrise, unless a slave has special permission from his or her master to the contrary—a permission which they seldom get, and one that gives to him that gives it the proud name of being a kind master. I do not recollect of ever seeing my mother by the light of day. She was with me in the night. She would lie down with me, and get me to sleep, but long before I waked she was gone. Very little communication ever took place between us. Death soon ended what little we could have while she lived, and with it her hardships and suffering. She died when I was about seven years old, on one of my master's farms, near Lee's Mill. I was not allowed to be present during her illness, at her death, or burial. She was gone long before I knew any thing about it. Never having enjoyed, to any considerable extent, her soothing presence, her tender and watchful care, I received the tidings of her death with much the same emotions I should have probably felt at the death of a stranger.

* * *

My father was a white man. He was admitted to be such by all I ever heard speak of my parentage. The opinion was also whispered that my master was my father; but of the correctness of this opinion, I know nothing; the means of knowing was withheld from me.

* * *

From *My Bondage and My Freedom* (1855)

* * *

But to return, or rather, to begin. My knowledge of my mother is very scanty, but very distinct. Her personal appearance and bearing are ineffaceably stamped upon my memory. She was tall, and finely proportioned; of deep black, glossy complexion; had regular features, and, among the other slaves, was remarkably sedate in her manners. There is in *"Prichard's Natural History of Man,"* the head of a figure[1]—on page 157—the features of which so resemble those of my mother, that I often recur to it with something of the feeling which I suppose others experience when looking upon the pictures of dear departed ones.

Yet I cannot say that I was very deeply attached to my mother; certainly not so deeply as I should have been had our relations in childhood been different. We were separated, according to the common custom, when I was but an infant, and, of course, before I knew my mother from any one else.

The germs of affection with which the Almighty, in his wisdom and mercy, arms the helpless infant against the ills and vicissitudes of his lot, had been directed in their growth toward that loving old grandmother, whose gentle hand and kind deportment it was the first effort of my infantile understanding to comprehend and appreciate. Accordingly, the tenderest affection which a beneficent Father allows, as a partial compensation to the mother for the pains and lacerations of her heart, incident to the maternal relation, was, in my case, diverted from its true and natural object, by the envious, greedy, and treacherous hand of slavery. The slave-mother can be spared long enough from the field to endure all the bitterness of a mother's anguish, when it adds another name to a master's ledger, but *not* long enough to receive the joyous reward afforded by the intelligent smiles of her child. I never think of this terrible interference of slavery with my infantile affections, and its diverting them from their natural course, without feelings to which I can give no adequate expression.

I do not remember to have seen my mother at my grandmother's at any time. I remember her only in her visits to me at Col. Lloyd's plantation, and in the kitchen of my old master. Her visits to me

1. An ancient sculpture of an Egyptian male.

there were few in number, brief in duration, and mostly made in the night. The pains she took, and the toil she endured, to see me, tells me that a true mother's heart was hers, and that slavery had difficulty in paralyzing it with unmotherly indifference.

My mother was hired out to a Mr. Stewart, who lived about twelve miles from old master's, and, being a field hand, she seldom had leisure, by day, for the performance of the journey. The nights and the distance were both obstacles to her visits. She was obliged to walk, unless chance flung into her way an opportunity to ride; and the latter was sometimes her good luck. But she always had to walk one way or the other. It was a greater luxury than slavery could afford, to allow a black slave-mother a horse or a mule, upon which to travel twenty-four miles, when she could walk the distance. Besides, it is deemed a foolish whim for a slave-mother to manifest concern to see her children, and, in one point of view, the case is made out—she can do nothing for them. She has no control over them; the master is even more than the mother, in all matters touching the fate of her child. Why, then, should she give herself any concern? She has no responsibility. Such is the reasoning, and such the practice. The iron rule of the plantation, always passionately and violently enforced in that neighborhood, makes flogging the penalty of failing to be in the field before sunrise in the morning, unless special permission be given to the absenting slave. "I went to see my child," is no excuse to the ear or heart of the overseer.

One of the visits of my mother to me, while at Col. Lloyd's, I remember very vividly, as affording a bright gleam of a mother's love, and the earnestness of a mother's care.

I had on that day offended "Aunt Katy," (called "Aunt" by way of respect,) the cook of old master's establishment. I do not now remember the nature of my offense in this instance, for my offenses were numerous in that quarter, greatly depending, however, upon the mood of Aunt Katy, as to their heinousness; but she had adopted, that day, her favorite mode of punishing me, namely, making me go without food all day—that is, from after breakfast. The first hour or two after dinner, I succeeded pretty well in keeping up my spirits; but though I made an excellent stand against the foe, and fought bravely during the afternoon, I knew I must be conquered at last, unless I got the accustomed reënforcement of a slice of corn bread, at sundown. Sundown came, but *no bread*, and, in its stead, their came the threat, with a scowl well suited to its terrible import, that she "meant to *starve the life out of me*!" Brandishing her knife, she chopped off the heavy slices for the other children, and put the loaf away, muttering, all the while, her savage designs upon myself. Against this disappointment, for I was expecting that her heart would relent at last, I made an extra effort to maintain my dignity; but when I saw all the other children around me with merry and satisfied faces, I could stand it no longer. I went out behind the house, and cried like a fine fellow! When tired of this, I returned to the kitchen, sat by the fire, and brooded over my hard lot. I was too hungry to sleep. While I sat in the corner, I caught sight of an ear of Indian corn on an upper shelf of the kitchen. I watched my chance, and got it, and, shelling off a few grains, I put it back again. The grains in my hand, I quickly put in some ashes, and covered them with embers, to roast them. All this I did at the risk of getting a brutal thumping, for Aunt Katy could beat, as well as starve me. My corn was not long in roasting, and, with my keen appetite, it did not matter even if the grains were not exactly done. I eagerly pulled them out, and placed them on my stool, in a clever little pile. Just as I began to help myself to my very dry meal, in came my dear mother. And now, dear reader, a scene occurred which was altogether worth beholding, and to me it was instructive as well as interesting. The friendless and hungry boy, in his extremest need—and when he did not dare to look for succor—found himself in the strong, protecting arms of a mother; a mother who was, at the moment (being endowed with high powers of manner as well as matter) more than a match for all his enemies. I shall never forget the indescribable expression of her countenance, when I told her that I had had no food since morning; and that Aunt Katy said she "meant to starve the life out of me." There was pity in her glance at me, and a fiery indignation at Aunt Katy at the same time; and, while she took the corn from me, and gave me a large ginger cake, in its stead, she read Aunt Katy a lecture which she never forgot. My mother threatened her with complaining to old master in my behalf; for the latter, though harsh and cruel himself, at times, did not sanction the meanness, injustice, partiality and oppressions enacted by Aunt Katy in the kitchen. That night I learned the fact, that I was not only a child, but *somebody's* child. The "sweet cake" my mother gave me was in the shape of a heart, with a rich, dark ring glazed upon the edge of it. I was victorious, and well off for the moment; prouder, on my mother's knee, than a king upon his throne. But my triumph was short. I dropped off to sleep, and waked in the morning only to find my mother gone, and myself left at the mercy of the sable virago, dominant in my old master's kitchen, whose fiery wrath was my constant dread.

I do not remember to have seen my mother after this occurrence. Death soon ended the little communication that had existed between us; and with it, I believe, a life—judging from her weary, sad, downcast countenance and mute demeanor—full of heartfelt sorrow. I was not allowed to visit her during any part of her long illness; nor did I see her for a long time before she was taken ill and died. The heartless and ghastly form of *slavery* rises between mother and child, even at the bed of death. The mother, at the verge of the grave, may not gather her children, to impart to them her holy admonitions, and invoke for them her dying benediction. The bondwoman lives as a slave, and is left to die as a beast; often with fewer attentions than are paid to a favorite horse. Scenes of sacred tenderness, around the deathbed, never forgotten, and which often arrest the vicious and confirm the virtuous during life, must be looked for among the free, though they sometimes occur among the slaves. It has been a life-long, standing grief to me, that I knew so little of my mother; and that I was so early separated from her. The counsels of her love must have been beneficial to me. The side view of her face is imaged on my memory, and I take few steps in life, without feeling her presence; but the image is mute, and I have no striking words of her's treasured up.

I learned, after my mother's death, that she could read, and that she was the *only* one of all the slaves and colored people in Tuckahoe who enjoyed that advantage. How she acquired this knowledge, I know not, for Tuckahoe is the last place in the world where she would be apt to find facilities for learning. I can, therefore, fondly and proudly ascribe to her an earnest love of knowledge. That a "field hand" should learn to read, in any slave state, is remarkable; but the achievement of my mother, considering the place, was very extraordinary; and, in view of that fact, I am quite willing, and even happy, to attribute any love of letters I possess, and for which I have got—despite of prejudices—only too much credit, *not* to my admitted Anglo-Saxon paternity, but to the native genius of my sable, unprotected, and uncultivated *mother*—a woman, who belonged to a race whose mental endowments it is, at present, fashionable to hold in disparagement and contempt.

* * *

I say nothing of *father*, for he is shrouded in a mystery I have never been able to penetrate. Slavery does away with fathers, as it does away with families. Slavery has no use for either fathers or families, and its laws do not recognize their existence in the social arrangements of the plantation. When they *do* exist, they are not the outgrowths of slavery, but are antagonistic to that system. The order of civilization is reversed here. The name of the child is not expected to be that of its father, and his condition does not necessarily affect that of the child. He may be the slave of Mr. Gross. He may be a *freeman*; and yet his child may be a *chattel*. He may be white, glorying in the purity of his Anglo-Saxon blood; and his child may be ranked with the blackest slaves. Indeed, he *may* be, and often *is*, master and father to the same child. He can be father without being a husband, and may sell his child without incurring reproach, if the child be by a woman in whose veins courses one thirty-second part of African blood. My father was a white man, or nearly white. It was sometimes whispered that my master was my father.

* * *

From *Life and Times of Frederick Douglass* (1892)

* * *

My grandmother's five daughters were hired out in this way, and my only recollections of my own mother are of a few hasty visits made in the night on foot, after the daily tasks were over, and when she was under the necessity of returning in time to respond to the driver's call to the field in the early morning. These little glimpses of my mother, obtained under such circumstances and against such odds, meager as they were, are ineffaceably stamped upon my memory. She was tall and finely proportioned, of dark, glossy complexion, with regular features, and amongst the slaves was remarkably sedate and dignified. There is, in Prichard's *Natural History of Man*, the head of a figure, on page 157, the features of which so resemble my mother that I often recur to it with something of the feelings which I suppose others experience when looking upon the likenesses of their own dear departed ones.

Of my father I know nothing. Slavery had no recognition of fathers, as none of families. That the mother was a slave was enough for its deadly purpose. By its law the child followed the condition of its mother. The father might be a white man, glorying in the purity of his Anglo-Saxon blood, and the child ranked with the blackest slaves. Father he might be, and not be husband, and could sell his own child without incurring reproach, if in its veins coursed one drop of African blood.

Douglass on His Escape from Slavery†

[When Douglass wrote yet again of his life, long after slavery had ended, he responded to earlier readers' curiosity about how he escaped. In the first edition of the *Life and Times of Frederick Douglass* (1881, rev. 1882), he tells this story well, but he does not fully suggest how

† From *Life and Times of Frederick Douglass* (Hartford, CT: Park, 1882), pp. 242–55.

well the escape was orchestrated by devoted antislavery people operating in what was called the Underground Railroad. This careful coordination is in evidence from the moment the taxi driver got him to the train, only at the last minute, through to the two Quakers being on hand to get the Douglasses onto the stagecoach for the last leg of their trip. Only in New York City, where he had trouble finding David Ruggles's house, did the plan falter briefly.]

In the first narrative of my experience in slavery, written nearly forty years ago, and in various writings since, I have given the public what I considered very good reasons for withholding the manner of my escape. In substance these reasons were, first, that such publication at any time during the existence of slavery might be used by the master against the slave, and prevent the future escape of any who might adopt the same means that I did. The second reason was, if possible, still more binding to silence—for publication of details would certainly have put in peril the persons and property of those who assisted. Murder itself was not more sternly and certainly punished in the State of Maryland than that of aiding and abetting the escape of a slave. Many colored men, for no other crime than that of giving aid to a fugitive slave, have, like Charles T. Torrey,[1] perished in prison. The abolition of slavery in my native State and throughout the country, and the lapse of time, render the caution hitherto observed no longer necessary. But, even since the abolition of slavery, I have sometimes thought it well enough to baffle curiosity by saying that while slavery existed there were good reasons for not telling the manner of my escape, and since slavery had ceased to exist there was no reason for telling it. I shall now, however, cease to avail myself of this formula, and, as far as I can, endeavor to satisfy this very natural curiosity. I should perhaps have yielded to that feeling sooner, had there been anything very heroic or thrilling in the incidents connected with my escape, for I am sorry to say I have nothing of that sort to tell; and yet the courage that could risk betrayal and the bravery which was ready to encounter death if need be, in pursuit of freedom, were essential features in the undertaking. My success was due to address rather than courage; to good luck rather than bravery. My means of escape were provided for me by the very men who were making laws to hold and bind me more securely in slavery. It was the custom in the State of Maryland to require of the free colored people to have what were called free papers. This instrument they were required to renew very often, and by charging a fee for this writing, considerable sums from time to time were collected by the State. In these papers the name, age, color, height, and form of the free man

1. Maryland antislavery reformer (1813–1846). In 1844 he was sentenced to prison for attempting to aid in the escape of several slaves [*editors*].

were described, together with any scars or other marks upon his person, which could assist in his identification. This device of slaveholding ingenuity, like other devices of wickedness, in some measure defeated itself—since more than one man could be found to answer the same general description. Hence many slaves could escape by personating the owner of one set of papers; and this was often done as follows: A slave nearly or sufficiently answering the description set forth in the papers, would borrow or hire them till he could by their means escape to a free state, and then, by mail or otherwise, return them to the owner. The operation was a hazardous one for the lender as well as the borrower. A failure on the part of the fugitive to send back the papers would imperil his benefactor, and the discovery of the papers in possession of the wrong man would imperil both the fugitive and his friend. It was therefore an act of supreme trust on the part of a freeman of color thus to put in jeopardy his own liberty that another might be free. It was, however, not unfrequently bravely done, and was seldom discovered. I was not so fortunate as to sufficiently resemble any of my free acquaintances as to answer the description of their papers. But I had one friend—a sailor—who owned a sailor's protection, which answered somewhat the purpose of free papers—describing his person, and certifying to the fact that he was a free American sailor. The instrument had at its head the American eagle, which gave it the appearance at once of an authorized document. This protection did not, when in my hands, describe its bearer very accurately. Indeed, it called for a man much darker than myself, and close examination of it would have caused my arrest at the start. In order to avoid this fatal scrutiny on the part of the railroad official, I had arranged with Isaac Rolls, a hackman, to bring my baggage to the train just on the moment of starting, and jumped upon the car myself when the train was already in motion. Had I gone into the station and offered to purchase a ticket, I should have been instantly and carefully examined, and undoubtedly arrested. In choosing this plan upon which to act, I considered the jostle of the train, and the natural haste of the conductor, in a train crowded with passengers, and relied upon my skill and address in playing the sailor as described in my protection, to do the rest. One element in my favor was the kind feeling which prevailed in Baltimore, and other seaports[2] at the time, towards "those who go down to the sea in ships." "Free trade and sailors' rights" expressed the sentiment of the country just then. In my clothing I was rigged out in sailor style. I had on a red shirt and a tarpaulin hat and black cravat, tied in sailor fashion, carelessly and loosely about my neck. My knowledge of ships and sailor's talk came much to my assistance, for I knew a ship from

2. Psalm 107.23.

stem to stern, and from keelson to cross-trees, and could talk sailor like an "old salt." On sped the train, and I was well on the way to Havre de Grace before the conductor came into the negro car to collect tickets and examine the papers of his black passengers. This was a critical moment in the drama. My whole future depended upon the decision of this conductor. Agitated I was while this ceremony was proceeding, but still externally, at least, I was apparently calm and self-possessed. He went on with his duty—examining several colored passengers before reaching me. He was somewhat harsh in tone, and peremptory in manner until he reached me, when, strangely enough, and to my surprise and relief, his whole manner changed. Seeing that I did not readily produce my free papers, as the other colored persons in the car had done, he said to me in a friendly contrast with that observed towards the others: "I suppose you have your free papers?" To which I answered: "No, sir; I never carry my free papers to sea with me." "But you have something to show that you are a free man, have you not?" "Yes, sir," I answered; "I have a paper with the American eagle on it, that will carry me round the world." With this I drew from my deep sailor's pocket my seaman's protection, as before described. The merest glance at the paper satisfied him, and he took my fare and went on about his business. This moment of time was one of the most anxious I ever experienced. Had the conductor looked closely at the paper, he could not have failed to discover that it called for a very different looking person from myself, and in that case it would have been his duty to arrest me on the instant, and send me back to Baltimore from the first station. When he left me with the assurance that I was all right, though much relieved, I realized that I was still in great danger: I was still in Maryland, and subject to arrest at any moment. I saw on the train several persons who would have known me in any other clothes, and I feared they might recognize me, even in my sailor "rig," and report me to the conductor, who would then subject me to a closer examination, which I knew well would be fatal to me.

Though I was not a murderer fleeing from justice, I felt, perhaps, quite as miserable as such a criminal. The train was moving at a very high rate of speed for that time of railroad travel, but to my anxious mind, it was moving far too slowly. Minutes were hours, and hours were days during this part of my flight. After Maryland I was to pass through Delaware—another slave State, where slave-catchers generally awaited their prey, for it was not in the interior of the State, but on its borders, that these human hounds were most vigilant and active. The border lines between slavery and freedom were the dangerous ones, for the fugitives. The heart of no fox or deer, with hungry hounds on his trail, in full chase, could have beaten more anxiously or noisily than did mine, from the time I left Baltimore till

I reached Philadelphia. The passage of the Susquehanna river at Havre de Grace was made by ferryboat at that time, on board of which I met a young colored man by the name of Nichols, who came very near betraying me. He was a "hand" on the boat, but instead of minding his business, he insisted upon knowing me, and asking me dangerous questions as to where I was going, and when I was coming back, etc. I got away from my old and inconvenient acquaintance as soon as I could decently do so, and went to another part of the boat. Once across the river I encountered a new danger. Only a few days before I had been at work on a revenue cutter, in Mr. Price's ship-yard, under the care of Captain McGowan. On the meeting at this point of the two trains, the one going south stopped on the track just opposite to the one going north, and it so happened that this Captain McGowan sat at a window where he could see me very distinctly, and would certainly have recognized me had he looked at me but for a second. Fortunately, in the hurry of the moment, he did not see me; and the trains soon passed each other on their respective ways. But this was not the only hair-breadth escape. A German blacksmith, whom I knew well, was on the train with me, and looked at me very intently, as if he thought he had seen me somewhere before in his travels. I really believe he knew me, but had no heart to betray me. At any rate he saw me escaping and held his peace.

The last point of imminent danger, and the one I dreaded most, was Wilmington. Here we left the train and took the steamboat for Philadelphia. In making the change here I again apprehended arrest, but no one disturbed me, and I was soon on the broad and beautiful Delaware, speeding away to the Quaker City. On reaching Philadelphia in the afternoon I inquired of a colored man how I could get on to New York? He directed me to the Willow street depot, and thither I went, taking the train that night. I reached New York Tuesday morning, having completed the journey in less than twenty-four hours. Such is briefly the manner of my escape from slavery—and the end of my experience as a slave. Other chapters will tell the story of my life as a freeman.

* * *

My free life began on the third of September, 1838. On the morning of the 4th of that month, after an anxious and most perilous but safe journey, I found myself in the big city of New York, a *free man;* one more added to the mighty throng which, like the confused waves of the troubled sea, surged to and fro between the lofty walls of Broadway. Though dazzled with the wonders which met me on every hand, my thoughts could not be much withdrawn from my strange situation. For the moment the dreams of my youth, and the hopes of my manhood, were completely fulfilled. The bonds that had held me to "old master" were broken. No man now had a right to call me his slave or assert mastery over me. I was in the rough and tumble of an outdoor world, to take my chance with the rest of its busy number. I have often been asked, how I felt when first I found myself on free soil. And my readers may share the same curiosity. There is scarcely anything in my experience about which I could not give a more satisfactory answer. A new world had opened upon me. If life is more than breath, and the "quick round of blood,"[3] I lived more in one day than in a year of my slave life. It was a time of joyous excitement which words can but tamely describe. In a letter written to a friend soon after reaching New York, I said: "I felt as one might feel upon escape from a den of hungry lions." Anguish and grief, like darkness and rain, may be depicted; but gladness and joy, like the rainbow, defy the skill of pen or pencil. During ten or fifteen years I had, as it were, been dragging a heavy chain, which no strength of mine could break; I was not only a slave, but a slave for life. I might become a husband, a father, an aged man, but through all, from the cradle to the grave, I had felt myself doomed. All efforts I had previously made to secure my freedom, had not only failed, but had seemed only to rivet my fetters the more firmly, and to render my escape more difficult. Baffled, entangled, and discouraged, I had at times asked myself the question, May not my condition after all be God's work, and ordered for a wise purpose, and if so, was not submission my duty? A contest had in fact been going on in my mind for a long time, between the clear consciousness of right, and the plausible make-shifts of theology and superstition. The one held me an abject slave—a prisoner for life, punished for some transgression in which I had no lot or part; and the other counseled me to manly endeavor to secure my freedom. This contest was now ended; my chains were broken, and the victory brought me unspeakable joy. But my gladness was short lived, for I was not yet out of the reach and power of the slaveholders. I soon found that New York was not quite so free, or so safe a refuge as I had supposed, and a sense of loneliness and insecurity again oppressed me most sadly. I chanced to meet on the street, a few hours after my landing, a fugitive slave whom I had once known well in slavery. The information received from him alarmed me. The fugitive in question was known in Baltimore as "Allender's Jake," but in New York he wore the more respectable name of "William Dixon." Jake in law was the property of Doctor Allender, and Tolly Allender, the son of the doctor, had once made an effort to recapture *Mr. Dixon*, but had failed for want of evidence to support his claim. Jake told me the circumstances of this attempt, and how narrowly he escaped being

3. From Philip James Bailey's poem "Festus" (1839).

sent back to slavery and torture. He told me that New York was then full of southerners returning from the watering-places north; that the colored people of New York were not to be trusted; that there were hired men of my own color who would betray me for a few dollars; that there were hired men ever on the lookout for fugitives; that I must trust no man with my secret; that I must not think of going either upon the wharves, or into any colored boarding-house, for all such places were closely watched; that he was himself unable to help me; and, in fact, he seemed while speaking to me, to fear lest I myself might be a spy and a betrayer. Under this apprehension, as I suppose, he showed signs of wishing to be rid of me, and with whitewash brush in hand, in search of work, he soon disappeared. This picture, given by poor "Jake," of New York, was a damper to my enthusiasm. My little store of money would soon be exhausted, and since it would be unsafe for me to go on the wharves for work, and I had no introductions elsewhere, the prospect for me was far from cheerful. I saw the wisdom of keeping away from the ship-yards, for, if pursued, as I felt certain I would be, Mr. Auld would naturally seek me there among the calkers. Every door seemed closed against me. I was in the midst of an ocean of my fellow-men, and yet a perfect stranger to every one. I was without home, without acquaintance, without money, without credit, without work, and without any definite knowledge as to what course to take, or where to look for succor. In such an extremity, a man has something beside his new-born freedom to think of. While wandering about the streets of New York, and lodging at least one night among the barrels on one of the wharves, I was indeed free—from slavery, but free from food and shelter as well. I kept my secret to myself as long as I could, but was compelled at last to seek some one who should befriend me, without taking advantage of my destitution to betray me. Such an one I found in a sailor named Stuart, a warm-hearted and generous fellow, who from his humble home on Center street, saw me standing on the opposite sidewalk, near "The Tombs."[4] As he approached me I ventured a remark to him which at once enlisted his interest in me. He took me to his home to spend the night, and in the morning went with me to Mr. David Ruggles, the secretary of the New York vigilance committee, a co-worker with Isaac T. Hopper, Lewis and Arthur Tappan, Theodore S. Wright, Samuel Cornish, Thomas Downing, Philip A. Bell[5] and other true men of their time.

4. New York City prison finished in 1838 and built in the style of ancient Egyptian architecture.
5. Black newspaper editor (1808–1889). Ruggles (1810–1849), see p. 74, n. 2. Hopper (1771–1852), white Quaker philanthropist. Arthur (1786–1865) and Lewis Tappan (1788–1873), brothers, wealthy white businessmen. Wright (1797–1847), prominent black clergyman. Cornish (1795–1859), black editor and clergyman. Downing (1819–1903), black businessman.

All these (save Mr. Bell, who still lives, and is editor and publisher of a paper called the *Elevator*, in San Francisco) have finished their work on earth. Once in the hands of these brave and wise men, I felt comparatively safe. With Mr. Ruggles, on the corner of Lispenard and Church streets, I was hidden several days, during which time my intended wife came on from Baltimore at my call, to share the burdens of life with me. She was a free woman, and came at once on getting the good news of my safety. We were married by Rev. J. W. C. Pennington,[6] then a well-known and respected Presbyterian minister. I had no money with which to pay the marriage fee, but he seemed well pleased with our thanks.

Mr. Ruggles was the first officer on the underground railroad with whom I met after coming North; and was indeed the only one with whom I had anything to do, till I became *such* an officer myself. Learning that my trade was that of a calker, he promptly decided that the best place for me was in New Bedford, Mass. He told me that many ships for whaling voyages were fitted out there, and that I might there find work at my trade, and make a good living. So, on the day of the marriage ceremony, we took our little luggage to the steamer John W. Richmond, which at that time was one of the line running between New York and Newport, R. I. Forty-three years ago colored travelers were not permitted in the cabin, nor allowed abaft the paddle-wheels of a steam vessel. They were compelled, whatever the weather might be, whether cold or hot, wet or dry, to spend the night on deck. Unjust as this regulation was, it did not trouble us much. We had fared much harder before. We arrived at Newport the next morning, and soon after an old-fashioned stage-coach with "New Bedford" in large, yellow letters on its sides, came down to the wharf. I had not money enough to pay our fare, and stood hesitating to know what to do. Fortunately for us, there were two Quaker gentlemen who were about to take passage on the stage,—Friends William C. Taber and Joseph Ricketson,[7]—who at once discerned our true situation, and in a peculiarly quiet way, addressing me, Mr. Taber said: "Thee get in." I never obeyed an order with more alacrity, and we were soon on our way to our new home. When we reached "Stone Bridge" the passengers alighted for breakfast, and paid their fares to the driver. We took no breakfast, and when asked for our fares I told the driver I would make it right with him when we reached New Bedford. I expected some objection to this on his part, but he made none. When, however, we reached New Bedford he took our baggage, including three music

6. Pennington (1807–1870), see p. 74, n. 5.
7. Member of a prominent, wealthy Quaker family and friend of Henry David Thoreau; active in the antislavery movement. Taber, Quaker proprietor of a New Bedford bookstore, also headed a large private library in that city.

books,—two of them collections by Dyer, and one by Shaw,—and held them until I was able to redeem them by paying to him the sums due for our rides. This was soon done, for Mr. Nathan Johnson[8] not only received me kindly and hospitably, but, on being informed about our baggage, at once loaned me the two dollars with which to square accounts with the stagedriver. Mr. and Mrs. Nathan Johnson reached a good old age, and now rest from their labors. I am under many grateful obligations to them. They not only "took me in when a stranger," and "fed me when hungry," but taught me how to make an honest living.[9]

Thus, in a fortnight after my flight from Maryland, I was safe in New Bedford,—a citizen of the grand old commonwealth of Massachusetts.

* * *

FREDERICK DOUGLASS

I Am Here to Spread Light on American Slavery[†]

[In 1845, shortly after the publication of *Narrative of the Life of Frederick Douglass*, the American Anti-Slavery Society sent Douglass to Great Britain. Douglass and the society's objective was to further consolidate their alliance with the still active antislavery movement. (Parliament had emancipated slaves in the West Indian colonies in 1831.) Many of the leaders of the society, particularly William Lloyd Garrison and Wendell Phillips, were especially proud of Douglass and eager to have him known in Great Britain. They were certain that he would do credit to the movement. Others, such as Maria Weston Chapman, in charge of arranging speaking tours, were not sorry to have him out of the country for a time. Douglass had gained so much self-confidence as an orator and a writer that he seemed to them too big for any black man's britches. All white antislavery people, however dedicated to the cause, were not free of racist attitudes.

Douglass went first to Dublin, where Richard D. Webb published the first European edition of the *Narrative* (Webb & Chapman, 1845). Next he went south to Cork, which had an active antislavery society, to give one of the first of scores of successful lectures throughout Ireland, Scotland, and England. In all of his talks, he told stories about slavery

8. Mr. and Mrs. Nathan Johnson were leaders of the substantial black community in New Bedford; the Johnsons were successful caterers; Nathan Johnson was the sole black member of Taber's private library.
9. Matthew 25:35.
† An address delivered in Cork, Ireland, on October 14, 1845. From the *Cork Southern Reporter*, October 16, 1845 (supplement). Cited in John W. Blassingame et al., eds., *The Frederick Douglass Papers* (New Haven, CT: Yale UP, 1979–1992), pp. 1:39–45.

similar to those told in the *Narrative*, but these stories often diverged as he reached to make rhetorical points.

As the editors of the *Douglass Papers* noted, "On the afternoon of 14 October 1845, approximately a week after arriving in Cork, Douglass delivered an antislavery lecture in the city courthouse. The *Southern Reporter* noted that long before the meeting was scheduled to begin, the building was 'densely crowded in every part.' The gallery was 'thronged with ladies' who seemed to 'take the liveliest interest in the proceedings.' The *Cork Examiner* (October 15, 1845) reported the presence of 'over one hundred ladies' and a 'large audience of respectable gentlemen and citizens.' Mayor Richard Dawden presided. After Cork resident and American abolitionist James Buffum introduced a series of antislavery resolutions, Douglass addressed the audience. According to the *Southern Reporter* Douglass's oratorical skills were a matter of 'admiration' and even 'astonishment.' The Maryland fugitive joined 'facility and power of expression' with 'a most impressive and energetic delivery.' It was, however, Douglass's extremely 'humorous method' of exposing the 'hypocrisy and duplicity' of American slaveholders which 'kept the meeting in a roar.'"]

* * *

Mr. Frederick Douglas[s] then came forward amid loud cheering. He said—Sir, I never more than at present lacked words to express my feelings. The cordial and manly reception I have met with, and the spirit of freedom that seems to animate the bosoms of the entire audience have filled my heart with feelings I am incapable of expressing. I stand before you in the most extraordinary position that one human being ever stood before his race—a slave. A slave not in the ordinary sense of the term, not in a political sense, but in its real and intrinsic meaning. I have not been stripped of one of my rights and privileges, but of all. By the laws of the country whence I came, I was deprived of myself—of my own body, soul, and spirit, and I am free only because I succeeded in escaping the clutches of the man who claimed me as his property. There are fourteen Slave States in America, and I was sold as a slave at a very early age, little more than seven years, in the southern part of Maryland. While there I conceived the idea of escaping into one of the Free States, which I eventually succeeded in accomplishing. On the 3rd Sept., 1838, I made my escape into Massachusetts, a free state, and it is a pleasing coincidence that just seven years after I stood up in the Royal Exchange in Dublin, to unfold to the people of that good City the wrongs and sufferings to which my race in America were exposed. (Applause.) On escaping into Massachusetts, I went to work on the quays, rolling oil casks, to get a livelihood, and in about three years after having been induced to attend an anti-slavery meeting at Nantucket, it was there announced that I should go from town to town to expose their nefarious system. For four years I was then engaged in discussing the slavery question, and during that time I had opportunities of arranging my thoughts and language. It was at last doubted if I had ever been a slave, and this doubt being used to injure the anti-slavery cause, I was induced to set the matter at rest by publishing the narrative of my life. A person undertaking to write a book without learning will appear rather novel, but such as it was I gave it to the public. (Hear, hear.) The excitement at last increased so much that it was thought better for me to get out of the way lest my master might use some stratagem to get me back into his clutches. I am here then in order to avoid the scent of the blood hounds of America, and of spreading light on the subject of her slave system. There is nothing slavery dislikes half so much as the light. It is a gigantic system of iniquity, that feeds and lives in darkness, and, like a tree with its roots turned to the sun, it perishes when exposed to the light. (Loud cheering.) We want to arouse public indignation against the system of slavery and to bring the concentrated execrations of the civilized world to bear on it like a thunderbolt. (Loud cheering.) The relation of master and slave in America should be clearly understood. The master is allowed by law to hold his slave as his possession and property, which means the right of one man to hold property in his fellow. The master can buy, sell, bequeath his slave as well as any other property, nay, he shall decide what the poor slave is to eat, what he is to drink, where and when he shall speak. He also decides for his affections, when and whom he is to marry, and, what is more enormous, how long that marriage covenant is to endure. The slaveholder exercises the bloody power of tearing asunder those whom God had joined together—of separating husband from wife, parent from child, and of leaving the hut vacant, and the hearth desolate. (Sensation.) The slave holders of America resort to every species of cruelty, but they can never reduce the slave to a willing obedience. The natural elasticity of the human soul repels the slightest attempt to enslave it. The black slaves of America are not wholly without that elasticity; they are men, and, being so, they do not submit readily to the yoke. (Great cheering.) It is easy to keep a brute in the position of a brute, but when you undertake to place a man in the same state, believe me you must build your fences higher, and your doors firmer than before. A brute you may molest sometimes with impunity, but never a man. Men—the black slaves of America—are capable of resenting an insult, of revenging an outrage, and of looking defiance at their masters. (Applause.) Oftentimes, when the poor slave, after recovering from the application of the scourge and the branding iron, looks at his master with a face indicating dissatisfaction, he is subjected to fresh punishment. That cross look must be at once repulsed, and the master whips, as he says "the d—l out of him;" for when a slave looks dissatisfied with his condition, according to his cruel taskmaster's idea, it looks as if he had the devil in him, and it must be whipped out. (Oh, oh.) The state of slavery is one of perpetual cruelty. When very young, as I stated, I was sold into slavery, and was placed under the control of a little boy who had orders to kick me when he liked, whenever the little boy got cross, his mother used to say "Go and whip Freddy." I however, soon began to reason upon the matter, and found that I had as good a right to kick Tommy, as Tommy had me. (Loud laughter and cheering.) My dissatisfaction with my condition soon appeared, and I was most brutally treated. I stand before you with the marks of the slave-driver's whip, that will go down with me to my grave; but, what is worse, I feel the scourge of slavery itself piercing into my heart, crushing my feelings, and sinking me into the depths of moral and intellectual degradation. (Loud cheering.) In the South, the laws are exceedingly cruel, more so than in the Northern States. The most cruel feature of the system in the Northern States is the slave Trade. The domestic slave trade of America is now in the height of its prosperity from the Annexation of Texas to our Union. In the Northern States they actually breed slaves, and rear them for the Southern markets; and the constant dread of being sold is often more terrible than the reality itself. Here the speaker proceeded to comment upon the law of America relative to the punishment of slaves, and read the following:—

"If more than seven slaves are found together in any road, without a white person—*twenty lashes* a piece. For visiting a plantation without a written pass—*ten lashes*. For letting loose a boat from where it is made fast—*thirty nine lashes*; and for the second offence, shall have his ear cut off. For having an article for sale without a ticket from his master—*ten lashes*. For being on horseback without the written permission of his master—*twenty five lashes*."

I saw one poor woman (continued the speaker) who had her ear nailed to a post, for attempting to run away, but the agony she endured was so great, that she tore away, and left her ear behind. (Great sensation.) This is the law of America after her Declaration of Independence—the land in which are millions of professed Christians, and which supports their religion at a cost of 20 million dollars annually, and yet she has three millions of human beings the subjects of the hellish laws I have read. We would not ask you to interfere with the politics of America, or invoke your military aid to put down American slavery. No, we only demand your moral and religious influence on the slave [holder] in question, and believe me the effects of that influence will be overwhelming. (Cheers.) We want to awaken the slave holder to a sense of the iniquity of his position, and to draw him from his nefarious habits. We want to encircle America with a girdle of Anti-slavery fire, that will reflect light upon the darkness of the slave institutions, and alarm their guilty upholders—(great applause). It must also be stated that the American pulpit is on the side of slavery, and the Bible is blasphemously quoted in support of it. The Ministers of religion actually quoted scripture in support of the most cruel and bloody outrages on the slaves. My own master was a Methodist class leader (Laughter, and "Oh"), and he bared the neck of a young woman, in my presence, and he cut her with a cow skin. He then went away, and when he returned to complete the castigation, he quoted the passage, "He that knoweth his master's will and doeth it not, shall be beaten with many stripes."[1] (Laughter.) The preachers say to the slaves they should obey their masters, because God commands it, and because their happiness depended on it. (A laugh.) Here the Speaker assumed the attitude and drawling manner so characteristic of the American preachers, amid the laughter of all present, and continued—Thus do these hypocrites cant. They also tell the slaves there is no happiness but in obedience, and wherever you see poverty and misery, be sure it results from disobedience. (Laughter.) In order to illustrate this they tell a story of a slave having been sent to work, and when his master came up, he found poor *Sambo* asleep. Picture the feelings, say they, of that pious master, his authority thrown off, and his work not done. The master then goes to the law and the testimony, and he there read the passage I have already quoted, and *Sambo* is lashed so that he cannot work for a week after. "You servants," continued the preacher, "To what was this whipping traceable, to disobedience, and if you would not be whipped, and if you would bask in the sunshine of your master's favour, let me exhort you to obedience. You should also be grateful that God in his mercy brought you from Africa to this Christian land." (Great laughter.) They also tell the wretched slaves that God made them to do the working, and the white men the thinking. And such is the ignorance in which the slaves are held that some of them go home and say, "Me hear a good sermon to day, de Minister make ebery thing so clear, white man above a Nigger any day." (Roars of laughter.) It is punishable with death for the second attempt to teach a slave his letters in America (Loud expression of disgust), and in that Protestant country the slave is denied the privilege of learning the name of the God that made him. Slavery with all its bloody paraphernalia is upheld by the church of the country. We want them to have the Methodists of Ireland speak to those of America, and say, "While your hands are red with blood, while the thumb

1. Paraphrase of Luke 12.47.

screws and gags and whips are wrapped up in the pontifical robes of your Church, we will have no fellowship with you, or acknowledge you [as] Christians." (Great applause.) There are men who come here and preach, whose robes are yet red with blood, but these things should not be.—Let these American Christians know their hands are too red to be grasped by Irishmen. Presbyterians, Episcopalians, Congregationalists, and Roman Catholics, stand forth to the world and declare to the American Church, that until she puts away slavery, you can have no sympathy or fellowship with them—(Applause). For myself I believe in Christianity. I love it. I love that religion which is from above, without partiality or hypocrisy—that religion based upon that broad, that world-embracing principle, "That whatever you would that men should do to you, do ye even so to them." (Loud cheering.)—In America Bibles and slave-holders go hand in hand. The Church and the slave prison stand together, and while you hear the chanting of psalms in one, you hear the clanking of chains in the other. The man who wields the cow hide during the week, fills the pulpit on Sunday—here we have robbery and religion united—devils dressed in angels' garments. The man who whipped me in the week used to attend to show me the way of life on the Sabbath. I cannot proceed without alluding to a man who did much to abolish slavery, I mean Daniel O'Connell.[2] (Tremendous cheers.) I feel grateful to him, for his voice has made American slavery shake to its centre.—I am determined wherever I go, and whatever position I may fill, to speak with grateful emotions of Mr. O'Connell's labours. (Cheering.) I heard his denunciation of slavery, I heard my master curse him, and therefore I loved him. (Great cheering.) In London, Mr. O'Connell tore off the mask of hypocrisy from the slave-holders, and branded them as the vilest of the vile, and the most execrable of the execrable, for no man can put words together stronger than Mr. O'Connell. (Laughter and cheering.) The speaker proceeded at some length, and related amusing anecdotes connected with his history in the United States. In one instance he was travelling to Vermont, and having arrived at a stage, they took in five new passengers. It being dark at the time, they did not know the colour of his (the Speaker's) skin, and he was treated with all manner of respect. In fact he could not help thinking at the time that he would be a great man if perpetual darkness would only take the place of day. (Laughter.) Scarcely however had the light gilded the green mountains of Vermont than he saw one of the chaps in the coach take a sly peep at him, and whisper to another "Egad after all 'tis a nigger." (Great laughter.) He had black looks for

2. O'Connell (1775–1847), Irish patriot and opponent of slavery who rallied Irish support crucial to the passage of Britain's Emancipation Act of 1833.

the remainder of the way, and disrespect. That feeling of prejudice had now changed, and he could now walk through Boston in the most refined company. The speaker concluded by saying that he would again address them during his stay in Cork.

FREDERICK DOUGLASS

What to the Slave Is the Fourth of July?†

[Frederick Douglass's "5th of July" speech, as it has come to be called, is perhaps his most famous. He was asked by his Rochester neighbors to give the traditional Independence Day address in 1852. As it turned out, the Fourth of July fell on a Sunday that year and celebrations of the holiday were, therefore, moved to the next day, July 5.

Douglass made this innocuous shift in dates into a powerful image of black protest. Other Americans could cheerfully celebrate their independence with a gala holiday year after year, but that independence, he pointed out, was denied black Americans. The Fugitive Slave Act, enacted as part of the Compromise of 1850, had greatly increased the fervor of northern white antislavery people, and Douglass took the occasion to thunder out his hatred not only of slavery but of the denial of rights to free African Americans as well.

This speech is a fine example of the scholarship that Douglass, who had no schooling, brought to his work. He gave his audience an elaborate discussion of the reach for independence by the patriots of 1776. Still more impressive are the rhetorical heights that he achieves.]

Mr. President, Friends and Fellow Citizens: He who could address this audience without a quailing sensation, has stronger nerves than I have. I do not remember ever to have appeared as a speaker before any assembly more shrinkingly, nor with greater distrust of my ability, than I do this day. A feeling has crept over me, quite unfavorable to the exercise of my limited powers of speech. The task before me is one which requires much previous thought and study for its proper performance. I know that apologies of this sort are generally considered flat and unmeaning. I trust, however, that mine will not be so considered. Should I seem at ease, my appearance would much misrepresent me. The little experience I have had in addressing public meetings, in country school houses, avails me nothing on the present occasion.

The papers and placards say, that I am to deliver a 4th [of] July oration. This certainly sounds large, and out of the common way, for

† An address delivered in Rochester, New York, on Monday, July 5, 1852. Cited in John W. Blassingame et al., eds., *The Frederick Douglass Papers* (New Haven, CT: Yale UP, 1979–1992), pp. 2:359–88.

me. It is true that I have often had the privilege to speak in this beautiful Hall, and to address many who now honor me with their presence. But neither their familiar faces, nor the perfect gage I think I have of Corinthian Hall, seems to free me from embarrassment.

The fact is, ladies and gentlemen, the distance between this platform and the slave plantation, from which I escaped, is considerable—and the difficulties to be overcome in getting from the latter to the former, are by no means slight. That I am here to-day is, to me, a matter of astonishment as well as of gratitude. You will not, therefore, be surprised, if in what I have to say, I evince no elaborate preparation, nor grace my speech with any high sounding exordium. With little experience and with less learning, I have been able to throw my thoughts hastily and imperfectly together; and trusting to your patient and generous indulgence, I will proceed to lay them before you.

This, for the purpose of this celebration, is the 4th of July. It is the birthday of your National Independence, and of your political freedom. This, to you, is what the Passover was to the emancipated people of God. It carries your minds back to the day, and to the act of your great deliverance; and to the signs, and to the wonders, associated with that act, and that day. This celebration also marks the beginning of another year of your national life; and reminds you that the Republic of America is now 76 years old. I am glad, fellow-citizens, that your nation is so young. Seventy-six years, though a good old age for a man, is but a mere speck in the life of a nation. Three score years and ten is the allotted time for individual men; but nations number their years by thousands. According to this fact, you are, even now, only in the beginning of your national career, still lingering in the period of childhood. I repeat, I am glad this is so. There is hope in the thought, and hope is much needed, under the dark clouds which lower above the horizon. The eye of the reformer is met with angry flashes, portending disastrous times; but his heart may well beat lighter at the thought that America is young, and that she is still in the impressible stage of her existence. May he not hope that high lessons of wisdom, of justice and of truth, will yet give direction to her destiny? Were the nation older, the patriot's heart might be sadder, and the reformer's brow heavier. Its future might be shrouded in gloom, and the hope of its prophets go out in sorrow. There is consolation in the thought that America is young. Great streams are not easily turned from channels, worn deep in the course of ages. They may sometimes rise in quiet and stately majesty, and inundate the land, refreshing and fertilizing the earth with their mysterious properties. They may also rise in wrath and fury, and bear away, on their angry waves, the accumulated wealth of years of toil and hardship. They, however, gradually flow back to the same old channel, and flow on as serenely as ever. But, while the river may not be turned aside, it may dry up, and leave nothing behind but the withered branch, and the unsightly rock, to howl in the abyss-sweeping wind, the sad tale of departed glory. As with rivers so with nations.

Fellow-citizens, I shall not presume to dwell at length on the associations that cluster about this day. The simple story of it is that, 76 years ago, the people of this country were British subjects. The style and title of your "sovereign people" (in which you now glory) was not then born. You were under the British Crown. Your fathers esteemed the English Government as the home government; and England as the fatherland. This home government, you know, although a considerable distance from your home, did, in the exercise of its parental prerogatives, impose upon its colonial children, such restraints, burdens and limitations, as, in its mature judgement, it deemed wise, right and proper.

But, your fathers, who had not adopted the fashionable idea of this day, of the infallibility of government, and the absolute character of its acts, presumed to differ from the home government in respect to the wisdom and the justice of some of those burdens and restraints. They went so far in their excitement as to pronounce the measures of government unjust, unreasonable, and oppressive, and altogether such as ought not to be quietly submitted to. I scarcely need say, fellow-citizens, that my opinion of those measures fully accords with that of your fathers. Such a declaration of agreement on my part would not be worth much to anybody. It would, certainly, prove nothing, as to what part I might have taken, had I lived during the great controversy of 1776. To say *now* that America was right, and England wrong, is exceedingly easy. Everybody can say it; the dastard, not less than the noble brave, can flippantly discant on the tyranny of England towards the American Colonies. It is fashionable to do so; but there was a time when to pronounce against England, and in favor of the cause of the colonies, tried men's souls. They who did so were accounted in their day, plotters of mischief, agitators and rebels, dangerous men. To side with the right, against the wrong, with the weak against the strong, and with the oppressed against the oppressor! *here* lies the merit, and the one which, of all others, seems unfashionable in our day. The cause of liberty may be stabbed by the men who glory in the deeds of your fathers. But, to proceed.

Feeling themselves harshly and unjustly treated by the home government, your fathers, like men of honesty, and men of spirit, earnestly sought redress. They petitioned and remonstrated; they did so in a decorous, respectful, and loyal manner. Their conduct was wholly unexceptionable. This, however, did not answer the purpose.

They saw themselves treated with sovereign indifference, coldness and scorn. Yet they persevered. They were not the men to look back.

As the sheet anchor takes a firmer hold, when the ship is tossed by the storm, so did the cause of your fathers grow stronger, as it breasted the chilling blasts of kingly displeasure. The greatest and best of British statesmen admitted its justice, and the loftiest eloquence of the British Senate came to its support. But, with that blindness which seems to be the unvarying characteristic of tyrants, since Pharoah and his hosts were drowned in the Red Sea, the British Government persisted in the exactions complained of:

The madness of this course, we believe, is admitted now, even by England; but we fear the lesson is wholly lost on our present rulers.

Oppression makes a wise man mad.[1] Your fathers were wise men, and if they did not go mad, they became restive under this treatment. They felt themselves the victims of grievous wrongs, wholly incurable in their colonial capacity. With brave men there is always a remedy for oppression. Just here, the idea of a total separation of the colonies from the crown was born! It was a startling idea, much more so, than we, at this distance of time, regard it. The timid and the prudent (as has been intimated) of that day, were, of course, shocked and alarmed by it.

Such people lived then, had lived before, and will, probably, ever have a place on this planet; and their course, in respect to any great change, (no matter how great the good to be attained, or the wrong to be redressed by it), may be calculated with as much precision as can be the course of the stars. They hate all changes, but silver, gold and copper change! Of this sort of change they are always strongly in favor.

These people were called tories in the days of your fathers; and the appellation, probably, conveyed the same idea that is meant by a more modern, though a somewhat less euphonious term, which we often find in our papers, applied to some of our old politicians.

Their opposition to the then dangerous thought was earnest and powerful; but, amid all their terror and affrighted vociferations against it, the alarming and revolutionary idea moved on, and the country with it.

On the 2d of July, 1776, the old Continental Congress, to the dismay of the lovers of ease, and the worshippers of property, clothed that dreadful idea with all the authority of national sanction. They did so in the form of a resolution; and as we seldom hit upon resolutions, drawn up in our day, whose transparency is at all equal to this, it may refresh your minds and help my story if I read it.

1. Ecclesiastes 7.7.

> "Resolved, That these united colonies *are*, and of right, ought to be free and Independent States; that they are absolved from all allegiance to the British Crown; and that all political connection between them and the State of Great Britain *is*, and ought to be, dissolved."

Citizens, your fathers made good that resolution. They succeeded; and to-day you reap the fruits of their success. The freedom gained is yours; and you, therefore, may properly celebrate this anniversary. The 4th of July is the first great fact in your nation's history—the very ring-bolt in the chain of your yet undeveloped destiny.

Pride and patriotism, not less than gratitude, prompt you to celebrate and to hold it in perpetual remembrance. I have said that the Declaration of Independence is the RING-BOLT to the chain of your nation's destiny; so, indeed, I regard it. The principles contained in that instrument are saving principles. Stand by those principles, be true to them on all occasions, in all places, against all foes, and at whatever cost.

From the round top of your ship of state, dark and threatening clouds may be seen. Heavy billows, like mountains in the distance, disclose to the leeward huge forms of flinty rocks! That *bolt* drawn, that *chain* broken, and all is lost. *Cling to this day—cling to it*, and to its principles, with the grasp of a storm-tossed mariner to a spar at midnight.

The coming into being of a nation, in any circumstances, is an interesting event. But, besides general considerations, there were peculiar circumstances which make the advent of this republic an event of special attractiveness.

The whole scene, as I look back to it, was simple, dignified and sublime.

The population of the country, at the time, stood at the insignificant number of three millions. The country was poor in the munitions of war. The population was weak and scattered, and the country a wilderness unsubdued. There were then no means of concert and combination, such as exist now. Neither steam nor lightning had then been reduced to order and discipline. From the Potomac to the Delaware was a journey of many days. Under these, and innumerable other disadvantages, your fathers declared for liberty and independence and triumphed.

Fellow Citizens, I am not wanting in respect for the fathers of this republic. The signers of the Declaration of Independence were brave men. They were great men too—great enough to give fame to a great age. It does not often happen to a nation to raise, at one time, such a number of truly great men. The point from which I am compelled to view them is not, certainly, the most favorable; and yet I cannot contemplate their great deeds with less than admiration. They were statesmen, patriots and heroes, and for the good they did, and the principles they contended for, I will unite with you to honor their memory.

They loved their country better than their own private interests; and, though this is not the highest form of human excellence, all will concede that it is a rare virtue, and that when it is exhibited, it ought to command respect. He who will, intelligently, lay down his life for his country, is a man whom it is not in human nature to despise. Your fathers staked their lives, their fortunes, and their sacred honor, on the cause of their country. In their admiration of liberty, they lost sight of all other interests.

They were peace men; but they preferred revolution to peaceful submission to bondage. They were quiet men; but they did not shrink from agitating against oppression. They showed forbearance; but that they knew its limits. They believed in order; but not in the order of tyranny. With them, nothing was "*settled*" that was not right. With them, justice, liberty and humanity were "*final*;" not slavery and oppression. You may well cherish the memory of such men. They were great in their day and generation. Their solid manhood stands out the more as we contrast it with these degenerate times.

How circumspect, exact and proportionate were all their movements! How unlike the politicians of an hour! Their statesmanship looked beyond the passing moment, and stretched away in strength into the distant future. They seized upon eternal principles, and set a glorious example in their defence. Mark them!

Fully appreciating the hardship to be encountered, firmly believing in the right of their cause, honorably inviting the scrutiny of an onlooking world, reverently appealing to heaven to attest their sincerity, soundly comprehending the solemn responsibility they were about to assume, wisely measuring the terrible odds against them, your fathers, the fathers of this republic, did, most deliberately, under the inspiration of a glorious patriotism, and with a sublime faith in the great principles of justice and freedom, lay deep the corner-stone of the national superstructure, which has risen and still rises in grandeur around you.

Of this fundamental work, this day is the anniversary. Our eyes are met with demonstrations of joyous enthusiasm. Banners and pennants wave exultingly on the breeze. The din of business, too, is hushed. Even Mammon seems to have quitted his grasp on this day. The ear-piercing fife and the stirring drum unite their accents with the ascending peal of a thousand church bells. Prayers are made, hymns are sung, and sermons are preached in honor of this day;

while the quick martial tramp of a great and multitudinous nation, echoed back by all the hills, valleys and mountains of a vast continent, bespeak the occasion one of thrilling and universal interest—a nation's jubilee.

Friends and citizens, I need not enter further into the causes which led to this anniversary. Many of you understand them better than I do. You could instruct me in regard to them. That is a branch of knowledge in which you feel, perhaps, a much deeper interest than your speaker. The causes which led to the separation of the colonies from the British crown have never lacked for a tongue. They have all been taught in your common schools, narrated at your firesides, unfolded from your pulpits, and thundered from your legislative halls, and are as familiar to you as household words. They form the staple of your national poetry and eloquence.

I remember, also, that, as a people, Americans are remarkably familiar with all facts which make in their own favor. This is esteemed by some as a national trait—perhaps a national weakness. It is a fact, that whatever makes for the wealth or for the reputation of Americans, and can be had *cheap!* will be found by Americans. I shall not be charged with slandering Americans, if I say I think the American side of any question may be safely left in American hands.

I leave, therefore, the great deeds of your fathers to other gentlemen whose claim to have been regularly descended will be less likely to be disputed than mine!

The Present

My business, if I have any here to-day, is with the present. The accepted time with God and his cause is the ever-living now.

> "Trust no future, however pleasant,
> Let the dead past bury its dead;
> Act, act in the living present,
> Heart within, and God overhead."[2]

We have to do with the past only as we can make it useful to the present and to the future. To all inspiring motives, to noble deeds which can be gained from the past, we are welcome. But now is the time, the important time. Your fathers have lived, died, and have done their work, and have done much of it well. You live and must die, and you must do your work. You have no right to enjoy a child's share in the labor of your fathers, unless your children are to be blest by your labors. You have no right to wear out and waste the

2. Stanza quoted from Henry Wadsworth Longfellow's poem "A Psalm of Life."

hard-earned fame of your fathers to cover your indolence. Sydney Smith[3] tells us that men seldom eulogize the wisdom and virtues of their fathers, but to excuse some folly or wickedness of their own. This truth is not a doubtful one. There are illustrations of it near and remote, ancient and modern. It was fashionable, hundreds of years ago, for the children of Jacob to boast, we have "Abraham to our father,"[4] when they had long lost Abraham's faith and spirit. That people contented themselves under the shadow of Abraham's great name, while they repudiated the deeds which made his name great. Need I remind you that a similar thing is being done all over this country to-day? Need I tell you that the Jews are not the only people who built the tombs of the prophets, and garnished the sepulchres of the righteous? Washington could not die till he had broken the chains of his slaves. Yet his monument is built up by the price of human blood, and the traders in the bodies and souls of men, shout—"We have Washington to *our father*." Alas! that it should be so; yet so it is.

> "The evil that men do, lives after them,
> The good is oft' interred with their bones."[5]

Fellow-citizens, pardon me, allow me to ask, why am I called upon to speak here to-day? What have I, or those I represent, to do with your national independence? Are the great principles of political freedom and of natural justice, embodied in that Declaration of Independence, extended to us? and am I, therefore, called upon to bring our humble offering to the national altar, and to confess the benefits and express devout gratitude for the blessings resulting from your independence to us?

Would to God, both for your sakes and ours, that an affirmative answer could be truthfully returned to these questions! Then would my task be light, and my burden easy and delightful. For *who* is there so cold, that a nation's sympathy could not warm him? Who so obdurate and dead to the claims of gratitude, that would not thankfully acknowledge such priceless benefits? Who so stolid and selfish, that would not give his voice to swell the hallelujahs of a nation's jubilee, when the chains of servitude had been torn from his limbs? I am not that man. In a case like that, the dumb might eloquently speak, and the "lame man leap as an hart."[6]

But, such is not the state of the case. I say it with a sad sense of the disparity between us. I am not included within the pale of

3. Anglican minister and master essayist and lecturer (1771–1845), whose skills were employed in the causes of Catholic emancipation and parliamentary reform.
4. Matthew 3.9.
5. Shakespeare, *Julius Caesar* 3.2 76–77.
6. Isaiah 35.6.

this glorious anniversary! Your high independence only reveals the immeasurable distance between us. The blessings in which you, this day, rejoice, are not enjoyed in common. The rich inheritance of justice, liberty, prosperity and independence, bequeathed by your fathers, is shared by you, not by me. The sunlight that brought life and healing to you, has brought stripes and death to me. This Fourth [of] July is *yours*, not *mine*. *You* may rejoice, I must mourn. To drag a man in fetters into the grand illuminated temple of liberty, and call upon him to join you in joyous anthems, were inhuman mockery and sacrilegious irony. Do you mean, citizens, to mock me, by asking me to speak to-day? If so, there is a parallel to your conduct. And let me warn you that it is dangerous to copy the example of a nation whose crimes, towering up to heaven, were thrown down by the breath of the Almighty, burying that nation in irrecoverable ruin! I can to-day take up the plaintive lament of a peeled and woe-smitten people!

"By the rivers of Babylon, there we sat down. Yea! we wept when we remembered Zion. We hanged our harps upon the willows in the midst thereof. For there, they that carried us away captive, required of us a song; and they who wasted us required of us mirth, saying, Sing us one of the songs of Zion. How can we sing the Lord's song in a strange land? If I forget thee, O Jerusalem, let my right hand forget her cunning. If I do not remember thee, let my tongue cleave to the roof of my mouth."[7]

Fellow-citizens; above your national, tumultous joy, I hear the mournful wail of millions! whose chains, heavy and grievous yesterday, are, today, rendered more intolerable by the jubilee shouts that reach them. If I do forget, if I do not faithfully remember those bleeding children of sorrow this day, "may my right hand forget her cunning, and may my tongue cleave to the roof of my mouth!" To forget them, to pass lightly over their wrongs, and to chime in with the popular theme, would be treason most scandalous and shocking, and would make me a reproach before God and the world. My subject, then fellow-citizens, is AMERICAN SLAVERY. I shall see, this day, and its popular characteristics, from the slave's point of view. Standing, there, identified with the American bondman, making his wrongs mine, I do not hesitate to declare, with all my soul, that the character and conduct of this nation never looked blacker to me than on this 4th of July! Whether we turn to the declarations of the past, or to the professions of the present, the conduct of the nation seems equally hideous and revolting. America is false to the past, false to the present, and solemnly binds herself to be false to the future. Standing with God and the crushed and bleeding slave on

7. This and the first quotation in the paragraph below are from Psalms 137.1–6.

this occasion, I will, in the name of humanity which is outraged, in the name of liberty which is fettered, in the name of the constitution and the Bible, which are disregarded and trampled upon, dare to call in question and to denounce, with all the emphasis I can command, everything that serves to perpetuate slavery—the great sin and shame of America! "I will not equivocate; I will not excuse;"[8] I will use the severest language I can command; and yet not one word shall escape me that any man, whose judgement is not blinded by prejudice, or who is not at heart a slaveholder, shall not confess to be right and just.

But I fancy I hear some one of my audience say, it is just in this circumstance that you and your brother abolitionists fail to make a favorable impression on the public mind. Would you argue more, and denounce less, would you persuade more, and rebuke less, your cause would be much more likely to succeed. But, I submit, where all is plain there is nothing to be argued. What point in the anti-slavery creed would you have me argue? On what branch of the subject do the people of this country need light? Must I undertake to prove that the slave is a man? That point is conceded already. Nobody doubts it. The slaveholders themselves acknowledge it in the enactment of laws for their government. They acknowledge it when they punish disobedience on the part of the slave. There are seventy-two crimes in the State of Virginia, which, if committed by a black man, (no matter how ignorant he be), subject him to the punishment of death; while only two of the same crimes will subject a white man to the like punishment. What is this but the acknowledgement that the slave is a moral, intellectual and responsible being? The manhood of the slave is conceded. It is admitted in the fact that Southern statute books are covered with enactments forbidding, under severe fines and penalties, the teaching of the slave to read or to write. When you can point to any such laws, in reference to the beasts of the field, then I may consent to argue the manhood of the slave. When the dogs in your streets, when the fowls of the air, when the cattle on your hills, when the fish of the sea, and the reptiles that crawl, shall be unable to distinguish the slave from a brute, *then* will I argue with you that the slave is a man!

For the present, it is enough to affirm the equal manhood of the negro race. It is not astonishing that, while we are ploughing, planting and reaping, using all kinds of mechanical tools, erecting houses, constructing bridges, building ships, working in metals of brass, iron, copper, silver and gold; that, while we are reading,

8. From the first issue of the *Liberator* (January 1, 1831), in which William Lloyd Garrison promised, "I am in earnest—I will not equivocate—I will not excuse—I will not retreat a single inch—and I will be heard."

writing and cyphering, acting as clerks, merchants and secretaries, having among us lawyers, doctors, ministers, poets, authors, editors, orators and teachers; that, while we are engaged in all manner of enterprises common to other men, digging gold in California, capturing the whale in the Pacific, feeding sheep and cattle on the hill-side, living, moving, acting, thinking, planning, living in families as husbands, wives and children, and, above all, confessing and worshipping the Christian's God, and looking hopefully for life and immortality beyond the grave, we are called upon to prove that we are men!

Would you have me argue that man is entitled to liberty? that he is the rightful owner of his own body? You have already declared it. Must I argue the wrongfulness of slavery? Is that a question for Republicans? Is it to be settled by the rules of logic and argumentation, as a matter beset with great difficulty, involving a doubtful application of the principle of justice, hard to be understood? How should I look to-day, in the presence of Americans, dividing, and subdividing a discourse, to show that men have a natural right to freedom? speaking of it relatively, and positively, negatively, and affirmatively. To do so, would be to make myself ridiculous, and to offer an insult to your understanding. There is not a man beneath the canopy of heaven, that does not know that slavery is wrong *for him.*

What, am I to argue that it is wrong to make men brutes, to rob them of their liberty, to work them without wages, to keep them ignorant of their relations to their fellow men, to beat them with sticks, to flay their flesh with the lash, to load their limbs with irons, to hunt them with dogs, to sell them at auction, to sunder their families, to knock out their teeth, to burn their flesh, to starve them into obedience and submission to their masters? Must I argue that a system thus marked with blood, and stained with pollution, is *wrong?* No! I will not. I have better employments for my time and strength, than such arguments would imply.

What, then, remains to be argued? Is it that slavery is not divine; that God did not establish it; that our doctors of divinity are mistaken? There is blasphemy in the thought. That which is inhuman, cannot be divine! *Who* can reason on such a proposition? They that can, may; I cannot. The time for such argument is past.

At a time like this, scorching irony, not convincing argument, is needed. O! had I the ability, and could I reach the nation's ear, I would, to-day, pour out a fiery stream of biting ridicule, blasting reproach, withering sarcasm, and stern rebuke. For it is not light that is needed, but fire; it is not the gentle shower, but thunder. We need the storm, the whirlwind, and the earthquake. The feeling of the nation must be quickened; the conscience of the nation must be roused; the propriety of the nation must be startled; the hypocrisy of the nation must be exposed; and its crimes against God and man must be proclaimed and denounced.

What, to the American slave, is your 4th of July? I answer: a day that reveals to him, more than all other days in the year, the gross injustice and cruelty to which he is the constant victim. To him, your celebration is a sham; your boasted liberty, an unholy license; your national greatness, swelling vanity; your sounds of rejoicing are empty and heartless; your denunciations of tyrants, brass fronted impudence; your shouts of liberty and equality, hollow mockery; your prayers and hymns, your sermons and thanksgivings, with all your religious parade, and solemnity, are, to him, mere bombast, fraud, deception, impiety, and hypocrisy—a thin veil to cover up crimes which would disgrace a nation of savages. There is not a nation on the earth guilty of practices, more shocking and bloody, than are the people of these United States, at this very hour.

Go where you may, search where you will, roam through all the monarchies and despotisms of the old world, travel through South America, search out every abuse, and when you have found the last, lay your facts by the side of the everyday practices of this nation, and you will say with me, that, for revolting barbarity and shameless hypocrisy, America reigns without a rival.

* * *

JAMES MONROE GREGORY

From Frederick Douglass, the Orator†

[In 1893, James Monroe Gregory, a professor of Latin at Howard University, wrote *Frederick Douglass, the Orator.* (When Douglass died in 1895, a revised edition was printed with additional chapters on Douglass's death, his funeral services, and his obituary tributes.) As a student of the classics, Gregory was well-equipped to analyze Douglass's oratory, although he had not heard him in his prime.]

* * *

By whatever standard judged Mr. Douglass will take high rank as orator and writer. It may be truly said of him that he was born an orator; and, though he is a man of superior intellectual faculties, he has not relied on his natural powers alone for success in this his chosen vocation. He is called a self-made man, but few college

† From *Frederick Douglass, the Orator* (New York: Thomas Y. Cromwell, 1893), pp. 89–92.

bred men have been more diligent students of logic, of rhetoric, of politics, of history, and general literature than he. He belongs to that class of orators of which Fox of England and Henry and Clay[1] in our own country are the most illustrious representatives. His style, however, is peculiarly his own.

Cicero says, "The best orator is he that so speaks as to instruct, to delight, and to move the mind of his hearers." Mr. Douglass is a striking example of this definition. Few men equal him in his power over an audience. He possesses wit and pathos, two qualities which characterized Cicero and which, in the opinion of the rhetorician Quintilian, gave the Roman orator great advantage over Demosthenes.[2] Judge Ruffin[3] of Boston, in his introduction to Mr. Douglass' autobiography, says: "Douglass is brimful of humor,—at times of the driest kind; it is of a quaint kind; you can see it coming a long way off in a peculiar twitch of his mouth; it increases and broadens gradually until it becomes irresistible and all-pervading with his audience." The humor of Mr. Douglass is much like that of Mr. Joseph Jefferson,[4] the great actor, who never makes an effort to be funny, but his humor is of the quiet, suppressed type. Like Mr. Jefferson, now he excites those emotions which cause tears, and now he stirs up those which produce laughter. Grief and mirth may be said to reside in adjoining apartments in the same edifice, and the passing from one apartment to the other is not a difficult thing to do.

The biographer of Webster[5] gives the following amusing anecdote to show the simplicity of expressing thought for which that Colossus of American intellect is distinguished in his speeches: "On the arrival of that singular genius, David Crockett,[6] at Washington, he had an opportunity of hearing Mr. Webster. A short time afterwards he met him and abruptly accosted him as follows: 'Is this Mr. Webster?' 'Yes,

1. Henry Clay (1777–1852), Whig senator from Kentucky; in the decades before the Civil War, he became famous as an orator and compromiser in such legislative events as the Missouri Compromise. Charles James Fox (1749–1806), English statesman, politician, and renowned orator. Patrick Henry (1736–1799), Virginia statesman and orator; one of the most influential politicians of the Revolutionary era. His most famous words to the Continental Congress in March of 1775: "Give me liberty, or give me death."
2. Celebrated Athenian orator (383–322 B.C.E.) whom Cicero admired. Cicero (106–43 B.C.E.), the greatest of the Roman orators. Marcus Fabius Quintilianus (35?–97? B.C.E.), celebrated Roman rhetorician in the style of Cicero.
3. George Lewis Ruffin (1834–1886); born of African descent but of free parentage, he studied law, graduated from Harvard, and in 1883 was appointed judge of a Boston municipal court, the only black justice to hold office in New England at that time.
4. Famous American actor (1829–1905) who brilliantly played a number of roles for over seventy years in theater companies in the United States, England, and Australia.
5. Daniel Webster (1782–1852), Whig senator from Massachusetts; famous orator, though not in the cause of antislavery.
6. Famous frontiersman from Tennessee (1786–1836) who represented Tennessee in the state legislature and in the U.S. Congress; he later became a legend after his heroic death at the Alamo in Texas.

sir.' 'The great Mr. Webster of Massachusetts?' continued he, with a significant tone. 'I am Mr. Webster of Massachusetts,' was the calm reply. 'Well, sir,' continued the eccentric Crockett, 'I had heard that you were a great man, but I don't think so; I heard your speech and *understood every word you said.*'"

President Lincoln gave this reply to the question asked, to what secret he owed his success in public debate: "I always assume that my audiences are in many things wiser than I am, and I say the most sensible things I can to them. I never found that they did not understand me."

The power of simple statement is one of the chief characteristics of Mr. Douglass' style of speaking, and in this respect he resembles Fox, the great British statesman, who, above all his countrymen, was distinguished on account of plainness, and, as I may express it, homeliness of thought which gave him great power in persuading and moving his audience.

Mr. Douglass' influence in public speaking is due largely to the fact that he touches the hearts of his hearers—that he impresses them with the belief of his sincerity and earnestness. His heart is in what he says. "Clearness, force, and earnestness," says Webster, "are the qualities which produce conviction. True eloquence, indeed, does not consist in speech; it cannot be brought from far; labor and learning may toil for it, but they will toil for it in vain. Words and phrases may be marshaled in every way, but they cannot compass it; it must exist in the man, in the subject, and in the occasion."

There have been those of brilliant minds who have gained some reputation as speakers; they have been successful in pleasing and amusing those they addressed, but their success stopped here. They could not reach the depths of the heart, because their own hearts were not touched. The poet Horace[7] admirably enforces this thought when he says: "If you wish me to weep, you must first yourself be deeply grieved."

But to be fully appreciated, Mr. Douglass must be seen and heard. This was also true of Henry Clay. One could form but a faint conception of his eloquence and grandeur by reading his speeches, and yet, as reported, they were both logical and argumentative. The fire and action of the man could not be transferred to paper. Mr. Douglass in speaking does not make many gestures, but those he uses are natural and spontaneous. His manner is simple and graceful, and there is nothing about his style artificial or declamatory.

* * *

7. Quintus Horatius Flaccus (65–8 B.C.E.), celebrated Roman poet.

ELIZABETH CADY STANTON

[Diary Entry on Douglass's Death][†]

[Of the many tributes paid Frederick Douglass on his death, perhaps the one that best captured the essence of the public man was what his old friend and fellow human rights reformer Elizabeth Cady Stanton (1815–1902) wrote in her diary the day after his death. She had known Douglass since the 1840s, the decade of the *Narrative* and the time of the speech that she recalls.]

NEW YORK, *February 21* [1895].

Taking up the papers to-day, the first word that caught my eye thrilled my very soul. Frederick Douglass is dead! What memories of the long years since he and I first met chased each other, thick and fast, through my mind and held me spellbound. A graduate from the "Southern Institution," he was well fitted to stand before a Boston audience and, with his burning eloquence, portray his sufferings in the land of bondage. He stood there like an African prince, majestic in his wrath, as with wit, satire, and indignation he graphically described the bitterness of slavery and the humiliation of subjection to those who, in all human virtues and powers, were inferior to himself. Thus it was that I first saw Frederick Douglass, and wondered that any mortal man should have ever tried to subjugate a being with such talents, intensified with the love of liberty. Around him sat the great antislavery orators of the day, earnestly watching the effect of his eloquence on that immense audience, that laughed and wept by turns, completely carried away by the wondrous gifts of his pathos and humor. On this occasion, all the other speakers seemed tame after Frederick Douglass. In imitation of the Methodist preachers of the South, he used to deliver a sermon from the text, "Servants, obey your masters,"[1] which some of our literary critics pronounced the finest piece of satire in the English language. The last time I visited his home at Anacosta [*sic*], near Washington, I asked him if he had the written text of that sermon. He answered, "No, not even notes of it." "Could you give it again?" I asked. "No," he replied; "or at least I could not bring back the old feelings even if I tried, the blessing of liberty I have so long enjoyed having almost obliterated the painful memories of my sad early days."

† From Theodore Stanton and Harriet Stanton Blach, eds., *Elizabeth Cady Stanton*, (New York: Harper & Brothers, 1922), pp. 2:311–12.

1. Cf. Colossians 3.22.

CRITICISM

WILLIAM S. McFEELY

[The Writing of the *Narrative*]†

[How the *Narrative* came to be is told in McFeely's biography of Douglass. No account is known to exist that describes exactly where he wrote the book, how many drafts he prepared, and other details that would illuminate the inception of this remarkable work.]

* * *

He was, in fact, determined to be something far beyond a curiosity when in 1844 he began to write a story of his life that would make the world pay him true attention. His book, he and his friends felt sure, not only would reach readers who had not heard him, but would also reinforce the picture in the mind's eye, the sonorous sound still in the ear, of those who had. Wendell Phillips, in particular, urged him to write his story, and in the spring of 1845 was telling his audiences to be on the lookout for it. The *Narrative of the Life of Frederick Douglass* would be a powerful antislavery tract, but it would also be far more than that.

In his writing, Douglass outran being a runaway. Never satisfied with the degree to which a nineteenth-century white world took the ex-slave seriously as an intellectual, he would have been profoundly gratified by the attention paid his work in the twentieth century. Read now only secondarily for what they tell us about slavery, his *Narrative* (1845) and *My Bondage and My Freedom* (1855) have earned the regard of critics, such as William L. Andrews, who see them as two in the series of great "I" narratives of that most remarkable of all decades of American letters. The *Narrative* carries none of the poetry of Whitman's first edition of *Leaves of Grass* (1855), but it too is a song of myself. There is not the epic tragedy of Melville's *Moby-Dick* (1851), and yet it is a story—not wholly unlike Ishmael's—of survival in a world at sea with evil. On the other hand, with its message of growing self-confidence, of self-reliance, the *Narrative* is kin to Emerson's essays. But perhaps Douglass's telling of his odyssey is closest cousin to Thoreau's account of his altogether safe escape to Walden Pond. That quietly contained, subversive tale has reverberated ever since its telling with a message of radical repudiation of corrupt society. Thoreau heard a Wendell Phillips lecture describing Douglass's exodus—and reporting that a written account was on its way—in the spring of 1845 as he was planning his sojourn outside

† From William S. McFeely, *Frederick Douglass* (New York: Norton, 1991), pp. 114–17.

Concord. Robert D. Richardson, Jr., who wrote Thoreau's intellectual biography, has said that it is not "an accident that the earliest stages of Thoreau's move to Walden coincide with . . . the publication of Douglass's narrative of how he gained his freedom. *Walden* is about self-emancipation."

In all three of his autobiographies, Douglass tantalizes us with the many things he leaves out; not the least of these is discussion of why and how he wrote them. His correspondence is equally void of references to what must have been a compelling exercise for him. We know that Phillips and others in the Anti-Slavery Society urged him to put his story into print, but whom did he talk to about the project, who helped, who was its editor? His later quarrels with his British publisher make it clear that he cared not only about the content—he resisted any censoring of material thought to be offensive to Christians—but also about the appearance of the front matter and the cover. Such concerns must have been with Douglass even at the time of the first printing of the first book.

But perhaps not. To a remarkable degree *Narrative of the Life of Frederick Douglass* does seem to have simply sprung from a man who had been telling the same story in much the same language from the antislavery platform for four years. And once he had created, with his voice and then his pencil, the Frederick Douglass of the *Narrative*, the author never altered either the character or the plot significantly. This, more than the fact that speaking came easier than writing for Douglass, explains why he wrote no books other than the autobiographies. He had but one character to craft, one story to tell. The two later books, *My Bondage and My Freedom* and *Life and Times of Frederick Douglass*, reveal important shifts in approach and detail, but the Frederick Douglass of the *Narrative* remains inviolate.

The *Narrative* is short and direct, from the "I was born" of its first line to its closing account of the Nantucket speech, describing how Douglass "felt strongly moved to speak" and was urged to do so as well: "It was a severe cross, and I took it up reluctantly. The truth was, I felt myself a slave, and the idea of speaking to white people weighed me down. I spoke but a few moments, when I felt a degree of freedom." The person we come to know in these brief pages is unforgettable. From the *Narrative* and the many other accounts of runaways published in Douglass's day, right down to Toni Morrison's *Beloved* in ours, there has been no escape from the slave in American letters. And for the fifty years following publication of the *Narrative* in 1845, there was no escape for the author from the runaway he had created.

It is easy when reading the *Narrative* to misjudge the reason for the author's many omissions—the nature of his relationships with his brothers and sisters, for example. His focused concentration on himself does invite the charge of insensitivity to others. But there were other, deeper reasons for such voids. We get a hint of them when he tells of slaves on a Wye House farm singing "most exultingly" when "leaving home: . . . they would sing, as a chorus, to words which to many would seem unmeaning jargon, but which, nevertheless, were full of meaning to themselves." There were some sounds of slavery that Douglass could not render in words that his readers would hear, private torments and horrors too deep in the well to be drawn up.

The book was published by the "Anti-Slavery Office" in Boston in June 1845 and priced at fifty cents. The *Liberator* had announced its publication in May, and Phillips and his allies in the literary world saw to it that reviews appeared promptly. By fall, 4,500 copies had been sold in the United States; soon there were three European editions, and within five years 30,000 copies were in the hands of readers. The inevitable charge appeared that a slave boy could not have written the book—Lydia Maria Child[1] (also falsely credited with having written Harriet Jacobs's *Incidents in the Life of a Slave Girl*) was one of many suspected of having been the ghost writer. But anyone who had heard Douglass—and by 1845 thousands of people had—knew that the language of the *Narrative* was the same as that of the man who so passionately told his tale from the platform.

WILLIAM L. ANDREWS

[Frederick Douglass and the American Jeremiad]†

* * *

When he wrote his *Narrative* in 1845, Frederick Douglass made a serious effort to appeal to white middle-class readers of the North by fashioning his autobiography into a kind of American jeremiad. This genre differs from that which Wilson J. Moses has labeled the black jeremiad in one crucial sense: while the latter was preoccupied with America's impending doom because of its racial injustices, the American jeremiad foretold America's future hopefully, sustained by the conviction of the nation's divinely appointed mission. The practitioners of both literary traditions tended to see

1. White New England abolitionist and author (1802–1880); between 1833 and 1860 she wrote, edited, and published many books, journals, and magazines on the abolition of slavery [*editors*].

† From William L. Andrews, *To Tell a Free Story: The First Century of Afro-American Autobiography, 1760–1865* (Urbana: U of Illinois P, 1986), pp. 123–32. Bracketed page numbers refer to this Norton Critical Edition.

themselves as outcasts, prophets crying in the wilderness of their own alienation from prevailing error and perversity. While the white Jeremiahs decry America's deviation from its original sacred mission in the New World, they usually celebrate the national dream in the process of lamenting its decline. The American jeremiad affirms and sustains a middle-class consensus about America by both excoriating lapses from it and rhetorically coopting potential challenges (such as those offered by Frederick Douglass) to it.[1]

* * *

With Herman Melville and Henry David Thoreau,[2] contemporary Jeremiahs who also addressed the national sin of slavery, Douglass confronted America with profoundly polarized emotions that produced in him a classic case of Du Boisian double consciousness.[3] As a fugitive slave orator in the early 1840s, he denounced the institutionalized racism that pervaded America and perverted its much-heralded blend of liberty, democracy, and Christianity. Following the Garrisonian line, his speeches poured contempt on the Constitution of the United States as a compact with slavery and condemned northern as well as southern Christians for being the slave's tyrants, "our enslavers."[4] The *Narrative*, however, goes to no such political or religious extremes. In that book, Douglass deploys the rhetoric of the jeremiad to distinguish between true and false Americanism and Christianity. He celebrates the national dream by concluding his story with a contrast between the thriving seacoast town of New Bedford, Massachusetts—where he was "surrounded with the strongest proofs of wealth" [76]—and the run-down Eastern Shore of Maryland, where "dilapidated houses, with poverty-stricken inmates," "half-naked children," and "barefooted women" testified to an unprogressive polity. Appended to Douglass's story is an apparent apology for his narrative's "tone and manner, respecting religion," but this quickly gives way to a final jeremiad against the pharisaical "hypocrites" of "the *slaveholding religion* of this land". [79] "I love the pure, peaceable, and impartial Christianity of Christ," Douglass proclaimed. All the more reason, therefore, for him to appropriate the

1. Wilson J. Moses, *Black Messiahs and Uncle Toms* (University Park: Pennsylvania State University Press, 1982), pp. 30–48, and Sacvan Bercovitch, *The American Jeremiad* (Madison: University of Wisconsin Press, 1978), p. 180. My discussion of the American jeremiad as a genre is dependent on Bercovitch's excellent study and draws liberally from it.
2. Melville (1819–1891) and Thoreau (1817–1862) were the authors of, respectively, *Moby-Dick* (1851) and *Walden* (1854) [*editors*].
3. In *The Souls of Black Folk* (1903), W. E. B. Du Bois (1868–1964) discusses the concept of African American "double-consciousness" [*editors*].
4. See Douglass's address, "Southern Slavery and Northern Religion" (Feb. 11, 1844), in Blassingame, ed., *Douglass Papers*, 1:25. Frederick Douglass, John W. Blassingame, and John R. McKivigan, eds., *The Frederick Douglass Papers* (New Haven, CT: Yale UP, 1979–92).

language of Jeremiah 6:29 for his ultimate warning to corrupters of the faith: "'Shall I not visit for these things? saith the Lord. Shall not my soul be avenged on such a nation as this?'" [82]. The *Narrative* builds a convincing case for Douglass's literary calling and his ultimate self-appointment as America's black Jeremiah.

Douglass's account of his rise from slavery to freedom fulfills certain features of the jeremiad's cultural myth of America. The *Narrative* dramatizes a "ritual of socialization" that Sacvan Bercovitch finds often in late eighteenth- and early nineteenth-century jeremiads: the rebellion of a fractious individual against instituted authority is translated into a heroic act of self-reliance, a reenactment of the national myth of regeneration and progress through revolution. The great rhetorical task of the jeremiad is to divest self-determinative individualism of its threatening associations with anarchy and antinomianism, the excesses of the unbridled self. In America the jeremiad made much of the distinction between rebellion and revolution. The rebel disobeys out of self-interest and defiance of the good of the community and the laws of Providence. His act parallels Lucifer's primal act of disobedience, which produced only discord and a (temporary) thwarting of the divine plan. The revolutionary, on the other hand, promotes in the secular sphere the same sort of upward spiral toward perfection that God demanded of each individual soul in its private progress toward redemption. The American jeremiad obviated the distinction between secular and sacred revolution in order to endow the former with the sanction of the latter, the better to authorize the national myth of the American Revolution. America was a truly revolutionary society in the sense and to the extent that its people—that is to say, those who had been accorded the status of personhood in the Constitution—remained faithful to God's plan for the progressive conversion of their land into a new order. Americans were therefore called to be revolutionaries, but revolutionaries in the service of an evolving divine order within which Americans could achieve corporate self-realization as God's chosen people.

As several critics have noted, Douglass's *Narrative* seems to have been consciously drawn up along structural and metaphorical lines familiar to readers of spiritual autobiographies.[5] The young Frederick is initiated into a knowledge of the depravity of man when he witnesses the hideous flogging of his aunt Hester. "It was the blood-stained gate, the entrance to the hell of slavery, through which I was

5. G. Thomas Couser discusses the "analogy between the process of conversion and that of liberation" in the *Narrative* in his *American Autobiography: The Prophetic Mode* (Amherst: University of Massachusetts Press, 1979), p. 53. See also Houston Baker's observation in *Long Black Song* (Charlottesville: University Press of Virginia, 1972), p. 78: "Douglass's work is a spiritual autobiography akin to the writings of such noted white American authors as Cotton Mather, Benjamin Franklin, and Henry Adams."

about to pass" [16]. Though seemingly damned to this southern hell, the eight-year-old boy is delivered by "a special interposition of divine Providence in my favor" from the plantation of Edward Lloyd in Talbot County to the Baltimore home of Hugh Auld. From that time forward, the boy is convinced that freedom—"this living word of faith and spirit of hope" [30]—would be his someday. The thought "remained like ministering angels to cheer me through the gloom." Douglass's faith in this intuitively felt heavenly promise of liberation undergoes a series of trials in his boyhood and early teens, when he is first led out of his "mental darkness" by Sophia Auld, who teaches him his letters, and then is thrust back into "the horrible pit" of enforced ignorance by her husband, who fears a mentally enlightened slave.

The middle chapters of the *Narrative* recount the slave youth's growing temptations to despair of deliverance from bondage. Returned to the rural region where he was born, Douglass discovers the hypocrisy of Christian slaveholders whose pretentions to piety mask their cruelty and licentiousness. He reaches a dark night of the soul in 1833, when the harsh regime of Edward Covey, "the snake," breaks him "in body, soul, and spirit." And yet, he undergoes "a glorious resurrection, from the tomb of slavery, to the heaven of freedom" [53] by violently resisting Covey's attempt to apprehend him, one August morning, for another infraction of the rules. Thus, "resurrected," the sixteen-year-old youth, "a slave in form" but no longer "a slave in fact," begins to put his revived faith in freedom and his "self-confidence" into practice. Hired out in 1834 to William Freeland, he starts a "Sabbath school" in which to teach slaves how to read the Bible and "to imbue their minds with thoughts of freedom" [59]. "My tendency was upward," states Douglass, firmly committed to following the road to freedom analogized in the *Narrative* in imagery reminiscent of *Pilgrim's Progress*.[6] The first escape attempt, appropriately timed for Easter, is foiled, but his second, in September 1838, succeeds.

The last pages of the *Narrative* describe the new freeman's call to witness for the gospel of freedom that had preserved, regenerated, and pointed him northward. A subscription to the *Liberator* sets his "soul" on fire for "the cause" of abolitionism. At an antislavery meeting in Nantucket in August 1841, "I felt strongly moved to speak," but Douglass is restrained by a sense of unworthiness before white people. Still the promptings of the spirit cannot be resisted, even though it is "a severe cross" for the new convert to take up. "I spoke but a few moments, when I felt a degree of freedom, and said what I desired with considerable ease." This liberation of the tongue climaxes the life-long quest of Frederick Douglass toward his divinely

6. An English spiritual allegory published by John Bunyan in 1678 [*editors*].

appointed destiny in the antislavery ministry. The special plan of Providence is now fully revealed at the end of the *Narrative*. Frederick Douglass is a chosen man as well as a freeman. His trials of the spirit have been a test and a preparation for his ultimate mission as a black Jeremiah to a corrupt white Israel. This autobiography, as Robert G. O'Meally has emphasized, is a text meant to be preached.[7]

Like all American jeremiads, the *Narrative* is a political sermon. Douglass's self-realization as a freeman and a chosen man takes place via a process of outward and sometimes violent revolution as well as inner evolution of consciousness. The strategy of Douglass's jeremiad is to depict this revolution as a "process of Americanization," to use once again a key phrase in Bercovitch's analysis of the genre. As Bercovitch notes, the jeremiad was responsible for rationalizing and channeling the revolutionary individualistic impulse in America so as to reconcile it with the myth of America's corporate destiny as a chosen people. This meant distinguishing firmly between the truly American revolutionary individualism and the rebellious, un-American individualism of the alien and seditious Indian, Negro, or feminist. Those marked by racial heritage as other had to *prove* that they were of "the people," the American chosen, by demonstrating in their own lives the rituals of Americanization that had converted them from non-persons, as it were, into members of the middle-class majority. "Blacks and Indians . . . could learn to be True Americans, when in the fullness of time they would adopt the tenets of black and red capitalism."[8] Douglass pledges allegiance to the economic tenets of the republic in his autobiography, entitled, appropriately enough, the narrative of "*An American Slave*." Douglass goes beyond his predecessors in the slave narrative, in using this orthodoxy to justify his revolution against slavery and its perverse, un-American profit motive.

John Seelye has pointed out some of the affinities between Douglass's *Narrative* and the cultural myth of America as dramatized in Franklin's memoir. Douglass is "Ben Franklin's specific shade," argues Seelye, though the ex-slave's story is "not a record of essays to do good but attempts to be bad, Douglass like Milton's Satan[9] inventing virtue from an evil necessity."[1] It is no small part of Douglass's rhetorical

7. Robert G. O'Meally, "Frederick Douglass' 1845 *Narrative:* The Text Was Meant to Be Preached," in Dexter Fisher and Robert B. Stepto, eds., *Afro-American Literature: The Reconstruction of Instruction* (New York: Modern Language Association, 1978), pp. 192–211. O'Meally concentrates on the relationship of the *Narrative* to black sermonic traditions. For a discussion of Douglass's actual experience as a preacher, see William L. Andrews, "Frederick Douglass, Preacher," *American Literature* 54 (Dec. 1982), 592–97.
8. Bercovitch, *American Jeremiad*, p. 160.
9. The antagonist in John Milton's epic poem *Paradise Lost* (1667) [*editors*].
1. John Seelye, "The Clay Foot of the Climber: Richard M. Nixon in Perspective," in William L. Andrews, ed., *Literary Romanticism in America* (Baton Rouge: Louisiana State University Press, 1981), p. 125.

art, however, to translate his badness into revolutionary necessity of a kind his white reader could identify with. Douglass's life, like Franklin's, describes a rising arc from country to city; then it follows a downward curve of expectations when the town slave is returned to the plantation; but it revolves upward once more, after the fight with Covey, carrying the black youth from Talbot County to Baltimore and finally to New York and New Bedford. When given the opportunity for self-improvement in the city, young Fred is every bit as enterprising as Father Ben. As a boy he overcomes adversity to learn reading and writing on his own. Discovery of an eloquence handbook entitled *The Columbian Orator* foreshadows the day when he will become one. But first he must become a man. The battle with Covey halts his regression into the slave's "beast-like stupor" and "revived within me a sense of my own manhood." "Bold defiance" replaces "cowardice"; significantly, the spheres of this defiance are intellectual and economic. As a Sabbath school teacher at Freeland's, Douglass uses as his text the Bible, and his aim is consistent with America's middle-class civil religion. He encourages his slave pupils to behave "like intellectual, moral, and accountable beings" rather than "spending the Sabbath in wrestling, boxing, and drinking whisky" [58]. Douglass domesticates a greater gesture of defiance, his first escape attempt, by analogizing it to the hallowed decision of Patrick Henry (ironically, a slaveholder) for liberty or death. "We did more than Patrick Henry," the fugitive advances of himself and his fellow runaways, because their liberty was more dubious and their deaths more certain if they failed. By implication, then, these dauntless blacks were more heroically American in their struggle for independence than was one of the most prominent delegates of the convention of 1776.

After Douglass's return to Baltimore in the spring of 1835 to be hired out in various employments, the *Narrative* concentrates increasingly on the economic humiliations of an upwardly aspiring "slave in form but not in fact." While apprenticed as a ship's carpenter, the slave is attacked and beaten by four white workers who felt it "degrading to them to work with me." Manfully, Douglass returns the blows in kind despite the adverse odds. Taught the calking trade, he "was able to command the highest wages given to the most experienced calkers," $1.50 a day. The money "was rightfully my own," Douglass argues. "I contracted for it; I earned it; it was paid to me." Yet every week Hugh Auld took it. "And why? Not because he earned it,—not because he had any hand in earning it,—not because I owed it to him,—nor because he possessed the slightest shadow of a right to it; but solely because he had the power to compel me to give it up" [68].

With Grandy, Lane, and Henson,[2] Douglass appeals to his reader's respect for contract and resentment of arbitrary power as a way of preparing his case for the final break with slavery. The right at issue here is pragmatic and economic, not abstract or romantic. Douglass analogizes Auld to a "grim-visaged pirate" and a "robber"—an outlaw, in other words—to banish him from a consubstantial relationship with the northern reader. Meanwhile, Douglass qualifies himself for acceptance as an economic revolutionary in the best American tradition. He works his way up the economic ladder in the South from country slave to city apprentice to the quasi-free status of one who "hired his time."

Hiring his time required Douglass to meet all his living expenses out of the income that he could make for himself, while still paying his master a fixed return of $3 per week. This was "a hard bargain," but still "a step toward freedom to be allowed to bear the responsibilities of a freeman" [71]. Here again, Douglass stresses how he qualified himself, step by step, for freedom and its "responsibilities" as well as its "rights." "I bent myself to the work of making money," adds Douglass, by way of proving his dedication to the quintessential responsibilities of an American free man. "I was ready to work at night as well as day, and by the most untiring perseverance and industry, I made enough to meet my expenses, and lay up a little money every week" [71]. The savings were used, presumably, to help Douglass in his flight to freedom, for less than a month after Auld halted the slave's hiring out (fearing that too much freedom would go to the black man's head), Douglass retaliated by taking the ultimate "step toward freedom."

One of the most unconventional features of the *Narrative* was Douglass's refusal to end his story with the stock-in-trade climax of the slave narrative. Watching the panting fugitive seize his freedom just ahead of snapping bloodhounds and clutching slavecatchers left white readers with a vicarious sense of the thrill of the chase as well as the relief of the successful escape. In the slave narrative a generation of readers found a factual parallel to the capture-flight-and-pursuit plots of their favorite romances by James Fenimore Cooper, William Gilmore Simms, and Robert Montgomery Bird.[3] Yet Douglass left only a hiatus in his story where the customary climax should have been, insisting, quite plausibly, that to recount

2. Moses Grandy, Lunsford Lane, and Josiah Henson were slave narrators. See Moses Grandy, *Narrative of the Life of Moses Grandy: Late a Slave in the United States of America*, ed. George Thompson (Boston: O. Johnson, 1844); Lunsford Lane, *The Narrative of Lunsford Lane* (Boston: J. G. Torrey, Printer, 1842); and Josiah Henson, *The Life of Josiah Henson Formerly a Slave, Now an Inhabitant of Canada*, ed. Samuel Atkins Eliot (Boston: A. D. Phelps, 1849) [*editors*].
3. Cooper, Simms, and Bird were popular 19th-century American novelists [*editors*].

his mode of escape would alert slaveholders to it and thus close it to others. The conclusion he chose for his *Narrative* indicates that in his mind the high point of a fugitive slave's career was not his arrival in the free states but his assumption of a new identity as a free man and his integration into the American mainstream.

Douglass notes graphically the initial terrors of the isolated fugitive in a strange and often hostile land, but his emphasis is on how quickly and happily he assimilated. He marries within two weeks of his arrival in New York. He and his wife Anna move immediately to New Bedford, where the morning after his arrival he receives from his Negro host a new name to denote his new identity in freedom. Two days later, he takes his first job stowing a sloop with a load of oil. "It was the first work, the reward of which was to be entirely my own." "It was to me the starting-point of a new existence" [78]. Everything falls into place for Douglass in New Bedford, where the American dream of "a new existence" is always possible for every man, black or white. New Bedford fulfills the ex-slave's socioeconomic quest; here every man pursues his work "with a sober, yet cheerful earnestness, which betokened the deep interest which he felt in what he was doing, as well as a sense of his own dignity as a man." Most marvelous of all, the black population of this paragon of industrial capitalism lives in "finer houses" and enjoys "more of the comforts of life, than the average of slaveholders in Maryland." True, Douglass admits, "prejudice against color" along the docks of New Bedford kept him from resuming his former trade as a calker. But a note to the text removes even this blemish from the image of the town as the epitome of progress and justice: "I am told that colored persons can now get employment at calking in New Bedford—a result of anti-slavery effort." Perhaps this is the reason for the mild manner and the absence of irony or bitterness with which Douglass brings up this lone instance of racism in the North. The refusal of New Bedford's calkers to work with him moves the narrator to none of the moral outrage that accompanies his recall of the same kind of treatment that he received from Baltimore's calkers. Now Douglass is more thick-skinned and matter-of-fact; his narrative business is not to complain about the barriers to his progress but to show how he, like his adopted city, overcame them. Now is the time for understatement: "Finding my trade of no immediate benefit, I threw off my calking habiliments, and prepared myself to do any kind of work I could get to do" [78].

For the next three years, Douglass had to support his family via whatever manual labor jobs he could find, including sawing wood, shoveling coal, sweeping chimneys, and rolling casks in an oil refinery. Yet the *Narrative* stresses only the bright side of this experience—Douglass's American ingenuity and industry—not the ugly side—New Bedford's economic repression of a trained black tradesman. Only in 1881, in his *Life and Times*, when Douglass no longer had the same rhetorical stake in a dramatic contrast between North and South, would he call the whole humiliating episode "the test of the real civilization of the community" of New Bedford, which the town plainly failed.[4] In 1845 New Bedford had to serve as Douglass's standard of "real civilization," of true Americanism, so that he as a jeremiad writer could have something by which to measure the South's fall from national grace.

Like earlier popular literary genres from which Afro-American autobiography sought authentication and other rhetorical advantages, the American jeremiad provided a structure for Douglass's vision of America that was both empowering and limiting at the same time. The jeremiad gave the ex-slave literary license to excoriate the South pretty much as he pleased so long as the ideals and values by which he judged that region's transgressions remained American. Thus while bitterly evoking the nightmare of slavery, Douglass's example invoked just as reverently the dream of America as a land of freedom and opportunity. In a letter to Douglass several weeks before the *Narrative* was published, Wendell Phillips, one of the most forthright abolitionist critics of racism in the North as well as slavery in the South, urged the autobiographer to include a comparison of the status of blacks in both sections of the country. "Tell us whether, after all, the half-free colored man of Massachusetts is worse off than the pampered slave of the rice swamps!" [11], Phillips requested, with his usual penchant for irony. In Douglass's jeremiad, however, such a topic was not tellable. In the spiritual autobiography and the success story, of which Douglass's *Narrative* is an amalgam, doubts about the achievement or significance of salvation and success are clear evidence that they have not been attained. Douglass's story, by contrast, is determined to declare New Bedford as more than one slave's attainable secular salvation in America. Such a declarative act brought into being New Bedford as Douglass needed it to be—a symbol of his belief in America as a free, prosperous, and progressive social order that thrived without caste distinctions or the exploitation of labor. For the sake of this symbol in his vision of America, Douglass could make his own exploitation in the New Bedford labor market seem like a useful lesson in the school of hard knocks, the sort of adversity that self-made men generally glory in. For the symbol's sake, Douglass would censor himself and say nothing of more humiliating Jim Crow experiences that he had been subjected to in the North, although he

4. *Life and Times of Frederick Douglass* (Hartford, Conn.: Park, 1881), p. 260.

had been recounting such incidents from the abolitionist platform for the past three years.[5]

The American jeremiad structured Douglass into a fixed bipolar set of alternatives with which to define the experience and aspirations of "an American slave." That which was not American was conceived of as an absence, un-Americanism, false Americanism. America was constantly being analyzed and measured against its opposite, which was only the negative function of the interpretive possibilities of the symbol.[6] To get outside this self-enclosed dualism, one had to liberate oneself from the symbol of America as a self-valorizing plenitude and from the binary oppositions that maintained the symbol within a field of meanings of its own making. Henry Louis Gates, Jr., has argued convincingly that in the first chapter of the *Narrative*, the binary oppositions that inform and enforce the culture of the slavocracy are "mediated" by the narrator so as to "reverse the relations of the opposition" and reveal that "the oppositions, all along, were only arbitrary, not fixed."[7] For instance, as both the son and slave of his father-master, the mulatto Douglass deconstructs the fundamental opposition between white people and black animals on which much of the rationale for slavery was based. That separation between white and black cannot hold because it is culturally, not naturally, determined. By the time we finish the last chapter of the *Narrative*, however, it becomes evident that Douglass is not bent on the same kind of critique of the binary oppositions that govern and validate the symbol of America. The *Narrative* turns, structurally and thematically, on such dualities as southern slavery versus northern freedom, "slaveholding religion" versus "Christianity proper," Baltimore versus New Bedford, compulsion versus contract, stagnation versus progress, deprivation versus wealth, violence versus order, community versus caste system. And very little mediation takes place between these fixed, shall we say "black-and-white," antitheses.[8] Indeed, Douglass suggests that the gap between these

5. For an example of Douglass's attacks on the racist Methodists of New Bedford, see his speech "The Church Is the Bulwark of Slavery" (May 25, 1842), in Blassingame, ed., *Douglass Papers*, 1: 19.
6. Bercovitch, *American Jeremiad*, pp. 177–78.
7. Henry Louis Gates, Jr., "Binary Oppositions in Chapter One of *The Narrative of the Life of Frederick Douglass, an American Slave, Written by Himself*," in Fisher and Stepto, eds., *Afro-American Literature*, pp. 226–27.
8. Douglass's "Appendix" does question distinctions between Christianity in the South and the North through statements like "I can see no reason, but the most deceitful one, for calling the religion of this land Christianity." In this respect, Douglass was following the Garrisonian line of attacking all northern churches that maintained any sort of denominational "union with slaveholders." However, this hypocrisy of the northern church when linked with the corruption of the southern gave Douglass all the more reason to write as a Jeremiah lamenting the decline of present-day religion when contrasted to its opposite, "Christianity proper."

poles of true and false Americanism is growing wider, as New Bedford's progress against racial discrimination seems to testify.

Thus as an American jeremiad, Douglass's *Narrative* deconstructs binary oppositions that uphold slavery in the South while reconstructing the pattern of his life around other sets of oppositions whose support of the myth of America he might as readily have questioned, too. In 1845, however, Douglass was still exploring the rhetorical possibilities of binary oppositions as a means of establishing his own identity relative to America, South and North. It is through his own experiments with rhetoric that we see Douglass's particular brand of "opposing self" at work. As a jeremiadic autobiographer, he has more than his own story to tell. He must preach in such a way as to discredit the false oppositions and hierarchies of value that have arisen as a consequence of slavery's perversions of the true oppositions between good and evil, the natural and the unnatural.

* * *

ROBERT D. RICHARDSON, JR.

From Henry Thoreau: A Life of the Mind†

* * *

On May 24, Anthony Burns, a runaway slave, was arrested in Boston. On the twenty-fifth the U.S. Congress passed the Kansas-Nebraska bill. On the twenty-sixth a Boston mob tried to rescue Burns from the courthouse. They failed, Burns was identified, taken to the harbor and put on a ship for return to the South. But it had taken a battalion of U.S. artillery, four platoons of marines, the sheriff's posse, twenty-two companies of state militia, and forty thousand dollars to return Anthony Burns to slavery. He was the last to be returned from Massachusetts. The public was greatly stirred up over the incident, Thoreau along with the rest. He began composing a lecture or speech on the danger of submitting to an unjust law. The subject grew on him, would not leave him alone. Out walking for lilies or for the serenity of a lake, the incident kept rising to mind. Eventually, on July 4, on the ninth anniversary of his move out to the pond for personal liberation, he delivered, in Framingham, his "Slavery in Massachusetts" talk.

It is strong stuff, not quite advocating violent disobedience but coming very close. The lecture was toned down a bit from the

† From Robert D. Richardson, Jr., *Henry Thoreau: A Life of the Mind* (Berkeley and Los Angeles: U of California P, 1986), pp. 314–16. Reprinted by permission of the University of California Press.

journal version in this regard. The question was not, he thought, whether the fugitive slave law was constitutional, but whether it was right. "I wish my countrymen to consider, that whatever the human law may be, neither an individual nor a nation can ever commit the least act of injustice against the obscurest individual, without having to pay the penalty for it." The law was wrong. It should not be obeyed. If the state said obey it, the state was wrong and should be disobeyed. Thoreau's language veered toward the violence he would still not openly call for. "Rather than do this [obey the fugitive slave law] I need not say what match I would touch, what system endeavor to blow up,—but as I love my life, I would side with the light, and let the dark earth roll from under me." The essay is strong in its denunciation of the governor, the courts, the papers ("I have heard the gurgling of the sewer through every column"), but it is important to remember that this essay reflects a wide segment of popular feeling of the time. There is no doubt Thoreau felt strongly about the issue, so strongly that he slipped into some old Christian rhetoric. In his notes as in his speech, Thoreau makes heavy and uncharacteristic use of heaven and hell, angels and devils, adopting, for the time and the cause, the rhetorical style of William Lloyd Garrison, Wendell Phillips, and Frederick Douglass:

> I dwelt before, perhaps, in the illusion that my life passed somewhere only *between* heaven and hell, but now I cannot persuade myself that I do not dwell *wholly within* hell. The site of that political organization called Massachusetts is to me morally covered with volcanic scoriae and cinders, such as Milton describes in the infernal regions.[1]

Freedom is one of the ideas we cannot do without, though various terms for freedom become stale or suspect. But whether called liberty by the revolutionary generation, emancipation by the Civil War generation, freedom in the first half of the twentieth century, or liberation, as now, it is only the terms that change, becoming valorized or discredited by turns. One of the important meanings of Thoreau's life, and of *Walden*, is the imperative of freedom or liberation. It is thus entirely fit that the final stages of the printing and publishing of *Walden* should coincide with Thoreau's renewed involvement in the antislavery movement, and the aftermath of the Anthony Burns affair. Nor is it an accident that the earliest stages of Thoreau's move to Walden coincided with the emergence of Frederick Douglass, and the publication of Douglass's narrative of how he gained his freedom. *Walden* is about self-emancipation, but

1. Henry D. Thoreau, *Reform Papers*, ed. Wendell Glick (Princeton: Princeton University Press, 1973), pp. 96, 101, 102, 106–7.

not at the expense of ignoring the problem of external, physical freedom. The Thoreau who sought his own freedom was, inevitably, involved in the political movement to abolish slavery, and his involvement grew rather than diminished as time went on.

* * *

HOUSTON A. BAKER, JR.

[The Economics of Douglass's *Narrative*]†

* * *

One of the most striking manifestations of the economic voice of Douglass's 1845 *Narrative* is the description of the wealthy slave-owner Colonel Lloyd's "finely cultivated garden, which afforded almost constant employment for four men, besides the chief gardener, (Mr. M'Durmond)" [21]. This garden, which is found at the outset of chapter 3, * * * is coded in a manner that makes it the most significant economic sign in the initial chapters of the *Narrative.* The entire store of the slaveholder's "Job-like" [22] riches is imaged by the garden, which was "probably the greatest attraction of the place [the Lloyd estate]" [21]. Abounding in "fruit of every description," the garden is "quite a temptation to the hungry swarms of boys, as well as the older slaves . . . few of whom had the virtue or the vice to resist it" [21].

* * *

In the case of Colonel Lloyd's garden the fruits of slave labor are *all* retained by the master. And any attempts by slaves to share such fruits are not only dubbed stealing, but also severely punished. Even so, "the colonel had to resort to all kinds of stratagems [beyond mere flogging] to keep his slaves out of the garden" [21].

The image of vast abundance produced by slaves but denied them through the brutality of the owner of the means of production (i.e., the land) suggests a purely economic transformation of a traditional image of the biblical garden and its temptations. Douglass heightens the import of this economic coding through implicit and ironic detailings of the determination of general cultural consciousness *by commerce.* The folkloric aphorism that a single touch of the "tar brush" defiles the whole is invoked in the *Narrative* as a humorous

† From *Blues, Ideology, and Afro-American Literature* (Chicago: U of Chicago P, 1984), pp. 44–50. Reprinted by permission of the University of Chicago Press. Bracketed page numbers refer to this Norton Critical Edition.

analogue for Colonel Lloyd's ideological and mystifying designation of those who are denied the fruits of the garden as *unworthy*. The colonel *tars* the fence around his garden, and any slave "caught with tar upon his person . . . was severely whipped by the chief gardener" [21].

The promotion of *tar* (of a *blackness* so sticky and entangling for American conscience that the Tar Baby story[1] of African provenance has been an enduring cultural transplant) to a mark of low status, deprivation, and unworthiness is commented upon by the narrator as follows: "The slaves became as fearful of tar as of the lash. They seemed to realize the impossibility of touching *tar* without being defiled" [21]. Blacks, through the *genetic* touch of the tar brush that makes them people of color, are automatically guilty of the paradoxically labeled "crime" of seeking to enjoy the fruits of their own labor.

The "increase in store" of a traditional American history takes on quite other dimensions in light of Douglass's account of the garden in chapter 3. Later in the *Narrative*, he writes of the life of slaves on Thomas Auld's farm: "A great many times have we poor creatures been nearly perishing with hunger, when food in abundance lay mouldering in the safe and smoke-house, and our pious mistress was aware of the fact; and yet mistress and her husband would kneel every morning, and pray that God would bless them in basket and store!" [41]. The keenly literate and secular autobiographical self that so capably figures the economics of Lloyd's garden—summing in the process both the nil financial gain of blacks, and their placement in the left-hand, or debit, column of the ledgers of American status—is the same self encountered when the narrator returns as a teenager to southern, agrarian slavery.

At the farm of Mr. Edward Covey, where he has been hired out for "breaking," the *Narrative* pictures four enslaved black men fanning wheat. Douglass comprises one of their number, "carrying wheat to the fan" [49]. The sun proves too much for the unacclimatized Douglass, and he collapses, only to be beaten by Mr. Covey for his failure to serve effectively as a mindless ("the work was simple requiring strength rather than intellect") cog in the machine of slave production. Seeking redress from his master (Mr. Thomas Auld) who hired him to Covey, Douglass finds that the profit motive drives all before it: "Master Thomas . . . said . . . that he could not think of taking me from . . . [Mr. Covey]; that should he do so, he would lose the whole year's wages" [51].

1. The best known of the southern African American animal fables first popularized by Joel Chandler Harris in *Uncle Remus, His Songs and His Sayings: The Folk-Lore of the Old Plantation* (New York: D. Appleton, 1881) [*editors*].

The most bizarre profit accruing to the owners in the Covey episode, however, is not slave wages, but slave offspring. If Colonel Lloyd would take the fruit of the slave's labor, Mr. Covey would take the very fruit of the slave's womb. He puts a black man "to stud" with one of his slave women and proclaims the children of this compelled union his property. This is a confiscation of surplus value with a vengeance. It manifests the supreme aberrancy of relationships conditioned by the southern traffic in human "chattel." At Covey's farm, produce, labor, wages, and profit create a crisis that Douglass must negotiate in the best available fashion. He resolves physically to combat Mr. Covey, the "man in the middle."

In contrast to a resolved young Douglass in Chapter 10 of the *Narrative* stands Sandy Jenkins, the slave mentioned earlier in this discussion who has a free wife. Sandy offers Douglass a folk means of negotiating his crisis at Covey's, providing him with "a certain *root*," which, carried "*always on* . . . [the] *right side*, would render it impossible for Mr. Covey or any other white man" to whip the slave [52]. What is represented by the introduction of Sandy Jenkins is a displacement of Christian metaphysics by Afro-American "superstition." Ultimately, this displacement reveals the inefficacy of trusting solely to any form of extra-secular aid for relief (or release) from slavery.

The root does not work. The physical confrontation does. Through physical battle, Douglass gains a measure of relief from Covey's harassments. Jenkins's mode of negotiating the economics of slavery, the *Narrative* implies, is not *a man's way*, since the narrator claims that his combat with Covey converted him, ipso facto, into *a man*. In the same chapter in which the inefficacy of Jenkins's way is implied, the text also suggests that Jenkins is the traitor who reveals the planned escape of Douglass and fellow slaves to their master Mr. Freeland. Sandy seems to represent the inescapable limiting conditions of Afro-American slavery in the South; he is the pure, negative product of an economics of slavery. Standing in clear and monumentally *present* (even to the extent of a foregrounding footnote) contrast to the Douglass of chapter 10, Sandy represents the virtual impossibility of an escape from bondage on the terms implied by the attempted escape from Freeland's.

At its most developed, *southern* extension, the literate abolitionist self of the *Narrative* engages in an act of physical revolt, forms a Christian brotherhood of fellow slaves through a Sabbath school, and formulates a plan for a *collective* escape from bondage. But this progress toward liberation in the agrarian South is foiled by one whose mind is so "tarred" by the economics of slavery that he betrays the collective. The possibility of collective freedom is thus foreclosed by treachery within the slave community. A communally dedicated Douglass ("The work of instructing my dear fellow-slaves was the sweetest engagement with which I was ever blessed," [58]) finds that revolt, religion, and literacy *all* fail. The slave does, indeed, *write* his "own pass" and the passes of his fellows, but the Sabbath school assembled group is no match for the enemy within.

What recourse, then, is available for the black man of talent who would be free? The *Narrative* answers in an economic voice similar to that found in *The Life of Olaudah Equiano.*[2] Returned to Baltimore and the home of Mr. Hugh Auld after a three-year absence, the teenaged slave is hired out to "Mr. William Gardner, an extensive shipbuilder in Fell's Point. I was put there to learn how to calk" [65]. In short space, Douglass is able "to command the highest wages given to the most experienced calkers" [68]. In lines that echo Vassa with resonant effect, he writes: "I was now of some importance to my master. I was bringing him from six to seven dollars per week. I sometimes brought him nine dollars per week: my wages were a dollar and a half a day" [68]. Having entered a world of real *wages*, Douglass is equivalent to the Vassa who realized what a small "venture" could produce. And like Vassa, the nineteenth-century slave recognizes that the surplus value his master receives is but stolen profit: "I was compelled to deliver every cent of that [money contracted for, earned, and paid for calking] to Master Auld. And why? Not because he earned it . . . but solely because he had the power to compel me to give it up" [68].

Like Vassa, Douglass has arrived at a fully commercial view of his situation. He, too, enters an agreement with his master that results in freedom. Having gained the right to hire his own time and to keep a portion of his wages, Douglass eventually converts property, through property, into humanity. Impelled by his commercial endeavors and the opportunities resulting from his free commerce, he takes leave of Mr. Auld. He thus removes (in his own person) the master's property and places it in the ranks of a northern humanity. "According to my resolution, on the third day of September, 1838, I left my chains and succeeded in reaching New York" [73]. By "stealing away," Douglass not only steals the fruits of his own labor (not unlike the produce of Colonel Lloyd's garden), but also liberates the laborer—the chattel who works profitlessly in the garden.

The necessity for Douglass to effect his liberation through flight results from the complete intransigence to change of southern patriarchs. Mr. Auld, as the young slave knows all too well, cannot

2. Olaudah Equiano, *The Interesting Narrative of the Life of Olaudah Equiano, or Gustavus Vassa, the African. Written by Himself* (London, 1789) [*editors*].

possibly conceive of the child of his "family," of the "nigger" fitted out to work only for his profit, as simply an economic investment. Instead of exchanging capital, therefore, Douglass appropriates his own labor and flees to the camp of those who will ultimately be Auld's adversaries in civil war.

The inscribed document that effectively marks Douglass's liberation in the *Narrative* is, I think, no less an economic sign than Vassa's certificate of manumission:

> This may certify, that I joined together in holy matrimony Frederick Johnson and Anna Murray, as man and wife, in the presence of Mr. David Ruggles and Mrs. Michaels.
>
> James W. C. Pennington
> *New York, Sept.* 15, 1838.

What Douglass's certificate of marriage, which is transcribed in full in chapter 11, signifies is that the black man has *repossessed* himself in a manner that enables him to enter the kind of relationship disrupted, or foreclosed, by the economics of slavery.

Unlike Sandy Jenkins—doomed forever to passive acquiescence and weekend visitation—Douglass enters a productive relationship promising a new bonding of Afro-American humanity. As a married man, who understands the necessity for *individual* wage earning (i.e., a mastery of the incumbencies of the economics of slavery), Douglass makes his way in the company of his new bride to a "New England factory village" where he quickly becomes a laborer at "the first work, the reward of which was to be entirely my own" [78].

The representation of New Bedford that the *Narrative* provides—with Douglass as wage-earning laborer—seems closely akin to the economic, utopian vision that closes Vassa's account: "Everything looked clean, new, and beautiful. I saw few or no dilapidated houses, with poverty-stricken inmates, no half-naked children and bare-footed women, such as I had been accustomed to see in . . . [Maryland]" [77]. Ships of the best order and finest size, warehouses stowed to their utmost capacity, and ex-slaves "living in finer houses, and evidently enjoying more of the comforts of life, than the average slaveholders in Maryland" complete the splendid panorama. Such a landscape is gained by free, dignified, and individualistic labor—the New England ideal so frequently appearing in Afro-American narratives. (One thinks, for example, of the DuBoisian vision in *The Souls of Black Folk* or of Ralph Ellison's Mr. Norton.[3]) * * * And presiding

3. A wealthy New Englander in Ralph Ellison's novel *Invisible Man* (New York: Random House, 1952) [*editors*].

over the concluding vision in both narratives is the figure of the black, abolitionist spokesman—the man who has arisen, found his "voice," and secured the confidence to address a "general public."

What one experiences in the conclusions of Vassa's and Douglass's narratives, however, is identity with a difference. For the expressive, married, economically astute self at the close of Douglass's work represents a convergence of the voices that mark the various autobiographical postures of the *Narrative* as a whole. The orator whom we see standing at a Nantucket convention at the close of Douglass's work is immediately to become a *salaried* spokesman, combining literacy, Christianity, and revolutionary zeal in an individual and economically profitable job of work. Douglass's authorship, oratory, and economics converge in the history of the *Narrative*'s publication and the course of action its appearance mandated in the life of the author.

Since his identity and place of residence were revealed in the *Narrative*, Douglass, who was still a fugitive when his work appeared, was forced to flee to England. In the United Kingdom, he sold copies of his book for profit, earned lecture fees, and aroused sufficient sympathy and financial support to purchase his freedom with solid currency. While his Garrisonian, abolitionist contemporaries were displeased by Douglass's commercial traffic with slaveholders, the act of purchase was simply the logical (and "traditionally" predictable) end of his negotiation of the economics of slavery.

What is intriguing for a present-day reading of the *Narrative*'s history is the manner in which ideological analysis reveals the black spokesperson's economic conditioning—that is, his necessary encounter with economics signaled by a commercial voice and the implications of this encounter in the domain of narrative transaction. The nineteenth-century slave, in effect, *publicly* sells his voice in order to secure *private* ownership of his voice-person. The ultimate convergence of the *Narrative*'s history is between money and the narrative sign. Exchanging words becomes both a function of commerce and a commercial function. Ideological analysis made available by the archaeology of knowledge, thus, reveals intriguingly commercial dimensions of Afro-American discourse.

DEBORAH E. McDOWELL

In the First Place: Making Frederick Douglass and the Afro-American Narrative Tradition†

* * *

. . . this man
shall be remembered . . .
. . . with lives grown out of his life, the lives
fleshing his dream of the needful, beautiful thing.
—Robert Hayden, "Frederick Douglass"‡

Students of the 1845 *Narrative* commonly designate the following as its key sentence: "You have seen how a man was made a slave, you shall see how a slave was made a man."[1] The clause that follows that pivotal comma—"you shall see how a slave was made a man"—captures with great prescience the focus of much contemporary scholarship on slavery. That focus is studiously on making the slave a man, according to cultural norms of masculinity. This accounts in part, as I will show below, for why Douglass is so pivotal, so mythological a figure. I am not out to argue for any distinction between Douglass "the myth" and Douglass "the man," but rather and simply to view him as a product of history, a construction of a specific time and place, developed in response to a variety of social contingencies and individual desires.

The process and production in literary studies of Douglass as "the first" have paralleled and perhaps been partly fueled by what revisionist historians have made of him. We might go even further to argue that "history" has operated as narrative, in the making of Douglass and his *Narrative*. And so we face constructions upon constructions. While the mythologization of Douglass and this text well antedates the 1960s, 1970s, and 1980s, these decades are especially crucial in efforts to understand this process.

These years were characterized by revisionist mythmaking, much of it prompted by Stanley Elkins's controversial book *Slavery: A*

† From "In the First Place: Making Frederick Douglass and the Afro-American Narrative Tradition," in *Critical Essays on Frederick Douglass*, ed. William L. Andrews (Boston: G. K. Hall, 1991), pp. 195–97, 201–8. Reprinted by permission of the author. Page numbers in brackets refer to this Norton Critical Edition.

‡ Robert Hayden, "Frederick Douglass," in *Collected Poems of Robert Hayden*, ed. Frederick Glaysher (New York: Liveright Publishing Corporation, 1966), p. 62. Copyright © 1966 by Robert Hayden. Reprinted with permission of Liveright Publishing Corporation.

1. Frederick Douglass, *Narrative of the Life of Frederick Douglass, An American Slave, Written by Himself* (New York: Signet/New American Library, 1968), 47. Subsequent references are to this edition and will be indicated in parentheses in the text. I will also make reference to *My Bondage and My Freedom* (New York: Dover, 1969) and *Life and Times of Frederick Douglass, Written by Himself* (New York: Pathway Press, 1941).

Problem in American Institutional and Intellectual Life (1959). I need not rehearse in detail Elkins's now-familiar Sambo thesis emphasizing the effects of black male emasculation in slavery.[2] Historians, armed with a mountain of supporting data, came forth to refute Elkins's data and his thesis. Among the most prominent of these revisionists was John Blassingame, whose *The Slave Community* was rightly celebrated for its attempt to write history from the perspective of slaves, not planters. Blassingame rejects Elkins's Sambo thesis as "intimately related to the planters' projections, desires, and biases,"[3] particularly their desire to be relieved of the "anxiety of thinking about slaves as men."[4]

Blassingame sets out to correct the record to show that the slave was not "half-man," "half-child,"[5] as the Elkins thesis tried to show, but a whole man. Blassingame doesn't simply lapse into the reflexive use of the generic "he," but throughout his study assumes the slave to be literally male, an assumption seen especially in his chapter titled "The Slave Family." There he opens with the straightforward observation: "The Southern plantation was unique in the New World because it permitted the development of a monogamous slave family," which was "one of the most important survival mechanisms for the slave." He continues, "the slave faced almost insurmountable odds in his efforts to build a strong stable family . . . his authority was restricted by his master . . . The master determined when both he and his wife would go to work [and] when or whether his wife cooked his meals." "When the slave lived on the same plantation with his mate he could rarely escape frequent demonstrations of his powerlessness." "Under such a regime," Blassingame adds, "slave fathers often had little or no authority." Despite that, the slave system "recognized the male as the head of the family."[6]

Blassingame is clearly not alone in revising the history of slavery to demonstrate the propensities of slaves toward shaping their lives according to "normative" cultural patterns of marriage and family life. But *The Slave Community* must be seen as a study of the institution that reflects and reproduces the assumptions of a much wider discursive network—scholarly and political—within which the black male is the racial subject.

2. Perhaps as influential as the Elkins book in sparking revisionist histories of slavery was Daniel P. Moynihan's federally commissioned *Moynihan Report: The Case for National Action* (1965). While Elkins virtually ignored black women in his study, attributing the failure of black males to achieve "manhood" to a paternalistic slave system that infantilized them, Moynihan assigns blame to black women for being the predominant heads of household.
3. John Blassingame, *The Slave Community* (New York: Oxford University Press, 1979), xi.
4. Blassingame, *The Slave*, 230.
5. Blassingame, *The Slave*, xi.
6. Blassingame, *The Slave*, 172, 152.

There have been few challenges to this two-decade-long focus on the personality of the male slave. In her book *Ar'n't I a Woman?* (which might have been more aptly titled, "Can a slave be a woman; can a woman be a slave?"), Deborah White critiques the emphasis on negating Samboism, which characterizes so much recent literature on slavery. She argues that "the male slave's 'masculinity' was restored by putting black women in their proper 'feminine' place."[7] bell hooks offers an even stronger critique of this literature, noting eloquently its underlying assumption that "the most cruel and dehumanizing impact of slavery on the lives of black people was that black men were stripped of their masculinity." hooks continues, "To suggest that black men were dehumanized solely as a result of not being able to be patriarchs implies that the subjugation of black women was essential to the black male's development of a positive self-concept, an ideal that only served to support a sexist social order."[8]

While I would not argue that students of Afro-American literature have consciously joined revisionist historians in their efforts to debunk the Elkins thesis, their work can certainly be said to participate in and reinforce these revisionist histories. And what better way to do this than to replace the Sambo myth of childlike passivity with an example of public derring-do, with the myth of the male slave as militant, masculine, dominant, and triumphant in both private and public spheres?[9]

But the Elkins thesis, and the revisionist histories it engendered, are only part of a larger chain of interlocking events that have worked to mythologize Frederick Douglass. These include the demand for African and African-American Studies courses in universities, the publishers who capitalized on that demand, and the academic scholars who completed the chain. A series of individual slave narratives has appeared, along with anthologies and collections of less-popular narratives. The more popular the narrative, the more frequent the editions, and Douglass's 1845 *Narrative* has headed the list since 1960. Scholarly interest in African-American literature has accelerated correspondingly and, again, the 1845 *Narrative* has been premier. Although in his 1977 essay, "Animal Farm

7. Deborah Gray White, *Ar'n't I a Woman* (New York: W. W. Norton, 1985), 22.
8. bell hooks, *Ain't I a Woman* (Boston: South End Press, 1981), 20–21.
9. Ronald Takaki's interpretation is an example of making Douglass a militant. In "Not Afraid to Die: Frederick Douglass and Violence," in *Violence and the Black Imagination* (New York: Capricorn, 1972), Takaki traces Douglass's rise to a political activist who advocated killing for freedom. In a forthcoming essay, "Race, Violence, and Manhood: The Masculine Ideal in Frederick Douglass's 'The Heroic Slave,'" Richard Yarborough discusses Douglass's obsession with manhood in his novella "The Heroic Slave." There manhood was virtually synonymous with militant slave resistance. In the popular realm, Spike Lee's controversial film *Do the Right Thing* is structured according to this ideology of masculinity, which ranks black leaders (assumed to be male) according to their propensities for advocating violence.

Unbound," H. Bruce Franklin could list in a fairly short paragraph critical articles on the 1845 *Narrative*, scarcely more than a decade later the book had stimulated a small industry of scholarship on its own.[1] Thus Douglass's assumed genius as a literary figure is the work of a diverse and interactive collective that includes publishers, editors, and literary critics who have helped to construct his reputation and to make it primary in Afro-American literature.

A major diachronic study of the production, reception, and circulation history of Douglass's 1845 *Narrative* is urgently needed; but even more urgent is the need for a thoroughgoing analysis of the politics of gender at work in that process. One could argue that the politics of gender have been obscured both by the predominance of nonfeminist interpretations of the *Narrative* and by the text itself. In other words, those who have examined it have tended, with few exceptions, to mimic the work of Douglass himself on the question of the feminine and its relation to the masculine in culture.

For example, in his most recent reading of the 1845 *Narrative*, Houston Baker assimilates the text to Marxist language and rhetoric, but a more conventional rhetoric of family resounds. Baker's reading foregrounds the disruption of the slave family and offers the terms of its reunion: economic solvency. "The successful negotiation of such economics," says Baker, "is, paradoxically, the *only* course that provides conditions for a reunification of woman and sable man."[2] He continues, "the African who successfully negotiates his way through the dread exchanges of bondage to the type of expressive posture characterizing *The Life's* conclusion is surely a man who has repossessed himself and, thus, achieved the ability to reunite a severed African humanity."[3] A sign of that self-repossession, Baker argues, is Douglass's "certificate of marriage." "As a married man," he concludes, Douglass "understands the necessity for *individual* wage earning."[4] "In the company of his new bride," he goes to a New England factory village where he participates "creatively in the liberation of his people."[5] This reading's implication in an old patriarchal script requires not a glossing, but an insertion and a backward tracking. However important Douglass's wage-earning capacities as a freeman are, one could say that the prior wage, if you

1. For a bibliographic essay on the various editions of the Douglass narrative as compared to other slave narratives, see Ruth Miller and Peter J. Katopes, "Slave Narratives," and W. Burghardt Turner, "The Polemicists: David Walker, Frederick Douglass, Booker T. Washington, and W. E. B. DuBois," in M. Thomas Inge, Maurice Duke, and Jackson R. Bryer, *Black American Writers: Bibliographical Essays,* Vol. 1 (New York: St. Martin's Press, 1978).
2. Houston Baker, *Blues, Ideology, and Afro-American Literature,* (Chicago: University of Chicago Press, 1984), 38.
3. Baker, *Blues,* 38.
4. Baker, *Blues,* 48.
5. Baker, *Blues,* 49.

will, was Anna Murray's, Douglass's "new bride." A freedwoman, Anna "helped to defray the costs for [Douglass's] runaway scheme by borrowing from her savings and by selling one of her feather beds."[6]

Mary Helen Washington is one of the few critics to insert Anna Murray Douglass into a discussion of the 1845 *Narrative*. She asks, "While our daring Douglass . . . was heroically ascending freedom's arc . . . who . . . was at home taking care of the children?"[7] But such questions are all too rare in discussions of the *Narrative*. Because critical commentary has mainly repeated the text's elision of women, I would like to restore them for the moment, to change the subject of the text from man to woman.

* * *

> For heart of man though mainly right
> Hides many things from mortal sight
> Which seldom ever come to light
> except upon compulsion.
> —Frederick Douglass,
> "What Am I to You"

Frances Foster is one of the few critics to describe the construction in the popular imagination of the slave woman as sexual victim, a pattern she sees in full evidence in male slave narratives. Foster observes a markedly different pattern in slave narratives written by women. Unlike the male narratives, which portray graphically the sexual abuse of slave women by white men, female narratives "barely mention sexual experiences and never present rape or seduction as the most profound aspect of their existence."[8]

The pattern that Foster describes is abundantly evident in all three of Douglass's autobiographies. One can easily argue that, with perhaps the exception of his mother and grandmother, slave women operate almost totally as physical bodies, as sexual victims, "at the mercy," as he notes in *My Bondage and My Freedom* "of the fathers, sons or brothers of [their] master" (60). Though this is certainly true, slave women were just as often at the mercy of the wives, sisters, and mothers of these men, as Harriet Jacobs records in *Incidents in the*

6. Waldo E. Martin, *The Mind of Frederick Douglass* (Chapel Hill: University of North Carolina Press, 1984), 15.
7. Mary Helen Washington, "These Self-Invented Women: A Theoretical Framework for a Literary History of Black Women," *Radical Teacher* (1980), 4. In a recent study David Leverenz also notes that "Douglass's whole sense of latter-day self, in both the *Narrative* and its revision, focuses on manhood; his wife seems an afterthought. He introduces her to his readers as a rather startling appendage to his escape and marries her almost in the same breath." See "Frederick Douglass's Self-Fashioning," in *Manhood and the American Renaissance* (Ithaca: Cornell University Press, 1989), 128.
8. Frances Foster, "'In Respect to Females. . . .' Differences in the Portrayals of Women by Male and Female Narrators," *Black American Literature Forum*, 15 (Summer 1981), 67.

Life of a Slave Girl.[9] But in Douglass's account, the sexual villains are white men and the victims black women. Black men are largely impotent onlookers, condemned to watch the abuse. What Douglass watches and then narrates is astonishing—the whippings of slaves, one after another, in almost unbroken succession.

A scant four pages into the text, immediately following his account of his origins, Douglass begins to describe these whippings in graphic detail. He sees Mr. Plummer, the overseer, "cut and slash the women's heads" and "seem to take great pleasure" in it. He remembers being often awakened by the heart-rending shrieks of his aunt as she is beaten. He sees her "tie[d] up to a joist and whip[ped] upon her naked back till she was literally covered with blood. The louder she screamed, the harder he whipped; and where the blood ran fastest, there he whipped longest. He would whip her to make her scream, and whip her to make her hush; and not until overcome by fatigue, would he cease to swing the blood-clotted cowskin" (25) [15].

Though the whippings of women are not the only ones of which Douglass's *Narrative* gives account, they predominate by far in the text's economy as Douglass looks on. There was Mr. Severe, whom "I have seen . . . whip a woman, causing the blood to run half an hour at the time" (29) [18]. There was his master, who he had seen "tie up a *lame* young woman, and whip her with a heavy cowskin upon her naked shoulders, causing the warm red blood to drip. I have known him to tie her up early in the morning and whip her before breakfast; leave her, go to his store, return at dinner and whip her again, cutting in the places already made raw with his cruel lash" (68–69) [43]. There was Mr. Weeden, who kept the back of a slave woman "literally raw, made so by the lash of this merciless, religious wretch" (87) [56]. As the *Narrative* progresses, the beatings proliferate and the women, no longer identified by name, become absolutized as a bloody mass of naked backs.

What has been made of this recital of whippings? William L. Andrews is one of the few critics to comment on the function of whippings in the text. In a very suggestive reading, he argues that Douglass presents the fact of whipping in "deliberately stylized, plainly rhetorical, recognizably artificial ways." There is nothing masked about this presentation. On the contrary, "Douglass's choice of repetition" is his "chief rhetorical effect." It constitutes his "stylistic signature" and expresses his "performing self." In the whipping passages, Andrews adds, "Douglass calls attention to himself as an

9. See "The Jealous Mistress" chapter in *Incidents in the Life of a Slave Girl.* Even Douglass himself says as much at another point. He notes that the mistress "is ever disposed to find anything to please her; she is never more pleased than when she sees them under the lash" (23).

unabashed artificer, a maker of forms and efforts that recontextualize brute facts according to requirements of self. The freeman requires the freedom to demonstrate the potency of his own inventiveness and the sheer potentiality of language itself for rhetorical manipulation."[1]

However intriguing I find Andrews's reading, I fear that to explain the repetition of whippings solely in rhetorical terms and in the interest of Douglass's self-expression leads to some troubling elisions and rationalizations, perhaps the most troubling elision being the black woman's body. In other words, Douglass's "freedom"—narrative and physical alike—depends on narrating black women's bondage. He achieves his "stylistic signature" by objectifying black women. To be sure, delineating the sexual abuse of black women is a standard convention of the fugitive slave narrative, but the narration of that abuse seems to function beyond the mere requirements of form. A second look at the first recorded beating, his Aunt Hester's, forces out a different explanation. His choice of words in this account—"spectacle," "exhibition"—is instructive, as is his telling admission that, in viewing the beating, he became both "witness and participant" (25) [15].

Critical commentary has focused almost completely on Douglass as witness to slavery's abuses, overlooking his role as participant, an omission that conceals his complex and troubling relationship to slave women, kin and nonkin alike. In calling for closer attention to the narration of whipping scenes, I do not mean to suggest that Douglass's autobiographies were alone among their contemporaries in their obsession with corporal punishment. As Richard Brodhead has observed, "Corporal punishment has been one of the most perennially vexed of questions in American cultural history," and it had its "historical center of gravity in America in the antebellum decades."[2] Both in antislavery literature and in the literature of the American Gothic, what Brodhead calls the "imagination of the lash" was pervasive. That much antislavery literature had strong sexual undercurrents has been well documented. As many critics have observed, much abolitionist literature went beyond an attack on slavery to condemn the South as a vast libidinal playground.

1. William L. Andrews, *To Tell a Free Story: The First Century of Afro-American Autobiography, 1760–1865* (Urbana: U of Illinois P, 1986), p. 134. Valerie Smith also offers an interesting reading of the whippings. They enable the reader to "visualize the blood that masters draw from their slaves . . . Passages such as [Douglass's Aunt Hester's beatings] provide vivid symbols of the process of dehumanization that slaves underwent as their lifeblood was literally sapped" (*Self-Discovery and Authority in Afro-American Narrative* [Cambridge: Harvard UP, 1987], pp. 21–22).
2. Richard Brodhead, "Sparing the Rod: Discipline and Fiction in Antebellum America," *Representations* 21 (Winter 1988), 67. See also David Leverenz, *Manhood and the American Renaissance* for a discussion of beatings in Melville's *Moby Dick* and *White Jacket*, and in *Uncle Tom's Cabin*.

My aim here, then, is not to argue that Douglass's repeated depiction of whipping scenes is in any way unique to him, but rather to submit those scenes to closer scrutiny for their own sake. In other words, the preponderance of this pattern in antebellum literature should not preclude a detailed examination of its representation in a smaller textual sampling. Neither is my aim to psychoanalyze Douglass, nor to offer an "alternative," more "correct" reading, but rather to reveal that Douglass often has more than one voice, one motivation, and one response to his record of black women's abuse in his *Narrative*.

Freud notes in *Beyond the Pleasure Principle* that "repetition, the reexperiencing of something identical, is clearly in itself a source of pleasure."[3] If, as Douglass observes, the slave master derives pleasure from the repeated act of whipping, could Douglass, as observer, derive a vicarious pleasure from the repeated narration of the act? I would say yes. Douglass's repetition of the sexualized scene of whipping projects him into a voyeuristic relation to the violence against slave women, which he watches, and thus he enters into a symbolic complicity with the sexual crime he witnesses. In other words, the spectator becomes voyeur, reinforcing what many feminist film theorists have persuasively argued: sexualization "resides in the very act of looking."[4] Thus "the relationship between viewer and scene is always one of fracture, partial identification, pleasure and distrust."[5]

To be sure, Douglass sounds an urgently and warranted moral note in these passages, but he sounds an erotic one as well that is even more clear if the critical gaze moves from the first autobiography to the second. In a chapter titled "Gradual Initiation into the Mysteries of Slavery," Douglass describes awakening as a child to a slave woman being beaten. The way in which Douglass constructs the scene evokes the familiar male child's initiation into the mysteries of sexuality by peeking through the keyhole of his parents' bedroom:

> My sleeping place was the floor of a little, rough closet, which opened into the kitchen; and through the cracks of its unplaned boards, I could distinctly see and hear what was going on, without being seen by my master. Esther's wrists were firmly tied and the twisted rope was fastened to a strong staple in a heavy wooden joist above, near the fireplace. Here she stood,

3. Sigmund Freud, *Beyond the Pleasure Principle*, Volume 18 of *Standard Edition of the Complete Psychological Works of Sigmund Freud* (London: The Hogarth Press, 1955), 36.
4. Jacqueline Rose, *Sexuality in the Field of Vision* (London: Verso, 1986), 112.
5. Rose, *Sexuality*, 27. See also Laura Mulrey, "Visual Pleasure and Narrative Cinema," *Screen* 16 (Autumn 1975), and Teresa De Lauretis, *Alice Doesn't: Feminism, Semiotics, Cinema* (Bloomington: Indiana University Press, 1984).

on a bench, her arms tightly drawn over her breast. Her back and shoulders were bare to the waist. Behind her stood old master, with cowskin in hand, preparing his barbarous work with all manner of harsh, coarse, and tantalizing epithets. The screams of his victim were most piercing. He was cruelly deliberate, and protracted the torture, as one who was delighted with the scene. Again and again he drew the hateful whip through his hand, adjusting it with a view of dealing the most pain-giving blow. Poor Esther had never yet been severely whipped, and her shoulders were plump and tender. Each blow vigorously laid on, brought screams as well as blood. (87–88).[6]

This passage in all its erotic overtones echoes throughout Douglass's autobiographies and goes well beyond pleasure to embrace its frequent symbiotic equivalent: power. It can be said both to imitate and articulate the pornographic scene, which starkly represents and reproduces the cultural and oppositional relation of the masculine to the feminine, the relation between seer and seen, agent and victim, dominant and dominated, powerful and powerless.[7]

Examining the narration of whipping scenes with regard to the sex of the slave reinforces this gendered division and illustrates its consequences. While the women are tied up—the classic stance of women in pornography—and unable to resist, the men are "free," if you like, to struggle. William Demby is a case in point. After Mr. Gore whips him, Demby runs to the creek and refuses to obey the overseer's commands to come out. Demby finally asserts the power over his own body, even though it costs him his life.

But clearly the most celebrated whipping scene of all is Douglass's two-hour-long fight with Covey, on which the 1845 *Narrative* pivots. Positioned roughly midway through the text, it constitutes also the midway point between slavery and freedom. This explains in part why the fight is dramatized and elaborated over several pages, an allotment clearly disproportionate to other reported episodes. When the fight is over, Douglass boasts that Covey "had drawn no blood from me, but I had from him" and expresses satisfaction at "repell[ing] by force the bloody arm of slavery." He concludes, "I had several fights, but was never whipped" (81–83) [53].

6. Such passages run throughout *My Bondage and My Freedom.* Even in the series of appendices to the text, Douglass keeps his focus riveted on the violation of the slave woman's body. In "Letter to His Old Master" [Thomas Auld], for example, he writes: "When I saw the slave-driver whip a slave-woman, cut the blood out of her neck, and heard her piteous cries, I went away into the corner of the fence, wept and pondered over the mystery." He then asks Auld how he would feel if his daughter were seized and left "unprotected—a degraded victim to the brutal lust of fiendish overseers, who would pollute, blight, and blast the fair soul . . . destroy her virtue, and annihilate in her person all the grace that adorns the character of virtuous womanhood?" (427–28).
7. See Susanne Kappeler, *The Pornography of Representation* (Minneapolis: University of Minnesota, 1986), 104.

The fight with Covey is the part of the *Narrative* most frequently anthologized, and it is a rare critical text indeed that ignores this scene. I agree with Donald Gibson that "most commentators on the conflict have . . . interpreted it as though it were an arena boxing match." Gibson attributes such a view to what he terms the "public focus" of Douglass's narrative, "which requires that the slave defeat the slaveholder."[8] I would add to Gibson's explanation that this defeat serves to incarnate a critical/political view that equates resistance to power with physical struggle, a view that fails to see that such struggle cannot function as the beginning and end of our understanding of power relations.

The critical valorization of physical struggle and subsequent triumph and control finds an interesting parallel in discussion of Douglass's narrative struggles, among the most provocative being that of Robert Stepto in *From Behind the Veil*. In discussing the relation of Douglass's *Narrative* to the "authenticating" texts by William Garrison and Wendell Phillips, Stepto argues that these ancillary texts seem on the surface to be "*at war* with Douglass's tale for authorial control of the narrative as a whole."[9] While Stepto grants that there is a tension among all three documents, Douglass's "tale *dominates* the narrative because it alone authenticates the narrative" (Emphases added).[1]

In examining the issue of authorial control more generally, Stepto argues: "When a narrator wrests this kind of preeminent authorial control from the ancillary voices in the narrative, we may say he controls the presentation of his personal history, and that his tale is becoming autobiographical."[2] He continues, "Authorial control of a narrative need not always result from an author's defeat of competing voices or usurpation of archetypes or pregeneric myths, but is usually occasioned by such acts. What may distinguish one literary history or tradition from another is not the issue of whether such battles occur, but that of who is competing with whom and over what."[3]

This competition for authorial control in African-American letters, Stepto argues, does not conform to the Bloomian oedipal paradigm, for "the battle for authorial control has been more of a race ritual than a case of patricide."[4] Stepto is right to note that competition among African Americans is "rarely between artist and artist," but

8. Donald Gibson, "Reconciling Public and Private in Frederick Douglass's *Narrative*," *American Literature*, 57 (December 1985), 562.
9. Robert Stepto, *From Behind the Veil: A Study of Afro-American Narrative* (Urbana: University of Illinois Press, 1979).
1. Stepto, *From Behind*, 17.
2. Stepto, *From Behind*, 25.
3. Stepto, *From Behind*, 45.
4. Stepto, *From Behind*, 45.

between "artist and authenticator (editor, publisher, guarantor, patron)."[5] Here, of course, Stepto could easily have inserted that these authenticators have generally been white males. Thus the battle for authorial control in Douglass's case was a battle between white and black males.

For Stepto, Douglass's ultimate control rests on his "extraordinary ability to pursue several types of writing with ease and with a degree of simultaneity."[6] But again, the explanation of Douglass's strength depends overmuch on a focus on style emptied of its contents. In other words, what is the "content" of Douglass's "syncretic phrasing," the "introspective analysis," the "participant observations" that make him a master stylist in Stepto's estimation? But, more important, does Douglass's "defeat" of competing white male voices enable him to find a voice distinct from theirs?

Since Douglass's authorial control is the logical outcome of his quest for freedom and literacy, one might approach that question from the angle of the thematics of literacy, of which much has been made by critics. Revealing perhaps more than he knew in the following passage, Douglass describes one of many scenes of stolen knowledge in the *Narrative.* Because his retelling of this episode is all the more suggestive in *My Bondage and My Freedom*, I've selected it instead. "When my mistress left me in charge of the house, I had a grand time; I got Master Tommy's copy books and a pen and ink, and, in the ample spaces between the lines, *I wrote other lines, as nearly like his as possible*" (172, emphasis added).[7]

This hand-to-hand combat between black and white men for physical, then narrative, control over bodies and texts raises the question of who is on whose side? For, in its allegiance to the dialectics of dominance and subordination, Douglass's *Narrative* is, and not surprisingly so, a by-product of Master Tommy's copybook, especially of its gendered division of power relations. The representation of women being whipped, in form and function, is only one major instance of this point but the representation of women, in general, shows Master Tommy's imprint.

Abounding in this copybook are conventional ideas of male subjectivity that exclude women from language. The scenes of reading are again cases in point. Throughout the narrative Douglass employs what Lillie Jugurtha aptly terms "eye dialogue." That is,

5. Stepto, *From Behind*, 45.
6. Stepto, *From Behind*, 20.
7. Compare this passage with the same scene in the 1845 *Narrative:* "When left thus, I used to spend the time in writing in the spaces left in Master Thomas's copy-book, copying what he had written. I continued to do this until I could write a hand very similar to that of Master Thomas. Thus, after a long, tedious effort of years, I finally succeeded in learning how to write" (58) [37].

he presents personal exchanges that have the appearance of dialogue without being dialogue. In the following account, Douglass describes the scene in which Mrs. Auld is ordered to cease teaching Frederick to read:

> Mr. Auld found out what was going on, and at once forbade Mrs. Auld to instruct me further, telling her, among other things, that it was unlawful, as well as unsafe, to teach a slave to read. To use his own words . . . he said, "If you give a nigger an inch, he will take an ell. . . . Learning would spoil the best nigger in the world . . . if you teach that nigger (speaking of myself) how to read, there would be no keeping him. It would forever unfit him to be a slave. He would at once become unmanageable, and of no value to his master. As to himself, it would do him no good, but a great deal of harm. It would make him discontented and unhappy." (49) [30–31]

In glossing this passage, Jugurtha perceptively notices that "there is no second speaker presented here, no Lucretia Auld responding to her husband . . . One pictures, though one does not hear, a husband and a wife talking . . . Unobtrusively, perspectives are multiplied. Monologue functions as dialogue."[8] That Sophia Auld was regarded by Douglass early on as a substitute mother figure, links her erasure in the foregoing passage to the erasure of his biological mother in the first part of the 1845 *Narrative* and, by extension, to the erasure of the feminine. In this secular rewriting of the sacred text, Mrs. Auld is exiled from the scene of knowledge, of symbolic activity. As a woman she is not permitted "to teach or to have authority over men; she is to keep silent" (I Timothy 2:11–12). What critics have learned from and done with Douglass has often constituted a correspondingly mimetic process where the feminine is concerned. In other words, the literary and interpretive history of the *Narrative* has, with few exceptions, repeated with approval its salient assumptions and structural paradigms. This repetition has, in turn, created a potent and persistent critical language that positions and repositions Douglass on top, that puts him in a position of priority. This ordering has not only helped to establish the dominant paradigm of African-American criticism, but it has also done much to establish the dominant view of African-American literary history. In that view, Douglass is, to borrow from James Olney, "the founding father" who "produced a kind of Ur-text of slavery and freedom that, whether individual writers were conscious of imitat-

8. Lillie Jugurtha, "Point of View in the Afro-American Slave Narratives by Douglass and Pennington," in John Sekora and Darwin Turner, eds., *The Art of Slave Narrative* (Western Illinois University, 1982), 113.

ing Douglass or not, would inform the Afro-American literary tradition from his time to the present."[9]

* * *

It is this choice of Douglass as "the first," as "representative man," as the part that stands for the whole, that reproduces the omission of women from view, except as afterthoughts different from "the same" (black men). And that omission is not merely an oversight, but given the discursive system that authorizes Douglass as the source and the origin, that omission is a necessity. But if, as [Edward] Said suggests, "'beginning' is an eminently renewable subject,"[1] then we can begin again. We can begin to think outside the model that circumscribes an entire literary history into a genetic model and conscripts Douglass in the interest of masculine power and desire. In other words, we might start by putting an end to beginnings, even those that would put woman in the first place.

JEANNINE MARIE DeLOMBARD

[Eye-Witness to the Cruelty][†]

* * *

The development of the slave narrative as a new genre of literature made African Americans' personal stories of slavery indispensable to the court of public opinion. The argument of Jane Johnson's lawyer that "no one is so competent to satisfy the Court" as the former slave and that "her declaration is the best evidence attainable, all others being but secondary" echoed the similar claims with which abolitionist editors had introduced slave narratives as the most powerful "evidence" they presented in their case against Southern slaveholders. In his preface to the first slave narrative published by the AASS, the *Narrative of James Williams* (1838), Quaker poet John Greenleaf Whittier opened his discussion of Southern inhumanity by citing "the testimony and admissions of slave-holders," which he acknowledged were "only [those] of the . . . wrong-doer himself" and must therefore be "partial and

9. Olney, "The Founding Fathers—Frederick Douglass and Booker T. Washington" in Deborah E. McDowell and Arnold Rampersad, eds., *Slavery and the Literary Imagination* (Baltimore: Johns Hopkins, 1989), 81.
1. Edward Said, *Beginnings: Intention and Method* (New York: Columbia University Press, 1985), 38.
† From Jeannine Marie DeLombard, *Slavery on Trial* (Chapel Hill: U of North Carolina P, 2007), pp. 109–23. Page numbers in brackets refer to this Norton Critical Edition.

incomplete."[1] He insisted that "for a full revelation of the secrets of the prison-house, we must look to the slave himself."[2] The representation of the former slave as testifying witness quickly became a staple of abolitionist discourse. A decade later, Henry Watson, who had been enslaved in Virginia and Mississippi, authorized his *Narrative* (1848) by reflecting that "twenty-six years, the prime of my life, had passed away in slavery, I having witnessed it in all its forms."[3] By the end of the period, fugitive slave J. H. Banks would emblazon the title page of his *Narrative* (1861) with the slogan, "I am a witness against American slavery and all its horrors," and Harriet A. Jacobs would preface *Incidents in the Life of a Slave Girl* by expressing a desire "to add [her] testimony to that of abler pens to convince the people of the Free States what Slavery really is."[4]

Although the *Narrative of the Life of Frederick Douglass, an American Slave* was one of many slave narratives that appeared during the antebellum period, from the beginning of his career, Douglass stood as the apotheosis of the slave witness. An abolitionist who reported on Douglass's first speech before an interracial audience put it this way in the *National Anti-Slavery Standard*: having long "indulged the hope that . . . we might have some repentant slaveholder, or powerful slave to testify 'that which they themselves did know,'" the reformers found that the "morning of the 12th instant fulfilled our hopes. One, recently from the house of bondage, spoke with great power. Flinty hearts were pierced, and cold ones melted by his eloquence. Our best pleaders for the slave held their breath for fear of interrupting him. . . . It seemed almost miraculous how he had been prepared to tell his story with so much power."[5] When, four years later, this same "powerful slave" published his *Narrative*, he recounted the acts of silent witnessing that had "prepared [him] to tell his story with so much power" before the court of public opinion. In the process, he provided the abolitionist movement, in critic John Sekora's astute formulation, "not so much a life story as an indictment, an anti-slavery document, the testimony of an eyewitness, precisely what Garrison sought."[6] For,

1. James Williams, *Narrative of James Williams: An American Slave, Who Was for Several Years a Driver on a Cotton Plantation in Alabama*, ed. John Greenleaf Whittier (New York: American Anti-Slavery Society; Boston: Isaac Knapp, 1838), pp. vii, xvi, xvii.
2. Ibid., xvii.
3. Henry Watson, *Narrative of Henry Watson, a Fugitive Slave* (Boston: Bela Marsh, 1848), 38.
4. Jourden H. Banks, *A Narrative of Events of the Life of J. H. Banks, an Escaped Slave, from the Cotton State, Alabama, in America*, ed. James W. C. Pennington (Liverpool: M. Rourke, Printer, 1861). Harriet A. Jacobs, *Incidents in the Life of a Slave Girl. Written by Herself*, ed. Lydia Maria Child (Boston: Published for the Author, 1861), 1–2.
5. *National Anti-Slavery Standard*, 26 Aug. 1841, qtd. in Gregory P. Lampe, *Frederick Douglass: Freedom's Voice, 1818–1845* (East Lansing: Michigan State UP, 1998), 61.
6. John Sekora, "'Mr. Editor, If You Please': Frederick Douglass, My Bondage and My Freedom, and the End of the Abolitionist Imprint." *Callaloo* 17:2 (Spring, 1994): 620.

in addition to its well-known portrayal of the journey from slavery to freedom as a passage from South to North, from brute to man, from illiteracy to authorship, and from damnation to salvation, Douglass's *Narrative* also depicts the transition from thralldom to liberty in juridical terms, as a move from silent victimization to defiant testimony.

Scholars of the genre have frequently noted how slave narratives drew on vivid forensic images to inspire white, Northern audiences to take action against slavery.[7] Others have demonstrated that such vicarious witnessing risked substituting cathartic complacency for action while tacitly reinforcing legal restrictions on slave testimony, either by allowing imaginative white identification to obscure actual black suffering or by endowing the mute, abject body of the slave with superlative evidentiary authority.[8] As important as these analyses have been in heightening critical appreciation for the rhetorical challenges facing formerly enslaved authors, the discussion has tended to focus on the responses of white audiences to portrayals of black suffering. By contrast, the reading of Douglass's *Narrative* offered here stresses not so much the transactional qualities of the ex-slave's witnessing but, instead, examines how the author's testimonial stance modeled a new form of black discursive and civic authority in the interstices of American law and antebellum print culture.[9]

As suggested in the previous chapter, the rhetorical decriminalization of the black subject in Jacksonian print culture seemingly necessitated that subject's virtually simultaneous rhetorical victimization as the surest means of detaching crime from race in order to authorize extralegal black testimony to white crimes. But even as the role of testifying eyewitness may have appeared to offer an opening wedge for broader black civic participation, the position of victim, like that of criminal, was a precarious one from which to

7. On the forensic image and its effects, see Kathy Eden, *Poetic and Legal Fiction in the Aristotelian Tradition* (Princeton: Princeton UP, 1986), 78–83, 90. On readers as vicarious witnesses in the slave narrative, see William L. Andrews, *To Tell a Free Story: The First Century of Afro-American Autobiography, 1760–1865* (Urbana: U of Illinois P, 1986), 134–38; John Carlos Rowe, "Between Politics and Poetics: Frederick Douglass and Postmodernity," *Reconstructing American Literary and Historical Studies*, eds. Gunter H. Lenz, Hartmut Keil, and Sabine Brock-Sallah (Frankfurt: Campus, 1990), 203–4; P. Gabrielle Foreman, "Sentimental Abolition in Douglass's Decade: Revision, Erotic Conversion, and Politics of Witnessing in Frederick Douglass's 'Heroic Slave' and My Bondage and My Freedom," *Sentimental Men: Masculinity and the Politics of Affect in American Culture*, eds. Mary Chapman and Glenn Hendler (Berkeley: U of California P, 1999).

8. See Philip Fisher, *Hard Facts: Setting and Form in the American Novel* (New York: Oxford UP, 1985), 103–22; Saidiya V. Hartman, *Scenes of Subjection: Terror, Slavery, and Self-making in Nineteenth-century America* (New York: Oxford UP, 1997), 17–23.

9. On the criminal trial as "a forum for narrative transactions," see Paul Gewirtz, "Victims and Voyeurs at the Criminal Trial," *Faculty Scholarship Series*. Paper 1707. (1996): 135–49.

assert civic agency, much less autonomous legal personhood.[1] In the court of law, the authority of witnesses is grounded in their corporeal experience: they gain a hearing on the basis of what they may have seen or heard. In the antebellum court of public opinion, the authority of slave witnesses was doubly predicated on their corporeality, in that they testified to the violence they had personally suffered or had seen inflicted on other pained, black bodies.[2] As Sánchez-Eppler has demonstrated, if slaves gained a hearing at the popular tribunal at the very moment when there appeared "a crack in the hegemonic rhetoric of political disembodiment" that had situated "authority" in "the impossible position of the universal and hence bodiless subject," they did so at the behest of "a political movement and a literature" that strove "to speak the body, but that in so representing the body" also "exploit[ed] and limit[ed] it."[3] The era's most self-conscious print construction of the slave as witness, Douglass's *Narrative*, probes this discursive dilemma by demonstrating how the seemingly liberating authority of the fugitive's testimony can only be sustained through ongoing association with the slave's definitive physical abjection.[4] A possible resolution to this dilemma appears in the *Narrative*'s final lines, with the introduction of the figure of the black advocate.

The *Narrative* charts the development of its author's testimonial authority by presenting three incidents of Southern violence in which the slave Frederick Bailey is "doomed to be a witness and a participant."[5] As Frederick grows from passive, silent, terrorized witness of legally sanctioned violence against other slaves into a brutalized victim who seeks but is denied legal redress, the *Narrative* charts the increasing incommensurability of the young slave's maturing civic consciousness with his legal status as human property. The story culminates with the fugitive's public antislavery testimony in the North—and, implicitly, with his published testimony in the *Narrative* itself—thereby figuring the court of public opinion as an alternative to the court of law as a forum for African American civic participation.

1. Hartman, *Scenes*, 101. See also Gewirtz, "Victims."
2. On rhetorics of corporeality in the slavery debate, see Steven Mailloux, "Re-Marking Slave Bodies: Rhetoric as Production and Reception," *Philosophy and Rhetoric* 35.2 (2001): 96–119.
3. Karen Sánchez-Eppler, *Touching Liberty: Abolition, Feminism, and the Politics of the Body* (Berkeley: U of California P, 1997), 1, 3, 8. For a complication of this point, see Russ Castronovo, *Necro Citizenship: Death, Eroticism, and the Public Sphere in the Nineteenth-Century United States* (Durham: Duke UP, 2001), 64.
4. For a similar conclusion regarding Douglass's engagement with Scottish Common Sense philosophy, see Maurice S. Lee, *Slavery, Philosophy, and American Literature: 1830–1860* (Cambridge: Cambridge UP, 2010), 93–132.
5. Douglass, *Narrative*, [15].

The *Narrative*'s editorial apparatus indicates that to be a Southern slave is not only to be denied physical autonomy, forced to perform backbreaking labor, and subjected to arbitrary violence but also to be a silent witness to such suffering. Garrison, playing his part of abolitionist advocate, focuses his opening argument on the laws mandating the silence of Southern slaves. Although similar laws limiting the admissibility of African American testimony existed in the North, Garrison's comments locate both violence and silence exclusively in the South.[6] Noting that "Mr. DOUGLASS has frankly disclosed . . . the names . . . of those who committed the crimes which he has alleged against them," Garrison quickly asserts, "Let it never be forgotten, that no slaveholder or overseer can be convicted of any outrage perpetrated on the person of a slave, however diabolical it may be, on the testimony of colored witnesses, whether bond or free. By the slave code, they are adjudged to be as incompetent to testify against a white man, as though they were indeed a part of the brute creation."[7] Alluding to Douglass's narrative allegation of slaveholders' "crimes" enables Garrison to expose the inadequacy of American law, which by rendering such testimony inadmissible effectively denies the criminality of such outrages. In a society in which "there is no legal protection in fact, whatever there may be in form, for the slave population; and any amount of cruelty may be inflicted upon them with impunity," the abolitionist editor appeals to popular legal consciousness by presenting the former slave's printed "testimony" to the court of public opinion as a corrective to both the legal sanction for slavery and the exclusion of African Americans from full participation in American law.[8]

In the "Letter from Wendell Phillips, Esq." that follows Garrison's introduction, the celebrated abolitionist lawyer and orator acknowledges to Douglass the absence of legal protection for fugitive slaves in the North: "The whole armory of Northern Law has no shield for you."[9] Nevertheless, Phillips suggests that in the abolitionist community of the North, Douglass "may tell [his] story in safety," anticipating that "some time or other, the humblest may stand in our streets, and bear witness in safety against the cruelties of which he has been the victim."[1] Together, Garrison and Phillips imply that if in the South, the speech of a slave witness is deferred indefinitely, in the North, witnessing and testimony can be reunited in

6. For Northern restrictions on African American testimony, see Jane H. Pease and William H. Pease, *They Who Would Be Free: Blacks' Search for Freedom, 1830–1861* (New York: Atheneum, 1974), 156–58.
7. Douglass, *Narrative*, [9].
8. Ibid., [9].
9. Ibid., [12].
1. Ibid.

the extralegal court of public opinion. In the South, enslaved eyes see black bodies beaten, whipped, raped, and murdered, but enslaved tongues remain silent; in the North, not only are African American eyes freed from witnessing such horrors, but African American tongues are free to testify against what Garrison refers to as "that crime of crimes,—making man the property of his fellow-man."[2] It is by testifying to the crimes he himself has endured or has witnessed his fellow bondspeople suffering, Garrison and Phillips suggest, that the fugitive slave attains true liberation.

Douglass's *Narrative* reinforces the abolitionist association of the South with silence. Young Frederick, lacking a legal record of his birth, quells his desire to ask his master for information on this point, knowing that "he deemed all such inquiries on the part of the slave improper and impertinent."[3] Similarly, Colonel Lloyd's long-suffering stablemen mutely attend their master's unfair harangues, for, "to all these complaints, no matter how unjust, the slave must never answer a word"; the place of the slave is not to speak but to "stand, listen, and tremble."[4] The fact that those who broke this code of silence were punished with beating and sale, Douglass explains, "had the effect to establish among the slaves the maxim, that a still tongue makes a wise head."[5]

The Maryland plantation's pervasive silence is broken by the inarticulate screams of tortured slaves, screams that are met with yet more silence.[6] In the *Narrative*'s first portrayal of Southern violence, Frederick receives his initiation into slavery through an act of witnessing. One of the most frequently quoted scenes in the *Narrative* describes how as a young boy Frederick witnessed the flogging of his Aunt Hester by their master, Captain Anthony:

> I have often been awakened at the dawn of day by the most heart-rending shrieks of an own aunt of mine, whom he used to tie up to a joist, and whip upon her naked back till she was literally covered with blood. No words, no tears, no prayers, from his gory victim, seemed to move his iron heart from its bloody

2. Ibid., [8].
3. Ibid., [13].
4. Ibid., [22].
5. Ibid., [23]. On Jacobs's treatment of these themes, see Deborah M. Garfield, "Earwitness: Female Abolitionism, Sexuality, and Incidents in the life of a Slave Girl," *Harriet Jacobs and Incidents in the Life of a Slave Girl*, eds. Deborah M. Garfield and Rafia Zafar (Cambridge: Cambridge UP, 1996). For a persuasive reading of Jacobs's silence as "a rejection of both the attestatory position of slave narrators and the seductive one typical of white women's romances" with reference to contract law, see Carla Kaplan, "Narrative Contracts and Emancipatory Readers," *Yale Journal of Criticism* 6:1 (Spring 1993): 97.
6. Significantly, Douglass portrays the slaves who sing tragically expressive songs as in transit, "on their way" from one of the many "out-farms" to "the home plantation," Great House Farm (*Narrative*, [19]).

> purpose. The louder she screamed, the harder he whipped. . . . He would whip her to make her scream, and whip her to make her hush. . . . I remember the first time I ever witnessed this horrible exhibition. I was quite a child, but I well remember it. I never shall forget it whilst I remember any thing. It was the first of a long series of such outrages, of which I was doomed to be a witness and a participant. It struck me with awful force. It was the blood-stained gate, the entrance to the hell of slavery, through which I was about to pass. It was a most terrible spectacle. I wish I could commit to paper the feelings with which I beheld it.[7]

From the beating of his Aunt Hester, Frederick learns that to be a slave is to be a silent "witness" to arbitrary yet authorized cruelty against one's friends and family. Indeed, his aunt's whipping, "awaken[ing]" him "at the dawn of day," opens Frederick's eyes to the meaning of slavery and establishes his position early in the *Narrative* as an eyewitness to its cruelty. This episode represents the "blood-stained gate, the entrance to the hell of slavery," because previously Frederick had lived with his maternal grandmother "out of the way of the bloody scenes that often occurred on the plantation" and therefore "had never seen any thing like it before."[8] Underscoring the *Narrative*'s persistent association of authorship with the visual through the homonym "scene"/"seen," Douglass suggests that this first act of witnessing introduces Frederick not only to his slave identity but also to the embodied subjectivity that is inherent in the role of the slave witness.[9] Douglass's account of Frederick's frightened response to the bloody scene of his aunt's whipping vividly emphasizes the enslaved witness's physical vulnerability: "I was so terrified and horror-stricken at the sight, that I hid myself in a closet, and dared not venture out till long after the bloody transaction was over."[1] Seeing violence inflicted on the body of another, the young slave instinctively hides his own vulnerable African American body. That the body Frederick sees whipped is a female one is not insignificant, for not only does this scene introduce the young slave to the identification of blackness with abject corporeality

7. Ibid., [15–16]. On critical treatments of this scene, see Deborah McDowell, "In the First Place: Making Frederick Douglass & the Afro-American Narrative Tradition," *Critical Essays on Frederick Douglass*, ed. William L. Andrews (Boston: G. K. Hall, 1991), 201–4; Hartman, *Scenes*, 3.
8. Douglass, *Narrative*, [15, 16].
9. On the slave's embodied subjectivity, see Sidonie Smith, *Identity, and the Body: Women's Autobiographical Practices in the Twentieth Century* (Bloomington: Indiana University Press, 1993), 5–17. See also Sánchez-Eppler, *Touching*, 1–10.
1. Douglass, *Narrative*, [16]. On the economic implications of this "bloody transaction," see Priscilla Wald, *Constituting Americans: Cultural Anxiety and Narrative Form* (Durham: Duke UP, 1995), 81; Houston A. Baker, Jr., *Blues, Ideology, and Afro-American Literature: A Vernacular Theory* (Chicago: University of Chicago, 1984), 39–55.

under slavery, but also it demonstrates how the feminization of blackness serves to ungender and thus to dehumanize the enslaved male body.[2] The terror is that as interchangeable commodities, one brutalized slave can stand in for another—that young Frederick can and will replace Aunt Hester at the joist.[3] As Douglass suggests, in the context of slavery, to observe such violence is to be "doomed to be" *both* "a witness and a participant."

Minimizing the distinction between witnessing and participating in Southern violence, the account of Aunt Hester's beating maximizes the gap between witnessing and testimony. This first witnessing scene, which Douglass characterizes as an "exhibition" and a "spectacle," establishes the separation of the visual from the verbal that will characterize subsequent representations of Southern violence in the *Narrative.* Unlike later scenes, this one is notable for its noisiness. We should note, however, that Aunt Hester's vocalizations are incoherent "shrieks" and "screams"; her more articulate "words" and "prayers" are negated by their ineffectuality and, in the text, by the anaphoric "no" that precedes these terms. Far from putting an end to the violence of slavery—the goal of black testimony in the North—the slave's inarticulate utterances only seem to provoke more violence in the South: "The louder she screamed, the harder he whipped."

Just as the shared experience of enslavement and physical vulnerability unites young Frederick with his aunt, the incapacity for coherent verbal expression that violence fosters links the adult Douglass with the abused slave woman. For although the author breaks Frederick's silence by describing Aunt Hester's flogging, he nevertheless implies that in this instance, the very act of witnessing precludes speech well after the event itself has passed; even the famously articulate Douglass cannot "commit to paper the feelings" with which he beheld this violent scene.[4] Here the trauma of

2. Robyn Wiegman, *American Anatomies: Theorizing Race and Gender* (Durham: Duke UP, 1995), 67. On the passage's psychosexual overtones, see Albert Stone, "Identity and Art in Frederick Douglass's Narrative," *Critical Essays on Frederick Douglass*, ed. William Andrews (Boston: G. K. Hall, 1991), 69; Eric J. Sundquist, *To Wake the Nations: Race in the Making of American Literature* (Cambridge: Belknap-Harvard UP, 1993), 99; Jenny Franchot, "The Punishment of Esther: Frederick Douglass and the Construction of the Feminine," *Frederick Douglass: New Literary and Historical Essays*, ed. Eric Sundquist (New York: Cambridge UP, 1990); Foreman, "Sentimental Abolition," 197–99. On the gendered implications of the abolitionist positioning of the former slave as slavery's eyewitness, see Jeannine DeLombard, "'Eye-Witness to the Cruelty': Southern Violence and Northern Testimony in Frederick Douglass's 1845 Narrative," *American Literature* 73:2 (2001): 250–51 and "Adding Her Testimony: Harriet Jacobs' Incidents as Testimonial Literature," *Multiculturalism: Roots and Realities*, ed. C. James Trotman (Bloomington: Indiana UP, 2002), 30–48.
3. See Hartman, *Scenes*, 11. See also Stephen M. Best, *The Fugitive's Properties: Law and the Poetics of Possession* (Chicago: U of Chicago P, 2004), 1–98.
4. Attuned to this scene's juridical overtones, Wald notes, "Douglass . . . participates in the scene by witnessing it, in the active sense of testifying rather than the more passive

witnessing threatens to overwhelm the ability to testify; the visual threatens to exceed, and thereby to suppress, the verbal. The remaining "bloody scenes," then, chart Frederick's quest to gain a hearing for his eyewitness testimony against slavery as well as Douglass's growing determination to "commit to paper" his increasingly detailed testimonial account of Southern violence. For it is only through such extralegal print testimony, the *Narrative* implies, that the black subject will be able to assert the civic identity denied to him as a slave.

The *Narrative*'s second witnessing scene powerfully illustrates how the act of observing violence against other slaves reinforces both the silence and the embodied subjectivity of the witnessing self through the logic of the slave's fungibility as a commodity.[5] Douglass describes how an overseer, aptly named Mr. Gore, shoots and kills the slave Demby for openly resisting punishment. In the middle of a whipping by Gore, Douglass explains, Demby had broken free and "plunged himself into a creek, and stood there at the depth of his shoulders, refusing to come out."[6] Warned that if he does not leave the water after three calls, he will be shot, Demby refuses, and Gore carries out his threat. As in his account of Aunt Hester's flogging, here Douglass emphasizes the scene's spectatorial aspect. The deliberate, dramatic pace at which it unfolds ("The first call was given. Demby made no response . . ." etc.) climaxes with the repressed reaction of the slaves forced to be passive witnesses to this violence: "A thrill of horror flashed through every soul upon the plantation."[7] And just as watching his Aunt Hester's whipping introduces young Frederick to his own physical vulnerability, Gore's murder of Demby is explicitly intended as an object lesson to the enslaved onlookers.[8] When asked by Frederick's master "why he resorted to this extraordinary expedient," Gore replies that Demby "was setting a dangerous example to the other slaves,—one which, if suffered to pass . . . would finally lead to the total subversion of all rule and order upon the plantation," for "if one slave refused to be corrected, and escaped with his life, the other slaves would soon copy the example; the result of which would be, the freedom

observing," thereby "bring[ing] the scene before a public whom he hopes to turn into a jury" (*Constituting*, 81). Although Douglass's testimonial writing represents a narrative intervention that encourages us to read Frederick's involvement as "a witness and a participant" in his aunt's whipping as an act of resistance rather than complicity, in this scene Douglass stresses young Frederick's passivity as a witness in order to emphasize the bifurcation of the visual and the verbal in the South. See also Foreman, "Sentimental Abolition," 196–98.

5. See Hartman, *Scenes*, 7–8.
6. Douglass, *Narrative*, [25].
7. Ibid., [25].
8. As Wiegman notes, complicating Foucault, nineteenth- and twentieth-century U.S. technologies of race combine spectacle and surveillance in the sense that specularity reinforces panopticism (*American*, 37–42). See also Hartman, *Scenes*, 7–8.

of the slaves, and the enslavement of the whites."[9] Demby's body serves as a surrogate for those of his fellow slaves: if that body is recalcitrant, the entire corporate body of the slaves will become resistant, resulting in a cataclysmic reversal of racial power relations. If, however, that body is successfully subdued through exemplary violence, the enslaved collective will become tractable, and plantation order will be preserved. As Gore understands, in the context of Southern slavery, to witness brutality is to experience it vicariously. The logic of Gore's monitory murder of Demby rests on the equation of the roles of "witness" and "participant," an equation that in turn rests on both the witness's physical vulnerability and the slave's commodity status.

In this second violent scene, Douglass emphasizes that in the South, black witnessing must always be silent. Noting that "the guilty perpetrator of one of the bloodiest and most foul murders goes unwhipped of justice, and uncensured by the community in which he lives," Douglass explains that Mr. Gore's "horrid crime was not even submitted to judicial investigation" because "it was committed in the presence of slaves, and they of course could neither institute a suit, nor testify against him."[1] The enforced silence of the slave witnesses means that just as the material evidence of Gore's crime is rendered invisible by the physical setting in which it occurs (Demby's "mangled body sank out of sight," the creek's running water "marked" only temporarily by his "blood and brains"), any testimonial evidence of Demby's murder is similarly effaced by the legal environment of the South, in which white violence evaporates in a haze of black silence.[2]

Even as Douglass's account of Demby's murder once again calls attention to the persistent separation of the seen from the said under slavery, however, it serves to narrow the gap between witnessing and testimony in the *Narrative.* Like the other terrorized slaves on Colonel Lloyd's plantation, Frederick is as powerless to take legal action against Demby's murderer as he is to intervene in the murder itself. An important distinction, however, sets this scene apart from the one in which he witnesses his Aunt Hester's flogging. Here, although the young slave is once again silenced by the trauma of witnessing, the adult fugitive is not. Unable to "institute a suit or testify against" Gore in a court of law, Douglass redresses Frederick's silence and that of the other enslaved witnesses with his retrospective print incrimination of the "guilty perpetrator": he thus exposes the murderous overseer before the court of public opinion

9. Douglass, *Narrative,* [25].
1. Ibid.
2. Ibid.

with his extralegal testimony that "Mr. Gore lived in St. Michael's, Talbot county, Maryland, when I left there; and if he is still alive, he very probably lives there now."[3] Following the *Narrative*'s trajectory from slavery in the South to freedom in the North, this scene places the narrator one step closer to the latter by associating him not only with the visual, as a frightened witness to Southern violence, but also with the verbal, as one prepared to give detailed factual testimony against the perpetrators of such violence. Appropriating the language of the jettisoned "judicial investigation," Douglass endows his enslaved self a legal consciousness that belies his property status as a "nigger"—"worth a half-cent to kill . . . and a half-cent to bury."[4]

Critics of the *Narrative* have traditionally stressed the structural and thematic importance of another violent scene, Frederick's fight with the slave-breaker Covey. Douglass himself highlights the encounter with his acclaimed chiasmus: "You have seen how a man was made a slave; you shall see how a slave was made a man."[5] This observation, together with Frederick's vow that "the white man who expected to succeed in whipping, must also succeed in killing me," appears to signal his achievement of masculinity, maturity, and physical autonomy and, therefore, to represent his symbolic emancipation.[6] But, as Douglass himself points out, Frederick "remained a slave for four years afterwards," encouraging us to read this scene not as the *Narrative*'s turning point but, like Frederick's earlier attainment of literacy, one of many steps on "the pathway from slavery to freedom."[7]

Instead of prefacing Frederick's liberating flight to the North, the fight with Covey introduces the abortive escape attempt that in turn brings Frederick into his first direct contact with law. Far from censuring the plantation justice represented by Covey's violence, the court of law effectively extends it by reinforcing legal restrictions on slave speech. When the would-be runaways are caught in their escape attempt, Henry literally eats Frederick's words by consuming in a biscuit the pass he had forged. Next, Frederick urges Henry to "own nothing."[8] Repeating the phrase twice more, Douglass writes, "And we passed the word around,

3. Ibid.
4. Ibid., [27].
5. Ibid., [49].
6. Ibid., [53]. See Jon-Christian Suggs, *Whispered Consolations: Law and Narrative in African-American Life* (Ann Arbor: U of Michigan P, 2000), 61; David Leverenz, *Manhood and the American Renaissance* (Ithaca: Cornell UP, 1989), 108–34; Franchot, "Punishment," 154; Richard Yarborough, "Race, Violence, and Manhood: The Masculine Ideal in Frederick Douglass's 'The Heroic Slave.'" *Frederick Douglass: New Literary and Historical Essays*, ed. Eric Sundquist (New York: Cambridge UP, 1990), 166–67.
7. Douglass, *Narrative*, [53, 31].
8. Ibid., [63].

'*Own nothing*;' and '*Own nothing*!' said we all."[9] Playing on the dual meaning of the verb "to own," as "to admit" and "to possess," Douglass's repetition alerts us to how silence mediates the slave's civic exclusion. As objects of property who literally can "own nothing," and especially not the property in whiteness through which to claim the procedural rights that will allow their speech to be exculpatory rather than incriminatory, Frederick and his comrades seek refuge in silence.[1] Due to the slave's double character, all he or she can "own," it would seem, is guilt. Under Southern law, the slave's testimonial speech can only be an admission of guilt, whether one's own or that of another slave. (And indeed, Douglass reports, "We found the evidence against us to be the testimony of one person," clearly an enslaved "informant.")[2] Thus, when the runaways "reached St. Michael's, [they] underwent a sort of examination"—Douglass's language here signaling that slaves were subject to a very different "sort" of legal proceeding than whites—in which the captured fugitives deny any intention to abscond.[3] When the slaves briefly break their silence, their few words are strategic rather than expressive: Frederick and his co-conspirators speak "more to bring out the evidence against" them "than from any hope of getting clear of being sold," the standard punishment for runaways.[4] The episode ends not with Frederick "safe in a land of freedom" as he had hoped but, rather, held fast by Southern slave law, immured "within the walls of a stone prison."[5] In the very next paragraph, however, Frederick's unexpected release returns him to Baltimore, where, in keeping with the *Narrative*'s testimonial trajectory, the book reaches its climax when an injury to the slave's eye propels his escape from Southern brutality, silence, and law.

As the final instance of violence Douglass recounts in the *Narrative*, this critically neglected scene depicts a crisis of witnessing that cannot be resolved in the South. Frederick, working as an apprentice in a racially mixed Fells Point shipyard, struggles to obey the journeymen carpenters' often conflicting orders. But when four armed white apprentices gang up on him, Frederick, keeping "the vow [he] made after the fight with Mr. Covey," fights back and is beaten badly.[6] He recounts his experience to his master, who immediately takes him to an attorney with the intention of suing his attackers, only to discover that blacks can neither institute a

9. Ibid.
1. See Cheryl I. Harris, "Whiteness as Property," *Harvard Law Review* 106:8 (1993): 1707–91.
2. Douglass, *Narrative*, [64].
3. Ibid.
4. Ibid.
5. Ibid., [65].
6. Ibid., [66].

suit nor testify against whites in a court of law. Significantly, this scene, which calls attention to the physical vulnerability and silence inherent in Frederick's role as an "eye-witness to the cruelty" of Southern violence, directly precedes the chapter in which Douglass recounts how Frederick "planned, and finally succeeded in making, [his] escape from slavery."[7]

Like the fight with Covey, the shipyard beating differs from the other bloody scenes in the *Narrative* in that Frederick, no longer merely a witness to the violence inflicted on the enslaved black body, becomes its direct target. In contrast to the Covey episode, however, this experience produces in Frederick a heightened awareness of the inescapability of the slave's embodied subjectivity. As the shipyard beating and its sequel suggest, it is precisely this definitive corporeality that denies the slave witness the right to testify against that violence, making it impossible for him to fulfill his civic responsibilities in the South. Frederick's eye injury represents not only the slave's physical vulnerability, but also the necessity of the would-be slave witness's escape to the North, for it is only there, the *Narrative* suggests, that the fugitive can replace silent victimization with resistant testimony.

Douglass introduces the shipyard scene with a montage of disparate body parts, thereby linking the ruthless exploitation of the black body to the violence of Southern slavery: "At times I needed a dozen pair of hands. . . . Three or four voices would strike my ear. . . . 'I say, Fred., bear a hand['] . . . 'I say, darky, blast your eyes, why don't you heat up some pitch?' . . . [']Damn you, if you move, I'll knock your brains out!'"[8] Douglass continues to focus on body parts in his description of Frederick's beating, associating the labor of the shipyard "hands" with the violence that white hands—and "fists"—commit: "I fell, and with this they all ran upon me, and fell to beating me with their fists. I let them lay on for a while, gathering strength. In an instant, I gave a sudden surge, and rose to my hands and knees. Just as I did that, one of their number gave me, with his heavy boot, a powerful kick in the left eye. My eyeball seemed to have burst. When they saw my eye closed, and badly swollen, they left me. With this I seized the handspike, and for a time pursued them. But here the carpenters interfered, and I thought I might as well give it up. It was impossible to stand my hand against so many. All this took place in the sight of not less than fifty white ship-carpenters."[9] Frederick, first prostrate under others' "fists," begins to rise heroically, only to rest servilely on his

7. Ibid., [68].
8. Ibid., [65–66].
9. Ibid., [66].

"hands and knees," finally concluding in the odd locution that completes his rise even as it signals his defeat, the impossibility of "stand[ing]" his "hand." Syllepsis links his white antagonists to Frederick's own degraded posture: Frederick "fell," and his aggressors "fell to beating him"; he lay on the ground, letting them "lay on" their blows; when his "left eye" shut, his attackers finally "left" him.

Crucial to this scene is the injury to Frederick's eye—the same eye that was opened at the dawn of day by his Aunt Hester's shrieks, the same eye that witnessed her flogging and Demby's murder. Now, when Frederick himself is the helpless target of slavery's violence, his own sight is disabled by a kick to his eye. The spectatorial distance that characterizes Douglass's description of Aunt Hester's whipping and Demby's murder has, quite literally, vanished, replaced with a new tactile immediacy. The momentarily blinded Frederick literally cannot see his own beating as a "terrible spectacle" or a "horrible exhibition," but he *can* attempt to witness this inhumanity after the fact by testifying against his white coworkers.

Following the shipyard scene, the visual and the verbal seem, at last, to come together in what appears to be a set-piece of slaveholding paternalism: Frederick tells "the story of [his] wrongs to Master Hugh," while his mistress, Sophia Auld, "moved . . . to tears" by Frederick's "puffed-out eye and blood-covered face," "bound up [his] head, covering the wounded eye with a lean piece of fresh beef."[1] Like Sophia's ministrations to his eye, Frederick's private testimony seems to restore his identity as a witness, not only to the cruelty of slavery but also to this rare instance of benevolence. As Master Hugh "listened attentively to [his] narration of the circumstances leading to the savage outrage, and gave many proofs of his strong indignation at it," Frederick finds that "it was almost compensation for [his] suffering to witness, once more, a manifestation of kindness from this, [his] once affectionate old mistress," whose flowing tears sympathetically (albeit colorlessly) mimic her slave's bleeding eye.[2]

Douglass disrupts this scene of benign plantation justice, however, by demonstrating the inadequacy of private redress to the public wrongs suffered by the slave. As a reminder that the gap between witnessing and testimony can never be closed in the South due to restrictions on slaves' courtroom speech, Frederick's restored status as witness is quickly overturned when Hugh Auld consults with Esquire Watson, an attorney: "His answer was, he could do nothing in the case, unless some white man would come forward and testify. He could issue no warrant on my word. If I had been killed in the

1. Ibid., [67].
2. Ibid.; Douglass critiques the kind of quietist sentimentalism discussed in Fisher, *Hard Facts*, 110.

presence of a thousand colored people, their testimony combined would have been insufficient to have arrested one of the murderers. Master Hugh, for once, was compelled to say this state of things was too bad. Of course, it was impossible to get any white man to volunteer his testimony in my behalf, and against the young white men. . . . There was nothing done, and probably nothing would have been done if I had been killed. Such was, and such remains, the state of things in the Christian city of Baltimore."[3] As Shoshana Felman has argued of the trials involving brutalized Los Angeles motorist Rodney King and wife-abuser O. J. Simpson, Frederick's encounter with Esquire Watson is, crucially, "about an *unseen* beating, about an inexplicable, recalcitrant relation between beating and blindness, beating and invisibility, an invisibility that cannot be dispelled in spite of the most probatory visual evidence."[4] But whereas for Felman (following Althusser) it is the jury in each case whose ideological blinders keep it from seeing beatings of the black citizen or the female spouse as physical manifestations of deep cultural hatred in the form of racism or misogyny, in this scene from the *Narrative*, it is the legal inadmissibility of black testimony that illustrates how justice can "in effect be blind—in ways other than the ones in which it is normally expected to be."[5] In the topsy-turvy world of the slaveholding South, the willful blindness of justice implies not impartiality but its reverse, (racial) discrimination. And through the legislated legal incompetence of the slave, law overlooks the very racist violence that endangers the sight of the would-be black witness.

As in his account of Demby's murder, here Douglass provides literary testimony that arraigns the slaveholding South's criminality before the popular tribunal as it protests the exclusion of blacks from the American legal system by directing attention to the inadmissibility of African American testimony in the American courtroom.[6] Frederick's legal exclusion represents the penultimate phase in his transformation from silent enslaved victim to outspoken antislavery witness. Denied the opportunity to give his testimony in a Southern court of law, Frederick must turn to the Northern court of public opinion.

In the logic of the antislavery movement's juridical metaphor, the attack on Frederick and its aftermath become a metaphor for the authorship of the *Narrative* itself. Just as earlier the murdered Demby stands in for "every soul on the plantation," Frederick

3. Douglass, *Narrative*, [67].
4. Shoshana Felman, *The Juridical Unconscious: Trials and Traumas in the Twentieth Century* (Cambridge: Harvard UP, 2002), 81.
5. Ibid., 80.
6. Here, as in the defense for the O. J. Simpson criminal trial, "law is invoked as part and parcel" of the racial "trauma" (ibid., 91).

embodies the "thousand[s] of colored people" beaten, silenced, and rendered invisible by white supremacy, represented here by the murderous, bullying white shipyard workers. Douglass's "narration" of the "outrage" of slavery is intended to provoke "indignation" in the attentive antebellum reader, who, like Frederick's master Hugh Auld, may well be complicit in the peculiar institution of slavery yet fair-minded enough to be persuaded by what Douglass pointedly calls the "facts in the case."[7] It is no coincidence that the beating immediately precedes Frederick's flight from slavery. Refusing to remain physically vulnerable and silent any longer, Frederick directly engages the legal system, personified by Esquire Watson. The inadequacy of plantation justice, the inadmissibility of his own eyewitness testimony, the refusal of the Southern attorney to represent him, the failure of any white coworkers to come forward as witnesses, and the highly racialized blindness of Southern justice precipitate, even require, Frederick's escape to the abolitionist North, where he encounters passionate white advocates for the slave and the opportunity to take the witness stand against the guilty perpetrators before the popular tribunal.

But even as the pivotal scene of Frederick's shipyard beating seems to justify the antislavery movement's adoption of the language of criminal litigation, it also threatens to undo the power of that rhetoric. This scene, with its emphasis on the eye's physicality, poses but does not resolve some disturbing questions about the reliability of the slave victim's firsthand testimony of Southern violence. Like the "lean piece of fresh beef" with which his wounded eye is covered, Frederick's injury reminds us of the corporeality and, hence, physiological vulnerability and fallibility of that organ. Although the reader, like Hugh Auld, is meant to be outraged by the injustice of a legal system in which slave testimony is inadmissible, Douglass's account of the assault potentially reinforces the well-documented anxieties of white readers about the veracity of African American accounts of slavery and the trustworthiness of their authors.[8] After all, how reliable is an eyewitness whose "eye [is] closed, and badly swollen"?[9]

Douglass strives to resolve this dilemma in his story's brief but subtle conclusion. The final image that the *Narrative* offers of its protagonist/narrator seems to represent the culmination of the witnessing scenes that have gone before: three years after his arrival in the North, the former bondsman, attending a Nantucket

7. Douglass, *Narrative*, [66].
8. See Marion Wilson Starling, *The Slave Narrative: Its Place in American History* (Washington, DC: Howard UP, 1988), 221–48; Andrews, *To Tell*, 97–166.
9. On vision and visuality in the witnessing scenes discussed here, see DeLombard, "Eye-Witness." [See p. 163 of this Norton Critical Edition—*editors*.]

antislavery convention, "felt strongly moved to speak."[1] Although he "felt [him]self a slave, and the idea of speaking to white people weighed [him] down," the fugitive "spoke but a few moments" before he "felt a degree of freedom, and said what [he] desired with considerable ease."[2] It is not his first, exhilarated view of New York nor his subsequent preaching and lecturing at "the colored people's meeting at New Bedford" that provides Douglass with "a degree of freedom" but the act, years later, of telling his story to a racially mixed audience.[3] The liberating experience of testifying in the North, the *Narrative* seems to imply, provides the discursive antidote to the oppressive trauma of witnessing in the South. Rising to address the Nantucket antislavery meeting in the *Narrative*'s closing lines, the fugitive completes his transformation from slave to freeman: no longer forced silently to witness violence in the South, he is now free publicly to testify in the North against that violence.

Intriguingly, however, Douglass vacates his testimonial role at the moment of its fulfillment. Instead of providing an account of that landmark Nantucket speech—an abbreviated version, as Garrison's preface makes clear, of the *Narrative* we hold in our hands—Douglass notes that "from that time until now, I have been engaged in pleading the cause of my brethren."[4] Shifting in the *Narrative*'s last sentence from the posture of the witness to that of advocate, Douglass locates his identity as slave victim and witness firmly in the South, implicitly resisting abolitionist pressure to retain that identity in the North. No longer the "powerful slave" whose moving testimony caused "the best pleaders for the slave" to catch their breath in Nantucket, Douglass now pleads his fellow slaves' cause himself. With this concluding image of professional black advocacy, Douglass claimed a role usually reserved for white antislavery activists, asserted a civic agency denied to African Americans in the North as well as the South, and thereby assumed a discursive authority as unprecedented in the court of public opinion as it had been in the court of law.

1. Douglass, *Narrative*, [79].
2. Ibid., [79].
3. Ibid.
4. Ibid.

HENRY LOUIS GATES, JR.

Introduction to *Picturing Frederick Douglass*[†]

Frederick Douglass was in love with photography. During the four years of civil war, he wrote more extensively on photography than any other American, even while recognizing that his audiences were "riveted" to the war and wanted a speech only on "this mighty struggle."[1] He frequented photographers' studios and sat for his portrait whenever he could. As a result of this passion, he also became the most photographed American of the nineteenth century.

It may seem strange, if not implausible, to assert that a black man and former slave wrote more extensively on photography, and sat for his portrait more frequently, than any of his American peers. But he did. Douglass gave four separate talks on photography ("Lecture on Pictures," "Life Pictures," "Age of Pictures," and "Pictures and Progress"), whereas Oliver Wendell Holmes, the Boston physician and writer who is generally considered the most prolific Civil War–era photo critic, penned only three.[2] We have also identified, after years of research, 160 separate photographs of Douglass, as defined by *distinct poses* rather than multiple copies of the same negative.[3] By contrast, scholars have identified 155 separate

† From Henry Louis Gates, Jr., "Introduction" to John Stauffer, Zoe Trodd, Celeste-Marie Bernier, *Picturing Frederick Douglass: An Illustrated Biography of the Nineteenth Century's Most Photographed American* (New York: Liveright, 2015), pp. ix–xvii.

1. Douglass, "Pictures and Progress," n.d. (c. November 1864–March 1865).
2. Holmes's three essays on photography are: "The Stereoscope and the Stereograph," *Atlantic Monthly* (June 1859): 738–48; "Sun-Painting and Sun-Sculpture; With a Stereoscopic Trip Across the Atlantic," *Atlantic Monthly* (July 1861): 13–29; and "Doings of the Sunbeam," *Atlantic Monthly* (July 1863): 1–16, although the last two are supplements to his 1859 essay. See Mark Durden, ed., *Fifty Key Writers on Photography* (New York: Routledge, 2013), p. 125; Alan Trachtenberg, ed., *Classic Essays on Photography* (New Haven, CT: Leete's Island Books, 1980), p. 71; and Alan Trachtenberg, *Reading American Photographs: Images as History, Mathew Brady to Walker Evans* (New York: Hill & Wang, 1989), pp. 17–20, 90–93.

   Douglass probably delivered more than four lectures on photography—one lecture for each speech he wrote—but we have not yet been able to identify when he gave them. The editors of the *Frederick Douglass Papers* suggest that he delivered "Pictures and Progress" (originally titled "Lecture on Pictures") on December 3, 1861, in Boston, and again on November 15 in Syracuse, retitled as "Life Pictures"; but "Life Pictures" is substantially different from "Lecture on Pictures." See John W. Blassingame, ed., *The Frederick Douglass Papers* (New Haven: Yale University Press, 1979–2012).
3. Circumstantial evidence suggests that there are many more than 160 separate poses of Douglass. For starters, we have not uncovered a single photograph taken of Douglass in Europe. That's a shocking fact, given how frequently he sat for his portrait in the United States—on average once every sixteen weeks from 1845 to 1895. He spent three and a half years in Europe (two years in 1845–47, six months in 1859–60, and a year from 1886 to 1887, mostly in Britain). It thus seems odd, given how much he loved photography, that he would not once sit for his portrait while in Europe.

photographs of George Custer, 128 of Red Cloud, 127 of Walt Whitman, and 126 of Abraham Lincoln.[4] Ulysses S. Grant is a contender, but no one has published the corpus of Grant photographs; one eminent scholar has estimated 150 separate photographs of Grant.[5] Although there are some 850 total portraits of William "Buffalo Bill" Cody and his Wild West Show, and 650 of Mark Twain, no one has analyzed how many of these are distinct poses, or photographs as opposed to engravings, lithographs, and other non-photographic media. Moreover, Cody and Twain were a generation younger, and

---

There are two likely reasons for this absence of images in European archives. First, digitization and documentation of holdings in European archives lag behind the United States. "Finding aids" or their equivalent, common in United States archives, often do not exist in Europe. As a result, scholars and even archivists have no idea what is in an archive until they look at each item.

Second, photography was far less popular in Britain than in the United States. Storefront photo galleries were rare, as were daguerreotypes, tintypes, ambrotypes, and cartes-de-visite, the most popular formats among the masses. In Britain, the calotype (or talbotype) was the preferred medium, and owing to cost and labor, it did not cater to the masses. More significantly, unlike in the United States, many if not most British photographers and their societies came from the upper class.

Douglass befriended aristocrats and elites, and there is evidence from his correspondence that he sat for his portrait while in England, even though we have not found any images. In 1859 he wrote a letter to Mrs. Cash in Huddersfield, referring to a photograph her daughter had taken of him in 1846: "Please, if you are seeing or writing to your daughter Ellenor, remember me kindly to her, tell her I am as much like the picture she took of me as the wear and tear of thirteen years will permit me to be"—Douglass to Mrs. Cash, December 1859, in Philip S. Foner, ed., *The Life and Writings of Frederick Douglass* (cited hereafter as *LWFD*), Vol. V (New York: International Publishers, 1975), p. 459.

Every critic, collector, dealer, and historian of British photography we contacted felt as we do: that it seems strange that Douglass would not have sat for his portrait while in Britain.

The second piece of circumstantial evidence suggesting that Douglass sat for many more than 160 portraits is that the archives of his rivals (Custer, Red Cloud, and Lincoln) reveal many clusters of five to seven or more photographs, all quite similar, which stemmed from a single photo shoot. These clusters are rare in the Douglass archive, suggesting that many more photographs exist than have been collected or archived. This is understandable, since photographs of Douglass did not become collectors' items among whites until the late twentieth century. Finally, it is likely that many photographs were lost in the fire that destroyed Douglass's Rochester home in 1872.

During the research for this book, we sometimes encountered claims that other photographs were of Douglass. For example, the collector Jackie Napoleon Wilson claimed in *Hidden Witness: African-American Images from the Dawn of Photography to the Civil War* (New York: St. Martin's Press, 1999), which is the catalog accompanying an exhibition of the same title held at the J. Paul Getty Museum, that a photograph of two men is the "earliest known" depiction of Douglass and was made in the early 1840s. But the daguerreotype, held by the Chrysler Museum of Art and taken by the white Virginian William A. Pratt, is actually titled "Freemen of Color" and is dated 1850. Neither man in the photograph is Douglass.

4. D. Mark Katz, *Custer in Photographs* (New York: Bonanza Books, 1985); Frank H. Goodyear III, *Red Cloud: Photographs of a Lakota Chief* (Lincoln: University of Nebraska Press, 2003), p. 1; Charles Hamilton and Lloyd Ostendorf, *Lincoln in Photographs: An Album of Every Known Pose* (Dayton, OH: Morningside House, 1985), p. ix; the Walt Whitman Archive, online at www.whitmanarchive.org/multimedia/gallery.html.
5. Harold Holzer is planning a book on the photographs of Grant. Although he has not yet analyzed and added up how many separate photographs there are, he estimates "about 150"—Holzer to Stauffer in conversation, Lincoln Forum, Gettysburg, PA, November 17, 2013.

many if not most of their portraits were taken after 1900, when the Eastman Kodak snapshot had transformed the medium, bringing photography "within reach of every human being who desires to preserve a record of what he sees," as Kodak declared.[6] In the world, the only contemporaries who surpass Douglass are the British royal family and other British celebrities: there are 676 separate photographs of Princess Alexandra, 655 of the Prince of Wales, 593 of Ellen Terry, 428 of Queen Victoria, and 366 of William Gladstone.[7]

Douglass's passion for photography, however, has been largely ignored. He is perhaps most popularly remembered as one of the foremost abolitionists, and the preeminent black leader, of the nineteenth century. History books have also celebrated his relationship with President Lincoln, the fact that he met with every subsequent president until his death in 1895, and that he was the first African American to receive a federal appointment requiring Senate approval. His three autobiographies (two of them bestsellers) helped transform the genre and are still read today.[8] Yet, because his photographic passion has been almost completely forgotten, historians have missed an important question: why was a man who devoted his life to ending slavery and racism and championing civil rights so in love with photography?

The first part of the answer is that Douglass embraced photography as a great *democratic* art. More than once he praised Louis Daguerre, the founder of the first popular form of photography, the daguerreotype, and hailed him as "the great discoverer of modern times, to whom coming generations will award special homage. . . .

6. George Eastman, "The Kodak Manual," George Eastman House, Rochester, NY, quoted in Beaumont Newhall, *The History of Photography, From 1839 to the Present*, rev. ed. (New York: Museum of Modern Art, 1988), p. 129; Buffalo Bill Museum Image Archive, online at http://images.buffalobill.org/; J. R. LeMaster and James D. Wilson, eds., *The Mark Twain Encyclopedia* (New York: Garland Publishing, 1993), pp. 575–77; and Milton Meltzer, *Mark Twain Himself: A Pictorial Biography* (New York: Thomas Y. Crowell, 1960).

7. John Plunkett, *Queen Victoria: First Media Monarch* (Oxford: Oxford University Press, 2003), p. 160, Table 1: Photographs registered at Stationer's Hall, 1862–1901. It is unclear from Plunkett's book whether his numbers are total photographs or separate poses of the royal family.

8. On Douglass transforming the genre of autobiography, see William L. Andrews, *To Tell a Free Story: The First Century of Afro-American Autobiography, 1760–1865* (Urbana: University of Illinois Press, 1986), pp. 97–144, 167–76, 184–88, 214–39; John Stauffer, *Giants: The Parallel Lives of Frederick Douglass and Abraham Lincoln* (New York: Twelve, 2008), pp. 72, 310; Henry Louis Gates, Jr., *Figures in Black: Words, Signs, and the "Racial" Self* (New York: Oxford University Press, 1987), chs. 3–4; Robert B. Stepto, *A Home Elsewhere: Reading African American Classics in the Age of Obama* (Cambridge, MA: Harvard University Press, 2010), ch. 1; Robert B. Stepto, *From Behind the Veil: A Study of Afro-American Narrative* (1979; Urbana: University of Illinois Press, 1991), pp. 16–41, 153–57, 184–90; David W. Blight, Introduction, *Narrative of the Life of Frederick Douglass*, 2nd ed. (Boston: Bedford/St. Martin's, 2003), pp. 1–26; and John Stauffer, Introduction, *Narrative of the Life of Frederick Douglass, an American Slave* (New York: Library of America, 2014), pp. ix–xxi.

What was once the special and exclusive luxury of the rich and great is now the privilege of all. The humblest servant girl may now possess a picture of herself such as the wealth of kings could not purchase fifty years ago."[9]

He wrote this after he and photography had come of age together. Born in February 1818, Douglass escaped from slavery on September 3, 1838, a year before Daguerre and Henry Fox Talbot created the first forms of photography. For the rest of his life, he would mark his new birth of freedom by celebrating it in place of his unknown birthday. He began his career as an abolitionist orator in 1841, just as technical improvements reduced exposure times, enabling the proliferation of daguerreotype portraits. Portraits fueled the demand for photography and constituted over 90 percent of all images in the medium's first five decades.[1]

He first sat for a photograph, a daguerreotype, around 1841. After publishing his best-selling autobiography, *Narrative of the Life of Frederick Douglass*, in 1845, he lectured throughout the British Isles for two years. There he received his legal freedom and was introduced to the *Illustrated London News*, the world's first (and hugely successful) pictorial weekly. The *Illustrated* disseminated photographs and sketches by cutting engravings from them, enabling readers to receive the news visually for the first time. In 1846, Douglass was twice featured in the paper and when he returned to the United States in 1847 to launch his own newspaper, *The North Star*, it was increasingly common for books to be illustrated with frontispiece engravings cut from photographs. Four years later, the American illustrated press was launched in Boston with *Gleason's Pictorial Drawing-Room Companion*, followed by the wildly popular *Frank Leslie's Illustrated Newspaper* in 1855 and *Harper's Weekly* in 1857. By then, there were photographic studios in every city, county, and territory in the free states, and new forms of photography to choose from, notably the tintype and ambrotype.

9. Douglass, "Lecture on Pictures" (1861) and "Pictures and Progress," n.d. (ca. November 1864–March 1865).

1. On Douglass celebrating September 3, 1838, the day he reached freedom in the free states, in place of his unknown birthday, see Douglass, *My Bondage and My Freedom*, ed. John Stauffer (New York: Modern Library, 2003), pp. 257–58; James McCune Smith, "Frederick Douglass in New York," *Frederick Douglass' Paper*, February 2, 1855; and John Stauffer, *The Black Hearts of Men: Radical Abolitionists and the Transformation of Race* (Cambridge, MA: Harvard University Press, 2001), p. 114.

On portraits constituting over 90 percent of American photographs in the early years, see Robert A. Sobieszek and Odette M. Appel, *The Daguerreotypes of Southworth and Hawes* (1976; New York: Dover Publications, 1980), p. x; Keith F. Davis, *The Origins of American Photography, 1839–1885: From Daguerreotype to Dry-Plate* (Kansas City: The Nelson-Atkins Museum of Art, 2007), pp. 173–74; and Roger Watson and Helen Rappaport, *Capturing the Light: The Birth of Photography* (New York: St. Martin's Press, 2013).

Virtually every Northerner could afford to have his or her portrait taken.[2]

From the 1850s on, the free states enjoyed a love affair with photography that surpassed every other nation on earth. The American South, however, lacked the cities, roads, entrepreneurship, and other aspects of a capitalist infrastructure that enabled photography to flourish in the North. Moreover, in their efforts to defend slavery, Southerners suppressed freedoms of speech, debate, and the press, including photography and visual images.[3]

Douglass quickly recognized this close connection between photography and freedom. He defined himself as a free man and citizen as much through his portraits as his words. The democratic art of photography echoed the freedom articulated in the nation's founding document. His own freedom had coincided with the birth of photography, and he became one of its greatest boosters.

The second reason for Douglass's love of photography is that he believed in its truth value, or objectivity. Much as his Bible referred to an unseen but living God, a photograph accurately captured a moment in time and space. Even more than truth-telling, the truthful *image* represented abolitionists' greatest weapon, for it gave the lie to slavery as a benevolent institution and exposed it as a dehumanizing horror. Like slave narratives (Douglass was a master of the genre), photographic portraits bore witness to African Americans' essential humanity, while also countering the racist caricatures that proliferated throughout the North.

Douglass paid close attention to such caricatures. He noted with scorn in 1872: "I was once advertised in a very respectable newspaper under a little figure, bent over and apparently in a hurry, with

2. *Gleason's Pictorial* became *Ballou's Pictorial Drawing-Room Companion* in 1855 and lasted until 1859. On the birth of visual culture and the popularity of photography in America, see Newhall, *History of Photography*, pp. 27–39; Miles Orvell, *American Photography* (New York: Oxford University Press, 2003), pp. 13–14; Robert Taft, *Photography and the American Scene: A Social History, 1839–1899* (1938; New York: Dover Publications, 1964), pp. 46–166; Trachtenberg, *Reading American Photographs*, pp. 3–20; Alan Trachtenberg, "Photography: The Emergence of a Keyword," and Barbara McCandless, "The Portrait Studio and the Celebrity: Promoting the Art," both in *Photography in Nineteenth-Century America*, ed. Martha A. Sandweiss (New York: Harry N. Abrams, 1991), pp. 16–47, 48–75; John Stauffer, "Daguerreotyping the National Soul: The Portraits of Southworth and Hawes," *Prospects* 22 (1997): 69–97; Stauffer, *Black Hearts of Men*, pp. 55–56; Mary Panzer, *Mathew Brady and the Image of History* (Washington, DC: Smithsonian Institution Press, 1997), pp. 23–38, 71–92; Joshua Brown, *Beyond the Lines: Pictorial Reporting, Everyday Life, and the Crisis of Gilded-Age America* (Berkeley: University of California Press, 2002), pp. 1–59; and Vicki Goldberg, *The Power of Photography, Expanded and Updated: How Photographs Changed Our Lives* (New York: Abbeville Publ., 1991), pp. 7–17.

3. On the comparative paucity of photography in the slave states, see Davis, *The Origins of American Photography*, pp. 48, 174; Brown, *Beyond the Lines*, p. 50; and John Stauffer, "The 'Terrible Reality' of the First Living-Room Wars," in *War/Photography: Images of Armed Conflict and Its Aftermath*, eds. Anne Wilkes Tucker and Will Michels (Houston: Museum of Fine Arts, 2012), pp. 84–85, 88 n. 42.

a pack on his shoulder, going North." And he was all too familiar with the wider tendency toward racist depictions of African Americans: "We colored men so often see ourselves described and painted as monkeys, that we think it a great piece of good fortune to find an exception to this general rule," he wrote in 1870.[4]

Photographers recognized that their medium lied—many self-consciously manipulated the image, solarizing it, airbrushing out unwanted subjects, or distorting it in other ways. But Douglass and most patrons of the art believed that the camera told the truth. Even in the hands of a racist white, it simultaneously created an authentic portrait and a work of art. Neither Douglass nor his peers recognized any contradiction between photography as an art and as a technology.[5]

Thirdly, Douglass believed that photography highlighted the essential humanity of its subjects. This was because of the medium's ability to produce portraits for the millions. Influenced by Aristotle's *Poetics* and the writings of Ralph Waldo Emerson and Thomas Carlyle, Douglass argued that humans' proclivity for pictures is what distinguished them from animals: "Man is the only picture-making animal in the world. He alone of all the inhabitants of earth has the capacity and passion for pictures."[6] He summarized the significance of a photograph of Hiram Revels, the first African American senator, by saying: "Whatever may be the prejudices of those who may look upon it, they will be compelled to admit that the Mississippi Senator is a man."[7]

Emphasizing the humanity of all people was central to Douglass's reform vision, since most white Americans believed that blacks were innately inferior, lacking in reason and rational thought. Furthering that view were the ethnologists (precursors of anthropologists),

4. Douglass, "Which Greeley Are We Voting For? An Address Delivered in Richmond Virginia on 24 July 1872," *TFDP* 1:4, pp. 303; Douglass, letter to Louis Prang, June 14, 1870, published in *Prang's Chromos: A Journal of Popular Art* (September 1870), reprinted in Katherine Morrison McClinton, *The Chromolithographs of Louis Prang* (New York: Clarkson N. Potter, 1973; cited hereafter as letter to Louis Prang), p. 37. Douglass also applied the language of photography more broadly. In a letter to Gerrit Smith on April 15, 1852, he noted that although he had met someone, the room was dark and "I did not get a very good daguerreotype of the man" (meaning strong visual image)—*TFDP* 3:1, pp. 529.
5. Douglass, "Pictures and Progress," pp. 164–165 in this volume; Stauffer, *Black Hearts of Men*, pp. 51–52; Nancy Armstrong, *Fiction in the Age of Photography: The Legacy of British Realism* (Cambridge, MA: Harvard University Press, 1999), pp. 1–74, 248–49.
6. Douglass, "Pictures and Progress"; Aristotle, *Poetics*, trans. Malcolm Heath (New York: Penguin Books, 1996), pp. 6–7 (3.1: "The Anthropology and History of Poetry, Origins."); W. J. T. Mitchell, "Representation," in Frank Lentricchia and Thomas McLaughlin, eds., *Critical Terms for Literary Study*, 2nd ed. (Chicago: University of Chicago Press, 1995), pp. 11–17; Thomas Carlyle, *On Heroes and Hero Worship and the Heroic in History* (1842; repr., London: Oxford University Press, 1951); and Ralph Waldo Emerson, *Representative Men: Seven Lectures* (1850; repr., Cambridge, MA: Harvard University Press, 1996).
7. Douglass, letter to Louis Prang, p. 37.

who argued that blacks had smaller craniums, and brains, than whites, and thus lacked whites' cognitive abilities. In an 1854 speech, "Claims of the Negro Ethnologically Considered," Douglass engaged ethnologists' methods of comparing craniums and blacks' and whites' comparative capacities for reason, but with limited success. After his "awakening" to the philosophical power of photography, however, he dismissed the ethnologists' methods out of hand. "Dogs and elephants are said to possess reason," he says. But they lack "imagination," the realm of thought enabling humans to create pictures of themselves and their world. Douglass exposed the ethnologists' faulty method of analysis: they "profess some difficulty in finding a fixed, unvarying, and definite line separating . . . the lowest variety of our species, always meaning the Negro—from the highest animal." The line separating humans from other animals was quite clear, Douglass emphasized, as philosophers from Aristotle forward had acknowledged: "man is everywhere a picture-making animal and the *only* picture-making animal in the world. The rudest and remotest tribes of men manifest this great human power and thus vindicate the brotherhood of man." The picture-making power was "a sublime, prophetic, and all-creative power."[8]

The fourth reason for Douglass's love of photography is that it inspired people to eradicate the sins of their society. The power of the imagination allowed people to appreciate pictures as accurate representations of some greater reality. It helped them try to realize their sublime ideals in an imperfect world. As Douglass put it in an adage inspired by his reading of Carlyle: "Poets, prophets, and reformers are all picture-makers—and this ability is the secret of their power and of their achievements. They see what ought to be by the reflection of what is, and endeavor to remove the contradiction." Douglass considered himself all three: a poet, prophet, and reformer. So did most other abolitionists. As a group, abolitionists and antislavery advocates, from Douglass and Lincoln to Whitman and Sojourner Truth, had their portraits taken with greater

8. Douglass, "Pictures and Progress"; Douglass, "Claims of the Negro Ethnologically Considered" (1854), *TFDP*, 1:2, pp. 497–524. On Douglass's limited success at attacking ethnologists on their own terms, and his awakening to the philosophical power of photography, see Catherine Kistler's superb essay, "Countering Ethnographic Racism with Rhetoric and Photography," in "English 90fd: The Rhetoric of Frederick Douglass and Abraham Lincoln," Harvard University (Fall 2013). On the ethnologists' arguments, see George M. Fredrickson, *The Black Image in the White Mind: The Debate on Afro-American Character and Destiny, 1817–1914* (1971; Middletown, CT: Wesleyan University Press, 1987), pp. 71–96; William Stanton, *The Leopard's Spots: Scientific Attitudes Toward Race in America, 1815–59* (Chicago: University of Chicago Press, 1960), pp. 24–112; Stephen Jay Gould, *The Mismeasure of Man* (New York: W. W. Norton & Co., 1996), pp. 62–104; and Ann Fabian, *The Skull Collectors: Race, Science, and America's Unburied Dead* (Chicago: University of Chicago Press, 2010), pp. 79–120.

frequency, distributed them more effectively, and were more taken with photography, than other groups. Photography inspired them to remove the contradictions between what ought to be and what was.[9]

Douglass recognized, however, that the power of photography depended upon its circulation in the public sphere. Photographs, like writing, needed to be published in books, newspapers, broadsides, and pamphlets in order to be disseminated. Whereas a daguerreotype or ambrotype offered a private viewing experience, its publication sent it into the world and made it public. Through the dissemination of his image and word, Douglass photographed and wrote himself into the public sphere, became the most famous black man in the Western world, and thus acquired cultural and political power. Indeed, his portraits and words sent a message to the world that he had as much claim to citizenship, with the rights of equality before the law, as his white peers. He knew, as James Russell Lowell put it, that "[t]he very look and bearing of Douglass are eloquent, and are full of an irresistible logic against the oppression of his race."[1] His likeness embodied his cause of racial equality. This is why he always dressed up for his sittings with photographers, appearing "majestic in his wrath," as one admirer said of his portrait, and why he labored to speak and write with such eloquence. He was widely considered one of, if not the, greatest orators in the Civil War era, more eloquent even than Lincoln or Emerson. It was through his images and words that he "out-citizened" white citizens, at a time when most whites did not believe that African Americans should be citizens.[2]

Douglass made every effort to circulate his photographs. He shared them with absent family members and close friends. In 1863, his son Charles requested a few autographed Douglass photos for himself and a friend. That same year, Julia Griffiths wrote Douglass

9. Douglass, "Pictures and Progress"; Carlyle, *On Heroes and Hero Worship and the Heroic in History;* Stauffer, *Black Hearts of Men*, pp. 50, 302 n. 6; Carl Peterson, "19th Century Photographers and Related Activity in Madison County, New York," *Madison County Heritage* 23 (1998): 15–25; Alan Trachtenberg, "The Daguerreotype: American Icon," in *American Daguerreotypes from the Matthew R. Isenburg Collection* (New Haven: Yale University Art Gallery, 1989), p. 16; John Wood, "Silence and Slow Time: An Introduction to the Daguerreotype," and Alan Trachtenberg, "Mirror in the Marketplace: American Responses to the Daguerreotype, 1839–1851," both in *The Daguerreotype: A Sesquicentennial Celebration*, ed. John Wood (Iowa City: University of Iowa Press, 1989), pp. 1–29, 60–73; John Wood, "The American Portrait," in *America and the Daguerreotype*, ed. John Wood (Iowa City: University of Iowa Press, 1991); and Panzer, *Mathew Brady*, pp. 23–38, 71–92.

1. James Russell Lowell, "The Prejudice of Color," February 13, 1846, in Lowell, *Anti-Slavery Papers*, Vol. 1 (Boston: Houghton Mifflin & Co., 1902), pp. 21–22.

2. Frederick S. Voss, *Majestic in His Wrath: A Pictorial Life of Frederick Douglass* (Washington, DC: Smithsonian Institution Press, 1995). On Douglass photographing and writing himself into the public sphere, see *Frederick Douglass' Paper*, August 3, 1855; Gates, *Figures in Black*, pp. 98–124; Blassingame, Introduction, *TFDP* 1:1, pp. xxi–lxix; and Stauffer, *Black Hearts of Men*, p. 46. On Douglass's preeminence as an orator, see Stauffer, *Giants*, pp. 67–96, 131–66.

from England to ask for a likeness to put in her new photo album.[3] Douglass also gave his portraits as gifts to new friends, for example to Susan B. Anthony.

His gifted photographs adorned the walls of homes for decades. In 1937, the educator Josephine Turpin Washington explained that she would show visitors a photograph she had kept since Douglass gave it to her as a birthday gift (presumably when she clerked for him in the Recorder of Deeds office during summer breaks from Howard University in the early 1880s).[4] So ubiquitous was Douglass on people's walls, even before his death, that artists depicted rooms with framed Douglass images. In 1889, the African American artist Henry Jackson Lewis, a cartoonist for the *Indianapolis Freeman*, made a sketch of his editor, Edward Elder Cooper, at work in his study. Above Cooper's desk are two portraits, one of himself and one of Douglass. Another drawing by Lewis featuring Douglass on the wall was published in *The Freeman*, as was one by Moses Tucker.[5]

Douglass used his photographs to garner subscriptions to his own newspaper, thereby disseminating them further. In late 1873, his *New National Era* repeatedly advertised the "inducement" of a "fine photograph" of himself, sized at 14×20 inches, to any new subscriber.[6]

His photographs also helped promote individuals and organizations devoted to black rights. In 1846, the Anti-Slavery Bazaar offered for sale an "excellent Daguerreotype of Frederick Douglass." Two years later, Ephraim Williams, a shoemaker, and James Knight, a porter, told Douglass that they had commissioned lithograph portraits of him (and other black abolitionists) "to be hung up in our parlors and the parlors of all men who are true to the bondman" as a way to pay tribute to "the reformers who have marched in the forefront, battling for our rights as men and as Americans." In October 1894, the black photographer James E. Reed agreed to sell photographs from a recent sitting—the last in Douglass's

3. Frederick Douglass Papers, Library of Congress (cited hereafter as FDP-LC), General Correspondence, 1863. See also Douglass enclosing a photograph with a letter on March 31, 1894, noting: "it will probably be the last occasion I may have to have a photograph taken, as I am fast approaching the sunset of life"—FDP-LC, General Correspondence, 1894, Mar. Douglass was wrong about this photograph being his last, going on to sit for several more in May and October that year. He also requested photographs from others. For one request, see Florence Blackall, March 31, 1894, FDP-LC, General Correspondence, 1894, Mar.

4. Josephine T. Washington, "Know Thyself!" *Pittsburgh Courier*, December 18, 1937, p. 19.

5. Henry Jackson Lewis, unpublished drawing, 1889, DuSable Museum of African American History, uncatalogued; Lewis, "The Race Problem," *Indianapolis Freeman*, March 30, 1889; Moses Tucker, "An Opossum Dinner," *Indianapolis Freeman*, December 21, 1889.

6. See, e.g., *The New National Era*, December 25, 1873.

life—to the public, and give the profits to Douglass's "Southern school".[7]

Douglass's photographs helped promote his talks, too. After the Civil War he became a speaker with the Redpath Lyceum Bureau, based in Boston and organized by the abolitionist James Redpath. The bureau used a lantern slide of Douglass to advertise his affiliation to the agency.

But Douglass faced a problem in trying to disseminate his portrait on a mass scale. The halftone process, which enabled photographs to be mass-produced, would not be perfected until the twentieth century. Although he had to rely instead on engravings cut from photographs for book and newspaper illustrations, he did not have quite the same faith in the objectivity of an engraver (or painter) as he did of a camera. In 1849 he discovered an engraving of himself, cut from another engraving that possibly stemmed from a painting, in *A Tribute for the Negro*, by the British abolitionist Wilson Armistead. The engraver had portrayed Douglass with a slight smile. Douglass was outraged, and in his newspaper he noted that his portrait had "a much more kindly and amiable expression than is generally thought to characterize the face of a fugitive slave." Although he was no longer a fugitive, he wanted the look of a defiant but respectable abolitionist. He then attacked the fallibility of engraving and painting: "Negroes can never have impartial portraits at the hands of white artists," he stated. "It seems to us next to impossible for white men to take likenesses of black men, without most grossly exaggerating their distinctive features. And the reason is obvious. Artists, like all other white persons, have adopted a theory respecting the distinctive features of Negro physiognomy." The vast majority of whites could not create "impartial" likenesses because of their preconceived notions of what African Americans looked like.[8]

Douglass's criticism of white artists highlights why he was so taken with photography. As an art and a technology, photography overcame whites' "preconceived notions" of African Americans; the camera, unlike an engraving or painting, represented them accurately. Douglass surmounted the problem of disseminating his photographs using an unreliable medium by hiring engravers he could trust. John C. Buttre was his preferred engraver.[9]

7. "Twelfth National Anti-Slavery Bazaar," *The Liberator*, January 23, 1846, 14; *TFDP* 3:1, 330; FDP-LC, General Correspondence, 1894, Nov.–Dec. and Undated. Reed likely refers to Booker T. Washington's Tuskegee Institute in Alabama, to which Douglass would sometimes encourage friends to donate in the 1890s. See, e.g., Louis R. Harlan, ed., *The Booker T. Washington Papers: 1889–95* (Urbana: University of Illinois Press, 1974), p. 396.
8. Douglass, "A Tribute for the Negro," *The North Star*, April 7, 1849.
9. Stauffer, *Black Hearts of Men*, p. 51.

Still, even a faithful engraving lacks the extraordinary detail of the photograph on which it was based. In fact, engravings may appear to us today as crude representations. But they and lithographs were the only available processes for disseminating a photograph in books and print media. Significantly, most Americans treated engravings cut from *photographs* as objective or "authentic," much as most people today interpret a halftone photograph in *The New York Times* as truthful. So did Douglass; if the engraving in Armistead's book had in fact been drawn from a painting, then there are no known instances of Douglass critiquing an engraving cut from a photograph of himself. The illustrated press, from the *Illustrated London News* to *Frank Leslie's* and *Harper's Weekly*, referred to engravings cut from photographs in their pages as "photographs," whereas engravings from sketches were called "sketches." Editors simply ignored the transfer process necessary to mass-produce an image. While the truthfulness of sketches from "eyewitness" artists was challenged, virtually no one "questioned the veracity of a photograph," or an engraving cut from it.[1]

By resolving the problem of circulating his "impartial" likeness, Douglass authorized millions of portraits to be sent into the world. With very few exceptions, these were public portraits—designed to bolster his public persona. For Douglass, photography was not a personal or sentimental tool, a way to visualize family relationships or friendships. The only photograph that falls into the category of private memento is a honeymoon shot from 1884 with his second wife Helen Pitts. The photographs of Douglass with friends visiting Mount Vernon in Virginia may also have been mementos, but these photographs may have been taken at the behest of a group member rather than Douglass himself.

The only body of work that captures something of his private life are the photos of Cedar Hill, his home in Anacostia, Washington D.C., after Reconstruction. He posed several times for photographs on his porch; in his library; and walking around the grounds. But he was rarely photographed with family members. There are no clearly identified images of Douglass with his first wife, Anna, or with any of his children. He was photographed with his second wife, Helen, seven times. The only grandchild who features in any photographs with Douglass is Joseph, of whom Douglass was particularly fond.[2]

1. Stauffer, "'Terrible Reality,'" p. 81; Goldberg, *Power of Photography*, p. 21; Brown, *Beyond the Lines*, pp. 49, 54–55.
2. Two photographs by William W. Core (cat. #90 and #91) may include some of Douglass's family members—possibly Anna or his adult children and grandchildren. But Core photographed Douglass's home from a distance, and although Douglass is recognizable, the other subjects are not, and they lack facial detail. In addition, cat. #156 shows Douglass with Charles Satchell Morris, who had worked as Douglass's secretary and married Douglass's granddaughter Annie Rosine Sprague in 1892. Annie had died in 1893. So although it doesn't depict a grandchild, the photograph does depict Douglass with his widowed grandson-in-law.

Even here, the photographs with Joseph reflect a professional collaboration. The two performed together in Boston in May 1894, Douglass giving a speech and Joseph performing violin solos before and after his grandfather's remarks. They sat for photographs during that Boston trip, then again in New Bedford after performing together. The photographs include Joseph playing his violin, and in one of these Douglass holds a piece of paper, perhaps related to the speech he was giving that day. The only known photographs of Douglass with any blood relative, then, are depictions of a professional and artistic collaboration as much as family portraits.

The sheer number of these public portraits, from his earliest known photograph as a young man with an Afro, circa 1841, to the postmortem portrait fifty-four years later, conveys not only Douglass's faith in photography but his understanding of the public identity he was crafting. By continually updating his public persona, he embraced what might be called a protomodernist conception of the self that paralleled his radical egalitarianism. Just as he rejected fixed social stations and rigid hierarchies, so too did he repudiate the idea of a fixed self. He imagined the self as continually evolving, in a state of constant flux, which exploded the very foundations of both slavery and racism. Of course slavery and racism both depend upon some individuals being "fatally fixed for life." Slavery creates a low ceiling above which no one can rise, and racism reflects the belief that some people are *permanently* superior to other people. Douglass's fluid conception of the self conjoined art and politics. He went so far as to say that "the moral and social influence of pictures" was more important in shaping national culture than "the making of its laws."[3]

* * *

3. Douglass, "Lecture on Pictures"; Lincoln uses the term "fatally fixed for life" in critiquing slavery and racism; see Roy Basler, ed., *The Collected Works of Abraham Lincoln* (New Brunswick, NJ: Rutgers University Press, 1953), Vol. 3, p. 478.

Frederick Douglass: A Chronology

1818	Born a slave in Talbot County (Eastern Shore), Maryland.
1824	Taken by grandmother to Wye House, where their master, Aaron Anthony, is manager. Befriended by manager's daughter, Lucretia Auld, wife of Thomas Auld.
1826	Sent to Baltimore to live with Thomas Auld's brother, Hugh Auld, and his wife, Sophia.
1827	Returned to Talbot County for distribution of Anthony's estate. Awarded to Thomas Auld. Returned to Hugh Auld in Baltimore.
1833–34	Sent back to Thomas Auld. Rented to Edward Covey as fieldhand.
1835	Rented to William Freeland. Plans escape with other young slaves. Caught. Escapes hanging or sale south. Sent back to Baltimore, where he works as a caulker in a shipyard. Meets Anna Murray.
1838	Escapes slavery. Marries Anna Murray in New York City. They settle in New Bedford, Massachusetts.
1839	Rosetta Douglass born. Douglass hears William Lloyd Garrison speech.
1840	Lewis Henry Douglass born.
1841	Makes first great public antislavery speech, Nantucket, Massachusetts. Begins tours as an agent of the New England Anti-Slavery Society. Moves to Lynn, Massachusetts.
1842	Frederick Douglass, Jr., born.
1844	Charles Remond Douglass born.
1845	Publishes *Narrative of the Life of Frederick Douglass.*
1845–47	Travels in Ireland, Scotland, and England, giving antislavery speeches.
1847	Moves to Rochester, New York. Publishes *North Star* (1847–51). Continues his speaking tours.
1849	Annie Douglass born.
1851	Publishes *Frederick Douglass' Paper* (1851–60).
1852	Gives "5th of July" speech.

1853	Publishes *The Heroic Slave*, a novella.
1855	Publishes *My Bondage and My Freedom.*
1859	Accused of being an accomplice of John Brown, goes to England, via Canada. Publishes *Douglass' Monthly* (1859–63).
1860	Annie Douglass dies. Douglass returns to Rochester.
1861	The Civil War begins. Douglass urges that the ending of slavery be the war's aim.
1863	Recruits for the African American 54th Massachusetts regiment.
1870	Publishes *New National Era* (1870–74).
1871	Secretary of commission sent to attempt to annex the Dominican Republic.
1872	Rochester house burned by arsonist. Moves to Washington, D.C.
1874	President of Freedman's Savings Bank, which fails.
1877	Marshall of District of Columbia.
1881	Recorder of Deeds, Washington, D.C. Publishes *Life and Times of Frederick Douglass.*
1882	Anna Murray Douglass dies.
1884	Marries Helen Pitts Douglass.
1889–91	United States Minister to Haiti.
1892	Publishes revised *Life and Times of Frederick Douglass.*
1893	Commissioner of the Republic of Haiti at the Chicago World's Fair.
1894	Gives last great speech, "Lessons of the Hour," opposing lynching.
1895	Dies in Washington, D.C. Buried in Rochester, New York.

Selected Bibliography

MAJOR WORKS BY FREDERICK DOUGLASS (CHRONOLOGICAL)

Narrative of the Life of Frederick Douglass, an American Slave, Written by Himself. Boston: American Anti-Slavery Society, 1845.

My Bondage and My Freedom. New York: Miller, Orton, & Mulligan, 1855.

Life and Times of Frederick Douglass, Written by Himself. Hartford, CT: Park, 1881. Rev. 1882.

Life and Times of Frederick Douglass, Written by Himself: His Early Life As a Slave, His Escape from Bondage, and His Complete History to the Present Time. Boston: De Wolfe, Fiske, 1892.

Life and Writings of Frederick Douglass. Ed. Philip S. Foner. 5 vols. New York: International, 1950–75.

Frederick Douglass on Women's Rights. Ed. Philip S. Foner. Westport, CT: Greenwood, 1976.

Douglass, Frederick, and John R. McKivigan. *The Frederick Douglass Papers.* New Haven, CT: Yale UP; Bloomington: Indiana UP, 1973–2012.

Autobiographies. Ed. Henry Louis Gates, Jr. New York: Library of America, 1994.

Oxford Frederick Douglass Reader. Ed. William L. Andrews. New York: Oxford UP, 1996.

MAJOR BIOGRAPHIES

• indicates a work included or excerpted in this Norton Critical Edition

Holland, Frederic May. *Frederick Douglass, the Colored Orator.* New York: Funk & Wagnalls, 1891.

Huggins, Nathan Irvin. *Slave and Citizen: The Life of Frederick Douglass.* Boston: Little, Brown, 1980.

• McFeely, William S. *Frederick Douglass.* New York: Norton, 1991.

Preston, Dickson J. *Young Frederick Douglass: The Maryland Years.* Baltimore: Johns Hopkins UP, 1980.

Quarles, Benjamin. *Frederick Douglass.* Washington, DC: Associated Publishers, 1948. Reprint, New York, 1969.

GENERAL HISTORICAL AND LITERARY STUDIES

• Andrews, William L., ed. *Critical Essays on Frederick Douglass.* Boston: G. K. Hall, 1991.

• ———. *To Tell a Free Story: The First Century of Afro-American Autobiography, 1760–1865.* Urbana: U of Illinois P, 1986.

• Baker, Houston A., Jr. *Blues, Ideology, and Afro-American Literature.* Chicago: U of Chicago P, 1984.

———. *The Journey Back.* Chicago: U of Chicago P, 1980.

Blassingame, John W. *The Slave Community.* 2nd ed. New York: Oxford UP, 1979.

———, ed. *Slave Testimony.* Baton Rouge: Louisiana State UP, 1977.

Blight, David W. *Frederick Douglass' Civil War.* Baton Rouge: Louisiana State UP, 1989.

Butterfield, Stephen. *Black Autobiography in America.* Amherst: U of Massachusetts P, 1974.

Davis, Charles T., and Henry Louis Gates, Jr., eds. *The Slave's Narrative.* New York: Oxford UP, 1985.

• DeLombard, Jeannine Marie. *Slavery on Trial: Law, Abolitionism, and Print Culture.* Chapel Hill: U of North Carolina P, 2007.

Dickson, D. Bruce, Jr., *The Origins of African American Literature, 1680–1865.* Charlottesville: UP of Virginia, 2001.

Dudley, David L. *My Father's Shadow: Intergenerational Conflict in African American Men's Autobiography.* Philadelphia: U of Pennsylvania P, 1991.

Ernest, John. *Chaotic Justice: Rethinking African American Literary History.* Chapel Hill: U of North Carolina P, 2009.

———. *Resistance and Reformation in Nineteenth-Century African-American Literature.* Jackson: UP of Mississippi, 1995.

Fisch, Audrey A., ed. *The Cambridge Companion to the African American Slave Narrative.* Cambridge: Cambridge UP, 2012.

Fisher, Dexter, and Robert B. Stepto, eds. *Afro-American Literature: The Reconstruction of Instruction.* New York: Modern Language Association, 1979.

Foster, Frances Smith. *Witnessing Slavery.* 2nd ed. Madison: U of Wisconsin P, 1993.

Fredrickson, George M. *The Black Image in the White Mind.* New York: Harper & Row, 1971.

Gates, Henry Louis, Jr. *Figures in Black.* New York: Oxford UP, 1987.

• Gregory, James Monroe. *Frederick Douglass, the Orator.* Springfield, MA: Wiley & Co. 1893.

Lee, Maurice S. *The Cambridge Companion to Frederick Douglass.* Cambridge: Cambridge UP, 2009.

Leverenz, David. *Manhood and the American Renaissance.* Ithaca, NY: Cornell UP, 1989.

Levine, Robert S. *Martin Delany, Frederick Douglass, and the Politics of Representative Identity.* Chapel Hill: U of North Carolina P, 1997.

———, and Samuel Otter, eds. *Frederick Douglass and Herman Melville: Essays in Relation.* Chapel Hill: U of North Carolina P, 2008.

Martin, Waldo E. *The Mind of Frederick Douglass.* Chapel Hill: U of North Carolina P, 1982.

McBride, Dwight A. *Impossible Witnesses: Truth, Abolitionism, and Slave Testimony.* New York: New York UP, 2001.

McDowell, Deborah E., and Arnold Rampersad, eds. *Slavery and the Literary Imagination.* Baltimore: Johns Hopkins UP, 1989.

Meier, August. *Negro Thought in America, 1880–1915.* Ann Arbor: U of Michigan P, 1966.

Patterson, Orlando. *Slavery and Social Death.* Cambridge: Harvard UP, 1982.

Quarles, Benjamin. *Black Abolitionists.* New York: Oxford UP, 1969.

• Richardson, Robert D. *Henry Thoreau: A Life of the Mind.* Berkeley: U of California P, 1986.

Ripley, C. Peter, et al., eds. *The Black Abolitionist Papers*, 5 vols., Chapel Hill: U of North Carolina P, 1985–1992.

———. "The Autobiographical Writings of Frederick Douglass," *Southern Studies* 24.1 (spring 1985): 5–29.

Sekora, John, and Darwin T. Turner, eds. *The Art of Slave Narrative.* Macomb: Western Illinois U, 1982.

Smith, Valerie. *Self-Discovery and Authority in Afro-American Narrative.* Cambridge: Harvard UP, 1987.

• Stanton, Elizabeth Cady. *Elizabeth Cady Stanton*, 2 vols. eds. Theodore Stanton and Harriet Stanton Blach. New York: Harper & Brothers, 1922.

• Stauffer, John, Zoe Trodd, Celeste-Marie Bernier. *Picturing Frederick Douglass: An Illustrated Biography of the Nineteenth Century's Most Photographed American.* New York: Liveright, 2015.

Stepto, Robert B. *From Behind the Veil: A Study of Afro-American Narrative.* Urbana: U of Illinois P, 1979.

Sundquist, Eric J., ed. *Frederick Douglass: New Literary and Historical Essays.* Cambridge: Cambridge UP, 1990.

———. *To Wake the Nations: Race in the Making of American Literature.* Cambridge: Harvard UP, 1993.

Walker, Peter F. *Moral Choices: Memory, Desire, and Imagination in Nineteenth-Century American Abolition.* Baton Rouge: Louisiana State UP, 1978.

Zafar, Rafia. *We Wear the Mask: African Americans Write American Literature, 1760–1870.* New York: Columbia UP, 1997.

15-16 } female sexuality
47

65, 66, 67 } — law
72. love } & religion
79-84 } —

123: Criminals

↳ of 13th

race law: prejudice made policy

STOP!

This is the back of the book. You wouldn't want to spoil a great ending!

This book is printed "manga-style," in the authentic Japanese right-to-left format. Since none of the artwork has been flipped or altered, readers get to experience the story just as the creator intended. You've been asking for it, so TOKYOPOP® delivered: authentic, hot-off-the-press, and far more fun!

DIRECTIONS

If this is your first time reading manga-style, here's a quick guide to help you understand how it works.

It's easy... just start in the top right panel and follow the numbers. Have fun, and look for more 100% authentic manga from TOKYOPOP®!

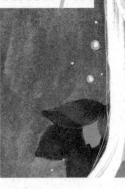

remember
benjamin

TOKYOPOP MANGA SUPPLEMENT

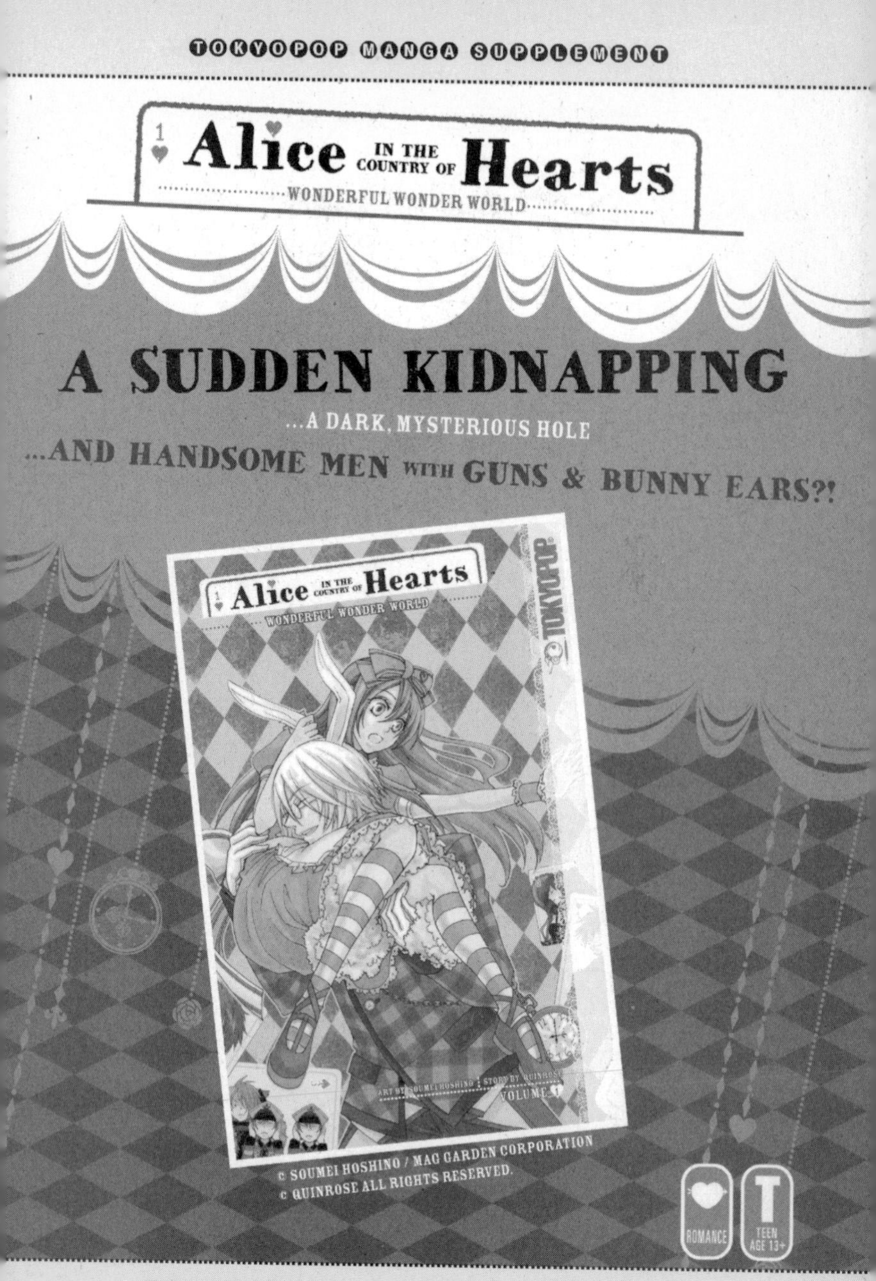

FOR MORE INFORMATION VISIT: www.TOKYOPOP.com

Happy
CAFE
Enjoy
VOL 2

In the next volume of...

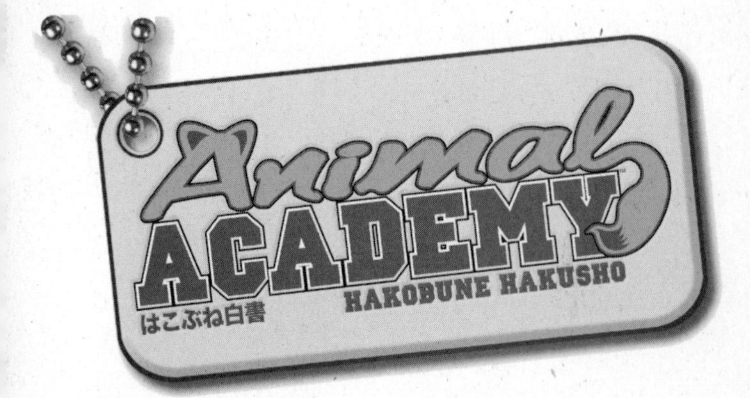

The rumor mill sure is turning at Morimori! Talk of love is in the air, but strangely, there's even more talk of ninjas, too. Plus, the mystery of the Sagami brothers deepens, and Fune finally gets to meet the very unusual school headmistress!

HAKOBUNE HAKUSHO.4

Minoru Watanuki →

- Raccoon dog (tanuki).
- Morimori High School 1st year White Class.
- Homeroom teacher.
- Species: Nyctereutes Procyonides.
- Rumor has it he used to drive a motorcycle. He's an excellent teacher for magical animals because he really cares about humans.

↖ Zenda Miyoshi

- Cat
- Morimori High School 3rd year student, Blue Class.
- Ranked 12th in attendance.
- Species: Felix catus.
- First became interested in humans a long time ago, when he was taken to a veterinarian. He believes ninjas were expert information gatherers.

Remember Both the Good and the Bad After Chapter 19
Oh I forgot!
?
SQUISH
Sorry, Miiko!
Sensei asked me to punish you for playing hooky.
Ouch!
Ow, ow, ow, ow, ow!
?
Miiko refused to speak to Neko for the rest of the day.
...
...
My bad.
PAT
Reset in half a day.
You shouldn't skip class without telling anyone!
It's so rude!
Words of wisdom from the class prez. ★
!!
S-sorry!

I should also mention that I have lots of modest readers
I'm so sorry! I don't quite know how old so-and is, but I hope you like this
Maybe there's no set age.
I'm so sorr writing such a long letter, but I'll wrap it up now.
Aw.
But I was enjoying it so much...
I'm sorry, but I'll try to do better from now on.
You don't need to apologize...
MODEST
There were letters from so many different people.
This must mean that there are a lot of nice people out there!
I'm just surrounded by good souls.
I know I've taken too long to say this, but thank you very much for picking up this book!
I hope you read it.
And I'd love to hear your feedback.
I just hope I'm expressing my appreciation well enough.
And sorry for not always writing back.
And that about wraps things up! I still have plenty of things to improve on!
Let's do this!
I hope we meet again next volume!
Bye bye!
Take care!
Thank you!! ♥
•I. nami
•O. miwa
•K. miwa
•M. yo-ki
•M. asami
Fan Mail: TOKYOPOP c/o Animal Academy Editor 5900 Wilshire Blvd, Suite 2000 Los Angeles, CA 90036

Postscript [4]

Hello! This is Moyamu Fujino!
And this is **volume 4!**
Time to celebrate!
This means I've done a total of 21 manga volumes!
Amazing! I can't thank you enough! It's like a dream come true!
20 volumes.
This whole shelf.
Yup!
friend
Huh? No way!
Wow...
Back
It sorta makes you realize just how long you've been drawing.
Couldn't do it without you, though!
th-thump th-thump
And so (is that segue okay?), let's talk about the letters I've received!
I'd like to thank everyone who wrote, whether you've known about me for a while or just stumbled across me in the bookstore!
It's great to hear your thoughts and opinions, and even get updates on recent events! It really makes you think about how quickly time flies.
Incredible!
Books!
Pictures!
Photos!
They all have so many ideas!
A CD!
Wow! Is this really okay?
Lots of people have sent me CDs, cassettes, and even MDs. To be honest, I don't think much about sound when I'm drawing manga, so this is a really refreshing change.
It was way before the drama CD came out, but once I posted stuff for "First King Adventure" on the net.
I'm a total web-n00b!

Behold my ninja club belt! (Not!)

Animal Academy 4 End

I don't care what you do anymore. Just take Fukuta-san and get out of here.
That'll fix everything.
She's in the way.

You must have a rough idea of what my task here is.
I wanted to ask more about you, but it's getting to be a pain.

Even if I can't prove it you're...
...the only one who could've written it.
Excuse me?
That's quite the accusation.
Cats and Raccoons: The Forbidden Love
Kamaba-san has nothing to do with this.
Oh?
I think you have nothing to do with this, Sasuke.

You're here to ask me what this is about.
But you know...
...I'm not in the journalism club.
Did you cut this out?
I thought it was strange that there were rumors that didn't start in my class.
PFFT!
......
ぱしっ
What are you so mad about?

I didn't know you...
...and Sasuke were so close.
Wha--?
It--it's nothing like that!
Well, he's the one who told me to go get you.
Huh?
Re--
Really?
I guess we're... sorta close...
Art Room
I already know.

Get away, you stinky fox!
......
A- anyway!
Have you seen Sasuke-kun?
Nope, haven't seen him.
He hasn't shown up yet.
Why're you looking for him?
You should know!
Remember how he disappeared the moment we got back?
......

Maybe he's at the art club?
He might be with Kamaba-san.
Let's go check it out.
......?
What's going on?
Um... sure?
ガラッ
......?
Kotaro!
Good morning!
Mornin'!
ぐいっ
Good to see you, Miiko!

Fukuta
Good morning, everyone!
Morning, Fukuta-nyan!
Suzu-nyan, too!
Are you feeling better?
Yep! Just fine!
Just needed a day of rest.
Did I miss anything?
Nope!
You're looking a lot better.
Wanna see yesterday's homework?
Good. It's all the same as always.
Oh, by the way...
...has anyone seen Sasuke-kun?

White-1
I've got to thank him.
White-1
Ahh...!

That's right.

I have to thank him for helping me back home.

Now, let's go to bed.
It's about time...
...I started being braver.
......
Yeah!
Fune?
I'm gonna do my best!

Um...
How do I say this to her?
......
Miiko...
......
Please don't forget...
...that dream you told me about.
Okay?

Don't worry about it. I'm just glad you're okay.
......
Good night!
ぱたん
Sorry about that, Miiko.
ぱっ
Don't treat me like I'm stupid!
I wasn't!
Yes, you were! I was in the middle of talking!
S- sorry.
Miiko wasn't finished yet!
......
Miiko...
なで

I'm really sorry, but...
...I was wondering what happened today.
Oh, don't apologize!
We're doing just fine!
Fune's a hu--
Mmph!
And, um, Kotaro-kun?
Kotaro?
He's fine. I think he'll be back in class tomorrow.
Really?
......
You'll be there tomorrow too, right?
Yup! Thanks...
...for coming to check on us.
Oh, it's nothing.

Strange dream I had, huh?
She thinks it was a dream?!
But I guess ...
...I should be glad...
...she thought it was...
... just a dream.
Miiko--
....
Ume-chan, how long have you been there?
Eep!
Um... excuse me.

You said you were human, Fune.
!!!!
That's what you said...
...and then you left.

Now's still--
Wait!
さっ
……
Thanks!
Thank you so much!
'Night!
Kotaro!
It's a secret, right?!

Why should I?
You weren't here!
Oh, great excuse...
のこのこ
MORIMORIGITEN
化ねこ・化きつね・化たぬき・化アニマル専門学校
MORIMORIGITEN
盛森

But...
...I'm glad.
She was sleeping!
Miiko, you didn't go to school today, did you?
What?

Purrrr...
......
Fune?
......
Welcome back.
......
streeetch
Wow, do I feel stupid.

I'm such an idiot!
Miiko's a magical animal...
...so I just assumed she'd be fine as long as she's here.
But who knows how she reacted to me leaving like that?!
ばん
Miiko--!

......
...all right.
You're sure you're okay?
I really am!
You'd tell me about it?
Uh huh!
You know, even teachers feel sad when we're left out.
...yes, sir.
By the way...
...why isn't Suzuhara with you?
Huh?

I won't lose my way again!

Fune was--
Well, we...
Er...
We got lost in the woods!
Is that all?
Y-yes. That's all.
I'm...
...really, really sorry, though!
But--
But...!
...I'm all right now!

Gah!!! Gh-ghost--!
Hold it right there.
Do you have any idea how worried I was?
Ow, ow, ow, ow!
You'd better apologize!
......
So, then...
...tell me why you skipped school today.
......
......

Let's head to the dorms!
Sensei must be angry.
Y- yeah.
He probably is.
I did play hooky all day.
Like that time I skipped class when I had a cold.
I wonder if he sent anyone to my room to get me.
If he did, I bet Miiko went to class like she was supposed to.
Watanuki-sensei can be pretty harsh when he's mad.
Tell me about it.

...huh
Gone
He went without me!
Wait for me!
......
Sure is quiet...
Well, class is over already.

Look, I found it!
We can get in through here!
I ended up...
...coming back.
どき どき
That's it.
It's okay.
It's okay.
It's okay.
It's okay.
It's okay.
Ko-
Kotaro.
Thanks for doing all this.

Report.19

Sparkly Beginnings

They were in the same class.
And even though they were different species, they had some things in common.
The color's name doesn't matter.
That's why she got cornered in the art club so often.
But...it's fun...
...and pretty.
All that matters is what you want to draw.
You can be so flaky sometimes, Kamaba-san.
...
Umemo
Be nice, Silvino.
It's okay. There are plenty of things I don't know
S-same here!
I don't know that much, really.
......
I know that all too well.
Umemo
Yeah.
Can you explain it?

Sasuke's in love?
You're right!
Whoa...!
A Steamy Romance Begins?!
Cats and Raccoons-- The Forbidden Love

First Yuichi Takuma, and now Neko Fukuta, probably.
We didn't even see where she left from, either.
What do you think?
It's too early to call this a failure.
More importan-tly...
...Sasuke Sagami in the freshman white class is your brother, isn't he?
I'd like to bring up the journalism club's cover story for tomorrow's issue.
Honestly, I don't trust their sources.
I don't like seeing this kind of trashy attack, especially when we've lost several students recently.
Here it is-- cross-species romance.

It's a great day, and it's time...
...to bring this ninja club meeting to order!
Attendance is a bit low, I see...
Now for today's report! Sound off!
This is where you tell us if anything unusual has happened.
Well, we've lost several freshmen.

I got back home safe and sound, after all.

How would Sasuke-kun know...
...where I was?
You'll catch a cold.
Does he know what I'm feeling, too?
Either way...
...I know I'll be okay, no matter how worried I get.

A black cat?
?
That's him there!
I just followed him...
...until I got here.
Sasuke-kun?

What would you have done if you couldn't find me, or if I'd said I wouldn't go back?
Huh...? Er...
......
I didn't think of that.
Really?
Ha ha.
That's Kotaro for you.
But I wonder...
...does he really understand that I'm human?
Not that it matters anymore.
But I'm really glad you came, Kotaro.
Did you get lost on the way?
This black cat led me here.

Okay.
Have a safe trip back.
Hey, Kotaro...

I'm sorry!
BOW
I'm heading back now.
You sure straight-ened out fast.
Is it because you're wearing your uniform?
Must be one tough school.
No, it's not that.
I...
I told myself I'd try my best.
I'll make sure...
...to call you and Dad and Ken...
...again soon.

Oh!
Sorry!
Don't move!
What are all these?
...sorry.
It's such...
...a simple thing.
But I feel like all of my drawing in the playground dirt...
...helped me get my feelings sorted out.
I'm sorry.
I may have run away 'cause I was so worried and confused...
...but I'm not ready...
...to give in yet.

I...
I'm going home!!!
I'm going home--!
What're you doing, Sis?
!
Ken! What about you?!
I'm heading home from school.

Miiko
...but...
......

Silvino
Urara
Reira
Uru
Rucha
Chosuke
Ume
Mokichi
Teacher
BOSS
Me
FRIENDS
Umako
Mino
Takuma
Shin
Ruka

So happy...
And now I see...
...how selfish I've been all this time.
Which, is it?
すくっ
ぱんっ
びくっ
....
ぎゅ——…
Leaving like that was selfish!
But...
...I already spilled everything to Miiko!
There's too much to deal with!

?
Yeah.
......
Heh heh.
The look on his face says...
..."you had to ask?"
I'm happy.

Takuma-kun...
...may not be near me anymore...
...and maybe I was a little selfish...
Miiko...
...I'm sorry for lying for so long, but I'm not really a cat.
So it's okay to have a friendship line...
...connecting you and me?

It doesn't matter if you're not human!
I mean...
...we're still friends!
Kota-ro...
It's really hard..
...to truly under-stand...
..how other eople feel...
...But it's okay to try to imagine it...
... right?

Scritch
Likes
Miiko
カリ…
Kotaro
Friends
Takuma
That's right.
They're lines of friendship--the things that connect us.

......
SCUFF
Shin.
Ruka.
SCUFF
Kama-boko.
SCUFF
Ko-taro--!
I can't keep track of so many names!
SCUFF
And Watanuki-sensei!
Give me a second!
......
What the heck am I doing...?
Mokichi!

......
You mean...
...you like her, right?
And how about this...?
Yuichi!

You're pretty cool, Kotaro.
How'd you draw such a solid line between us?
......
That's not all...
ズル
ズル
...how about this?
It's Miiko.
....

The line...
......
What is it?
....

ズルル
ル
ル
...I came here to stop you, Fune.
What does this line...
...even mean?
Is it something bad?
I don't really know, but...
...is it wrong?
It's not dividing us.

Um...
...doesn't this shock you at all?
It seems like it should.
SWISH
......
But...

I...I can't cross it.
"It's because I'm human."
"I'm sorry."
But...
...you...
...were there.
At Morimori.
I was, but now...
...I just ...
...I don't think I can be there any-more.
I mean ...

It seems wrong for me to go to a school to learn to be human.
That's why...
Why what?
......
......
A rock?
There's a line dividing us.

So you're saying...
...you went to Morimori even though you're human?
I don't know how else to put it, Kotaro.
......
But...
...you're still *Fune,* right?
......

......
I know.
Current Situation
Searching?
Left?
?
They were close friends.
Just trust me.
White-1

I'm sure she'll be back.
Just yesterday I told her she could talk to me about anything.
I want it to be that way, but...
...maybe I'm not all that reliable.
......
She'll come back.
So when she does...
......
...please welcome her home.

I ran into your brother ...
...this morning before class.
He said Fukuta might be leaving the school.
We're in the same club, and she wanted to talk to me about something important...
I was just heading ov to see the headmaste
......
She'd never leave Morimori!

Watanuki-sensei!
What're you going to do about the three students who missed class today?
What's the matter, Sasuke?
This is sudden.
I'm just concerned because nobody's asking about them.
That, and...
...I saw Kotaro-kun slipping out late last night. Looks like they might've had a rendezvous planned.
Maybe they got lost in the woods.
....

Report.18
The Kotaro Araki
Equation

......
...you what?
......
Sniff Sniff
......
What're you talking about?
......
Guess the cat's out of the bag.

...didn't you know...
......
...I'm human?

Come on, Fune!
Let's go home to Morimori!
Wait a minute!
Um...
I mean...

You're here!
Fune!!
Huh...?! Wh-what're you doing here, Kotaro?!
ぎゅむっ
It's Fune!
What a relief!
I've been looking all over for you.

I might have the wrong cat...
...but it looks so familiar.
That black cat...
But...
Get a grip!
Of course he's not here.
I must be seeing things.
Everyone's in class right now.
He can't be h--

Wait up!
Can it...?
No way! It can't be him!
......?!!
SLUMP
......
Didn't watch my step...

....
Sasuke-kun...?
Hey--!

I couldn't say anything to anyone.
I'm just running away.
But...
...what should I do now?
Mrow!
!

Thanks for the food!
ガタッ
So soon?
Did I say something wrong?
Nope, it's nothing.
I'm going for a walk!
What's gotten into you?
I'll be back soon!
FUKUTA
How do I decide what to do?
I wondered if it was all a dream...
...but I don't want that to be true!
Takuma-kun must be having an even harder time.
And my being here doesn't change anything.

Um... what're you doing, Mom?
I'll forget if I don't write it down.
So, was this kid you were close with a boy or a girl?
A boy.
Memo Memo
Oh--! Should we talk about the birds and the bees?
It's not like that.
....

"Let's go!"
"I think that's wonderful."
"Are you ready..."
"...to join the ninja club?!"
"Fukuta-san!"
Well, it sounds like you're settling in just fine.
Am I right?
That's wonder-ful.
... yeah.
But recently ...
...there was someone I was getting close to.
......

So you get along, then?
Y-yeah.
I think so.
This is awkward.
I'm glad to hear it!
"I'm so glad!"
......
Yeah.
She's really cute, and...
...there's a guy with a huge crush on her.
"Mean Fune!"
"You're so bossy."

COUGH COUGH
Drink some tea!
Let's see...
...it's kind of a strange school...
...but it's fun.
The end.
How is it strange?
Well...
I mean my classmates.
How so?
Um... there's my roommate.
We're in a dorm...
...and she's really sensitive about smells and stuff.
I mean, I'm handling it okay.
I used to be pickier, but now things don't bother me as much.

Ah!
There's the kettle!
ガタ
guess not much has changed after all.
The food is still the same.
It tastes and smells so familiar.
......
もぐ もぐ
So?
How's school been?
URK.

ぱく
......
How is it?
She's staring at me.
I wonder if it was Mom...
...who patted my head when I was sleeping.
She always used to do that.
It's so embarras-sing.

Um...
I'm home.
Oh!
Still in your pajamas?
I just got up.
Okay!
Time to eat!

...I over-slept.
It's so quiet.
It kinda feels like everything that's happened was just one long dream.
Maybe I'll go back t bed.
ガチャガチャ
Wow, it's bright.
I'm back!
Welcome home, Neko!

Is that you, Mom?
It's good to be home.
......
Dear Neko,
Welcome home! You can heat up some stew for lunch! I'll be back around 2, so make sure to leave some snacks for Ken. See you later!
Love, Mom

Someone's petting me.
It tickles.
Miiko...
She always liked to be petted.
Oh...

Because it's hot these days!
So I'm just your personal heater...?
What's a heater?
Never mind.
You're weird.
You're so smart, Fune!
Fune and Miiko are best friends!
Pet me!
But only if your hands are clean...

Those two...
...do they like each other or not?
I hope they're sleeping well...
...to-night.
Good night, every-one.
Miiko!
It's morning! Wake up!
Good morning!
Morning...
Miiko, you've been sleeping by yourself more lately!

......
"You don't have to force yourself to be here."

I never even told anyone I was leaving.
The least I can do is listen...
...to what's bothering you.
I wonder if Sensei will be upset.
And Miiko...
I hope she gets to sleep okay.
Kotaro and Ume-chan must already be in bed.
There's still school tomorrow.
"I'll make sure..."
"...you don't have to leave the school."
Sasuke-kun...

It's summer break!
Right?
Huh?
?
Am I wrong?
....
Nope, you got it!
Summer break starts early in high school!
... really?
Uh huh! Totally!
And by the way, that's my spoon.
I'm glad I came home...
...but...
...I still left Morimori.
What do I do now?

I'm already in high school...
...and Ken's only in fourth grade!
And he's using my spoon.
What?
Eyeing my ice cream?
I don't care about your ice cream!
......
Aha! I figured out why you came home!

Ahhh...
I'm so anxious...
Ken, what're you still doing up?
Hmm?
I've started watching these...
...fun five-minute educational shows. They explain stuff really clearly.
They're only on at night.
Huh.
I had no idea he was into that.
They really do explain it all in just five minutes!
I know, right?

......
Where're Mom and Dad?
Dad's not home yet, and Mom's asleep.
Of course.
You really should've called first, you know.
We haven't fixed up your room since you left.
The futon's good to go, though.
That's fine.
FUKUTA
How about a bath?
Definitely!
And Sis...
....
Welcome home.

Ken...?
What're you doing?
Um... looking for my keys.
Keys?
Heh.
......
......
Aren't you coming in?
うい――ん…
Y--
Yes!
Ken's always got it together.
Hey... Did you grow?
Why? Do I look taller?
And what are you doing out so late?
I was craving ice cream, so I went to the corner store.
But...

Everything...
The train, the traffic lights, even the crosswalks—it feels like it's been forever since I left.
Doesn't help that it's night.
....
!
My house keys!
Ohh, where did I put them...?
Huh?
Sis?

All right! (I made it!)
......
Hmm...
I feel kinda weird.

ガタン
ガタン
Oh!
Just two more stops.
Yeah...
This is the way home.
Not long now!
I'm going home!
Just a little further...
...and I'll be there!

I won't let you down!
...huh?

......
Heh heh.
Take care!
Mom, Dad, Ken...thank you.

Sorry I can't make it to your opening ceremony.
Don't worry bout it!
I promise I'll do great in high school!
You're leaving for school already, Sis?
Oh, Ken! You're awake?
Yawn.
We just got up.
Hey...
You're heading out, Neko?
Wow! Dad, you never get up this early!
I couldn't miss...
...the first day of your new school year, could I?

You're sure you're not forgetting anything?
Yup! I'm all set!
That backpack is huge! You really don't need a ride?
I'll be fine, Mom!
What about you? Aren't you going to be late for work?
......
I'll just sleep in today. ☆
Are you serious--?
Are you sure that's okay?!
Don't worry. At least let me see you off!
After all, today's my only chance.
04 32

Report.17

The Door to Anywhere and its Key

The Tanabata story says two lovers were banished to opposite sides...
...of the Milky Way because they neglected their duties.
I ran through the dark without looking away...
SLIP
ズルッ
Oof!
...tripping again and again.
But nothi could ke me fron running.
...in the direction he'd pointed in that day.
Lights kept flickering in and out.
I felt as if I was running through a dream...
I realized they were so blurry because I was crying too hard to see them.
...and then I jumped aboard the train.

Oh!
It's the...
...Milky Way...
That's when I realized...
...I'd come back to the same field as before.

What do I do?
What do you say at a time like this?
Please let me out? Please open up? I want to go? None of those are right.
What is it? What is it?!
My head's spinning.
I can't even think straight!
Spinning and spinning and spinning...

Oh yeah ... I can't leave...
... through here.
So what do I do now?

I can't be the one who does it!
It has to be you!
......
Hurry and stop Fukuta-san!
Or else she'll end up just like Takuma-kun!
ばっ
?
What's going on?
Murm murm

......
What now?!
Huff...
......
H-hurry! You...have to go...
Find Fukuta-san...!

Sasuke?
......
He untie: him-self?
Oh, he broke the branch.
He sure is des-perate.
Not that it makes any difference.
MORIMORIGI TEN
!

......
パキ
...huh?

That's right.

It's too much.

Too much has hap-pened.

They're magical animals. We're just too different--!

And I can't accept that the weird student handbook is just some perfectly normal thing.

It's wrong for me to be here!

......
It's true.
......
ぎゅっ
Take...
Take care, okay...?
SLAM

I'm...
...hu-
man!

....
I'm sorry, Miiko.
It's...
...because I'm a human.
....
Fune?
はっ

もす
もす もす
ぎゅっ!
ぎゅっ!
Fune? What are you doing?
I'm... ...pack-ing.
I think.
How come?
......

"It's okay."
"You don't have to be here."
What do I do?
I'm really starting to doubt myself.
SLAM
Fune!
Where'd you go?

You...
...really think so?
I dunno.
Was I really...
...trying too hard?
I...

I know...
...you're trying really hard, Fukuta-san.
You don't have to force yourself to be here.
You don't have to fight so hard.

Eep--!
MORIMORIGITEN
His grip...
...on my shoulder...
...kinda...
That hurts ...

"If there's any way I can help, just tell me."
I'm sorry.
"Although I don't know how useful I'd be."
I'm sorry, but...
But I'm...
I'm a...
...human.

"I promise I'll do my best!"
Fukuta-san?
Oh!
You okay?
Um, yeah! Totally fine!
Are you sure?
O-of course I'm sure!
"You don't need to pretend, you know."

I was so sure he belonged here.
I never thought he'd just... leave.
Takuma-kun was a magical animal.
....
... yeah.
That's right, huh?
But...
...what about me?
I get the feeling that...
...I don't belong here.
Kotoko
Toko
Koyanagi
Umako
Suzuhara
Miiko
Takaku
Urara
Tsukigusa
Mino
Tome
Rin
Fukuta
Neko

Me? Well...
I came out to look at the stars.
Wow, you're a romantic!
Listen, I'm sorry.
Huh?
I heard about what hap-pened...
...with Takuma-kun.
Oh, that!
It's not your fault!
I didn't mean for things to end up like this.
I really am sorry.

I don't even know what to think anymore...
Fukuta-san?
....
Ahh--! Yusuke-kun!
Hello? Personal space?
What're you doing out here?
I-I was just heading back from the school.
I...
...forgot something...
...there.
You forgot something?
Really...?
Like a text-book?
You sure are a good student.
I-if you say so.
What about you, Yusuke-kun?

Shiver
Will I be able to...
...go back to the way things used to be?
Back to my friends and family?
Neko Fukuta
I...

ザァ
GOD

Why do I...
...have to keep this thing?
I have to keep it for three whole years?
Until graduation?
How come?
Maybe..
...it's more special tha
I thought.
What did I...
...do?
There's something...
May-be...
...I al-ready did...
... some-thing.
What do I do?
What...?

Just so we're clear, Sasuke...
...don't even think about getting in my way.
That's right.
Maybe I should talk to Sasuke-kun about this.
But then again...
...may-be...
...I shouldn't show it to just anyone.
Techni-cally it doesn't even belong to me.
I won-der...
...if Sasuke-kun would know any-thing?
It didn't seem like he had his own, though.

Or if it wasn't either of those things...
...then maybe it wandered off on its own.
This is all turning into a bigger hassle than I expected.
Even the opening in the barrier has gotten shaky and unstable.
おとっ
And there are way too many humans wandering around.

Well, if it isn't Sasuke.
What're you up to?
......
What was with you earlier?
Did you lose something?
Yeah, you could say that.
You don't just *lose* something that big, though.
......
So either *you* took it or some freak stole it.

It isn't here.
In that case...
たっ
......
Hmm?

As for Miiko, who was left behind...
...
ぽんっ
rustle
カサ
!
......
Fune?
?

What *is* it for...
... exactly?
It'll do a lot for you.
... huh?
Oh, well.
The least I can do is listen to what's bothering you.
なで
なで
Talking it out will make you feel better.
....
......
?
Doesn't remember why she came running in a panic in the first place.

Giving it back!
Oh! I forgot to thank you for letting me borrow it!
Huh?
Aren't you supposed to hang on to that for all three years?
Uh...
Three years?
Is...
Is that true?
I think so...
... yeah.
Until graduation...
......
I'm... supposed to keep this?
?
Isn't that what it's for?

W-Watanuki-sensei!
S-s-s-something came out of my book!
Hm? Fukuta?
Why haven't you gone home yet?
I just ran over from the dorm! You've got to listen!
Something's wrong with my book!
There're things going in and out of it!
White-1

Report. 16

re: Reality World

Spinning through the darkness.

スゥ…
にゃ――……
…………!!
ガサッ!
バサッ
MORIMORIGITEN
盛森

Kimura
Sasuke Sagami
Input Unknown
8/29
Yuichi Takuma
2/28
Tagoori
Input Unknown
!
My tears--!
ura
8/
Sagami
2/
4/
8/
7/
6/
Fushi
......
......
......
...who's there?

......
I've never gone in.
Is that the truth?
I just said I didn't do it!
What's with you?
I see.
Never mind. No big deal.
...what gives?
......
It's nothing.

Clack
Ah!
Sasuke.
Were you in my room?
What do you mean?
Well? Did you go in or not?
Your life could depend on the answer.

I second that.
You're making it hard for the whole class.
Sigh...
SLAM
..........!
WHUMP
!

Kotaro never used to get angry, even if you swiped his lunch.
He took everything in stride.
Right back atcha!
He treated everyone like a friend.
You know, I think he was talking about an enemy at lunch.
An enemy?
What kind of enemy?!
Kotaro Araki is under the impression someone drove Yuichi Takuma away.
That "someone" is now his enemy.
Ranmaru Fushi...
...your bad attitude abou Yuichi Takum is backfiring on you.
You really shouldn't say you're happy that he's gone.
You're not doing yourself any favors.
......

Girls' Dorm
Boys' Dorm
Go away!
I'm not changing rooms!
Come in here again and I'll bite you!
Stupid Kotaro!
He's been acting like a jerk ever since Takuma left!
Calm down, Ranmaru.
Chill.

......
Huh?
?
Takuma
Tagoori
Sasuke
Yuichi
Shin
H-how did that happen...?
8 / 13
8 / 29
2 / 28
4 / 10
スゥ
Mokichi
Sasuke
Yuichi
Shin
... circles?

Please don't erase him...

FSSST

Araki
Kara
Kino
Kim
Sag
Tak
Tag
No
Fu
M

Kotaro
Silvino
Kagekuma
Mokichi
Sasukei
Yuichi
Shin
Takahiko
Ranmaru
Harabei
O

drip
drip

Araki
Karamatsu
Kinoshita
Kimura
Sagami
Takuma
Tagoori
Nagao
Fushi
Mat

a
ei
ni
in
akahiko
Ranmaru

I'm signing up for basketball!
Please don't...! Please don't disappear!

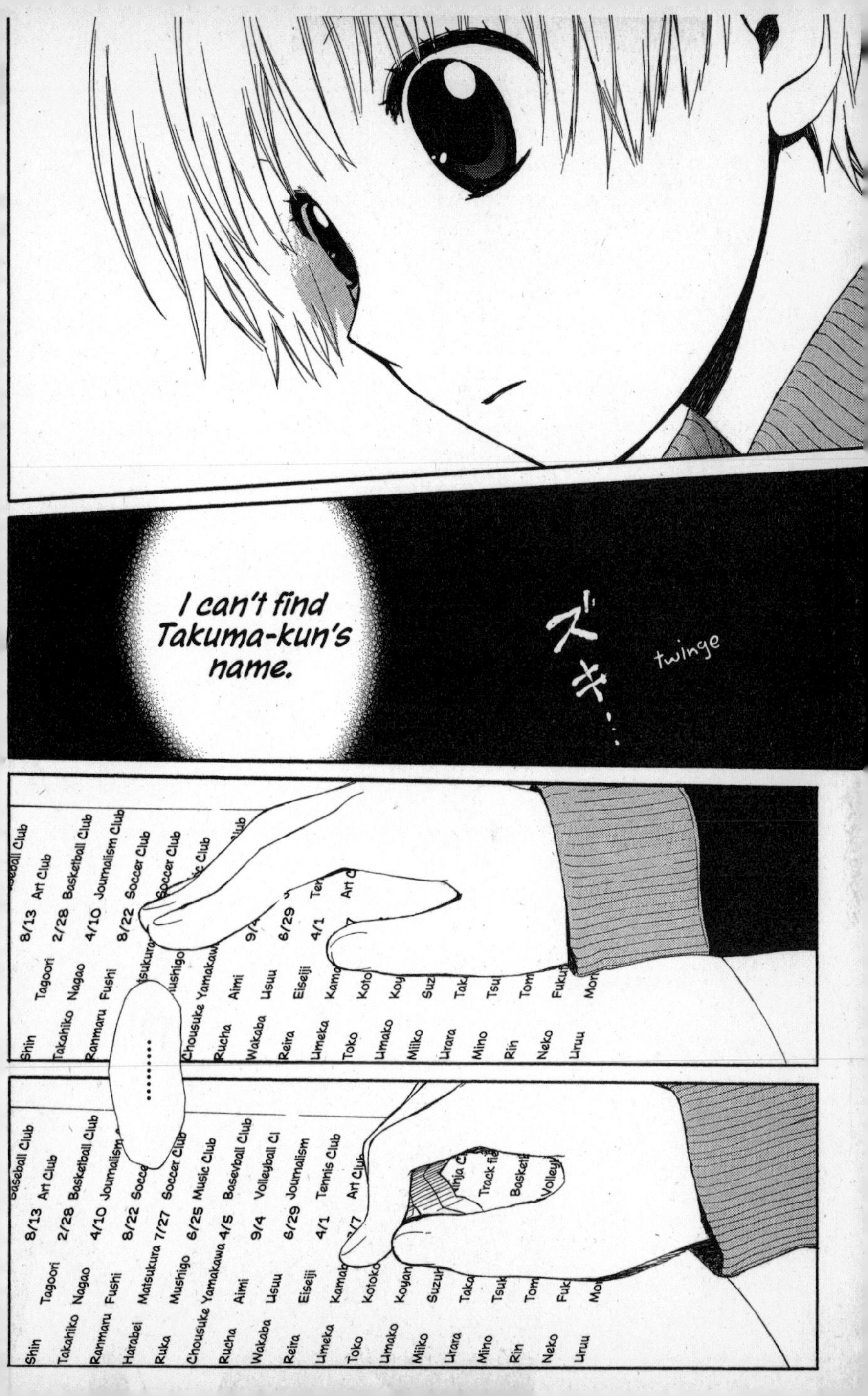
I can't find Takuma-kun's name.
ズキ…
twinge
……….

Sasuke-kun?

きょろ きょろ

You could've just *given* it to me...

Honestly...

......

......

The first-year white class.

Aha!

3
4
5

Baseball Club
Art Club

Basketball Club
Journalism Clu
Soccer Club
Soccer Club
Music Club
Baseball Club
Volleyball Cl
Journalism
Tennis Club
Art Club

2/28
8/13

2/28
4/10
8/22
7/27
6/25
4/5
9/4
6/29
4/1
3/7
3/2
9/5
9/9
4/19

Bask
Club
Ninja Club
Sewing Club

8/27
3/12
2/22
3/20

Found it.

I'm beat!
......
Today was a real workout.
I wonder what Kotaro's wish was?
I bet it was about Takuma-kun.
!

Please work.

I hope some of Miiko's "I want to see you"...
...is meant for Takuma-kun.
Heave, ho!
Heave, ho!
Please come back
Neko Fukuta

I want to see you.
...wow!
Miiko!
Your writing's a lot better!
!
You can read it?
I sure can!
......

Please come back.
Neko Fukuta
Maybe i every-one...
...makes the same wish, he really will come back.
......

...that's it!
A shrine archway!
Wait, what am I doing?
Why the heck did I draw that?
Well, no harm done.
Did everyone get a piece of paper?
Good! Now write down your wish and sign it.
My wish!
....

I never knew there was a shrine all the way out here.
Hmm... I wonder...
....

How would it feel to suddenly learn you're not human?
It was so hard listening to everyone talk about Takuma-kun...
...when they didn't know the first thing about him.
So hard.
Snap out of it!

Fukuta-san?
Yeah, Ume-chan?
You don't need to pretend, you know.
Was I? I didn't notice...
I was so surprised when you hit Ranmaru-kun!
Oh ...
That.
If there's any way I can help, just tell me.
Although I don't know how useful I'd be.
Thanks.
Sorry for scaring you earlier.
Oh, I wasn't scared ...
I'm sure lots of the others feel the same way as you and Kotaro-kun.
You think so?
I mean... Takuma-kun gave up trying to become human halfway.
That's hard to deal with.
We're ...
...not talking about the same thing...

I should've told him not to go.
Should I have just said, "Okay, see you later"?
But that just would've made it harder for him.
If I'd just held on to his hand...
I'm so confused, I can't even think straight.
...we could have talked it out.
What're you doing?
Trying not to yawn.
Gather 'round, everyone!
I can't get all choked up like that!

I swear ...
...whoever it is, I'll kick his butt.
That was pretty cool, Kotaro.
?
Thanks.
And me...?
I'm still not over it.
Oh, no.
I'm tearing up again.
Takuma-kun...

Think it was Ranmaru?
Nah.
メキ
メキ
メキ
メキ
Although we kinda had a fight yesterday, too.
I can't quite figure it out...
I really don't get what Yuichi was thinking.
But...
...I do know the enemy's close by.
"Enemy"?
Daily Dose of Miiko.
......
He almost had you, Miiko.
ぐい！

Now, as I was saying...
...I expect you all to help each other with the assignment.
七夕
Tanabata Festival
I really do think...
...something happened to Yuichi.
Somebody must've done something so bad to him that he *had* to leave!

べしっ
Hey! That hurt!
Oops!
S-sorry. My hand slipped.
Ranmaru-kun, no fighting in class!
I didn't do anything!
ガタッ
So why'd Takuma leave, anyway?
Why're you still talking about it?
If you'd all kindly be quiet!

I didn't even say anything!
You're just gonna ask when Takuma's coming back.
You've asked every single day!
If you're so sad without a roommate, I'll trade with you.
So it was you, Ranmaru!
Say what?
Yuichi wouldn't have left for no reason!
I know you're behind it!
What --?!
I didn't do nothin'!
Takuma left of his own free will!
Don't blame me!
Anyway, I never liked him from day one!
He always acted like some kind of *human*--

So now...
...I'd like you...
...to find a nice tall bamboo stalk...
...and cut it, so you can each...
...make your own wishes.
Wow, they all got serious fast.
Without further ado...
Good luck!
Watanuki-sensei?
Give it a rest, Kotaro.
We don't need to hear it ***again***.

I can't hold them back.
Yuichi Takuma is gone.
The legend says that once a year, on August 7th during the Tanabata festival...
...your wish will come true if you tie it to a bamboo stalk.

What's that stuff coming out of your eyes?

Report.15 Tears on the Page

カラ
カラ
tak
But one person...
...was missing.

It was just another morning.
Same old school.
Same old classroom.
White-1
Same seat by the window.
Everything was exactly like the day before.
rattle

Volume 4
by
MOYAMU FUJINO

HAMBURG // LONDON // LOS ANGELES // TOKYO

Animal Academy: Hakobune Hakusho Volume 4

Created by Moyamu Fujino

Translation - Katherine Schilling
English Adaptation - Ysabet Reinhardt MacFarlane
Retouch and Lettering - Star Print Brokers
Copy Edit - Soo-Kyung Kim
Production Artist - Rui Kyo
Cover Layout - Stephanie Gonzaga
Graphic Designer - Louis Csontos

Editor - Lillian Diaz-Przybyl
Print Production Manager - Lucas Rivera
Managing Editor - Vy Nguyen
Senior Designer - Louis Csontos
Art Director - Al-Insan Lashley
Director of Sales and Manufacturing - Allyson De Simone
Associate Publisher - Marco F. Pavia
President and C.O.O. - John Parker
C.E.O. and Chief Creative Officer - Stu Levy

A TOKYOPOP® Manga

TOKYOPOP Inc.
5900 Wilshire Blvd. Suite 2000
Los Angeles, CA 90036

E-mail: info@TOKYOPOP.com
Come visit us online at www.TOKYOPOP.com

ISBN: 978-1-4278-1098-4

First TOKYOPOP printing: April 2010

10 9 8 7 6 5 4 3 2

Printed in the USA

[4]

HAKOBUNE はこぶね白書 HAKUSHO

Cartoon by
MOYAMU FUJINO
藤野もやむ

At one point, Acid Phreak compared cracking computer systems to walking into a building where the door was unlocked. Barlow responded by saying he kept the door to his house unlocked, and Acid challenged Barlow to e-mail his address to him. Barlow replied in the *Harper's* conference:

```
''Acid. My house is at 372 North Franklin Street in Pinedale,
Wyoming. If you're heading north on Franklin, you go about two
blocks off the main drag before you run into a hay meadow on the
left. I've got the last house before the field. The computer is
always on . . . And is that really what you mean? Are you merely
just the kind of little sneak that goes around looking for easy
places to violate? You disappoint me, pal. For all your James
Dean-on-Silicon rhetoric, you're not a cyberpunk. You're just a
punk.''
```

The next day, Phiber Optik posted Barlow's credit history in the *Harper's* conference. He had hacked TRW, the private company that stores the key details of everybody's credit history in online computer systems that are supposed to be secure.

The arguments continued, the WELL conference ended, and the *Harper's* editors started cutting down the hundreds of pages of online rhetoric to paper-publishable size. Before the article was published, however, *Harper's* took Optik, Acid, and Barlow to dinner in Manhattan. As Barlow noted at the time, "They looked to be as dangerous as ducks." They didn't exactly become immediate friends after meeting face-to-face, but Barlow and the crackers did find some common ground—a commitment to individual liberty as a core value.

Cut back to Pinedale: "And, as I became less their adversary and more their scoutmaster," Barlow recalled when he told his story, first online and then in print, "I began to get 'conference calls' in which six or eight of them would crack pay phones all over New York and simultaneously land on my line in Wyoming. . . . On January 24, 1990, a platoon of Secret Service agents entered the apartment which Acid Phreak shares with his mother and 12-year-old sister. The latter was the only person home when they burst through the door with guns drawn. They managed to hold her at bay for about half an hour until their quarry happened home."

Among the others raided as part of a separate investigation was Craig Neidorf, whose crime was to publish sections of an allegedly purloined document in *Phrack*, an online newsletter he distributed electronically.

Another related raid resulted in the seizure of some key business equipment of Steve Jackson, whose Austin company published a fictional board game that law enforcement officials were convinced was a computer crime manual. The news was all over the Net. Law had come to cyberspace in a big way, and they were busting all the wrong people. More frighteningly, they were intimidating people just for the crime of disseminating information, and they were doing it on a nationally coordinated basis.

Acid and a few other young men across the United States were part of the now-notorious Operation Sun Devil, involving more than 150 federal agents, local and state law enforcement agencies, and the security arms of three or four regional telephone companies. Some of the arrests made around the same time had to do with the illegal electronic possession of a document that turned out to be publicly available for less than $100. The plot was already sinister enough when Barlow got his call from Agent Baxter of the FBI. Baxter, who operated out of an office in Rock Springs, Wyoming, one hundred miles away from Pinedale, wanted to get together with Barlow as soon as possible to talk about some kind of mysterious—at least to him—conspiracy to steal the trade secrets of Apple Computer.

A word of explanation is always in order when discussing high-tech crimes, because many involve theft or vandalism of intangible property such as private credit records, electronic free speech, or proprietary software. Apple computers all include in their essential hardware something known as a ROM chip that contains, encoded in noneraseable circuits, the special characteristics that make an Apple computer an Apple computer. The ROM code, therefore, is indeed a valuable trade secret to Apple; although it is stored in a chip, ROM code is computer software that can be distributed via disk or even transmitted over networks. If you knew that code, you could make your own ROMs and bootleg Apple computers. Well-known figures in the PC industry had been receiving unsolicited computer disks containing pieces of that code, accompanied by a manifesto by some group that called itself the NuPrometheus League. (Barlow swears that Agent Baxter repeatedly pronounced it the "New Prosthesis League.")

Agent Baxter's puzzlement was the heart of the encounter between him and Barlow. Not only Agent Baxter, but his sources of information, seemed exceedingly unclear about the nature of whatever it was they were supposed to be investigating. It turned out that Barlow had been contacted by the FBI because his name was on the roster of an annual private gathering called the Hackers' Conference. Baxter reported that he had been informed that the Hackers' Conference was an underground organization of computer outlaws that was probably part of the same grand conspiracy as the NuPrometheus League.

Hacker used to mean something different from what it means now. Steven Levy's 1984 book *Hackers: Heroes of the Computer Revolution* was about the unorthodox young programmers who created in the 1960s and 1970s the kind of computer technology that nonprogrammers used in the 1980s and 1990s. Although they kept odd hours and weren't fashion plates, and although they weren't averse to solving lock-picking puzzles, the original hackers were toolmakers, not burglars.

The first Hackers' Conference was a gathering of the traditional kind of hacker, not the system cracker that the mass media have since identified with the word *hacker*. I've attended enough Hackers' Conferences myself to know they are innocent events that celebrate the best in what used to be known as Yankee ingenuity, more like Nerdstocks than saboteur summits. Something seems weirdly and dishearteningly wrong when the FBI is investigating the kind of people that gave America whatever it retains of a competitive edge in the PC business.

That wasn't the only thing Baxter was unclear about. John Draper, known since the 1970s as Captain Crunch, is old enough to be Acid Phreak's father, but he still claims respect and notoriety as the original "phone phreak" who actually predated computer crackers. He's still a (legitimate) computer programmer (who created, among other things, the first word processor for IBM's first personal computer). Crunch, as he is known these days, is an amiable and unorthodox fellow who mostly stays in his apartment and writes programs. Baxter told Barlow, who probably had to physically restrain himself from the kind of involuntary laughter that spews beverages on people's shirts, that Draper was "the CEO of Autodesk, Inc., an important Star Wars contractor." And Draper was suspected of having "Soviet contacts."

Just about everything Baxter told Barlow was wrong, and Barlow knew it. There was a wacky near-miss element to the way Baxter was wrong. It was true that Draper had once worked at Autodesk as a programmer, but that was as close to being the CEO of Autodesk that he ever got; the real CEO of Autodesk, John Walker, definitely was on the Hackers' Conference list of attendees himself. Autodesk makes computer-aided design software for personal computers and was in the process of developing a cyberspace toolkit for architects and designers, but it was hardly a top-secret defense contractor. John Draper did have some Russian programmer friends, but by 1990, the Evil Empire was in the throes of disintegration.

Baxter's story was hilariously misinformed enough to make anybody worry about how well the FBI is doing against the real techno-criminals, the nuclear terrorists and large-scale data thieves. So Barlow sat Baxter down at a computer, showed him what computer source code looked like, demonstrated e-mail, and downloaded a file from the WELL. Baxter, Barlow reported, "took to rubbing his face with both hands, peering up over his fingertips and alternating 'It sure is something, isn't it?' with statements such as 'Whooo-ee.' "

There was controversy on the WELL about Barlow's online recollections of his candid conversations with Agent Baxter. The most radical faction in the online discussion insisted that Barlow was acting as an informant for the FBI. Barlow's point was that if everybody in law enforcement was acting on completely erroneous information about cyberspace technology, travesties of justice were inevitable.

Another person on the Hackers' Conference roster, who had actually received some of the purloined ROM code, unsolicited, and properly reported it to the authorities, was Mitchell Kapor. Kapor had cofounded Lotus Development Corporation, one of the first and most successful software companies of the PC era, and had codesigned Lotus 1-2-3, one of the most successful PC programs of all time. He had sold the company years ago for multiple tens of millions of dollars, and the WELL was one of the places he now could be found, talking about software design, intellectual property, and civil liberties in cyberspace. He, too, was concerned with the Sun Devil arrests and what that might mean for the perhaps short-lived liberties presently enjoyed in cyberspace. He too, had been contacted by the FBI.

In late spring 1990, while he was flying in his jet cross-country, Kapor realized he was almost directly over Barlow's ranch. He had been following Barlow's reports on the WELL; they had met in person for the first time at a WELL party—introduced, as a matter of fact, by Blair Newman. Kapor called Barlow from his jet and asked Barlow if he was interested in a drop-in visit.

Kapor landed, he and Barlow started talking about the Sun Devil arrests, the NuPrometheus affair, the recent state of high aggressiveness by federal law enforcement authorities in cyberspace, and law enforcement's correspondingly high state of puzzlement about what was really going on in the world of high-tech communications. They founded the Electronic Frontier Foundation (EFF) that afternoon in Barlow's Pinedale kitchen.

Within a few days, Kapor had put Barlow in touch with the distinguished constitutional law firm that had made it possible for the *New York Times* to publish the Pentagon Papers. Kapor, concerned about the nature of the Sun

Devil arrests and what they signaled for civil liberties in cyberspace, offered to support the costs of legal defense.

Within days of the Pinedale meeting, Steve Wozniak, cofounder of Apple Computer, and John Gilmore, Unix telecommunications wizard and one of the first employees of the enormously successful Sun Microsystems, offered to match Kapor's initial contributions. A board of directors was recruited that included, among others, WELL founder Stewart Brand. The EFF endowment was intended from the beginning to be a great deal more than a defense fund.

The EFF founders saw, as the first reporters from the mass media did not, that Sun Devil was not just a hacker bust. The EFF founders agreed that there was a good chance that the future of American democracy could be strongly influenced by the judicial and legislative structures beginning to emerge from cyberspace. The reasons the EFF spoke out regarding Acid, Optik, and Scorpion as well as Neidorf and Jackson had to do with the assumptions made by the Secret Service about what they could and could not do to citizens. "The Electronic Frontier Foundation will fund, conduct, and support legal efforts to demonstrate that the Secret Service has exercised prior restraint on publications, limited free speech, conducted improper seizure of equipment and data, used undue force, and generally conducted itself in a fashion which is arbitrary, oppressive, and unconstitutional," Barlow declared in an early manifesto. "In addition, we will work with the Computer Professionals for Social Responsibility and other organizations to convey to both the public and the policy-makers metaphors which will illuminate the more general stake in liberating Cyberspace."

System cracking is serious business. Someday, some data vandal is going to do real damage to something important, like a 911 response system, or air traffic control, or medical records. But Acid Phreak and his buddies weren't the culprits. And the way they were busted sent a chill down the spine of every sysop of every one of the forty to fifty sixty thousand BBSs in America.

The legal defense team blew a fatal hole in the 911 case when an expert who happened to monitor the public EFF conference on the WELL offered a key piece of expert knowledge: the document that was so highly valued that hundreds of law enforcement officers were protecting it on behalf of a large corporation could be obtained legally from the publications department of that corporation for an amount that would merit something more akin to a petty theft misdemeanor charge than a guns-drawn raid. The problem soon turned out to be one of education: not even the deep pockets of the EFF founders and the best legal expertise they could buy could be effective against a system in which very few people involved in enforcing the law or defending suspects understood the kind of place—cyberspace—in which the alleged crimes took place.

It wasn't just the legal system that had been taken by surprise. New social and civil rights and responsibilities, utterly untested by case law, have been emerging from CMC technology, along with the online cultures that have been growing in it. To most citizens and lawmakers in 1990, online newsletters and ROM code and the constitutional implications of computer networks were remote and incomprehensible issues. In that atmosphere of confusion and ignorance, most people thought the EFF was defending hackers, period; the rights of electronic speech and assembly that the EFF founders were so concerned about were invisible to the majority of the population. Someone had to do a better job of explaining to citizens that they were in danger of losing rights they didn't know they possessed.

***

The EFF began its public outreach via a conference on the WELL, inviting both the prosecutors and the defendants in the Sun Devil busts to engage in a dialogue with cryptographers, criminologists, hackers, crackers, and attorneys about the kind of law enforcement that is proper and improper in cyberspace. The Computers, Freedom, and Privacy conference was organized independently by some of the people who had participated in the EFF's online discussions on the WELL and the EFF's node on the Net, bringing the former online and courtroom opponents together face-to-face.

By fall 1992, the EEF's office in Washington was directed by Jerry Berman and the Cambridge office was directed by ex-WELL director Cliff Figallo. They hired a legal director and a publications director. They began holding press conferences, attending congressional hearings, publishing online and mailing paper pamphlets, and seeking members via the Net. By the end of 1992, however, tension emerged between the Cambridge office, where the educational and community-building efforts were focused, and the Washington, D.C. office, where the political lobbying efforts were based. The EFF board, deciding that the organization should focus its energy on lobbying and legal support, closed its Cambridge office in 1993. By that time, the Computers, Freedom, and privacy conference and other allied organizations, such as Computer Professionals for Social Responsibility, were in position to pick up the outreach and community-building tasks that the EFF was no longer supporting.

At the end of January 1993, the Steve Jackson case came to a dramatic climax. The EFF and Steve Jackson Games had filed suit against the Secret Service. Jackson's publishing business, almost two years later, had not recovered from the confiscation of computer equipment belonging to Steve Jackson Games. We followed the trial on the Net. Shari Steele from the EFF's legal team relayed news from the site of the trial in Austin to the Net:

Hi everybody.

I really don't have much time to write, but I just witnessed one of the most dramatic courtroom events. The judge in the Steve Jackson Games trial just spent 15 minutes straight reprimanding Agent Timothy Foley of the United States Secret Service for the behavior of the United States regarding the raid and subsequent investigation of Steve Jackson Games. He asked Foley, in random order (some of this is quotes, some is paraphrasing because I couldn't write fast enough):

How long would it have taken you to find out what type of business Steve Jackson Games does? One hour? In any investigation prior to March 1st (the day of the raid) was there any evidence that implicated Steve Jackson or Steve Jackson Games, other than Blankenship's presence? You had a request from the owner to give the computers and disks back. You knew a lawyer was called. Why couldn't a copy of the information contained on the disks be given within a matter of days? How long would it have taken to copy all disks? 24 hours? Who indicated that Steve Jackson was running some kind of illegal activity? Since the equipment was not accessed at the Secret Service office in Chicago after March 27, 1990, why wasn't the equipment released on March 28th? Did you or anyone else do any investigation after March 1st into the nature of Mr. Jackson and his business? You say that Coutorie told you it was a game company. You had the owner standing right in front of you on March 2nd. Is it your testimony that the first time that you realized that he was a publisher and had business records on the machine was when this suit was filed?

The government was so shaken, they rested their case, never

even calling Barbara Golden or any of their other witnesses to the stand. Closing arguments are set for this afternoon. It truly was a day that every lawyer dreams about. The judge told the Secret Service that they had been very wrong. I'll try to give a full report later. Shari

The verdict came in on March 12, 1993, a significant legal victory for Steve Jackson Games and the EFF, although certainly not the last battle in this struggle. The judge awarded damages of $1,000 per plaintiff under the Electronic Communications Privacy Act and, under the Privacy Protection Act, awarded Steve Jackson Games $42,259 for lost profits and out-of-pocket costs of $8,781. The method in which law enforcement authorities had seized Jackson's computers was ruled to be an unlawful search and seizure of a publisher.

It remains to be seen whether the online civil libertarians can build a broad-based movement beyond the ranks of the early adapters and whether even a well-organized grassroots movement can stand up to the kind of money and power at stake in this debate. But at least the battle over fundamental civil rights in cyberspace has been joined, and organizations like the EFF, Computer Professionals for Social Responsibility, and Computers, Freedom, and Privacy are beginning to proliferate. If these organizations succeed in gaining supporters outside the circles of technically knowledgeable enthusiasts, citizens might gain powerful leverage at a crucial time. There comes a time when small bands of dedicated activists need wide support; in cyberspace, that time has arrived.

The online community has a responsibility to the freedom it enjoys, and if it wants to continue to enjoy that freedom, more people must take an active part in educating the nontechnical population about several important distinctions that are lost in the blitz of tabloid journalism. Most important, people in cyberspace are citizens, not criminals, nor do the citizens tolerate the criminals among them; however, law enforcement agencies have a commitment to constitutional protections of individual rights, and any breach of those rights in the pursuit of criminals threatens the freedoms of other citizens' rights to free speech and assembly.

The constitutional government of the United States has proved to be a flexible instrument for two centuries, but cyberspace is very new and we are moving into it quickly. Any freedoms we lose now are unlikely to be regained later. The act of simply extending the Bill of Rights to that portion of cyberspace within U.S. jurisdiction would have an enormously liberating impact on the application of CMC to positive social purposes everywhere in the world.

Grassroots and Global: CMC Activists

Are virtual communities just computerized enclaves, intellectual ivory towers? The answer must lie in the real world, where people try to use the technology for the purpose of addressing social problems. Nonprofit organizations on the neighborhood, city, and regional levels, and nongovernmental organizations (NGOs) on the global level, can be seen as modern manifestations of what the enlightenment philosophers of democracy would have called "civil society." The ideal of building what one pioneer, Howard Frederick, calls a "global civil society" is one clear vision of a democratic use of CMC. Nonprofits and NGOs that use CMC effectively are concrete evidence of ways this technology can be used for humanitarian purposes.

Nonprofits and NGOs are organizationally well-suited to benefit from the leverage offered by CMC technology and the people power inherent in virtual communities. These groups feed people, find them medical care, cure blindness, free political prisoners, organize disaster relief, find shelter for the homeless—tasks as deep into human nonvirtual reality as you can get. The people who accomplish this work suffer from underfunding, overwork, and poor communications. Any leverage they can gain, especially if it is affordable, will pay off in human lives saved, human suffering alleviated.

Nonprofit organizations and volunteer action groups dealing with environmentalism, civil rights, physical and sexual abuse, suicide prevention, substance abuse, homelesslness, public health issues, and all the other people problems in modern society that aren't addressed adequately by the government, the justice system, or the private sector generally operate on a shoestring, with volunteer labor. Few of them have people with enough computer expertise to set up a mailing list database or an e-mail network, so they end up spending five times as much money by paying a service or misusing volunteers to do their mailings.

Dan Ben-Horin tapped the social consciousness of experts on the WELL, matching computer-literate mentors with nonprofit organizations. The scheme worked so well that it turned into a well-funded nonprofit organization itself—CompuMentor. Here is the story of the birth of CompuMentor, in Ben-Horin's own words:

> The CompuMentor project began four and a half years ago when I couldn't get my new 24-pin printer to print envelopes without smudging. I had just started logging onto the WELL, so I posted my printer

question in the IBM conference. The answers I received were not only informal but also profuse, open-hearted, full-spirited. The proverbial thought balloon instantly appeared. These computerites on the WELL wanted to share their skills.

I had recently spent more than four years as ad director of Media Alliance of San Francisco, where I had started a technical assistance facility called Computer Alliance. Computer Alliance offered training to nonprofit groups and individuals who traveled to Fort Mason in San Francisco for instruction. From various conversations with nonprofit organizations, as well as my own experience as a fledgling computerist, I knew how easy it is to take a great class and then forget a crucial part of the lesson on the drive home.

My own learning had really commenced when my next-door neighbor expressed a willingness to help me whenever I needed him. And I needed him frequently. Now, here on the WELL was a whole community of helpful electronic next-door neighbors.

Of course, few nonprofit organizations are online with their personal computers. Was there a way to connect the online computer guides with the nonprofit organizations that needed guidance? I sent a flier ('Do you need computer help?') to thirty nonprofit organizations, eighteen of which responded, 'You betcha and how.' Then, on the WELL, I started asking folks if they wanted to adopt a nonprofit organization. A dozen folks said they were willing to visit nonprofit organizations as computer mentors. In addition, two dozen more said they would be glad to handle phone queries. One WELLbeing suggested we call the project ENERT—for Emergency Nerd Response Team—but we opted for the more bland CompuMentor.

By December 1990, CompuMentor had set up 968 matches with 446 nonprofit organizations, from a database of 668 volunteer mentors. A few examples of the kinds of organizations CompuMentor helped set up include DES Action of San Francisco, California Rural Legal Assistance, St. Anthony's Dining room, and Women's Refuge in Berkeley. CompuMentor has gone national since then and continues to secure funding from charitable foundations that know leverage when they see it.

Environmental activists have been among the most successful of the early adapters of CMC technology. Among the first online environmental activists was Don White, director of Earth Trust, a worldwide nonprofit organization that concentrates on international wildlife protection and environmental problems that "fall between the cracks of local and national environmental movements." According to White, "Recent EarthTrust programs include shutting down Korea's illegal whaling operations, expeditions to South America to save Amazon wildlife, acoustic and communications research on whales and dolphins, and groundbreaking work against deep-sea gillnetting fleets."

EarthTrust is an extremely low-overhead transnational organization that exists almost entirely as a network of volunteers scattered around the globe. Some volunteers are in cities where national governments can be lobbied; many are in remote locations where they can verify "ground truth" about logging, mining, fishing operations, and toxic waste disposal. EarthTrust provides its branch offices with inexpensive personal computers, printers, modems, and accounts with MCImail, a global electronic mail service. Each basic electronic workstation costs less than $1,000. The professionals in the field and those in the offices can coordinate communications inexpensively.

Environmental scientists and activists are dispersed throughout the world, generally don't have the money to travel to international conferences, and are compartmentalized into academic institutions and disciplines. The uses of electronic mailing lists and grassroots computer networks began to spread through the scientific and scholarly parts of the ecoactivist grapevine through the late 1980s. Just as virtual communities emerged in part as a means of fulfilling the hunger for community felt by symbolic analysts, the explosive growth in electronic mailing lists covering environmental subjects has served as a vehicle for informal multidisciplinary discussions among those who want to focus on real-world problems rather than on the borders between nations or academic departments.

By 1992, there were enough online environmentalist efforts to support the publication of a popular guidebook to CMC as a tool for environmental activism, *Ecolinking: Everyone's Guide to Online Environmental Organization. Ecolinking* is a combination of CompuMentor-in-a-book that instructs activists in the arcana of going online, and a directory that lists the key information about different BBSs and networks that already exist.

Among the subjects of FidoNet echoes (ongoing, BBS-network-based, international computer conferences on specific subjects), *Ecolinking* lists hazardous waste management, Indian affairs, sustainable agriculture, global environmental issues, health physics, geography, hunger, radiation safety, Native American NewsMagazine, Native American Controversy, and technology education, as well as other interest areas.

The struggle for preservation of the earth's biodiversity, which is threatened on a massive scale by human destruction of old-growth ecosystems, is an environmental-political issue that requires the concerted efforts of a number of different disciplines and nationalities. Ecologists, ethologists, biologists, anthropologists, activists around the world, have been using parts of the Net to coordinate scientific and political efforts. *Ecolinking* notes the example of Aldo de Moor, a fourth-year information management student in the Netherlands who created the Rain Forest Network Bulletin on BITNET as an online think tank for evaluating ecological action plans from both scientific and political perspectives—an incubator for potential environmental solutions.

The importance of BITNET is its reach throughout the world's research establishments. Originally funded by NSF and implemented by IBM, BITNET (Because It's Time Network) links more than two thousand academic and research organizations worldwide, in thirty-eight countries, mostly through automatic Listservs, electronic mailing lists that automatically move written discussions around to those who subscribe; the latest rounds of every discussion show up in the subscribers' electronic mailboxes, and the subscribers can send responses around to the rest of the list by replying to the e-mail. The European version of BITNET is called EARN (European Academic Research Network), which begat PLEARN, the Polish network that sprang up the moment communism crumbled.

BITNET mailing lists are gatewayed to the Internet. This means that this "invisible college" already has tremendous reach in the scholarly and scientific world across national as well as disciplinary boundaries. The dozens of BITNET mailing lists, from Agroforestry to Weather Spotters (and including such forums as the Brineshrimp Discussion List, the National Birding Hotline Cooperative, the Genomic-Organization Bulletin Board, and the Dendrochronology Forum), have created a web of interdisciplinary communications and a worldwide forum for sharing knowledge about environmental issues among tens of thousands of experts.

The increasing "networkability" of the nonprofits and NGOs that are springing up around the world, specifically in the area of environmental action and peacework, is what gave birth to the largest and most effective activist network in the world, the Institute for Global Communications, which includes EcoNet, PeaceNet, GreenNet, ConflictNet, and others worldwide.

The NGO movement represents another example of the kinds of organizations that global voice telecommunications made possible in the first place, and which have the potential to thrive in a CMC networked world. Just as nonprofit organizations focus on those social problems that fall between the cracks of local or regional institutions, public and private, NGOs address the issues that national and international institutions, public and private, don't seem to address. The Red Cross is the paradigm example. Amnesty International is a contemporary example of an NGO that has had real impact.

Howard Frederick, present news director of the Institute for Global Communications, believes that NGOs are the global equivalent to the institutions of civil society that the first theoreticians of modern democracy envisioned. In an online discussion that took place via a BITNET Listserv (and which was compiled into a book by MIT Press), Frederick asserted:

> The concept of *civil society* arose with John Locke, the English philosopher and political theorist. It implied a defense of human society at the national level against the power of the state and the inequalities of the marketplace. For Locke, civil society was that part of civilization—from the family and the church to cultural life and education—that was outside of the control of government or market but was increasingly marginalized by them. Locke saw the importance of social movements to protect the public sphere from these commercial and governmental interests.

Frederick pointed out in our online discussions that big money and powerful political interests have "pushed civil society to the edge," leaving those who would constitute such a culture with no communications media of their own. Frederick believes that CMC has changed the balance of power for NGOs on the global level, the way Dave Hughes believes CMC changes the balance of power for citizens on the community level:

> The development of communications technologies has vastly transformed the capacity of global civil society to build coalitions and networks. In times past, communication transaction clusters formed among nation-states, colonial empires, regional economies and alliances—for example, medieval Europe, the Arab world, China and Japan, West African kingdoms, the Caribbean slave and sugar economies. Today new and equally powerful forces have emerged on the world stage—the rain forest protection movement, the human rights movement, the campaign against the arms trade, alternative news agencies, and planetary computer networks.

NGOs, according to Frederick and others, face a severe political problem that arises from the concentration of ownership of global communication media in the hands of a very small number of people. He cited Ben Bagdikian's often-quoted prediction that by the turn of the century "five to ten corporate giants will control most of the world's important newspapers, magazines, books, broadcast stations, movies, recordings and videocassettes." These new media lords are not likely to donate the use of their networks for the kinds of information that NGOs tend to disseminate. Yet rapid and wide dissemination of information is vitally important to grassroots organizing around global problems.

The activist solution to this dilemma has been to create alternate planetary information networks. The Institute for Global Communications (IGC), then, was conceived as a kind of virtual community for NGOs, an enabling technology for the continued growth of global civil society. Again, the distributed nature of the telecommunications network, coupled with the availability of affordable computers, made it possible to piggyback an alternate network on the mainstream infrastructure.

In 1982, an environmental organization in California, the Farallones Institute, with seed money from Apple Computer and the San Francisco Foundation, created EcoNet to facilitate discussion and activism on behalf of worldwide environmental protection, restoration, and sustainability. In 1984, PeaceNet was created by Ark Communications Institute, the Center for Innovative Diplomacy, Community Data Processing, and the Foundation for the Arts of Peace. In 1987, PeaceNet and EcoNet joined together as part of IGC. In 1990, ConflictNet, a network dedicated to supporting dispute mediation and nonviolent conflict resolution, joined IGC.

IGC worked with local partners to establish sister networks in Sweden, Canada, Brazil, Nicaragua, and Australia. Eventually, GlasNet in the former Soviet Union affiliated with IGC. In 1990, the different member organizations formed the Association for Progressive Communications (APC) to coordinate what had become a global network of activist networks. By 1992, APC networks connected more than fifteen thousand subscribers in ninety countries.

APC networks experienced a radical surge in activity during the Gulf War. As the most highly news-managed war of the media age, the Gulf War created a hunger for alternative sources of information, a hunger that was met by the kinds of alternatives offered by APC. During the attempted coup in the Soviet Union in 1990, Russian "APC partners used telephone circuits to circumvent official control," according to Frederick. "Normally, the outdated Russian telephone system require hordes of operators to connect international calls by hand and callers must compete fiercely for phone lines. But the APC partner networks found other routes for data flow. While the usual link with Moscow is over international phone lines, APC technicians also rigged a link over a more tortuous route. That plan saw Soviet news dispatches gathered through a loose network of personal computer bulletin board systems in Moscow and Leningrad. The dispatches which were sent by local phone calls to the Baltic states, then to NordNet Sweden, and then to London-based GreenNet, which maintains an open link with the rest of the APC."

To those of us who had the Net's window on the world during the major international political crises of the past several years, the pictures we were able to piece together of what actually might be happening turned out to be considerably more diverse than the one obtainable from the other media available through conventional channels—the newspaper, radio, and television. Within hours of the crucial events in China in 1989 and Russia in 1991, the Net became a global backchannel for all kinds of information that never made it into the mass media. People with cellular telephones report via satellite to people with computers and modems, and within minutes, witnesses on the spot can report what they see and hear to millions of others. Imagine how this might work ten years from now, when digital, battery-operated minicams are as ubiquitous as telephones, and people can feed digitized images as well as words to the Net.

Information and disinformation about breaking events are pretty raw on the Net. That's the point. You don't know what to think of any particular bit of information, how to gauge its credibility, and nobody tells you what to think about it, other than what you know from previous encounters, about the reliability of the source. You never really know how to gauge the credibility of the nightly news or the morning paper, either, but most of us just accept what we see on television or read in the paper.

With the Net, during times of crisis, you can get more information, of extremely varying quality, than you can get from conventional media. Most important, you get unmediated news that fills in the important blank spots in the pictures presented by the mass media. You can even participate, if only as an onlooker. During the Gulf War, we on the WELL were spellbound readers of reports relayed via BITNET to Internet by an Israeli researcher, who was in a sealed room with his family, under missile attack. We asked him questions in the WELL's many-to-many public conference that were sent to him, and his answers returned, via Internet e-mail.

None of the evidence for political uses of the Net thus far presented is earthshaking in terms of how much power it has now to influence events. But the somewhat different roles of the Net in Tiananmen Square, the Soviet coup, and the Gulf War, represent harbingers of political upheavals to come. In February 1993, General Magic, a company created by the key architects of Apple's Macintosh computer, revealed their plans to market a technology for a whole new kind of "personal intelligent communicator." A box the size of a checkbook with a small screen, stylus, and cellular telephone will enable a person anywhere in the world to scribble a message on the screen and tap the screen with the stylus, sending it to anyone with a reachable e-mail address or fax machine. The same device doubles as a cellular phone. Apple, AT&T, Matsushita, Philips, Sony, and others have already announced their plans to license this technology. When the price drops to $25, what will that do to the mass media's monopoly on news? What kinds of Tiananmen Squares or Rodney King incidents will emerge from this extension of cyberspace?

Access to alternate forms of information and, most important, the power to reach others with your own alternatives to the official view of events, are, by their nature, political phenomena. Changes in forms and degrees of access to information are indicators of changes in forms and degrees of power among different groups. The reach of the Net, like the reach of television, extends to the urbanized parts of the entire world (and, increasingly, to far-flung but telecom-linked rural outposts). Not only can each node rebroadcast or originate content to the rest of the Net, but even the puniest computers can process that content in a variety of ways after it comes in to the home node from the Net and before it goes out again. Inexpensive computers can copy and process and communicate information, and when you make PCs independent processing nodes in the already existing telecommunications network, a new kind of system emerges.

Cities in Cyberspace

If electronic democracy is the theory, Santa Monica's Public Electronic Network (PEN) is a vivid example of the practice. And the PEN Action Group's SHWASHLOCK proposal is a classic case history, illustrating how citizens can agree on a common problem, use their collective resources to propose a solution, and convince the city's official government to help put the solution into practice. It's also an example of how the nonvirtual realities of modern cities can be influenced in concrete ways by the focused use of virtual communities. The scale of the example is small, and the city is one of the wealthier enclaves in the world, but SHWASHLOCK is what scientists call an "existence proof" for theories of virtual civil society-building.

The name of the proposal is an acronym for "SHowers, WASHing machines, LOCKers," the three elements that PEN members, including several homeless participants, agreed that homeless job-seekers most needed. Having determined that they wanted to address in some way what a Santa Monica Chamber of Commerce survey pinpointed as "the city's number-one problem"—homelessness—PEN members formed an action group that began having face-to-face meetings long with their ongoing virtual meetings. In August 1989, an artist, Bruria Finkel, posted her idea for providing a needed service. Homeless people cannot effectively seek employment without a place to shower in the morning and a free laundry service to help make them presentable, as well as a secure place to store personal belongings. And no city or nonprofit services provided those key elements.

The PEN Action Group discovered that hot showers in public parks were not open until noon, and nonprofit service agencies were reluctant to set up lockers because they didn't want to police their contents. Online with service providers and city officials, the Action Group found no clear consensus on how to implement what all agreed to be a promising new service. PEN enthusiast Michele Wittig, a psychology professor, proposed forming a group to directly address the homelessness issue. Existing social service providers weren't happy with the prospect of this new online group competing for shrinking social service budgets, so the SHWASHLOCK advocates decided to raise funds for an existing agency, which agreed to administer a laundry voucher system. Another obstacle was overcome when a city council member introduced the Action Group to a locker manufacturer who agreed to donate lockers to the city on a trial basis.

In July 1990, the Santa Monica city council, responding to the PEN Action Group's formal proposal, allocated $150,000 to install lockers and showers under the Santa Monica pier, and agreed to open public showers elsewhere at 6:00 A.M. The homeless members of the Action Group continued to ask for some kind of job bank as well, to provide job leads. PEN members decided to try to grow a network: a PEN terminal was donated to a homeless drop-in center already staffed by job counselors, and two graduate students earned course credits for finding job listings. PEN was doing what it was designed to do: enabling citizens to discuss their own agendas, surface problems of mutual concern, cooperatively design solutions, and make the ideas work in the city's official government.

Santa Monica is an exceptional city in terms of local citizen interest, stemming from the renter's rights movement in the early 1980s. The citizens' organizations that helped pass a historically stringent rent-control ordinance also helped elect a city council that was publicly committed to opening up the government to wider citizen participation. The city council, inspired by the way an American company had helped a Japanese city use CMC to resist destruction of a local forest, hired the same American company to help them design a municipal CMC system. Metasystems Design Group (MDG), the Alexandria, Virginia, company that helped Santa Monica set up the Caucus computer conferencing software, is well aware of the culture-altering potential of CMC technology and deliberately blends organizational development work with CMC systems engineering.

MDG's Lisa Carlson was one of the early true believers in social transformation via networking; she practices what she preaches to the extent that it is hard to find any significant CMC system in the world that doesn't have a contribution from her. Another partner in MDG, Frank Burns, was Colonel Burns of the U.S. Army's delta force in the early 1980s, when I first met him at a conference on education and consciousness. He explained to me that the largest educational institution in the world, the U.S. Army, needed to find out if it could learn anything from the human potential movement. Before he retired to become a toolmaker for electronic activists, Burns came up with the army's highly successful recruitment slogan, "Be All That You Can Be."

If you can convince the army to model itself after Esalen, even in a tiny way, you probably have some knack for facilitating changes in organizations. MDG has always coupled an awareness of the community with its knowledge of CMC tools. CMC was seen by the city and by MDG as a tool to increase citizen participation in local government. The specific changes that they hoped would come about were not designed into the system, for they were supposed to emerge from the CMC-augmented community itself. Four years later, those who started the system began to realize what they should have designed into the system, which those who replicate their efforts ought to take into account—the common problem in cyberspace of the hijacking of discussions by a vociferous minority.

PEN was launched in 1989. Ken Phillips, director of the Information Systems Department in Santa Monica City Hall, was the systems instigator and chief architect. When the city wouldn't pay for his plan, he obtained donations of $350,000 worth of hardware from Hewlett-Packard and $20,000 worth of software from MDG. The city distributed free accounts to city residents who would register for the service. Personal computers at home, terminals at work, and the dozens of public terminals provided to libraries, schools, and city buildings enable Santa Monicans to read information provided by the city, exchange e-mail with other citizens or city hall officials, and participate in public conferences. The police department runs the Crimewatch conference. "Planning" is a forum for discussions of land use, zoning, and development; "Environment" is where air quality, water pollution, and recycling programs are discussed; "Santa Monica" covers rent control, community events, and information about city boards and commissions.

Other forums allow discussion of topics far afield from municipal concerns. MDG, well aware of Oldenburg's ideas about informal public spaces, made sure there was enough virtual common space for people to create their own formal and informal discussions in addition to following the ones established by the system's organizers. MDG knew from experience with other organizations that you have to be careful not to structure a citizen participation system too elaborately in advance, that it is important to give the people who use the system both the tools and the power to change the structure of discussion as well as its content.

Giving the power of expression to citizens and connecting their forum to city officials does not guarantee that all projects will turn out as positively as SHWASHLOCK. Pamela Varley, a casewriter for Harvard's Kennedy School of Government, wrote a full case study of PEN, a version of which was published in MIT's *Technology Review* in 1991. Varley quoted several enthusiasts who acknowledged the real excitement they found in using the system. Don Paschal, who was homeless when he started using the system, used one of the phrases online activists often use: "It's been a great equalizer." People did seem to talk across social barriers. But violent disagreements broke out and spread, according to other informants. "PEN's egalitarianism, however," wrote Varley, "also makes the system vulnerable to abuse. PENners quickly discover that they must contend with people who feel entitled to hector mercilessly those with whom they disagree." She quoted PEN's Ken Phillips saying that it was like trying to hold a meeting while "allowing somebody to stand in a corner and shout."

Women had trouble online with a small number of men who would badger all females as soon as they joined the system, with public and private unwanted attention, innuendo, and violence fantasies that used the initials of women on PEN. A support group, PEN Femmes, emerged and immediately made a point of welcoming women and encouraging them to participate. As women became more visible online, harassment subsided, according to Varley.

Varley noted that "PEN's biggest disappointment has been the domination of its conference discussions by a small number of users. More than 3,000 people are signed up for PEN, but only 500 to 600 log on each month and most never add any comments to the conference discussion. PENners talk about the '50 hard core' users whose names appear again and again in the conference discussions." Varley quoted Phillips as saying, "I recommend to people that if they're going to do a system like this that they start with a group of community leaders, and let them set the tone of the system."

WELLite Kathleen Creighton also spent some time exploring PEN and interviewing PEN members in 1992 about what did and what did not work about the system. Creighton's informants agreed with Varley's, that some people had more time on their hands to harangue city officials online, and those with the worst manners had a powerfully negative impact on the process of communication between citizens and city officials. "Folks' expectations were very high and they counted on a dialogue with city employees," Creighton reported. "Except that city employees don't like being criticized or being held accountable. So users would ask the city folks questions, or PEN staff questions (which is just as bad) and not get any answers. So people got pissed off. Then they realized there was no penalty for being assholes (there isn't because the feeling is that the City of Santa Monica is barred from restricting speech—well, that's the feeling of *some*). And the powers that be told Ken Phillips years ago he couldn't have moderators."

Valuable lessons derived from the PEN experience: People want a means of communicating more than they want access to information; make databases of useful information available, but emphasize citizen-to-citizen communication as well. Citizens can put items on the city agenda, but if you plan to involve city officials, make clear to everyone what can and cannot be accomplished through this medium in terms of changing city policies, and set up some rules of polite communication within a framework of free speech. Free speech does not mean that anyone has to listen to vile personal attacks. Having both moderated forums and totally unmoderated forums for hot subjects is one technique for maintaining a place for reasoned discourse without stifling free expression. The people who use the system can design these rules, but if the PEN experience has anything to teach, it is that citizens can't hope to work with city hall without a flame-free zone for such discussions.

Another manifestation of municipal online systems is the Free-Net concept, pioneered in Cleveland and spreading outward from the American heartland. Cleveland Free-Net and the National Public Telecomputing Network movement grew out of a 1984 research project conducted at Case Western Reserve University. Dr. Tom Grundner, then associated with the university's Department of Family Medicine, tested the applicability of CMC to the delivery of community health information. With a single telephone line, he set up a BBS known as St. Silicon's Hospital, where citizens could pose their questions to a board of public health experts and receive answers within twenty-four hours. The popularity of the project attracted financial support from AT&T and the Ohio Bell Company, which funded a larger project.

Grundner designed a full-scale CMC system as a community information resource for fields far beyond public health alone. The governor of Ohio opened Free-Net in July 1986. The first phase of the experiment attracted seven thousand registered users and more than five hundred calls a day. In 1989, a new system opened, offering access via forty-eight telephone lines, including a connection to Case Western Reserve University's fiber-optic network and, eventually, Internet. People from anywhere in the world can read Free-Net discussions, although only citizens of the Free-Net municipality can participate actively. In 1987, the Youngstown FreeNet went online. In 1990, TriState Online in Cincinnati, the Heartland FreeNet in Peoria, Illinois, and the Medina County FreeNet, a rural system, went online.

In 1989, the participating organizations decided to create the National Public Telecomputing Network (NPTN), modeled after the National Public Radio and Public Broadcasting Systems in the United States—user-supported, community-based, alternative media. Although the system itself is funded by citizens and by nonprofit funding sources, the core idea of NPTN is that access to the network by citizens should be free. Again, if this combination of organizational vision and CMC technology continues to succeed, yet another approach to building an online civil society could spread beyond the early adapters.

The direction of CMC technology might take a different turn, however. The transition from a government-sponsored, taxpayer-supported, relatively unrestricted public forum to a privately owned and provided medium has accelerated recently, and this transition might render moot many of the fantasies of today's true believers in electronic democracy and global online culture. When the telecommunications networks becomes powerful enough to transmit high-fidelity sound and video as well as text, the nature of the Net—and the industry that controls it—might change dramatically.

Events of the spring and summer of 1993, when entertainment conglomerates, software companies, and telephone companies started jumping into bed with each other promiscuously, may have signalled the beginning of the end of the freewheeling frontier era of Net history. April and May saw a flurry of top-level agreements among the biggest communications and entertainment companies in the world. Every week in June seemed to feature a new bombshell. During a period of a few months, the big players that had been maneuvering behind the scenes for years went public with announcements of complex, interlocking alliances. The results of these deals will influence powerfully the shape of the Net in the late 1990s.

Nobody is sure yet who the winners and losers will be, or even where the most successful markets will turn out to be, but the nature of these interindustry alliances and the announced intentions of the partners paint a picture of what Big Money sees in the Net today: a better-than-ever conduit for delivering prepackaged entertainment to the home tomorrow. Everything that has been discussed in this book seems to be missing from that picture.

Will the enormously lucrative home video and television markets finance the many-to-many communications infrastructure that educators and activists dream about? Or will it all be pay-per-view, with little or no room for community networks and virtual communities?

In the late spring of 1993, U.S. West, one of the Regional Bell Operating Companies, announced their intention to invest $2.5 billion in Time-Warner Inc., the world's largest entertainment company, toward the goal of creating advanced cable and information networks. Time-Warner announced another partnership a few weeks later with Silicon Graphics Company to create computer-switched "video on demand." Suddenly, the most highly touted implication of these high-tech business partnerships was the miraculous ability to download tonight's video rental instead of walking a block and a half to the video rental store.

More than technology has been changing: the nature of the partnerships that emerged in early 1993 could be signs of a major shift in the structures of many traditional businesses, triggered by the shifts in our modes of communication made possible by the new technologies. IBM and Apple joined forces in a partnership that would have been unthinkable a few years ago; the IBM-Apple joint venture, Kaleida Labs, has been developing multimedia software to merge text, sound, graphics, and video in next-generation PCs. Kaleida in turn made deals with Motorola to provide microchips, and with Scientific Atlanta, a firm that makes decoders for cable television systems. Scientific Atlanta also has a partnership with Time-Warner.

The buzzphrase about these new digital channels slated to emerge from these alliances was not "virtual community," but "five hundred television channels." Newspapers started concentrating on the plans that many companies announced to put the control system for the Net connection in the cable box atop the television set—the "battle for the set-top." A reporter for the *San Francisco Chronicle* described these business alliances under the headline, "Future TV Will Shop for You and Talk for You," and began the article this way: "Imagine a television that talks to you, enables you to communicate with the kids who go to bed before you get home, and that helps you select a movie." Will set-top Net boxes bring the mass audiences into many-to-many contact? Or will grassroots conviviality be marginalized by high production values?

The information highways, as many print and broadcast journalists began to describe them, were suddenly seen as ever-more-effective conduits for broadcasting more of the same old stuff to more people, with most interactivity limited to channel selection. *Time* and *Newsweek* magazines both did cover stories on information superhighways. Neither of the major newsmagazines mentioned the potential for many-to-many communications between citizens.

The most powerful alliance was disclosed in June 1993. Microsoft, the company started by home-brew PC hobbyist Bill Gates, dominates the PC software market. Tele-Communications Inc. is the world's largest cable television company. On June 13, John Markoff reported on the first page of the *New York Times* that Time-Warner, Microsoft, and Tele-Communications Inc. were forming a joint venture that, in Markoff's words, "would combine the worlds of computing and television and perhaps shape how much of popular culture is delivered." Markoff quoted James F. Moore, an expert consultant: "This has tremendous economic and social importance; it is the gateway for popular culture. . . . This is the substitute for newspapers and magazines and catalogs and movies, and that gives it enormous economic potential for those who control the gateway."

The day after Kaleida announced their deal with Scientific Atlanta to develop set-top controllers, Microsoft announced a deal with Intel Corporation, the world's largest chip maker, and General Instrument, a manufacturer of cable converters. Telecommunications industry pundits began speculating that the future Net was going to be a hybrid of cable company conduits, telephone company money, and entertainment company content.

The largest chip maker in the world, the largest personal computer software vendor in the world, the largest entertainment company in the world, the largest cable television company in the world, the largest computer hardware manufacturers in the world—the Net these players are building doesn't seem to be the same Net the grassroots pioneers predicted back in the "good old days" on the electronic frontier. It is possible that the leaders of one or more of these institutions will have the vision to recognize that they are in the business of selling the customers to each other, as well as the business of selling them CDs and videos. But those who are used to thinking of CMC as a largely anarchic, dirt-cheap, uncensored forum, dominated by amateurs and enthusiasts, will have to learn a new way of thinking.

Electronic democracy is far from inevitable, despite the variety of hopeful examples you can find if you look for them. There are those who believe the whole idea is a cruel illusion, and their warnings are worth consideration—especially by the most enthusiastic promoters of CMC activism. The next chapter looks more closely at criticisms of the notion of electronic democracy.

chapter ten

DISINFORMOCRACY

Virtual communities could help citizens revitalize democracy, or they could be luring us into an attractively packaged substitute for democratic discourse. A few true believers in electronic democracy have had their say. It's time to hear from the other side. We owe it to ourselves and future generations to look closely at what the enthusiasts fail to tell us, and to listen attentively to what the skeptics fear.

For example, the rural BBSs and networks of nonprofit organizations represent only part of the picture of the nascent CMC industry. Consider another case history: Prodigy, the service that IBM and Sears spent a reported $1 billion to launch, is advertised on prime-time television as an information-age wonder for the whole family. For a flat monthly fee, Prodigy users can play games, make airplane reservations, send electronic mail to one another (although not to other networks), and discuss issues in public forums. In exchange for the low fees and the wide variety of services, users receive a ribbon of advertising matter at the bottom of their screens.

Prodigy's approach represents an alternate branch of CMC that did not evolve from the old ARPANET networks or the grassroots BBS culture, but from a surprisingly old and often-failed attempt to apply the broadcast paradigm to CMC, known as videotex. The idea is that people will pay, and even subject themselves to advertising, in exchange for information presented on a screen that the human viewer can browse by means of a telephone touchpad, keyboard, or other control device. The problem, as failed videotex experiments funded by governments (Britain's Prestel) and newspapers (Knight-Ridder's Viewtron) have demonstrated over and over, is that people aren't all that interested in information on screens, if that is all you have to sell—unless you also offer a way for people to interact with one another. Minitel, part of France Télécom's Télétel version of videotex, was so successful because of the chat services, the *messageries,* that were available along with the canned information.

Prodigy is modeled on the old consumers-as-commodity model that works for mass-market magazines. You use the services and contents of the magazine or television network (or online service) to draw a large population of users, who give you detailed information about their demographics, and then you sell access to those users to advertisers. You tailor the content of the magazine or television program or online service to attract large numbers of consumers with the best demographics, you spend money on polls and focus groups to certify the demographics of your consumers, and then advertising agencies buy access to the attention of those consumers you've "captured." This is the economic arm of the broadcast paradigm, extended to cyberspace. With a reported one million users, and both parent companies in trouble, it is not at all clear whether Prodigy will reach the critical mass of users to repay the investment, but this notion of online subscribers as commodities isn't likely to go away. It's based on one of the most successful money-making schemes in history, the advertising industry.

As a model of a future in which CMC services come to be dominated by a few very large private enterprises, Prodigy previews two key, chilling aspects of online societies that are far from the innocent dreams of the utopians. First there was a wave of paranoia among Prodigy subscribers, much discussed on the Net, regarding the way Prodigy's software works: to use the service, you grant Prodigy's central computers access to a part of your desktop computer (the infamous STAGE.DAT file that shows up on Prodigy users' computer disks) whenever you connect with the service via modem. The idea that Prodigy might be capable of reading private information off your personal computer from a distance, even though there was no proof that Prodigy was actually doing any such thing, stemmed from Prodigy's use of a technology that could, in principle, be used for such a purpose. The prospect of giving up parts of our privacy in exchange for access to information is the foundation of a school of political criticism of communications technologies that I'll come back to.

More chilling is the fact that all public postings on Prodigy are censored; there are actually banks of people sitting in front of monitors somewhere, reading postings from Prodigy subscribers, erasing the ones with offensive content. This measure dealt effectively with the outbreak of racist and anti-Semitic invective. It also dealt effectively with free and open public discussions among Prodigy subscribers of Prodigy's own policies. Prodigy's users sign a contract that gives Prodigy the right to edit all public messages before they are posted, and at the same time the contract absolves Prodigy of responsibility for the content of the messages that are posted by declaring them to be in the public domain. Then Prodigy subscribers used Prodigy's free e-mail feature to create mailing lists to get around Prodigy censorship. Private e-mail is protected by the Electronic Communications Privacy Act of 1986, which requires a court order for any third party to read a private message. So Prodigy management changed the pricing for e-mail, cutting off free messages after thirty per month, surcharging twenty-five cents for each additional message.

Prodigy as a private publisher claims First Amendment protection from government interference, so Prodigy users can't go to court to claim their rights to free speech without stepping on Prodigy's rights. Publishers in the United States have a right to publish what they want to publish; with the exception of libel, the courts have no business restraining editors from using their judgment. If you don't like Prodigy, you can go elsewhere—as long as there is an elsewhere. The presence of competition is the key. The Prodigy situation might be a preview of what could happen if a small number of large companies manages to dominate a global telecommunications industry that is now a competitive market of small and medium-size businesses that manage to survive and thrive along with the giants.

As long as BBSs remain legal and telephone carriers don't start charging by the amount of data users send and receive (instead of the amount of time they use the telephone connection), there will be a grassroots alternative to the giant services. But what if some big company comes along in the future and uses its deep pockets, economies of scale, and political power to squeeze out the WELLs and Big Sky Telegraphs and low-cost Internet access providers? Such tactics are not unknown in the history of the telecommunications industry. The telecommunications industry is a business, viewed primarily as an economic player. But telecommunications gives certain people access to means of influencing certain other people's thoughts and perceptions, and that access—who has it and who doesn't have it—is intimately connected with political power. The prospect of the technical capabilities of a near-ubiquitous high-bandwidth Net in the hands of a small number of commercial interests has dire political implications. Whoever gains the political edge on this technology will be able to use the technology to consolidate power.

There might be a fork in the road of technology-dependent civilization, somewhere in the mid- to late 1990s, forced by the technical capabilities of the Net. Two powerful and opposed images of the future characterize the way different observers foresee the future political effects of new communications technology. The utopian vision of the electronic agora, an "Athens without slaves" made possible by telecommunications and cheap computers and implemented through decentralized networks like Usenet and FidoNet, has been promoted by enthusiasts, including myself, over the past several years. I have been one of the cheerleaders for people like Dave Hughes and Mitch Kapor as they struggled to use CMC to give citizens some of the same media powers that the political big boys wield. And I admit that I still believe that this technology, if properly understood and defended by enough citizens, does have democratizing potential in the way that alphabets and printing presses had democratizing potential.

The critiques of the cheerleading for unproven technologies such as computer conferencing bear serious attention, and so do the warning signals from Prodigy, and the disturbing privacy issues that are raised by some of the same technologies that promise citizens so many benefits. What if these hopes for a quick technological fix of what is wrong with democracy constitute nothing more than another way to distract the attention of the suckers while the big boys divide up the power and the loot? Those who see electronic democracy advocates as naive or worse point to the way governments and private interests have used the alluring new media of past technological revolutions to turn democratic debate into talk shows and commercials. Why should this new medium be any less corruptible than previous media? Why should contemporary claims for CMC as a democratizing technology be taken any more seriously than the similar-sounding claims that were made for steam, electricity, and television?

Three different kinds of social criticisms of technology are relevant to claims of CMC as a means of enhancing democracy. One school of criticism emerges from the longer-term history of communications media, and focuses on the way electronic communications media already have preempted public discussions by turning more and more of the content of the media into advertisements for various commodities—a process these critics call commodification. Even the political process, according to this school of critics, has been turned into a commodity. The formal name for this criticism is "the commodification of the public sphere." The public sphere is what these social critics claim we used to have as citizens of a democracy, but have lost to the tide of commodization. The public sphere is also the focus of the hopes of online activists, who see CMC as a way of revitalizing the open and widespread discussions among citizens that feed the roots of democratic societies.

The second school of criticism focuses on the fact that high-bandwidth interactive networks could be used in conjunction with other technologies as a means of surveillance, control, and disinformation as well as a conduit for useful information. This direct assault on personal liberty is compounded by a more diffuse erosion of old social values due to the capabilities of new technologies; the most problematic example is the way traditional notions of privacy are challenged on several fronts by the ease of collecting and disseminating detailed information about individuals via cyberspace technologies. When people use the convenience of electronic communication or transaction, we leave invisible digital trails; now that technologies for tracking those trails are maturing, there is cause to worry. The spreading use of computer matching to piece together the digital trails we all leave in cyberspace is one indication of privacy problems to come.

Along with all the person-to-person communications exchanged on the world's telecommunications networks are vast flows of other kinds of personal information—credit information, transaction processing, health information. Most people take it for granted that no one can search through all the electronic transactions that move through the world's networks in order to pin down an individual for marketing—or political—motives. Remember the "knowbots" that would act as personal servants, swimming in the info-tides, fishing for information to suit your interests? What if people could turn loose knowbots to collect all the information digitally linked to *you*? What if the Net and cheap, powerful computers give that power not only to governments and large corporations but to everyone?

Every time we travel or shop or communicate, citizens of the credit-card society contribute to streams of information that travel between point of purchase, remote credit bureaus, municipal and federal information systems, crime information databases, central transaction databases. And all these other forms of cyberspace interaction take place via the same packet-switched, high-bandwidth network technology—those packets can contain transactions as well as video clips and text files. When these streams of information begin to connect together, the unscrupulous or would-be tyrants can use the Net to catch citizens in a more ominous kind of net.

The same channels of communication that enable citizens around the world to communicate with one another also allow government and private interests to gather information about them. This school of criticism is known as Panoptic in reference to the perfect prison proposed in the eighteenth century by

Jeremy Bentham—a theoretical model that happens to fit the real capabilities of today's technologies.

Another category of critical claim deserves mention, despite the rather bizarre and incredible imagery used by its most well known spokesmen—the hyper-realist school. These critics believe that information technologies have already changed what used to pass for reality into a slicked-up electronic simulation. Twenty years before the United States elected a Hollywood actor as president, the first hyper-realists pointed out how politics had become a movie, a spectacle that raised the old Roman tactic of bread and circuses to the level of mass hypnotism. We live in a hyper-reality that was carefully constructed to mimic the real world and extract money from the pockets of consumers: the forests around the Matterhorn might be dying, but the Disneyland version continues to rake in the dollars. The television programs, movie stars, and theme parks work together to create global industry devoted to maintaining a web of illusion that grows more lifelike as more people buy into it and as technologies grow more powerful.

Many other social scientists have intellectual suspicions of the hyper-realist critiques, because so many are abstract and theoretical, based on little or no direct knowledge of technology itself. Nevertheless, this perspective does capture something about the way the effects of communications technologies have changed our modes of thought. One good reason for paying attention to the claims of the hyper-realists is that the society they predicted decades ago bears a disturbingly closer resemblance to real life than do the forecasts of the rosier-visioned technological utopians. While McLuhan's image of the global village has taken on a certain irony in light of what has happened since his predictions of the 1960s, "the society of the spectacle"—another prediction from the 1960s, based on the advent of electronic media—offered a far less rosy and, as events have proved, more realistic portrayal of the way information technologies have changed social customs.

The Selling of Democracy: Commodification and the Public Sphere

There is an intimate connection between informal conversations, the kind that take place in communities and virtual communities, in the coffee shops and computer conferences, and the ability of large social groups to govern themselves without monarchs or dictators. This social-political connection shares a metaphor with the idea of cyberspace, for it takes place in a kind of virtual space that has come to be known by specialists as the public sphere.

Here is what the preeminent contemporary writer about the public sphere, social critic and philosopher Jurgen Habermas, had to say about the meaning of this abstraction:

> By "public sphere," we mean first of all a domain of our social life in which such a thing as public opinion can be formed. Access to the public sphere is open in principle to all citizens. A portion of the public sphere is constituted in every conversation in which private persons come together to form a public. They are then acting neither as business or professional people conducting their private affairs, nor as legal consociates subject to the legal regulations of a state bureaucracy and obligated to obedience. Citizens act as a public when they deal with matters of general interest without being subject to coercion; thus with the guarantee that they may assemble and unite freely, and express and publicize their opinions freely.

In this definition, Habermas formalized what people in free societies mean when we say "The public wouldn't stand for that" or "It depends on public opinion." And he drew attention to the intimate connection between this web of free, informal, personal communications and the foundations of democratic society. People can govern themselves only if they communicate widely, freely, and in groups—publicly. The First Amendment of the U.S. Constitution's Bill of Rights protects citizens from government interference in their communications—the rights of speech, press, and assembly are communication rights. Without those rights, there is no public sphere. Ask any citizen of Prague, Budapest, or Moscow.

Because the public sphere depends on free communication and discussion of ideas, as soon as your political entity grows larger than the number of citizens you can fit into a modest town hall, this vital marketplace for political ideas can be powerfully influenced by changes in communications technology. According to Habermas,

> When the public is large, this kind of communication requires certain means of dissemination and influence; today, newspapers and periodicals, radio and television are the media of the public sphere. . . . The term "public opinion" refers to the functions of criticism and control or organized state authority that the public exercises informally, as well as formally during periodic elections. Regulations concerning the publicness (or publicity [Publizitat] in its original meaning) of state-related activities, as, for instance, the public accessibility required of legal proceedings, are also connected with this function of public opinion. To the public sphere as a sphere mediating between state and society, a sphere in which the public as the vehicle of publicness—the publicness that once had to win

> out against the secret politics of monarchs and that since then has permitted democratic control of state activity.

Ask anybody in China about the right to talk freely among friends and neighbors, to own a printing press, to call a meeting to protest government policy, or to run a BBS. But brute totalitarian seizure of communications technology is not the only way that political powers can neutralize the ability of citizens to talk freely. It is also possible to alter the nature of discourse by inventing a kind of paid fake discourse. If a few people have control of what goes into the daily reporting of the news, and those people are in the business of selling advertising, all kinds of things become possible for those who can afford to pay.

Habermas had this to say about the corrupting influence of ersatz public opinion:

> Whereas at one time publicness was intended to subject persons or things to the public use of reason and to make political decisions subject to revision before the tribunal of public opinion, today it has often enough already been enlisted in the aid of the secret policies of interest groups; in the form of "publicity" it now acquires public prestige for persons or things and renders them capable of acclamation in a climate of nonpublic opinion. The term "public relations" itself indicates how a public sphere that formerly emerged from the structure of society must now be produced circumstantially on a case-by-case basis.

The idea that public opinion can be manufactured and the fact that electronic spectacles can capture the attention of a majority of the citizenry damaged the foundations of democracy. According to Habermas,

> It is no accident that these concepts of the public sphere and public opinion were not formed until the eighteenth century. They derive their specific meaning from a concrete historical situation. It was then that one learned to distinguish between opinion and public opinion. . . . Public opinion, in terms of its very idea, can be formed only if a public that engages in rational discussion exists. Public discussions that are institutionally protected and that take, with critical intent, the exercise of political authority as their theme have not existed since time immemorial.

The public sphere and democracy were born at the same time, from the same sources. Now that the public sphere, cut off from its roots, seems to be dying, democracy is in danger, too.

The concept of the public sphere as discussed by Habermas and others includes several requirements for authenticity that people who live in democratic societies would recognize: open access, voluntary participation, participation outside institutional roles, the generation of public opinion through assemblies of citizens who engage in rational argument, the freedom to express opinions, and the freedom to discuss matters of the state and criticize the way state power is organized. Acts of speech and publication that specifically discuss the state are perhaps the most important kind protected by the First Amendment to the U.S. Constitution and similar civil guarantees elsewhere in the world. Former Soviets and Eastern Europeans who regained it after decades of censorship offer testimony that the most important freedom of speech is the freedom to speak about freedoms.

In eighteenth-century America, the Committees of Correspondence were one of the most important loci of the public sphere in the years of revolution and constitution-building. If you look closely at the roots of the American Revolution, it becomes evident that a text-based, horseback-transported version of networking was an old American tradition. In their book *Networking*, Jessica Lipnack and Jeffrey Stamps describe these committees as

> a communications forum where homespun political and economic thinkers hammered out their ideological differences, sculpting the form of a separate and independent country in North America. Writing to one another and sharing letters with neighbors, this revolutionary generation nurtured its adolescent ideas into a mature politics. Both men and women participated in the debate over independence from England and the desirable shape of the American future. . . .
>
> During the years in which the American Revolution was percolating, letters, news-sheets, and pamphlets carried from one village to another were the means by which ideas about democracy were refined. Eventually, the correspondents agreed that the next step in their idea exchange was to hold a face-to-face meeting. The ideas of independence and government had been debated, discussed, discarded, and reformulated literally hundreds of times by the time people in the revolutionary network met in Philadelphia.
>
> Thus, a network of correspondence and printed broadsides led to the formation of an organization after the writers met in a series of conferences and worked out a statement of purpose—which they called a "Declaration of Independence." Little did our early networking grandparents realize that the result of their youthful idealism, less than two centuries later, would be a global superpower with an unparalleled ability to influence the survival of life on the planet.

As the United States grew and technology changed, the ways in which these public discussions of "matters of general interest," as Habermas called them—slavery and the rights of the states versus the power of the federal government were two such matters that loomed large—began to change as well. The text-based media that served as the channel for discourse gained more and more power to reshape the nature of that discourse. The communications media of the nineteenth century were the newspapers, the penny press, the first generation of what has come to be known as the mass media. At the same time, the birth of advertising and the beginnings of the public-relations industry began to undermine the public sphere by inventing a kind of buyable and sellable phony discourse that displaced the genuine kind.

The simulation (and therefore destruction) of authentic discourse, first in the United States, and then spreading to the rest of the world, is what Guy Debord would call the first quantum leap into the "society of the spectacle" and what Jean Baudrillard would recognize as a milestone in the world's slide into hyper-reality. Mass media's colonization of civil society turned into a quasi-political campaign promoting technology itself when the image-making technology of television came along. ("Progress is our most important product," said General Electric spokesman Ronald Reagan, in the early years of television.) And in the twentieth century, as the telephone, radio, and television became vehicles for public discourse, the nature of political discussion has mutated into something quite different from anything the framers of the Constitution could have foreseen.

A politician is now a commodity, citizens are consumers, and issues are decided via sound-bites and staged events. The television camera is the only spectator that counts at a political demonstration or convention. According to Habermas and others, the way the new media have been commoditized through this evolutionary process from hand-printed broadside to telegraph to penny press to mass media has led to the radical deterioration of the public sphere. The consumer society has become the accepted model both for individual behavior and political decision making. Discourse degenerated into publicity, and publicity used the increasing power of electronic media to alter perceptions and shape beliefs.

The consumer society, the most powerful vehicle for generating short-term wealth ever invented, ensures economic growth by first promoting the idea that the way to be is to buy. The engines of wealth depend on a fresh stream of tabloids sold at convenience markets and television programs to tell us what we have to buy next in order to justify our existence. What used to be a channel for authentic communication has become a channel for the updating of commercial desire.

Money plus politics plus network television equals an effective system. It works. When the same packaging skills that were honed on automobile tail fins and fast foods are applied to political ideas, the highest bidder can influence public policy to great effect. What dies in the process is the rational discourse at the base of civil society. That death manifests itself in longings that aren't fulfilled by the right kind of shoes in this month's color or the hot new prime-time candidate everybody is talking about. Some media scholars are claiming a direct causal connection between the success of commercial television and the loss of citizen interest in the political process.

Another media critic, Neal Postman, in his book *Amusing Ourselves to Death*, pointed out that Tom Paine's *Common Sense* sold three hundred thousand copies in five months in 1776. The most successful democratic revolution in history was made possible by a citizenry that read and debated widely among themselves. Postman pointed out that the mass media, and television in particular, had changed the mode of discourse itself, by substituting fast cuts, special effects, and sound-bites for reasoned discussion or even genuine argument.

The various hypotheses about commodification and mode of discourse focus on an area of apparent agreement among social observers who have a long history of heated disagreements.

When people who have become fascinated by BBSs or networks start spreading the idea that such networks are inherently democratic in some magical way, without specifying the hard work that must be done in real life to harvest the fruits of that democratizing power, they run the danger of becoming unwitting agents of commodification. First, it pays to understand how old the idea really is. Next, it is important to realize that the hopes of technophiles have often been used to sell technology for commercial gain. In this sense, CMC enthusiasts run the risk of becoming unpaid, unwitting advertisers for those who stand to gain financially from adoption of new technology.

The critics of the idea of electronic democracy have unearthed examples from a long tradition of utopian rhetoric that James Carey has called "the rhetoric of the 'technological sublime.'" He put it this way:

> Despite the manifest failure of technology to resolve pressing social issues over the last century, contemporary intellectuals continue to see revolutionary potential in the latest technological gadgets that are pictured as a force outside history and politics. . . . In modern futurism, it

> is the machines that possess teleological insight. Despite the shortcomings of town meetings, newspaper, telegraph, wireless, and television to create the conditions of a new Athens, contemporary advocates of technological liberation regularly describe a new postmodern age of instantaneous daily plebiscitory democracy through a computerized system of electronic voting and opinion polling.

Carey was prophetic in at least one regard—he wrote this years before Ross Perot and William Clinton both started talking about their versions of electronic democracy during the 1992 U.S. presidential campaign. If the United States is on the road to a version of electronic democracy in which the president will have electronic town hall meetings, including instant voting-by-telephone to "go directly to the people" (and perhaps bypass Congress?) on key issues, it is important for American citizens to understand the potential pitfalls of decision making by plebiscite. Media-manipulated plebiscites as political tools go back to Joseph Goebbels, who used radio so effectively in the Third Reich. Previous experiments in instant home polling and voting had been carried out by Warners, with their Qube service, in the early 1980s. One critic, political scientist Jean Betheke Elshtain, called the television-voting model an

> interactive shell game [that] cons us into believing that we are participating when we are really simply performing as the responding "end" of a prefabricated system of external stimuli. . . . In a plebiscitary system, the views of the majority . . . swamp minority or unpopular views. Plebiscitism is compatible with authoritarian politics carried out under the guise of, or with the connivance of, majority views. That opinion can be registered by easily manipulated, ritualistic plebiscites, so there is no need for debate on substantive questions.

What does it mean that the same hopes, described in the same words, for a decentralization of power, a deeper and more widespread citizen involvement in matters of state, a great equalizer for ordinary citizens to counter the forces of central control, have been voiced in the popular press for two centuries in reference to steam, electricity, and television? We've had enough time to live with steam, electricity, and television to recognize that they did indeed change the world, and to recognize that the utopia of technological millenarians has not yet materialized.

An entire worldview and sales job are packed into the word *progress,* which links the notion of improvement with the notion of innovation, highlights the benefits of innovation while hiding the toxic side-effects of extractive and lucrative technologies, and then sells more of it to people via television as a cure for the stress of living in a technology-dominated world. The hope that the next technology will solve the problems created by the way the last technology was used is a kind of millennial, even messianic, hope, apparently ever-latent in the breasts of the citizenry. The myth of technological progress emerged out of the same Age of Reason that gave us the myth of representative democracy, a new organizing vision that still works pretty well, despite the decline in vigor of the old democratic institutions. It's hard to give up on one Enlightenment ideal while clinging to another.

I believe it is too early to judge which set of claims will prove to be accurate. I also believe that those who would prefer the more democratic vision of the future have an opportunity to influence the outcome, which is precisely why online activists should delve into the criticisms that have been leveled against them. If electronic democracy advocates can address these critiques successfully, their claims might have a chance. If they cannot, perhaps it would be better not to raise people's hopes. Those who are not aware of the history of dead ends are doomed to replay them, hopes high, again and again.

The idea that putting powerful computers in the hands of citizens will shield the citizenry against totalitarian authorities echoes similar, older beliefs about citizen-empowering technology. As Langdon Winner (an author every computer revolutionary ought to read) put it in his essay "Mythinformation,"

> Of all the computer enthusiasts' political ideas, there is none more poignant than the faith that the computer is destined to become a potent equalizer in modern society. . . . Presumably, ordinary citizens equipped with microcomputers will be able to counter the influence of large, computer-based organizations.
>
> Notions of this kind echo beliefs of eighteenth-century revolutionaries that placing fire arms in the hands of the people was crucial to overthrowing entrenched authority. In the American Revolution, French Revolution, Paris Commune, and Russian Revolution the role of "the people armed" was central to the revolutionary program. As the military defeat of the Paris Commune made clear, however, the fact that the popular forces have guns may not be decisive. In a contest of force against force, the larger, more sophisticated, more ruthless, better equipped competitor often has the upper hand. Hence, the availability of low-cost computing power may move the baseline that defines electronic dimensions of social influence, but it does not necessarily alter the relative balance of power. Using a personal computer makes one no more powerful vis-à-vis, say, the National Security Agency than flying a hang glider establishes a person as a match for the U.S. Air Force.

The great power of the idea of electronic democracy is that technical trends in communications technologies can help citizens break the monopoly on their attention that has been enjoyed by the powers behind the broadcast paradigm—the owners of television networks, newspaper syndicates, and publishing conglomerates. The great weakness of the idea of electronic democracy is that it can be more easily commodified than explained. The commercialization and commoditization of public discourse is only one of the grave problems posed by the increasing sophistication of communications media. The Net that is a marvelous lateral network can also be used as a kind of invisible yet inescapable cage. The idea of malevolent political leaders with their hands on the controls of a Net raises fear of a more direct assault on liberties.

Caught in the Net: CMC and the Ultimate Prison

In 1791, Jeremy Bentham proposed, in *Panopticon; or, the Inspection House,* that it was possible to build a mechanism for enforcing a system of social control into the physical structure of a building, which he called the Panopticon. His design for this building was intended to be very general, an architectural algorithm that could be used in prisons, schools, and factories. Individual cells are built into the circumference of a circular building, around a central well. An inspection tower atop the well, in conjunction with a method for lighting the cells and leaving the inspection tower dark, made it possible for one person to monitor the activity of many people, each of whom would know he or she was under surveillance, none of whom would know exactly when. And the inspectors are similarly watched by other unseen inspectors. It was precisely this mental state of being seen without being able to see the watcher that Bentham meant to induce. When you can induce that state of mind in a population, you don't need whips and chains to restrain them from rebelling.

Historian and political philosopher Michel Foucault, in *Discipline and Punish,* examined the social institutions by which powerful people control the potentially rebellious masses. Foucault felt that the Panopticon as an idea as well as a specific architectural design was an important one, for it was a literal blueprint for the way future tyrants could use surveillance technologies to wield power. Just as the ability to read and write and freely communicate gives power to citizens that protects them from the powers of the state, the ability to surveil, to invade the citizens' privacy, gives the state the power to confuse, coerce, and control citizens. Uneducated populations cannot rule themselves, but tyrannies can control even educated populations, given sophisticated means of surveillance.

When you think of privacy, you probably think of your right to be undisturbed and possibly unembarrassed by intrusions into your personal affairs. It does not seem, on the surface, to be a politically significant phenomenon. Kevin Robins and Frank Webster, in their article "Cybernetic Capitalism: Information, Technology, Everyday Life," made the connection between Bentham, Foucault, and the evolution of the telecommunications network:

> We believe that Foucault is right in seeing Bentham's Panopticon as a significant event in the history of the human mind. We want to suggest that the new communication and information technologies—particularly in the form of an integrated electronic grid—permit a massive extension and transformation of that same (relative, technological) mobilization to which Bentham's Panoptic principle aspired. What these technologies support, in fact, is the same dissemination of power and control, but freed from the architectural constraints of Bentham's stone and brick prototype. On the basis of the "information revolution," not just the prison or factory, but the social totality, comes to function as the hierarchical and disciplinary Panoptic machine.

The Panopticon, Foucault warned, comes in many guises. It is not a value-neutral technology. It is a technology that allows a small number of people to control a large number of others. J. Edgar Hoover used it. So did Mao tse-Tung. You don't need fiber optics to institute a surveillance state—but it sure makes surveillance easier when you invite the surveillance device into your home.

Critics of those who pin their hopes for social change on computer technology also point out that information and communications technologies have always been dominated by the military, and will continue to be dominated by the military, police, and intelligence agencies for the foreseeable future. A computer is, was, and will be a weapon. The tool can be used for other purposes, but to be promoted as an instrument of liberation, CMC technology should be seen within the contexts of its origins, and in full cognizance of the possibly horrific future applications by totalitarians who get their hands on it.

The first electronic digital computer was created by the U.S. Army to calculate ballistics equations for artillery. The military and intelligence communities, particularly in the United States, have always benefited from a ten- to twenty-year technological lead on civilian applications of the computer technology. The U.S. National Security Agency, the ultra-secret technosnoop headquarters that applies computers to signals intelligence and codebreaking, and the U.S. National Laboratories at Livermore and Los Alamos, where thermonuclear weapons and antimissile defenses are designed, have long been the owners of the most powerful collections of computing power in the world.

Computer and communications technologies outside the military sphere are applied with great effectiveness by public and private police agencies. One example that I saw with my own eyes is suggestive of the range of goodies available to police forces: at a laboratory outside Tokyo, I saw a video camera on a freeway zero in on the license plate of a speeder, use shape-recognition software to decode the license number, and transmit it to police computers, where a warrant search could be conducted. No human in the loop—the camera and computer determine that a crime has been committed and instantly identify the suspect. Just as grassroots citizens' networks have been interconnecting into a planetary Net, police information networks have been evolving as well. The problem there is that law enforcement officers have the authority to shoot you dead; if they shoot you on the basis of misinformation propagated on a Net (and it is far easier to broadcast bad information than to recall it), the Net helped kill you. Jacques Vallee, in the very beginning of his prophetic 1982 book *The Network Revolution,* told the true cautionary tale of the innocent Frenchmen who died under police gunfire as the result of a glitch in a poorly designed police computer network.

The more spectacularly overt images of a Panoptic society—the midnight knock on the door, the hidden microphones of the secret police—are genuine possibilities worth careful consideration. Now it isn't necessary to plant microphones when a remote and inaudible command can turn any telephone—while it is on the hook—into a microphone. The old scenarios aren't the only ones, now. Privacy has already been penetrated in more subtle, complex ways. This assault on privacy, invisible to most, takes place in the broad daylight of everyday life. The weapons are cash registers and credit cards. When Big Brother arrives, don't be surprised if he looks like a grocery clerk, because privacy has been turning into a commodity, courtesy of better and better information networks, for years.

Yesterday, you might have gone to the supermarket and watched someone total up the bill with a bar code reader. Perhaps you paid with an ATM card or credit card or used one as identification for a check. Last night, maybe the data describing what you bought and who you are were telecommunicated from the supermarket to a central collection point. This morning, detailed information about your buying habits could have been culled from one database and sold to a third party who could compile it tomorrow into another electronic dossier somewhere, one that knows what you buy and where you live and how much money you owe. Next week, a fourth party might purchase that dossier, combine it with a few tens of millions of others on an optical disk, and offer to sell the collection of information as a marketing tool.

All of the information on the hypothetical mass-dossier disk is available from public sources; it is in their compilation, the way that information is sorted into files linked to real citizens, that intrusion is accomplished. On each CD-ROM disk will be a file that knows a lot about your tastes, your brand preferences, your marital status, even your political opinions. If you contributed to a freewheeling Usenet newsgroup, all the better, for your political views, sexual preferences, even the way you think, can now be compiled and compared with the other information in your dossier.

The capabilities of information-gathering and sorting technologies that can harvest and sift mind-numbing quantities of individual trivial but collectively revealing pieces of information are formidable today. This Panoptic machinery shares some of the same communications infrastructure that enables one-room schoolhouses in Montana to communicate with MIT professors, and enables overseas Chinese dissidents to disseminate news and organize resistance. The power to compile highly specific dossiers on millions of people will become even more formidable over the next several years as the cost of computing power drops and the network of electronic transactions becomes more richly interconnected. The commodization of privacy is piggybacking on the same combination of computers and communications that has given birth to virtual communities. The power to snoop has become democratized.

When our individual information terminals become as powerful as supercomputers, and every home is capable of sending and receiving huge amounts of information, you won't need a dictatorship from above to spy on your neighbors and have them spy on you. Instead, you'll sell pieces of each other's individuality to one another. Entrepreneurs are already nibbling around the edges of the informational body politic, biting off small chunks of privacy and marketing it. Information about you and me is valuable to certain people, whether or not we actively choose to disclose that information. We've watched our names migrate from magazine subscription lists to junk mail assaults, but we haven't seen the hardware and software that has evolved for gathering and exploiting private information for profit.

The most insidious attack on our rights to a reasonable degree of privacy might come not from a political dictatorship but from the marketplace. The term "Big Brother" brings to mind a scenario of a future dictatorship held together by constant electronic surveillance of the citizenry; but today's technologies allow for more subtlety than Orwell could have been foreseen. There are better ways to build Panopticons than the heavy-handed Orwellian model. If totalitarian manipulators of populations and technologies actually do achieve dominance in the future, I predict that it will begin not by secret police kicking in your doors but by allowing you to sell yourself to your television and letting your supermarket sell information about your transactions, while outlawing measures you could use to protect yourself. Instead of just telephone taps, the weapons will include computer programs that link bar codes, credit cards, social security numbers, and all the other electronic telltales we leave in our paths through the information society. And the most potent weapon will be the laws or absence of laws that enable improper uses of information technology to erode what is left of citizens rights to privacy.

"Marketplace," a CD-ROM that contained the collected available information about you, your family, and 120 million other people, was announced in 1991 by Lotus. After public criticism, Lotus decided not to market the product. Interactive television systems are being installed now, systems that allows customers to download videos and upload information about their tastes, preferences, and opinions. With high-speed digital communication capabilities of future fiber-optic networks, there will be even more ways to move information about you from your home to the databases of others, with and without your consent.

Informational dossiers about individuals are marketing gold mines for those who know how to make money by knowing which magazines you subscribe to, what kind of yogurt you eat, and which political organizations you support. Invisible information—your name, address, other demographic information—is already encoded in certain promotional coupons you get in the mail. Ultimately, advertisers will be able to use new technologies to customize the television advertising for each individual household. Advertising agencies, direct mail marketers, and political consultants already know what to do with your zip code, your social security number, and a few other data. These professional privacy brokers have begun to realize that a significant portion of the population would freely allow someone else to collect and use and even sell personal information, in return for payment or subsidies.

Here is one obvious answer to the inequity of access to Net resources and the gap between information-rich and information-poor. Some people would be able to afford to pay for "enhanced information services." Others would be able to use those services in exchange for a little information-monitoring. For answering a few questions and allowing certain of your transactions to be monitored, for example, you would be granted a certain number of hours of service, or even paid for the information and the right to use it. Why should anybody go to the trouble of seizing our rights of privacy when so many of us would be happy to sell them?

Selling your privacy is your right, and I'm not suggesting that anyone stop you. In fact, it might be a viable solution to the problems of equity of access. There is, in medicine, the notion of informed consent, however, which obligates your physician to explain to you the risks and potential side effects of recommended medical procedures. I'd like people to know what it is they are giving away in exchange for convenience, rebates, or online hours on the latest MUD. Do people have a right to privacy? Where does that right begin and end? Without adequate protections, the same information that can flow laterally, from citizen to citizen, can be used by powerful central authorities as well as by grassroots groups.

The most important kind of protection for citizens against technology-assisted invasion of privacy is a set of principles that can help preserve individual autonomy in the digital age. Laws, policies, and norms are the various ways in which such principles, once articulated and agreed on, are enforced in a democratic society. But high technology is often very good at rendering laws moot. Another kind of protection for citizens is the subject of current intense scrutiny by cyberspace civil libertarians, a technical fix known as citizen encryption. A combination of principles, laws, policies, and technologies, if intelligently designed and equitably implemented, offer one more hopeful scenario in which citizens can continue to make use of the advantages of the Net without falling victim to its Panoptic potential.

Gary Marx, a professor of sociology at MIT, is an expert on technology and privacy. Marx suggests that

> an important example of the kind of principles needed is the Code of Fair Information developed in 1973 for the U.S. Department of Health, Education, and Welfare. The code involves five principles:
>
> There must be no personal-data record keeping whose very existence is secret.
>
> There must be a way for a person to find out what information about him is in a record and how it is being used.
>
> There must be a way for a person to prevent information that was obtained for one purpose from being used or made available for other purposes without his consent.
>
> There must be a way for a person to correct or amend a record of identifiable information about himself.

> Any organization creating, maintaining, using, or disseminating records of identifiable personal data must assure the reliability of the data for their intended use and must take precautions to prevent misuses of the data.

The highly interconnected, relatively insecure networks, with their millions and billions of bits per second, are a tough environment to enforce rules based on these suggested principles. Many of the nuances of public conferencing or private e-mail or hybrid entities such as e-mail lists will require changes in these principles, but this list is a good way to focus societal debate about values, risks, and liberties. If the profit or power derived from Net-snooping proves to be significant, and the technicalities of the Net make it difficult to track perpetrators, however, no laws will ever adequately protect citizens. That's why a subculture of computer software pioneers known as cypherpunks have been working to make citizen encryption possible.

Encryption is the science of encoding and decoding messages. Computers and codebreaking go back a long way. Alan Turing, one of the intellectual fathers of the computer, worked during World War II on using computational strategies to break the codes created by Germany's Enigma machine. Today, the largest assemblage of computer power in the world is widely acknowledged to be the property of the U.S. National Security Agency, the top-secret contemporary high-tech codebreakers. Computers and mathematical theories are today's most important weapons in the war between codemakers and codebreakers. Like computers themselves, and CMC, the mathematical complexities of encryption have begun to diffuse from the specialists to the citizens.

A tool known as public-key encryption is causing quite a stir these days, not just because it enables citizens to encode messages that their recipients can read but are not readable by even the most computationally powerful codebreakers, but also because citizen encryption makes possible two extremely powerful antipanoptic weapons known as digital cash and digital signature. With digital cash, it is possible to build an electronic economy where the seller can verify that the buyer's credit is good, and transfer the correct amount of money, without the seller knowing who the buyer is. With digital signature, it is possible in the identity-fluid online world to establish certainty about the sender of a message. This has important implications for intellectual property and online publishing, as well as personal security.

Key is a cryptographers' term for the codebook that unlocks a particular code. Until recently, code keys, whether made of metal or mathematical algorithms, were top secret. If someone steals your key, your messages are compromised. Public-key encryption makes use of recent mathematical discoveries that enable a person to keep one key private and distribute to everyone and anyone a public key. If anyone wants to use that person's public key, only the owner of the private key can read the message; both public and private keys are necessary, and the private key cannot be discovered by mathematical operations on the public key. Because encryption is based on precise mathematical principles, it is possible to demonstrate that a particular encryption scheme is inherently strong enough to survive brute-force mathematical assault by powerful supercomputers.

Public-key encryption as it exists today is unbreakable by all but the most powerful computers, such as those owned by the National Security Agency. Policy debate and legal challenges have revolved around citizens' rights to use mathematically unbreakable encryption. The National Security Agency sees this as a security nightmare, when it can no longer do its job of picking strategic signals out of the ether and inspecting them for content that threatens the security of the United States. Certain discoveries in the mathematical foundations of cryptography are automatically classified as soon as a mathematician happens upon them. John Gilmore, one of the founders of the EFF, recently filed suit against the National Security Agency for its classification and suppression in the United States of fundamental cryptography texts that are undoubtedly known to America's enemies. A few days after Gilmore filed suit and informed the press, the agency astonished everybody by declassifying the documents.

Think of digital cash as a kind of credit card that allows you to spend whatever credit you legitimately have without leaving a personal identifier linked to the transaction. The same techniques could be used to render other aspects of personal information—medical and legal records—far less vulnerable to abuse. Different applications of encryption technology already are being considered as safeguards against different kinds of panoptic danger. But ubiquitous encryption poses important problems: will citizen encryption, by making it impossible for any individual or group to crack encrypted messages, give the upper hand to criminals and terrorists, or will it force law enforcement and intelligence agencies to shift resources away from signals intelligence (monitoring communications) and into other, possibly even more invasive surveillance techniques? The impact of citizen encryption, for good or ill, looms as one of those unexpected applications of higher mathematics—like nuclear fission—that has the potential to change everything. There's still time to talk about it.

The third school of criticism builds on the foundation of commodification of the public sphere but veers off into a somewhat surrealistic dimension. Highly abstruse works of contemporary philosophy, much of it originating in France, have been proposing certain ideas about the psychological and social effects of previous communications technologies that raise disturbing resonances with the nature of CMC technologies.

The Hyper-realists

Hyper-realists see the use of communications technologies as a route to the total replacement of the natural world and the social order with a technologically mediated hyper-reality, a "society of the spectacle" in which we are not even aware that we work all day to earn money to pay for entertainment media that tell us what to desire and which brand to consume and which politician to believe. We don't see our environment as an artificial construction that uses media to extract our money and power. We see it as "reality"—the way things are. To hyper-realists, CMC, like other communications technologies of the past, is doomed to become another powerful conduit for disinfotainment. While a few people will get better information via high-bandwidth supernetworks, the majority of the population, if history is any guide, are likely to become more precisely befuddled, more exactly manipulated. Hyper-reality is what you get when a Panopticon evolves to the point where it can convince everyone that it doesn't exist; people continue to believe they are free, although their power has disappeared.

Televisions, telephones, radios, and computer networks are potent political tools because their function is not to manufacture or transport physical goods but to influence human beliefs and perceptions. As electronic entertainment has become increasingly "realistic," it has been used as an increasingly powerful propaganda device. The most radical of the hyper-realist political critics charge that the wonders of communications technology skillfully camouflage the disappearance and subtle replacement of true democracy—and everything else that used to be authentic, from nature to human relationships—with a simulated, commercial version. The illusion of democracy offered by CMC utopians, according to these reality critiques, is just another distraction from the real power play behind the scenes of the new technologies—the replacement of democracy with a global mercantile state that exerts control through the media-assisted manipulation of desire rather than the more orthodox means of surveillance and control. Why torture people when you can get them to pay for access to electronic mind control?

During the events of May 1968, when students provoked a revolt in the streets of Paris against the Gaullist regime, a radical manifesto surfaced, written by Guy Debord. *The Society of the Spectacle* made a startling tangential leap from what McLuhan was saying at around the same time. Cinema, television, newspapers, Debord proclaimed, were all part of worldwide hegemony of power in which the rich and powerful had learned to rule with minimal force by turning everything into a media event. The staged conventions of the political parties to anoint politicians who had already been selected behind closed doors were a prominent example, but they were only part of a web of headlines, advertisements, and managed events.

The replacement of old neighborhoods with modern malls, and cafés with fast-food franchises, was part of this "society of the spectacle," precisely because they help destroy the "great good places" where the public sphere lives. More than twenty years later, Debord looked back and emphasized this aspect of his earlier forecasts:

> For the agora, the general community, has gone, along with communities restricted to intermediary bodies or to independent institutions, to salons or cafés, or to workers in a single company. There is no place left where people can discuss the realities which concern them, because they can never lastingly free themselves from the crushing presence of media discourse and of the various forces organized to relay it. . . . What is false creates taste, and reinforces itself by knowingly eliminating any possible reference to the authentic. And what is genuine is reconstructed as quickly as possible, to resemble the false.

Another French social critic, Jean Baudrillard, has been writing since the 1960s about the increasingly synthetic nature of technological civilization and a culture that has been irrevocably tainted by the corruption of our symbolic systems. This analysis goes deeper than the effects of media on our minds; Baudrillard claims to track the degeneration of meaning itself. In Baudrillard's historical analysis, human civilization has changed itself in three major stages, marked by the changes in meaning we invest in our symbol systems. More specifically, Baudrillard focused on the changing relationship between *signs* (such as alphabetical characters, graphic images) and *that which they signify*. The word *dog* is a sign, and English-speakers recognize that it refers to, signifies, a living creature in the material world that barks and has fleas. According to Baudrillard, during the first step of civilization, when speech and then writing were created, signs were invented *to point to reality.* During the second step of civilization, which took place over the past century, advertising, propaganda, and commodification set in, and the sign begins *to hide reality.* The third step includes our step into the hyper-real, for now we are in an age when signs begin *to hide the absence of reality.* Signs now help us pretend that they mean something.

Technology and industry, in Baudrillard's view, succeeded over the past century in satisfying basic human needs, and thus the profit-making apparatus that controlled technology-driven industry needed to fulfill desires instead of needs. The new media of radio and television made it possible to keep the desire level of entire populations high enough to keep a consumer society going. The way this occurs has to do with sign systems such as tobacco commercials that link the brand name of a cigarette to a beautiful photograph of a sylvan scene. The brand name of a cigarette is woven into a fabric of manufactured signifiers that can be changed at any time. The realm of the hyper-real. Virtual communities will fit very neatly into this cosmology, if it turns out that they offer the semblance of community but lack some fundamental requirement for true community.

Baudrillard's vision reminded me of another dystopian prophecy from the beginning of the twentieth century, E. M. Forster's chilling tale "The Machine Stops." The story is about a future world of billions of people, each of whom lives in a comfortable multimedia chamber that delivers necessities automatically, dispenses of wastes, and links everyone in the world into marvelously stimulating web of conversations. The only problem is that people long ago forgot that they were living in a machine. The title of the story describes the dramatic event that gives the plot momentum. Forster and Baudrillard took the shadow side of telecommunications and considered it in light of the human capacity for illusion. They are both good cautionary mythmakers, marking the borders of the pitfalls of global, high-bandwidth networks and multimedia virtual communities.

Virtual communitarians, because of the nature of our medium, must pay for our access to each other by forever questioning the reality of our online culture. The land of the hyper-real begins when people forget that a telephone only conveys the illusion of being within speaking distance of another person and a computer conference only conveys the illusion of a town hall meeting. It's when we forget about the illusion that the trouble begins. When the technology itself grows powerful enough to make the illusions increasingly realistic, as the Net promises to do within the next ten to twenty years, the necessity for continuing to question reality grows even more acute.

What should those of us who believe in the democratizing potential of virtual communities do about the technological critics? I believe we should invite them to the table and help them see the flaws in our dreams, the bugs in our designs. I believe we should study what the historians and social scientists have to say about the illusions and power shifts that accompanied the diffusion of previous technologies. CMC and technology in general has real limits; it's best to continue to listen to those who understand the limits, even as we continue to explore the technologies' positive capabilities. Failing to fall under the spell of the "rhetoric of the technological sublime," actively questioning and examining social assumptions about the effects of new technologies, reminding ourselves that electronic communication has powerful illusory capabilities, are all good steps to take to prevent disasters.

If electronic democracy is to succeed, however, in the face of all the obstacles, activists must do more than avoid mistakes. Those who would use computer networks as political tools must go forward and actively apply their theories to more and different kinds of communities. If there is a last good hope, a bulwark against the hyper-reality of Baudrillard or Forster, it will come from a new way of looking at technology. Instead of falling under the spell of a sales pitch, or rejecting new technologies as instruments of illusion, we need to look closely at new technologies and ask how they can help build stronger, more humane communities—and ask how they might be obstacles to that goal. The late 1990s may eventually be seen in retrospect as a narrow window of historical opportunity, when people either acted or failed to act effectively to regain control over communications technologies. Armed with knowledge, guided by a clear, human-centered vision, governed by a commitment to civil discourse, we the citizens hold the key levers at a pivotal time. What happens next is largely up to us.

AFTERWORD

When *The Virtual Community* went to press in the summer of 1993, the subtitle reflected the zeitgeist of that moment—"*Homesteading on the Electronic Frontier.*" By the time the book arrived in bookstores in November 1993, the media were buzzing about something called "the information superhighway." By the beginning of 1994, the information superhighway metaphor had saturated mass culture.

The heretofore underground online subculture was reported, hyped, spoofed, incisively analyzed, and grossly misinterpreted by the networks and national news magazines, intellectual and technical publications, *Doonesbury* gags and cartoons in *The New Yorker*, jokes on sitcoms—the modern American media food chain. In a few months, the public image of cyberspace changed from homesteaders on the frontier to highway developers. (By mid-1994, Net cognoscenti were calling it "the infobahn.")

The public is waking up. So are the biggest players in the telecommunications industry. Something has happened recently in the minds of the people who control the largest communications and entertainment corporations in the world, something significant enough to shape the market strategies of NTT (Nippon Telephone and Telegraph) and Time-Warner, Microsoft and Sprint, Viacom and Disney, Apple and IBM.

The grassroots movements described in *The Virtual Community* are beginning to intersect with movements that originated in boardrooms and government offices. The big players in business and government are newer at CMC than the Internet pioneers and BBSers, but they bring a lot more weight to bear on the market and on political regimes when they devote their resources to it.

When a representative of a regional Bell operating company called me in the summer of 1992 to find out whether his CEO ought to pay attention to (then senator) Albert Gore's National Education and Research Network legislation, I was astonished to realize that the highest levels of American telecommunications industries had not awakened to the revolution that was overtaking them, an impression that grew stronger as I talked with managers in other telecommunications companies. Then it all changed rapidly.

By the summer of 1993, telephone companies were merging and flirting with cable companies, software companies were entering joint ventures with entertainment companies, newspapers were establishing media laboratories.

Events related to the emergence of a new global communications infrastructure have been moving rapidly in Japan, as well as in the United States —in fact, events have been moving rapidly in Japan *because* events have been moving rapidly in the United States. Computer networks and virtual communities were futuristic fantasies when I talked about them with NTT researchers two years ago. Researchers were eager to speculate, but many-to-many communications technology wasn't yet part of their companies' business strategy.

Japan's largest players seem to have restructured their entire global telecommunications strategy in response to America's information superhighway initiative. NTT researchers told me in 1994 that their company was refocusing its energies on Internet-like interactive services to individuals, rather than just the few-to-many applications for high-bandwidth networks they had been developing previously.

The battle over whether Japan joins the Net in a big way—which was still unpredictably far in the future when Izumi Aizu, Joichi Ito, and I discussed it two years ago—broke out in earnest in late 1993, when TWICS drew the ire of a government ministry by offering full worldwide Internet access to all subscribers. Their access was suddenly cut off, then restored after unexpected publicity. A power struggle between the old guard, with its bureaucratic networks in Tokyo ministries, and the grassroots Internet activists in the universities and virtual communities elsewhere in Japan was joined. In the case of TWICS, the old guard didn't listen, and when the young generation of activists tried to end-run them, the old boys got angry.

When I attended my third Hypernetwork Conference in Oita, in 1994, COARA had become an Internet site, and Governor Hiramatsu talked of adding "Broadband ISDN" services (billions of bits per second) to Oita Prefecture's free network. Research managers from Techno-Japan, Inc., who had in years past listened to me futurize about citizen-to-citizen, many-to-many networks at previous conferences, were joined by their bosses, who were talking openly about finding their companies' places in the emerging "global information superhighway."

Two powerful forces drove the rapid emergence of the superhighway notion in 1994. First, the proposed mergers of multibillion-dollar companies (and sometimes their decisions not to merge, as happened to Bell Atlantic and TCI) are always news. Tens of billions of dollars start to add up to real money, not just in the minds of the public who read about it in the newspaper, but in the minds of the people who control companies. It doesn't matter that most people in the world had never heard of networked desktop communications before last year; everybody in the world understands what tens of billions of dollars means.

The second driving force behind the superhighway idea continued to be Vice President Gore. In late 1993, the Clinton-Gore administration began to present their vision, to be backed up by legislative and regulatory actions, of a "National Information Infrastructure"—known inside the Beltway as the "NII." But the U.S. government's entry into the discussion was punctuated by continuing front-page news from the business world.

The Bell-Atlantic/TCI proposed merger galvanized public attention for months. In early 1994, in the wake of an FCC-imposed cut in cable rates, the merging parties called off the deal. Barely had the news stories about the failure of the merger begun to fade when in March 1994, the dark prince of cyberspace, Bill Gates, the young Microsoft software magnate, announced he was teaming up with another very rich young boy-wizard of the info-industry, Craig McCaw. McCaw had just sold his cellular communications company, and Gates was positioning Microsoft for the new era.

The Gates-McCaw company, Teledesic, was set up to bypass the cables and fiber optics the other companies were fighting over. Gates and McCaw proposed making voice communications and enhanced data services available worldwide (especially in formerly hard-to-reach areas) through a network of 840 low-orbit satellites that would transfer information to and from the earthbound portion of the Net via ultra-high radio frequencies.

One week after the Gates-McCaw announcement, NTT announced a partnership with Gates to develop services "to allow users to access multimedia information on a communications network in Japan," according to a March 24 Reuters announcement. By the end of 1994, Gates has emerged as the man to watch. Gates is feared by those who favor wide-open competition because he has the understanding, the platform, the money, the power, and the will to go for a dominant position in the emerging industry, the way he achieved a dominant position in the personal computer software industry. Whether or not he manages to make himself the John D. Rockefeller of cyberspace, Bill Gates rang the bell that woke up the big money. It looks like he plans to keep ringing it.

Vice President Gore seemed to have listened to both the big money and the grassroots activists, judging from the proposals he outlined in a speech to the National Press Club in December 1993. He talked about a National Information Infrastructure (NII) that would be a platform for economic growth and competition, but would also serve the public good. Gore pledged the Clinton-Gore administration to five "guiding principles": The administration, Gore proclaimed, would act through legislative and regulatory initiatives to encourage private investment, provide and protect competition, provide open access to the network, avoid creating information "haves and have-nots," and encourage flexible and responsive government action.

The first principle represented a major policy shift. As an advocate of NREN in the Senate, Gore had spoken forcefully for a strong government role in building and regulating the new technology. In the early days of the Clinton-Gore administration, Gore clashed with industry figures over the role of the government in the emerging media. Gore was signaling a policy shift when he emphasized in his Press Club speech that private industry was going to build the new infrastructure. When Gore promised to remove some of the regulations that restrained cable and telephone companies from certain kinds of services, he was offering to deregulate something that had remained tightly controlled even during the deregulatory heyday of Reagan and Bush.

If the first principle could have been dictated by TCI's Tom Malone or Microsoft's Bill Gates, the second principle, a commitment to "protect competition," could have been written by Mitch Kapor. In fact, Gore acknowledged Kapor, the Electronic Frontier Foundation, and the EFF's "Open Platform" proposal in his declaration of principles. The vice president agreed with the industrialists that they should be cut loose to compete and build something far too big for the government to build or administer. But immediately after that, with his second guiding principle, Gore agreed with the Open Platform activists that the huge players in the telecommunications marketplace should be prevented from controlling the content of the communications they carry, and should be restrained from using their wealth to squeeze out competition from entrepreneurs and other smaller businesses.

By combining the offer to deregulate companies that were hungry to invest big money in the new media with a commitment on the part of the administration to protect competition, Gore proposed a compromise that was strongly influenced by the political realities of 1994. From the administration side, Gore knew that if they did not make the NII happen before the next election, the telecommunications industry's biggest players would be tempted to wait for the possibility of a Republican administration in 1997 that presumably would deregulate without restraining the biggest players.

From the industry side of the same problem, the technology and the industry were moving too quickly for major players to hesitate for long. The outcome of the next presidential election is always far from clear when there are still two years until it is held. And a lot can happen in a volatile global industry. Especially now that the Japanese are starting to wise up.

Gore stressed, in his third guiding principle, the need to design an information infrastructure that would not further exacerbate the split between the information-and-education haves and have-nots. He called upon the private sector to take the initiative in helping pay for extending the information highway into every school, library, and hospital in America. Those who have hopes of using CMC technology as a tool for restoring community and conviviality applauded this point. Evidence of great economic disparities and hardships by the less well-educated is not disputed. Everybody knows that a two-tiered society is in trouble and headed for bigger trouble. It is more cost-effective to educate people than to incarcerate them later. But nobody wants to pay for it. Perhaps Gore will succeed in luring the private sector into putting up a few billion to extend their infrastructure to a few repositories of public interest. It seems certain that taxpayers aren't going to pay for it, even though an equal-access superhighway might sound like a good idea in theory.

The "flexible and responsive government action" mentioned by Gore was the vaguest of the principles, but it was an acknowledgment that a major overhaul of communications policy is underway at the same time that the technological basis for the regulated industries is itself changing: cable television companies turn out to be high-bandwidth communication carriers that want to add voice and data communications to their entertainment fare, and telephone companies want to provide interactive multimedia point-click-and-buy services.

To complicate the picture, an "interactive television" vision of the new media emerged in 1994 as a Hollywood–Madison Avenue–Silicon Valley hybrid that might be a huge ball of hype or the beginning of yet another epic wealth-gathering scheme: imagine stopping the action in a sitcom or movie of the week, zooming in on an actor's sweater, clicking on it to get more information, and clicking on it again to buy it and arrange shipping. The final digital commodification of entertainment will open vast new horizons to the consumer society via the same technologies that online activists can use for political work and educators employ to link remote classrooms and online libraries. Everything is happening at once. A good time to be flexible.

Although Gore acknowledged the EFF Open Platform vision in regard to the importance of competitiveness in the telecommunications market, he and the administration very quickly clashed about the matter of allowing citizens to have access to strong encryption. The "Clipper Chip" proposal that Clinton inherited from a multiyear National Security Agency effort, began to sound more sinister as more was disclosed about it. The Clipper Chip is an encryption technology built into a microchip that can be manufactured in telephones and other communication devices. People who use Clipper-equipped devices can engage in secure communications.

The fly in the ointment is that the federal government holds the keys to a backdoor to everybody's Clipper Chip, which it can use to decode private conversations whenever it needs to defend national security. Remember J. Edgar Hoover? Wouldn't he have enjoyed that? Back to the FBI in a moment—they are indeed in the game.

The most ominous thing about the Clipper proposal, to many, is the fact that the government doesn't have to get the key to your private communications to learn a lot about you; Clipper devices emit identification signals that allow government traffic analysts to track where and when the devices were used. Clipper defenders pointed out that the government wasn't restraining people from using stronger forms of encryption, but citizen-encryption advocates, like gun owners, feel like they are on a slippery slope. By creating a de facto standard through the purchasing power of the federal government, the administration can make Clipper an accepted part of the landscape before most people understand what it is.

Civil libertarians point out that it is incumbent upon the government to make a case for taking any right that belongs to citizens; it is not upon the citizens to make a case for restraining the government. The fact that encryption involves esoteric mathematics doesn't help the issue. It will take time, at best, to explain the implications of these technical issues to the citizens whose liberties will be affected.

Along with the Clipper proposal put forward by the Clinton-Gore administration in 1993 and pushed in 1994 despite wide opposition from cryptography experts, civil libertarians, and mainstream businesspeople was the revival of the "Digital Telephony" Bill. The FBI was at it again, trying to force the telephone companies to install FBI-operable central snooping power in the new digital communications networks. Remember the Panopticon? Keep in mind that fewer than one thousand legal wiretaps are granted every year for investigation of serious crimes, out of the millions of crimes and billions of conversations. Instead of obtaining a court order and going to the telephone company to install a tap, the FBI would like the telephone company to, in effect, give them the power to tap any conversation they deem necessary. Everything is happening at once. The Net is liberating; the Net is a trap.

John Perry Barlow "schmoozed" his way onto Air Force Two after Gore made a much-publicized follow-up to his Press Club speech at an Information Superhighway Summit in early 1994. Gore evaded his questions about the civil liberty implications of Clipper and Digital Telephony. And White House staffers who had been friendlier about other NII issues began to use the "if you knew what we know" justification for sticking with a policy that could put a national digital surveillance state into place. It wasn't the Clinton administration that Barlow, the Wyoming libertarian, feared—it was putting certain kinds of power in the hands of any government.

Barlow responded with a hot rant, which proliferated through the Net for weeks before it appeared in print in *Wired* magazine:

> ...we could shortly find ourselves under a government that would have the automated ability to log the time, origin, and recipient of every call we made, could track our physical whereabouts continuously, could keep better account of our financial transactions than we do, and all without a court-ordered warrant. Talk about crime prevention!
>
> Worse, under some vaguely defined and surely mutable "legal authority," they also would be able to listen to our calls and read our e-mail without having to do any backyard rewiring. They wouldn't need any permission at all to monitor overseas calls.
>
> If there's going to be a fight, I'd rather it be with this government than the one we'd likely face on that hard day.
>
> Hey, I've never been a paranoid before. It has always seemed to me

> that most governments are too incompetent to keep a good plot strung together all the way to quitting time. But I am now very nervous about the government of the United States of America.
>
> Because Bill 'n' Al, whatever their other new-paradigm virtues, have allowed the old-paradigm trogs of the Guardian Class to define as their highest duty the defense of America against an enemy that exists primarily in the imagination—and is therefore capable of anything.
>
> To assure absolute safety against such an enemy, there is no limit to the liberties we will eventually be asked to sacrifice. And, with a Clipper Chip in every phone, there will certainly be no technical limit on their ability to enforce those sacrifices.
>
> In his Los Angeles speech, Gore called the development of the NII "a revolution." And it is a revolutionary war we are engaged in here. Clipper is a last ditch attempt by the United States, the last great power from the old Industrial Era, to establish imperial control over cyberspace. If they win, the most liberating development in the history of humankind could become, instead, the surveillance system that will monitor our grandchildren's morality. We can be better ancestors than that.

Just as CMC decentralizes control of communication and publication, it decentralizes surveillance as well. Before we argue about the best way to build utopia, it might be time for citizens to unite against the encroachments of tyranny in the guise of technology. Telltale chips are embedded in our purchases, bar codes track our smallest transaction, electronic telltales in our credit cards and telephones broadcast our location and activities, and powerful, high-bandwidth information superhighways carry information into—and out of—our homes. If there is a chance to stop the installation of a Panoptic super-surveillance state, that time is before it is installed. If Barlow is to be believed, that time is now.

Along with the economic and political infrastructures and the enabling technologies, the human interface to the Net is changing rapidly. It took Joi Ito, on my last trip to Tokyo, to show me the visible window into the Net. What had previously been a silent alphanumeric abstraction for years popped into full sensory reality for me.

Joichi Ito's family stone might record the names of twenty-seven generations, but Joi is a distinctly twenty-first-century lad. After a late dinner in Roppongi, on a rare snowy night in Tokyo in early 1994, we went to his apartment to kill some time on the Net before the Tokyo rave scene woke up. A Mosaic page painted itself on his PowerBook screen. Along the left side were postage-stamp pictures of galaxies and pop groups. Next to the pix were headlines and subheads. Even before he issued a command, I knew I was looking at a new world. I literally jumped the first time Joi pointed at the picture of a pop group and music came out of his computer's speaker.

"I've been teaching myself hypertext markup language," he remarked. Joi is always teaching himself something I've never heard about before. This language is a code that gives him the power to broadcast video, graphics, and text stored on his computer to tens of millions of Internet nodes.

I remember my first sight of a Macintosh in 1984. I remember the first time I logged on to the WELL in 1985. I remember the vertigo of reading through the names of three thousand newsgroups. I've learned to recognize those moments when a technological breakthrough sucks us all into a new dimension. Mosaic in Joi's hands had that instantly recognizable look of the future to it. Mosaic might be the "killer app"—the unexpected application of a technology that drives the technology to become a mass medium, like spreadsheets were for personal computers. It definitely has a beat you can dance to.

Outside Joi Ito's apartment, in the streets of Harajuku, Tokyo teenagers were cycling through a well-designed media loop: Fashion designers and retailers decide what trend to sell next month, their new look is transmitted at precisely timed intervals to the appropriate tribes via popular magazines and "idol" singers. Joi Ito, however, rolls his own media.

A Mosaic home page looks like the table of contents from a full-color slick-paper magazine. There are menus directing you to some of Joi's personal information—multimedia self-portraits. There's a video of Joi jumping out of an airplane. But Joi wanted to soar higher.

"First, let's see space," he said, and Joi clicked on the menu item for "Hubble Pictures." It took a minute to suck down the image from its home on a computer fifteen time zones away. Then a detailed color image of a distant galaxy, beamed to Earth from the Hubble Space Telescope that morning, popped up on his screen.

"How about the weather?" I pick one of the little pictures of parts of planet Earth—the North Pacific, because that's where we were at that moment. In a few seconds, I was watching a weather movie on the screen, beamed down from a satellite an hour before.

MTV.COM's server was cool. This was a digital outpost that MTV had set up on the Internet. Clicking on an icon on Joi's screen connected his computer in Tokyo to MTV's Internet site in the United States. I browsed album covers, tried a few samples of the songs on the albums. There's a short video of a VJ (I guess he's now an "EJ") blasting off in a rocketship, to the accompaniment of Elton John's "Rocketman."

Joi Ito's *Tomogaya* is a Net-zine, an online multimedia version of an only slightly older cultural phenomenon that bubbles up from populations that have access to communications technology. Zines came from a generation that doesn't care about the mass media. Zinesters want to get together with a few friends, jam with Xerox machines and computer paint programs, print it out at night on the boss's laser printer, and put it out there for a select cult audience.

Joi and his Nethead friends have their own ideas of where technoculture is headed. They want to play the Net like their parents wanted to play electric guitar. I watch where they're pointing because they might know something about where we're going.

The battle for the shape of the Net is joined. Part of the battle is a battle of dollars and power, but the great lever is still *understanding*—if enough people can understand what is happening, I still believe that we can have an influence. Whether we live in a Panoptic or democratic Net ten years from now depends, in no small measure, on what you and I know and do now. The outcome remains uncertain. What the Net will become is still, in large part, up to us.

BIBLIOGRAPHY

Allison, Jay. "Vigil." *Whole Earth Review* 75 (Summer 1992):4.

Amara, Roy, John Smith, Murray Turoff, and Jacques Vallee. "Computerized Conferencing, a New Medium." *Mosaic* (National Science Foundation) (January–February 1976).

Anderson, Benedict. *Imagined Communities: Reflections on the Origin and Spread of Nationalism*. London: Verso, 1983.

Bagdikian, Ben. "The Lords of the Global Village." *The Nation* (12 June 1989): 805.

———. *The Media Monopoly*. Boston: Beacon Press, 1983.

Baran, Paul. "On Distributed Communications." In *Rand Memoranda*, vols. 1–11. Santa Monica, Calif.: Rand Corporation, August 1964.

———. "On Distributed Communications Networks." *IEEE Transactions on Communications Systems* CS–12 (1964): 1–9.

Barlow, John. "Jackboots and Infobahn." *Wired* (April 1994): 40.

Barlow, John Perry. "Crime and Puzzlement." *Whole Earth Review* 68 (Fall 1990): 44.

Bartle, Richard. "Interactive Multi-User Computer Games." Internal study for British Telecom, Colchester, England, 1990.

Baudrillard, Jean. *Selected Writings*. Edited by Mark Poster. Stanford, Calif.: Stanford University Press, 1988.

Bellah, Robert N., R. Madsen, W. Sullivan, A. Swindler, and S. Tipton. *Habits of the Heart: Individualism and Commitment in American Life*. Berkeley, Calif.: University of California Press, 1985.

———. *The Good Society*. New York: Knopf, 1991.

Bentham, Jeremy. *Works*, vol. 4. Edited by J. Bowring. Edinburgh: William Tait, 1843.

Brand, Stewart. *II Cybernetic Frontiers*. New York: Random House, 1974.

———. *The Media Lab: Inventing the Future at MIT*. New York: Penguin, 1987.

Bruckman, Amy. "Identity Workshops: Emergent Social and Psychological Phenomena in Text-Based Virtual Reality." Master's thesis, MIT Media Laboratory, 1992.

Bruckman, Amy, and Mitchel Resnick. "Virtual Professional Community: Results from the MediaMOO Project." Paper submitted to the Third International Conference on Cyberspace. Austin, Texas, March 1993.

Bruhat, Thierry. "Messageries Electroniques: Grétel à Strasbourg et Télétel a Vélizy." In *Télématique: Promenades ans les Usages.* Edited by Marie Marchand and Clair Ancelin. Paris: La Documentation Francaise, 1984.

Carey, James. "The Mythos of the Electronic Revolution." In *Communication as Culture: Essays on Media and Society.* Winchester, Mass.: Unwin Hyman, 1989.

Carpignano, Paolo, Robin Anderson, Stanley Aronowitz, and William Difazio. "Chatter in the Age of Electronic Reproduction: Talk Television and the Public Mind." *Social Text* 25, no. 6 (1990).

Christensen, Ward, and Randy Seuss. "Hobbyist Computerized Bulletin Boards." *Byte* (November 1978): 150.

Christensen, Ward. "History: Me, Micros, Randy, Xmodem, CBBS." Posting on Chinet conferencing system, 18 March 1989.

Clapp, T. J. Burnside. "Weekend-Only World." Fesarius Publications, 1987.

Coate, John. "Innkeeping in Cyberspace." Paper read at the Directions in Advanced Computing Conference. Berkeley, Calif., 1991.

Congress of the United States, Office of Technology Assessment. *Critical Connections: Communication for the Future.* Washington, D.C.: United States Government Printing Office, 1990.

Curtis, Pavel. Panel on MUDs at the Directions in Advanced Computing Conference. Berkeley, Calif., 1991.

Curtis, Pavel, and David A. Nichols. *MUDs Grow Up: Social Virtual Reality in the Real World.* Palo Alto, Calif.: Xerox PARC, 1993.

Debord, Guy. *Comments on the Society of the Spectacle.* London: Verso, 1992.

Elshtain, Jean Betheke. "Interactive TV—Democracy and the QUBE Tube." *The Nation* (7–14 August 1982): 108.

Engelbart, Douglas C. "A Conceptual Framework for the Augmentation of Man's Intellect." In *Vistas in Information Handling,* vol. 1. Edited by Paul William Howerton and David C. Weeks. Washington, D.C.: Spartan Books, 1963, pp. 1–29.

———. "Intellectual Implications of Multi-Access Computing." Proceedings of the Interdisciplinary Conference on Multi-Access Computer Networks, April 1970.

———. "NLS Teleconferencing Features: The Journal and Shared-Screen Telephoning." *IEEE Digest of Papers* (CompCon) (Fall 1975): 175–76.

Evenson, Laura. "Future TV Will Shop for You and Talk for You." *The San Francisco Chronicle,* 8 June 1993.

Feenberg, Andrew. "From Information to Communication: The French Experience with Videotext." In *The Social Contexts of Computer-Mediated Communication.* Edited by Marin Lea. Englewood Cliffs, N.J.: Simon & Schuster/Harvester-Wheatsheaf, 1992.

Forster, E. M. "The Machine Stops." In *The Eternal Moment and Other Stories.* New York: Harcourt Brace Jovanovich, 1929.

Foucault, Michel. *Discipline and Punish: The Birth of the Prison*. Translated from the French by Alan Sheridan. New York: Pantheon, 1977.

Frederick, Howard. "Computer Networks and the Emergence of Global Civil Society." In L. Harasim, ed., *Global Networks, Computers and International Communication*. Cambridge, Mass.: MIT Press, 1993.

Geertz, Clifford. *The Interpretation of Cultures: Selected Essays*. New York: Basic Books, 1973, p. 44.

Gergen, Kenneth J. *The Saturated Self: Dilemmas of Identity in Contemporary Life*. New York: Basic Books, 1991.

Gibson, William. *Neuromancer*. New York: Ace, 1984.

Goffman, Erving. *The Presentation of Self in Every Day Life*. Garden City, N.Y.: Doubleday, 1959.

Habermas, Jürgen. *The Theory of Communicative Action*. Vol. 1, *Reason and the Rationalization of Society*. Translated by Thomas McCarthy. Boston: Beacon Press, 1984.

———. Extensive discussion of the public sphere was published in *Strukturwandel der Öffentlichkeit* (Neuwied, 1962). A discussion of this book, translated into English, appeared in *New German Critique* no. 3 (Fall 1974): 45-55.

———. *Communication and the Evolution of Society*. Translated by T. Mc Carthy. Boston: Beacon Press, 1979.

Hart, Jeffrey, R. Reed, F. Bar. "The Building of the Internet: Implications for the Future of Broadband Networks." *Telecommunications Policy* (November 1992): 666–89.

Hauben, Michael. "The Social Forces Behind the Development of Usenet News." Unpublished paper, Columbia University, 1992.

Hiltz, Starr Roxanne, and Murray Turoff. *The Network Nation: Human Communication via Computer*. Reading, Mass.: Addison-Wesley, 1978, p. 102.

Hiramatsu, Morihiko. "Towards a More Autonomous Region through Informatization and Revitalization." Speech given at the Apple Hakone Multimedia and Arts Festival, Hakone, Japan, 1 August 1992.

Jenkins, Henry. *Textual Poachers: Television Fans and Participatory Culture*. New York and London: Routledge, 1992.

Kiesler, Sara. "The Hidden Messages in Computer Networks." *Harvard Business Review* (January–February 1986).

Kiesler, Sara, Jane Siegel, and Timothy McGuire. "Social Psychological Aspects of Computer-Mediated Communication." *American Psychologist* 39, no. 10 (October 1984): 1123–34.

Kumon, Shumpei. "Japan as a Network Society." In *The Political Economy of Japan*. Vol. 3, *The Social and Cultural Dynamics*. Edited by Shumpei Kumon and Henry Rosovsky. Stanford, Calif.: Stanford University Press, 1992, pp. 109–41.

Kumon, Shumpei, and Izumi Aizu. "Co-emulation: The Case for a Global Hypernetwork Society." In *Global Networks: Computers and International Communication*. Edited by Linda Harasim. Cambridge, Mass.: MIT Press, 1993.

Krol, Ed. *The Whole Internet User's Guide & Catalog.* Sebastopol, Calif.: O'Reilly & Assoc., 1992.

LaQuey, Tracy. *The Internet Companion: A Beginner's Guide to Global Networking.* Reading, Mass.: Addison-Wesley, 1992.

Laurel, Brenda. *Computers as Theater.* Menlo Park, Calif.: Addison-Wesley, 1991.

Licklider, J. C. R. "Man-Computer Symbiosis." *IRE Transactions on Human Factors in Electronics* HFE-1 (March 1960): 4–11.

Licklider, J. C. R., Robert Taylor, and E. Herbert. "The Computer as a Communication Device." *International Science and Technology* (April 1968).

Lipnack, Jessica, and Jeffrey Stamps. *Networking: The First Report and Directory.* Garden City, N.Y.: Doubleday, 1982.

Marchand, Marie. *A French Success Story: The Minitel Saga.* Translated by Mark Murphy. Paris: Larousse, 1988.

Markoff, John. "U.S. Said to Play Favorites in Promoting Nationwide Computer Network." *The New York Times* (18 December 1991).

———. "Microsoft and Two Cable Giants Close to an Alliance." *The New York Times* (13 June 1993).

Marx, Gary T. "Privacy and Technology." *The World and I* (September 1990).

Morningstar, Chip, and F. Randall Farmer. "The Lessons of Lucasfilm's Habitat." In *Cyberspace: First Steps.* Edited by Michael Benedikt. Cambridge, Mass.: MIT Press, 1991.

Nora, Simon, and Alain Minc. *L'informatisation de la société.* Paris: Editions du Seuil, 1978.

Odasz, Frank. "Big Sky Telegraph." *Whole Earth Review* 71 (Summer 1991): 32.

Oldenburg, Ray. *The Great Good Place: Cafés, Coffee Shops, Community Centers, Beauty Parlors, General Stores, Bars, Hangouts, and How They Get You through the Day.* New York: Paragon House, 1991.

Olson, Mancur. *The Logic of Collective Action.* Cambridge, Mass.: Harvard University Press, 1965.

Peck, M. Scott. *The Different Drum: Community-Making and Peace.* New York: Touchstone, 1987.

Postman, Neal. *Amusing Ourselves to Death: Public Discourse in the Age of Show Business.* New York: Viking Penguin, 1985.

Quarterman, John. *The Matrix: Computer Networks and Conferencing Systems Worldwide.* Bedford, Mass.: Digital Press, 1990.

———. "How Big Is the Matrix?" *Matrix News* 2, no. 2. Matrix Information and Directory Services, Austin, Texas, 1992.

———. "The Global Matrix of Minds." In *Global Networks: Computers and International Communication.* Edited by Linda Harasim. Cambridge, Mass.: MIT Press, 1993.

Quittner, Joshua. "Internet Faces Gridlock." *Newsday* (1 November 1992).

Rapaport, Mathew J. *Computer-Mediated Communications.* New York: Wiley, 1991.

Reich, Robert. *The Work of Nations: Preparing Ourselves for 21st-Century Capitalism.* New York: Random House, 1991.

Reid, Elisabeth. "Electropolis: Communications and Community on Internet Relay Chat." Electronically distributed version of honors thesis for the Department of History, University of Melbourne, 1991.

Rheingold, Howard. *Tools for Thought.* New York: Simon & Schuster, 1985.

———. *Virtual Reality.* New York: Summit, 1991.

———. "Electronic Democracy." *Whole Earth Review* 71(Summer 1991): 4.

Rhodes, Sarah N. *The Role of the National Science Foundation in the Development of the Electronic Journal.* Washington, D.C.: National Science Foundation, Division of Information Science and Technology, 1976.

Robins, Kevin, and Frank Webster. "Cybernetic Capitalism: Information, Technology, Everyday Life." In *The Political Economy of Information.* Edited by V. Mosco and J. Wasko. Madison, Wisc.: The University of Wisconsin Press, 1988.

———. "Athens without Slaves . . . or Slaves without Athens? The Neurosis of Technology." In *Science as Culture*, vol. 1. London: Free Association Books, 1987.

Sculley, John, with John A. Byrne. *Odyssey: Pepsi to Apple—A Journey of Adventure, Ideas, and the Future.* New York: Harper & Row, 1987.

Smith, Marc. "Voices from the WELL: The Logic of the Virtual Commons." Master's thesis, Department of Sociology, UCLA, 1992.

Sproull, Lee, and Sara Kiesler. *Connections: New Ways of Working in the Networked World.* Cambridge, Mass.: MIT Press, 1991.

Sterling, Bruce. *Hacker Crackdown.* New York: Bantam, 1992.

Stone, Allucquere Roseanne. "Will the Real Body Please Stand Up? Boundary Stories about Virtual Cultures." In *Cyberspace: First Steps.* Edited by Michael Benedikt. Cambridge, Mass.: MIT Press, 1991.

Tribe, Laurence H. "The Constitution in Cyberspace." *The Humanist* (September–October 1991).

Turkle, Sherry. *The Second Self: Computers and the Human Spirit.* New York: Simon & Schuster, 1984.

Turoff, Murray, and Starr Roxanne Hiltz. "Meeting through Your Computer." *IEEE Spectrum* (May 1977): 58–64.

Uncapher, Willard. "Rural Grassroots Telecommunication: Big Sky Telegraph and Its Community." Master's thesis, Annenberg School for Communication, University of Pennsylvania, 1991.

———. "Trouble in Cyberspace." *The Humanist* (September–October 1991).

Vallee, Jacques. *The Network Revolution: Confessions of a Computer Scientist.* Berkeley, Calif.: And/Or Press, 1982.

Van Gelder, Lindsy. "The Strange Case of the Electronic Lover." Reprinted in *Com-*

puterization and Controversy. Edited by Charles Dunlop and Robert Kling. San Diego, Calif.: Academic Press, 1991.

Varley, Pamela. "What's Really Happening in Santa Monica." *Technology Review* (November/December 1991).

Winner, Langdon. *The Whale and the Reactor.* Chicago: University of Chicago Press, 1986, p. 112.

Wittig, Michelle. "Electronic City Hall." *Whole Earth Review* 71 (Summer 1991): 24.

Wolfe, Tom. *The Electric Kool-Aid Acid Test.* New York: Farrar, Straus and Giroux, 1968.

Yoshida, Atsuya, and Jun Kakuta. "People Who Live in an On-Line Virtual World." Department of Information Technology, Kyoto Institute of Technology, Matsugasaki, Sakyoku, Kyoto 606, Japan, 1993.

INDEX